The Players in the Money Game!

Poke Jeffers:

A Georgia boy with the clear, cool eyes of a hunter. But in the big-money jungle, he becomes the hunted.

Israel Padawer:

To him money was the blood his family had shed in the war in Europe. And his wife knew that nothing else would ever warm his blood again.

Noel Bigelow:

He held a winning hand in a cut-throat game. And he was prepared to hold on to it the dirtiest way he knew.

Carol Tracey:

Some man had to take the woman in her out from behind the ticker tape veil. But when he did, he might find more than he'd bargained for.

50 WALL STREET

Vartanig G. Vartan

AN AVON BOOK

AVON BOOKS
A division of
The Hearst Corporation
959 Eighth Avenue
New York, New York 10019

First Avon Printing, April, 1969

Cover design by Milton Charles

Printed in the U.S.A.

For Cinnie

1

Wall Street was like a waiting oven this Monday morning in August. At six o'clock the Street stood silent and gray, almost cold with disuse. It was deserted except for the pigeons nodding and gurgling and scurrying about in the half gloom. They foraged delicately along the gutters and streamed upon the sidewalks, a soft bobbing blanket of feathers.

Soon the cramped summer heat would begin oozing forth from the gray stone slabs of awakening buildings. In a few hours the huge sad flags—the bank standards tolerating the Stars and Stripes—would be hoisted to wait for the first teasing breeze.

The short connecting streets tumbled into Wall at odd angles. It was almost as though the daytime heat actually had shifted their courses, leaving the night to solidify the prankish designs.

Wall Street's topmost towers edged slowly from battleship gray to a dull rose. Far below stalked the pigeons; they were canny, proud, almost jaunty in this private early hour while they still kept their kingdom. On mincing feet the pigeons tracked crusts of bread and fragments of giant golden pretzels. Their cooing, an urgent sound, almost vulgar in its intensity, throbbed against the oven slabs of the buildings which were touched now with a faint warning glow.

Thatcher Kimbridge played absently with the sugar tongs. Seated alone in the dining room of his town house in the East Sixties, he was savoring something that he alone knew. It gave him a curious sensation of monopoly for a few moments, not unlike the thrill a scientist might feel upon discovering some new drug in his laboratory.

In less than two hours he planned to make an announcement to his fellow partners. Thereupon, the firm of Kimbridge & Co. slowly and irrevocably would begin to turn, like a liner at sea setting upon a newly charted course.

Thatcher Kimbridge cleared his throat in rehearsal. "Gentlemen, I believe the time has come to change Kimbridge & Co. from a partnership to a corporation. And in preparation for such a move"—the first murmurs of astonishment would be rising from around the table—"I propose we take one of the younger men, preferably a producer from this office, into the firm as a partner."

Yes, he reflected, carefully replacing the sugar tongs in their bowl, it would come as quite a shock to his partners. But it was the right decision, he was convinced of that. Kimbridge & Co. would remain alive after all of them had passed on. How simple a thing it was, he marveled, to achieve immortality by incorporation.

He glanced over the first page of *The New York Times,* not reading any of the articles but digesting every headline with the same thoroughness he had applied shortly before to two soft-boiled eggs, toast, and ginger marmalade, and then he turned to the obituary page. Staring out at him was a picture of Garrett Anderton, a photograph with the worry lines erased by an air brush. So Garrett was dead. . . .

Garrett Anderton had come to his office only two weeks ago. He was the president of a specialty chemical company for which Kimbridge & Co. had managed the initial public offering. Garrett wanted to raise new capital for expansion and he had sought out Thatcher's advice. Was a rights offering to stockholders or a convertible debenture issue the best route for his company to take? The two men had talked over the situation, and Thatcher's tentative recommendation had been in favor of straight debentures so that stockholder equity would not be diluted.

Thatcher took out the old-fashioned fountain pen that once belonged to his father and made a notation on a pad beside his coffee cup. The funeral service was tomorrow—Tuesday—at four o'clock. Good, he thought automatically, after the market closes.

"I beg your pardon, sir." It was Pinckney, the chauffeur, standing discreetly in the archway leading to the front hall. "Will you be wanting anything today?"

"No, Pinckney, I think not. Thank you."

"Very good, sir."

Pinckney went into the hall. Thatcher saw him pick up the silver card tray and begin to polish it between his gray hands.

This was a private ritual they performed every weekday morning. Thatcher always shared a taxi downtown with a lawyer friend, leaving the car at his wife's disposal. Edith Kimbridge, a red notebook in her purse engraved T.T.D. for "Things To Do," tra-

11

versed Manhattan like some benevolent marauder—shopping trips, flower shows, lunch at the Colony or the York Club, teas, charity-ball arrangements, hospital work, or simply visiting friends. And all the time, here at the house, the plants and flowers waited patiently for her touch.

It had been Jared Kimbridge's custom to ride to Wall Street each morning in the Silver Cloud now parked in the garage adjoining the town house. He always sat bolt upright in the back seat, his arms crossed, staring straight ahead through the tinted windshield and occasionally barking advice to Pinckney on how best to negotiate the traffic. In late afternoon the Rolls would be waiting at the fire hydrant directly in front of 50 Wall.

Thatcher put down his newspaper. An object in the hall caught his eye and it served to remind him that he never would comprehend the bargaining processes of his wife's mind. She insisted on comparison shopping for every head of lettuce she bought, surveying Gristede's and the food chains with the zeal of an accountant, and sometimes when she was in a hurry she would enlist the aid of poor Pinckney in checking the prices.

That damn Guardi painting! It had arrived a few days ago from England—the shimmering canal and gondolas and men in red hats and Venetian palaces that reminded Thatcher of ornate post offices—and now it hung in a heavy gilt frame. There were two other Guardis on the same wall out of his line of vision.

"Dammit, Edith," he had said when she tried to prepare him for her latest acquisition, "why do you always agree to that identical price? Don't tell me the market for Guardi paintings has stood absolutely still all this time. Don't you see? I wouldn't mind if you

12

had to pay ten thousand *more* this time. You shouldn't hold to the same bid all the time. Guardi paintings must fluctuate in price just like stocks—"

"Now, Thatch," she said sweetly, "there you go. Comparing everything under the sun to the stock market. This is art. It's *different*." She tilted her head, admiring the latest arrival on the wall. "Notice, dear, how the gondolas guide your eye along the canvas?"

It was useless, of course. Furthermore, she used her own money to buy the paintings, so that he could not even accuse her of extravagance. There was one final point: he did not possess the capacity to remain irritated with Edith for more than ten minutes. He might as well try to breathe without oxygen.

"The size of the committee," he had told her last night at dinner, "should not go beyond six or seven men if it is to work with maximum effectiveness. Beyond that point it tends to fragment into smaller groups. Now take a look at the big corporations. A company may have fifteen men on its board of directors, but the executive committee—only three or four men—does the really important work. They decide on a stock split or a dividend increase and the rest of the board simply goes along with their decision on the meeting day." Edith sat watching him quietly. "A committee," he went on, "is only as strong as the chairman. But now then"—he hunched forward—"a chairman ought to get suspicious any time he gets a unanimous vote out of his group. A little opposition is a healthy sign. All shades of opinion exist among people, even corporate directors, and on a really important matter you're bound to run into some conflict. Let's say, then, that the chairman tries to bludgeon the group into some course of action. What happens? The whole project usually spoils. The chairman has to

13

count on one thing. He's got to have the honest backing of a majority."

When he sat back, quite exhausted, Edith had reached out for his hand. She remained silent, and it was only then that Thatcher realized he had been reviewing the strategy he planned to use with his partners this morning. The fingers on his hand had tightened then and Edith said, "What you said makes excellent sense. But you drop your voice at times. If you were speaking to a group of men around a conference table, I'm not sure they all could have heard you. Just remember that, darling."

Thatcher rose from the table and he remembered then about old Arthur Crimmins. The day after he paid two hundred and forty thousand for a Cezanne as a gift to the Metropolitan he had gone downtown and cut the salary of every employee at his brokerage house by 5 per cent. Thatcher passed through the hall, making a conscious effort to ignore the serene row of Guardis.

Outside, on the stoop, he glanced into the garage. The red door was up and Pinckney, wearing work gloves now, was polishing the license plate.

"Good-by, Pinckney," he called.

The chauffeur straightened up. "Good-by, sir," Pinckney said. The license plate beside him bore nondescript letters, no longer the black initials JK.

Thatcher began to walk down the street, still quiet at this hour, and he noticed the doorway brasses shining in the sun. He remembered then a summer morning such as this when Edith had run out of the apartment house—they were living on Madison Avenue at the time, near a shop that always kept riding boots and saddle gear in its window—and seized his hand impulsively. They had been married nearly a year and she was carrying Brit at the time.

14

"What is it?" he asked, surprised by her appearance. "I haven't forgotten anything? I have my brief case." He held it up for her to see.

"No, Bunny," she said. "You haven't forgotten anything." She tilted her head. "I just wanted to have one more look at you, that's all."

The previous September her father had provided a wedding reception at Newport that was so elaborate even the old-timers clucked their approval. Each of Edith's ten bridesmaids had received a pin in the shape of a sea horse, with a crown of diamonds and one ruby eye. And here she stood on the sidewalk, smiling at him idiotically, still in her housecoat and slippers, her hair blowing across her cheeks as though she were a schoolgirl on a picnic, and she was calling him by her new pet name, Bunny.

Edith had straightened his tie and crinkled her nose at him, and the memory of her radiance now squeezed his heart. She stretched on her toes and kissed him.

"God bless you, Bunny," she said and shyly ran a finger across his brief case.

She turned and ran back into the apartment building. The doorman on duty, a dour Scotsman with a pointed chin who had fought in the Boer War, had grinned at Thatcher. It was the only time he ever saw the man smile.

Remembering the episode, he shook his head and then quickened his pace so that the taxi would not be kept waiting.

Thatcher Kimbridge was a slim, neat man who, in his early sixties, still walked with the light wary step of a boxer. At Yale, in fact, he had been captain of the boxing team—not that the sport particularly appealed to him but because he had thought, quite erroneously, it might please his father and now he carried

15

a dislocated nose to show for his efforts. The nose was broken in the first round of a match his senior year, fighting a left-handed Yugoslav from Harvard, but Thatcher had stuck out the full three rounds, not saying anything about the pain to his seconds. He had won on points and, when he grew older, the sinister bend to the nose lent a certain distinction to his neat, thin face with its candid gaze and receding line of straight black hair.

In contrast to Edith, who had pale skin and a tendency to freckle furiously whenever she got as close to the beach as the Episcopal Church in Southampton, his skin was the color of bronze. Jared Kimbridge had been even thinner than Thatcher; he possessed the same dark coloring and a face like a hatchet. Brittin Kimbridge seemed to have sprung from some other stock. He was a husky youth, tall, with sloping shoulders—a slugger's shoulders, Thatcher had often thought to himself—and the arms of a blacksmith. Brit had been a second lieutenant in the Marine Corps and one week before the cease-fire in Korea he was killed by a sniper's bullet.

Thatcher was approaching Park Avenue. The taxi waited at the corner. Thatcher hurried the last few steps, almost breaking into a run. He nodded to the driver, whose left arm was resting on an orange bath towel draped over the door, and climbed inside quickly.

"Morning, Ralph," he said to the man on the back seat who was reading a newspaper.

"Yep," the man replied, folding away his paper. "Another hot one."

The taxi pulled away from the curb and headed for the East River Drive. The time was seven thirty-one.

Cool air from the river whipped inside the speeding taxi. On the right there surfaced the midtown sky-

16

line, the Chrysler Building first and then the Empire State Building, only to be blotted shortly from view by the squat new skyscrapers closer to the river. Beside the white-laned drive the generating stations of Consolidated Edison rose up like old Irish castles.

Thatcher was tempted to mention the incorporation plan to his companion. Ralph, after all, was a close personal friend who could be trusted to remain silent. That, in a sense, was his business. Ralph Creek was a corporation lawyer who specialized in antitrust work and Thatcher respected his tough, sensible mind. Since his law firm did no work for Kimbridge & Co., Ralph could render an impartial opinion. Actually, the brokerage house retained two law firms, one to handle underwriting and the other for general legal affairs. But Thatcher, wishing to move with the utmost secrecy in the preliminary stages of his plan, had consulted only his personal attorneys. They had agreed that incorporation was a sound step for Kimbridge & Co. Next he employed an auditing firm to conduct its own study. The auditors had given him their report last Wednesday; now Thatcher had cost figures to back up his rhetoric.

Ralph Creek crossed his legs. "Afraid you'll be riding alone tomorrow, Thatch," he said. "Got to fly down to Washington in the morning. Damn!" he exploded, "the whole trip's probably a wildgoose chase. I'm supposed to sound out Justice on a merger for my client. The companies don't compete in any product lines but, hell, I know what Justice is going to say. They'll trot out the Clayton Act and start preaching about *potential* competition. Hah!"

The lawyer had turned to face Thatcher Kimbridge. Creek's left eyelid drooped and it lent an air of perpetual skepticism to his lined biscuit-colored face.

"Well, you can never tell," Thatcher said with a little laugh. "One of these days those trust busters may surprise you."

"No, they won't. Miracles like that don't happen any more. In the old days it was different. The Solicitor General's Office and the S.E.C., they got the best young talent in the land, back in the thirties. But not any more. Those smarty-pants lawyers have the bit in their teeth nowadays." He rapped his knuckles against the door. "Premerger clearance. What a laugh! They wouldn't clear the way for the sun to rise if they could help it!"

The two men fell silent. Every time two listed companies merge, Thatcher was thinking, it meant one less stock to trade. But that was his problem as a stock broker; no use mentioning it to Ralph.

"You know," the lawyer said a few minutes later, "whenever I get down to Washington and take a cab from the airport I always notice how damn *low* that city is. All the buildings appear to be stunted. The Washington Monument is about the only thing with some respectable height to it."

"Yes," said Thatcher, nodding in sympathy. "It's a city that can make a man nervous. I even worry about the stock market more than usual when Congress is in session."

Ahead of them the towers of Wall Street bulked hard and clear and permanent. To Thatcher this view was infinitely more satisfying than the skyline of midtown Manhattan. The buildings seemed to turn on an axis now as the drive bent around the river. And then Thatcher thought about something else. For months after he had received the news of Brit's death this Wall Street skyline inevitably had assumed one pattern in his mind: tombstones looming in a graveyard.

Suddenly he remembered the smell of Brit as a

baby, that wondrous mixture of milk and powder and baby flesh. And as Edith nursed him, Brit's tiny fingers would curl and uncurl in delight.

In front of Trinity Church, Thatcher hopped out of the taxi so that Ralph Creek could continue on to his office at the foot of Broadway.

"Have a good trip," Thatcher said.

"Thanks," Creek replied humorlessly. "You might as well tell me to have a good slug of arsenic." He shut the door. "Okay, Thatch. See you Wednesday."

The light filtered down upon Wall Street in flat, irregular planes so that to Thatcher Kimbridge the buildings from this angle had a strangely foreshortened appearance, as if viewed through the telescopic lens of a camera.

The morning crowd rushed along the deep, hot shadows, tilting down the slight incline that ran east from Broadway for the first block. This incline, with the East River only a few short blocks away, conveyed the impression of a tremendously busy gangplank.

A minute later, as he was walking past the Morgan Guaranty building, Thatcher suddenly stopped. He reached out and touched one of the pockmarks on the huge granite blocks. The pitted impression, a memento of the Wall Street explosion, felt gritty and warm to his touch. He had always liked the sure strength of this building even though it was no taller than his own town house and he could understand the bank's proud attitude toward the explosion scars. When the building had been remodeled, the blast marks were left undisturbed except for a steam washing.

He had been in college at the time, but he remembered the date as clearly as his own birthday. The sixteenth of September, 1920. "Bloody Thursday," that

19

day was called, to distinguish it from "Black Thursday," the twenty-fourth of October, 1929, the day that touched off the Crash. He remembered that date, too.

His father had described the explosion when Thatcher came down from New Haven the following weekend. At the instant of the detonation Jared Kimbridge had been only a block away. He had just left the Stock Exchange and was walking along Pine Street on his way to lunch. The force of the blast had knocked his father down but he was unhurt. Running toward the scene of the explosion—"most of the people were busy going in the opposite direction," his father had said—Jared Kimbridge saw the huge cone of acrid smoke, the color of mustard, that was starting to blot out the sky. When his father reached Wall Street, he had bent down to help a man who was moaning in pain. The sidewalk beside the bank was sprinkled with glass. The man held up his arm to Jared Kimbridge—and then the man's flesh and suit peeled off together in his father's hands. "As easily as the skin comes off a grape," that was the way he had described it to Thatcher.

On the sidewalk now a pigeon cocked its head inquisitively at Thatcher. The pigeon had black feathers and a shining crimson neck. He rubbed the coarse grit between his fingers and a few grains of it fell upon the pigeon accidentally. The pigeon strutted away disdainfully.

Somehow he could not shake off the memories of Brit and of his father this morning. He could hear his father's voice so clearly. . . .

It had a strange quality, that voice. It was soft on the surface, almost fragile, a voice that could hide its hardness like a steel razor gliding beneath a fluff of lather. As a child he had been fascinated by the spectacle of his father shaving with a bone-handled straight razor. The razor and his father's voice, they were so alike.

"Mind you," he could hear his father saying, "the House of Morgan helped to put us in business. During the panic of oh-seven old Pierpont Morgan kept scrambling to keep the trust companies from going bust. Why, you could have walked right across Wall Street on the heads of the depositors, there were so many of them. Morgan swore he'd break any of the big-time bear operators if they took advantage of the situation. They were good boys, though. But I figured to myself, what could I lose?" Thatcher could remember the voice taking on hardness here. "I was only a clerk in an investment house. I got my hands on some money and sold short like crazy. Later on, Morgan heard about what I had done. He never spoke to me after that the few times we were in the same room. But what did I care? I covered my short positions just before the market rallied. The money I made right then, mind you, put Kimbridge & Co. into business."

The gamble had paid off. Kimbridge & Co. opened its doors in 1907, just three days before Christmas. In Thatcher's files there was a faded photograph of that first office.

It showed a glass-domed ticker on a wooden stand beside a high wire basket. There was a carpet with a wild floral design on the floor and a chalk board covered part of one wall. A clerk with garters on his shirt sleeves posed self-consciously in front of the board. On the right, almost sliced out of the picture by the photographer, was the only other employee of the firm—his father. He was sitting in a rocking chair with his face in profile, peering in complete absorption at the board.

Thatcher felt a twinge of pride now at the image of his father, a brash upstart, standing up to the mighty

21

Morgan, a man who used to stride along with a flat-topped black derby clamped on his fierce head and a long cigar in a paper holder clenched between his teeth. *You* got out of his way when he walked down Wall Street.

Thatcher permitted himself a thin smile. Personally, he got along splendidly with the officers of the Morgan bank; one of them he respected in addition as an astute bridge player. As for Kimbridge & Co., it customarily enjoyed a high syndicate bracket in underwritings managed by Morgan Stanley & Co. His firm, Thatcher Kimbridge knew, possessed the essential ingredients: impeccable respect in Wall Street and a highly efficient distribution system for placing securities with clients.

"Hey, Thatch!" a voice called out. "Come on now. That building's not for sale!"

He turned to see David Hillyer regarding him with a bemused expression.

"Good morning, David." Thatcher Kimbridge managed to make his tone cordial.

Hillyer had a pink round face and oddly slanted eyes. His eyes always reminded Thatcher Kimbridge of two capers set in a dish of Jello. The truth was that he disliked—no, dammit, he actually despised—David Hillyer, the senior partner of Hillyer & Hunt. Not because of his appearance nor because the man represented competition. Hillyer & Hunt maintained a private dining room for its partners and Thatcher believed it a sin for a brokerage house to waste space in this fashion. He thought of various purposes for which this space might be used. Additional desk space for the Syndicate Department. A library for the Commodity Department. Why, the entire mail and stencil room of Kimbridge & Co. would fit into David Hillyer's absurd dining room!

He nodded brusquely to the figure on the sidewalk. The stories he kept hearing about David Hillyer invariably brought an acid taste to his mouth. A closed-circuit television console in Hillyer's own office to show the stock tape, a console fashioned from an antique English commode. The brass telescope behind the desk pointed across the harbor to the lower torso of the Statue of Liberty; a special lens was said to produce extraordinary effects.

"Looks like another hot day," declared Thatcher Kimbridge and strode toward the curb. It was almost time to meet with his partners.

2

On the twenty-ninth floor Thatcher Kimbridge entered the reception room and found it empty. Miss Grissom, the receptionist, evidently was somewhere inside.

He paused momentarily, gazing at the marble walls with their black streaks running through the yellowish stone. The streaks reminded him of the black veins on the hands of an old man. His father's hands. Jared Kimbridge would not permit his portrait to hang in the reception room—that stipulation was in his will, too—but his influence lingered in a far more subtle sense. Yes, thought Thatcher, his father's hands still cupped this room and every nook and cranny of the offices within.

He could hear his father's voice . . . "In April of ninety-eight—mind you, I was practically a kid then— I bought one hundred shares of St. Paul at $85 a share. That was right after the explosion of the *Maine*. I figured the railroads would take off. Well, I held on to that doggone stock until the next January when it sold for $130. It was a standard stock so brokers never asked for more than five dollars a share in margin money. My margin never was exhausted because St. Paul kept right on climbing. I turned a profit of 800 per cent in nine months. On an investment of $500. First stock I ever owned. . . ." The straight razor plunged triumphantly into a bowl of steaming water.

"Oh, Mr. Kimbridge! You gave me a start. I didn't see you at first, standing there so still."

The receptionist had entered from the board room and she hovered now, with a slightly flustered air, beside her desk. On the desk was a vase filled with eucalyptus. The leaves on the curving branches had a white powdery surface and gave off the musty odor of church pews.

"Good morning, Miss Grissom," he said.

"Oh, Mr. Kimbridge, I've just been in talking with Mr. Merriam. Miss Donahue called a few minutes ago and she sounded just terrible. Anyway, she won't be in today. But Mr. Merriam said his secretary could take the notes at the meeting this morning. So it's all arranged." She stood a bit straighter. "I hope you don't mind, Mr. Kimbridge."

"No . . . no, of course not. Thank you very much, Miss Grissom. Please ask Mr. Merriam to come to my office when he's finished dictating his morning report for the message wire."

He walked slowly into the board room, trying to shrug off his feeling of irritation. His secretary out ill, today of all days. He realized that, quite unconsciously, he had been depending upon the presence of Miss Donahue as a sort of silent ally. This was going to be a meeting where he would need all of the support he could muster. As the recorder of the minutes,

Miss Donahue did nothing more than take down the discussions in shorthand, of course, but he had grown to depend upon her. She was a large and quite homely woman in her late fifties and she had been his secretary since 1937, the year of the big market break. That was after his previous secretary had gotten married and moved to Denver. Thatcher did not enjoy interviewing the applicants and, finally, when Miss Donahue appeared he had asked her—he never knew quite why—if she voted regularly. "Of course, sir," she had replied, bringing down her heavy chin for emphasis, "and not only for the candidates. I vote 'yes' for every bond issue. I happen to believe strongly in bond issues for the good of the people." He had hired her on the spot, without even inquiring about her typing and shorthand ability.

He glanced automatically at the quotations board. The Friday figures curled like bits of cold spaghetti. On the far side of the board room, beyond the empty cubicles of the customers' men, fluorescent lights blinked on. Thatcher saw a clerk at the duplicating machine. The clerk would be wearing plastic gloves to keep the purple ink stain off his hands, Thatcher knew, and across the dim, soundless room he seemed quite unreal.

The managing partner paused for a few moments, feeling the pull of the board room. It was deceptively peaceful, the way Thatcher often had imagined wartime airdromes at dawn. He walked slowly down the aisle and turned into the corridor leading to the bull pen.

He entered the first office on the left, the office that his father had occupied. Jared Kimbridge had spurned the corner office, which was larger and had window views on two sides, in order that he might leave his door ajar and observe the comings and goings of his partners. Thatcher had moved into the office upon his father's death, not because of any similar motivation but simply because he believed this to be the space the managing partner should occupy. The corner office belonged to Seth Voorhees.

Thatcher's office was a large, austerely furnished room with a desk to the left of the door and a conference table to the right. There was a stock ticker beside the desk whose edge seemed actually to have been chewed. His father had used this plain, flat desk and spent hours at a time with his shoes hoisted against the edge and a green eyeshade on his head as he riffled the stock tape. For diversion his father sometimes read the moving tape upside down. In his father's hands the tape could hiss and dart and sometimes swell up like a giant paper boil.

Thatcher went over to the stock ticker and flicked the "on" switch. There was a humming noise and he absently fingered the blank tape. Miss Donahue's absence had thrown his resolve off balance. Was it somehow a warning, he wondered, to shelve his plan of incorporation?

"Morning, Thatch," said Howard Merriam.

The research partner walked over to the conference table and took his customary seat. He was a tall, angular man with patches of gray in his thick black eyebrows; with his stooped shoulders and slightly harassed air he seemed more like a classics professor than a Wall Street partner. There was nothing fancy about him. He was the only partner in Kimbridge & Co. who did not belong to a luncheon club and he was the closest friend Thatcher had in the firm.

"Hello, Howard. What do you hear?"

"Well, *Reader's Digest* is coming out with a piece on cosmetics companies in next month's issue. A friend of mine sent over an advance proof."

Thatcher nodded absently. The tape rustled in his fingers.

"My girl will be in as soon as she types up the dictation," Merriam said.

"Yes," said Thatcher. "That's just fine. What's her name?"

"Miss Leone. Ursula Leone."

"Isn't she about to have a baby?"

"She's six months along. And big as a house, I must say. You remember, Thatch. We agreed to waive the four-month pregnancy rule in her case. They don't have much money."

"This is their first child?"

"I should hope so," Merriam said, smiling. "They've only been married eight months."

"Yes," Thatcher said, "I'm sure she will be satisfactory. You've explained our routine here to her? Fine."

In a few minutes the other partners began drifting into the office. By the time Ursula Leone entered all seven men had taken their seats.

She came in shyly and flushed as Thatcher explained to the other partners why she was taking Miss Donahue's place.

My God, thought the managing partner, she looks just like a penguin. That same waddling walk. She took the solitary chair placed to one side of the conference table.

Thatcher Kimbridge coughed and gave a quick nod that included the assembled partners. The time was exactly eight-fifteen. "All right, gentlemen," he said. The dawn patrol meeting, as it was popularly known to the employees, had begun.

Thatcher sat at the head of the table, the far end of which was pushed against the wall. Seated clockwise to his left were Andy Kraft, Red Hooker, and Fred Lincoln. On the right side Seth Voorhees sat opposite

Fred Lincoln. Julian Everly and Howard Merriam, who was at Thatcher's immediate right, completed the group.

"Andy," said Thatcher Kimbridge, "what have you got for us?"

"The errors report," replied the back-office partner. He had thinning brown hair and a chalky face that bore the pepper marks of an accidental shotgun blast in his youth. When he talked he had the habit of looking past the other person, as if his mind were searching out an arithmetical answer on the opposite wall. Kraft smoothed out a piece of paper with a clinical gesture. "Volume is playing hob with us," he said. "The figure for the latest month runs four point two errors per thousand transactions."

Thatcher grunted. "Year ago?" he asked. His fingers were drumming on the table.

"We were batting a bit better then," said Kraft. "Errors per thousand were three point five."

"What's the trouble?" said Thatcher.

"The extra help," said Kraft. "You hire a girl today who's nineteen years old and pay her a decent salary. But she doesn't have that old college try. Even with all our new equipment, we're not maximizing potential."

Thatcher stared at the back-office partner. Kraft was dressed in his customary blue suit—"CPA blue," Seth Voorhees had once described it—and plain blue tie.

"Andy," said Thatcher, "let's go over the trouble spots again and see where we can cut down on our errors. I'm counting on an improvement next month— no matter what happens to volume."

"Okay, Thatch. I'll do my best."

"Red?"

The commodity partner passed a hand over his

lumpy bald head and said with a grin, "Know any reliable rain makers?"

"Afraid not," said Thatcher.

"That's too bad. Some of our largest commodities customers are short soybeans. I put them in last Tuesday. So now they're praying for rain. A soaking good rain in the right part of the Middle West now would mean a big soybean harvest. Our clients stand to make a killing." Hooker looked around the table. "I'm not hard to please. I'll even settle for a reliable rumor of rain."

"I'll let you know," said Thatcher, "if I come across a rain maker who looks like he can accommodate you. Fred?" He was anxious to hurry the meeting along.

The bond partner had been drawing a diagram on his pad. This did not mean that Lincoln was not paying attention. Thatcher recognized the sign; it meant his partner was on edge this morning.

When this happened, it was Fred Lincoln's habit to plot out an imaginary golf course, set down incredibly difficult hazards, and then proceed to play the course on paper. Across the table, Thatcher could see the bold design on the pad: Lady Fingers, five traps encircling a green with a long, curving approach.

I know what's bugging him, thought Thatcher with a sudden surge of sympathy. Fred Lincoln was sweating out a 12:30 P.M. sale in Spokane municipal bonds. It was a competitive bidding and Kimbridge & Co. was co-manager for one of the syndicates. If the Kimbridge & Co. group were awarded the deal, Fred Lincoln had to sell his bonds before the closing of orders at four o'clock this afternoon for the underwriting to be rated a success. A deal in the middle of the day made it that much tougher for the winning bidders. It meant losing an hour out of the vital four-hour selling period, an hour when the men at the banks and insurance companies who might buy the bonds were still at lunch. If they won the deal, Lincoln and his assistants would spend that afternoon giving the bond scales out over the telephone—and sweating blood. Institutions, even the biggest ones, were just like sheep. They might decide to snap up the bonds and then again they were just as likely to play coy. Fred Lincoln never knew until he picked up the telephone.

Lincoln laid his pencil carefully across the pad. "The bill market is improving a bit," he said to Thatcher. "The pension funds are loaded with cash, but heaven only knows when they'll jump in—or where." He paused and rattled loose golf tees in his pocket. "But we've got Spokane coming up today," he said.

"Yes, I know," said Thatcher softly. "Good luck." He looked over at Seth Voorhees, and tensed slightly.

Voorhees, who was far-sighted, customarily wore half glasses while he was on the trading floor or wherever he might be required to glance at reading material. These half glasses, in a thin tortoiseshell frame, were set firmly on his nose and when he stared back across the top rim at Thatcher the spectacles emphasized the dark, probing eyes of the floor partner.

"By the way, Seth," said Thatcher finally, "I noticed on a ticket Friday that you bought five hundred Honeywell for the firm's account. Something special going on there?"

"I wouldn't know," said Voorhees. "The block was offered on the floor and I saw who the seller was. I simply don't trust the judgment of that firm. When they sell a stock, it's usually a good buy, I've found. So now we own some Honeywell and we're ahead a point and three-eighths. If I can get another point for that stock this morning, I'll sell."

31

"Nothing else?" said Thatcher. He kept turning the speech over in his mind.

"Nothing else," said Voorhees.

"Julian," said Thatcher to the underwriting partner, "I suppose you know that Garrett Anderton died? Funeral's tomorrow. Four o'clock. St. Bartholomew's."

"Yes," said Everly. "I'll be there. Already marked it on my calendar." He touched his mustache lightly.

"Howard," said the managing partner, "what have you got for us?"

"I've got a stock market that can't make up its mind," replied Merriam. He frowned. "It's still making a line. Frankly, I've never seen anything quite like this. And it hasn't been showing its hand since last spring. One thing I can promise you," he said slowly. "When this market finally decides to move—up *or* down—it will be a humdinger. But right now the trading range looks as flat as this table."

Thatcher nodded. Now it was time for him to spring his surprise. He glanced around the group. Fred Lincoln was fiercely diagramming a new hole; from Thatcher's angle it appeared as impregnable as Fort Knox. Seth Voorhees kept eyeing Thatcher steadily.

The managing partner of Kimbridge & Co. hunched slightly forward in his chair. His palms were damp. "Gentlemen . . ."

Thatcher's voice, or so it seemed to him during the next minute, carried that strange, funereal quality he had always associated with the loudspeaker system at the Yale Bowl.

When he finished, a frozen silence filled the room. He saw Andy Kraft's eyes blinking rapidly behind his rimless glasses. Fred Lincoln's pencil was poised like a putter caught in the middle of its swing. But none of the partners said anything. There was a cough that seemed somehow to register disagreement. The cough came from Voorhees.

Then came the first articulate reaction. "Holy Mary," breathed Ursula Leone.

"Well," Julian Everly said finally. "Well, well. And what brought this on, Thatch?" Everly always liked to get directly to the heart of a matter; he even answered his own telephone.

"You certainly have the right to ask," Thatcher said. "After all"—he tried to smile but found it impossible to do so—"it's your money, too."

"Thanks," replied Everly, and Thatcher recognized the change in his partner's tone. Everly was using his corporate underwriting voice; he wasn't willing to commit himself. It was the same voice that asked the president of a new company, whenever Everly was approached for a prospective financing, "What exactly have you got that no other company has got?"

Thatcher Kimbridge felt the tension and he knew now that he was going to have to sell his idea to his partners. Well, dammit, he was ready.

"Gentlemen," he said, "I've worked over this matter very carefully from both the legal and the accounting point of view. With a corporation we can achieve permanence of capital for the first time in our existence. We can retain half our earnings instead of starting off each year from scratch. That means if a storm comes, a prolonged break in the stock market, say, we can ride out the storm. In short, Kimbridge & Co.—pardon me—Kimbridge & Co., *Inc.*, is guaranteed to remain alive. The way things now stand, if one of us dies, a chunk of capital can go right out of our business. By accumulating capital under the corporate form—"

"We'd be cutting down on our current income," Voorhees broke in. "Aren't you forgetting that detail, Thatch?"

"No, Seth, not at all. I grant you that in a corporation the current income for all of us would take a drop. But we'd be building for the future. Why, we could set up an earned surplus and build that up through nondistributed earnings. Just think what it would mean! We could fund a really good training program for new producers, instead of depending on the hand-to-mouth method we've always used. We could start a profit-sharing plan for employees—"

"Why not just hand the entire business over to them?" Voorhees snapped. "Aren't you leaving the partners out of your calculations, Thatch?"

"No, I'm not," answered Thatcher Kimbridge. "Every person would be on salary, that's true, but the important thing is that we would be able to stabilize our income. In both the good years *and* the bad."

"There'd still be bonuses?" This was Red Hooker unlimbering his guns.

"Yes," Thatcher replied carefully. "We could make provisions for that to continue."

"What about our venture capital deals?" Hooker persisted. "Could we still work those?"

"Yes, certainly," said Thatcher. He smiled a little then; he had been hoping for this question and he had guessed that it would come from the commodity partner. "And we'd get a break there, too. We wouldn't have to set up a separate investment account for each deal. Sometimes I think we drown in paper work as a partnership. Gentlemen," he said apologetically, remembering to raise his voice so that every man could hear him clearly, "I almost forgot to mention one point. The corporate rate would become our ceiling on taxes."

"Uh, Thatch," said Andy Kraft tentatively. "There's one other thing worth mentioning. Am I not correct

34

in assuming that we would enjoy a certain new immunity under a corporation? I mean, there would be only a limited liability for each of us here?"

"That is correct," said Thatcher. "But frankly I don't regard it as a compelling reason for incorporation. I personally would prefer unlimited liability." It was ironic, he thought, that a man who had never sold a share of stock or a bond would be the person to react instinctively in terms of protecting his estate. But a sense of victory began to stir within Thatcher; he realized that he had gained the support of the back-office partner. He had the same feeling about Red Hooker, too. If the firm could go on working its private deals, Hooker might grumble a bit but he would vote for incorporation in the end.

"What about our clients?" asked Julian Everly. "I can't help but think that the institutions would prefer to deal with us as partners." Everly surveyed the other men. "Somehow," he said, shaking his head, "I can't get used to the idea of thinking of you fellows as vice presidents."

"Nonsense," Thatcher cut in. "That part of it isn't really changing. After all, we're not going to grow beards. What difference does a title make? We'd be the same management offering the same services to our clients."

"True enough," said Voorhees. "But, dammit, I don't like the idea of our sacrificing current income in order to lay up riches for the future. I prefer to take our chances with the market and with getting our share of trading volume. That way we stand to make a killing in a real good year. And to hell with a lower corporate tax rate!"

Thatcher understood what lay behind the hostility of the floor partner. Seth Voorhees, after all, was paying alimony to two of his former wives and every one of his children attended expensive schools. On a current basis, therefore, Voorhees always required more income than any of his partners.

But was there something else? Thatcher turned the thought over in his mind as he watched Voorhees remove his glasses and chew the tip of the frame.

"Aren't we becoming afraid to live a little dangerously?" asked Voorhees. The glasses flapped ominously in his mouth as he spoke.

Thatcher did not reply immediately. The statement apparently had been addressed to the group in general. But Thatcher felt a premonition of danger. Could it be that Voorhees was opening the door to an old battle that neither had ever mentioned? Voorhees had fought him once for Edith's hand—and Thatcher knew he had never been forgiven for winning. This realization fortified his own resolve. Voorhees was using a bridge gambit. Bridge was a game where, as in love and as in the stock market, you lost if you hesitated too long before playing your cards. Your opponent knew then who held the king.

"I don't really think, Seth," the managing partner said quite calmly, "that this is a matter of living dangerously or not living dangerously. What we've got to face up to is what's best in the long run for the firm itself."

Howard Merriam looked quickly at the other two men and then he said, "Why can't we approach this thing gradually? I know of several firms that have set up corporate units for their underwriting business while keeping the parent organization as a partnership."

"That's quite true," agreed Everly. "A good idea, too. That way all of us could become officers of the underwriting corporation on a salary basis without disturbing our profits from the partnership."

"No," said Thatcher. "It's all or nothing. A halfway measure simply avoids the basic issue." He realized that he was losing Everly's support. But Howard Merriam would go along with him in the final analysis, Thatcher was sure of that. Howard was the man upon whose backing he most relied. Quickly he added up the score in his mind. Howard, Red, Andy—they would vote for incorporation. That left the other three partners either as doubtfuls or as openly opposed to incorporation. His own vote would tilt the scales in favor of incorporation. But would it also mean an undeclared war among the partners?

"A lot of what you say makes sense, Thatch," said Voorhees, "but aren't you forgetting one item?" He was reaching inside a trouser pocket.

"What's that?" asked Thatcher.

"Jared," replied Voorhees. The name was almost hissed. "Jared would never buy your plan to incorporate this firm."

"What my father would have done is academic here!"

"No," said Voorhees patiently, "it's not academic at all." He sounded as though he were admonishing a wayward child. "You can't really believe that Jared would go along with this idea. Why, most brokerage houses are carbon copies of one another these days. But Kimbridge & Co. *is* different. If we incorporate, we'll lose that quality. We might as well close up shop—or let one of the big wire houses take us over."

Voorhees rested a clenched fist on the table. Slowly he opened his fingers and in his palm lay a large coin. It was his tossing coin, a bronze coin the size of a silver dollar with the head of a bull on one side and the hindquarters of a bear on the other side. It had been Jared Kimbridge's tossing coin originally, the coin he flipped on the floor of the Stock Exchange after he had yelled "Take it!" simultaneously with some other broker; Jared, who habitually chose the bull's head, would toss to decide which one won the transaction. Jared had willed the tossing coin to Voorhees, although Thatcher would have preferred owning that piece of bronze more than the town house in which he lived.

Very deliberately Voorhees placed the coin on its edge and flicked it with a forefinger. Every eye in the room was on the coin as it spun on the table and finally settled with a *warbulla-warbull-warbuulaah* sighing sound.

"Heads," announced Voorhees simply. "That ought to settle our discussion. After all, gentlemen, it's very dangerous to offend a sign from the grave—"

"I repeat that my father's wishes remain academic!" Thatcher half shouted. He glared at Seth Voorhees across the table for a long moment and then began to rub the side of his nose. With a shrug, Voorhees reached for the coin.

"Look," said Red Hooker anxiously, "maybe we can come around this thing from another side. I know how we've all been resisting this idea of taking some younger men into the partnership. That's why we lose a branch manager every year or two. Another firm comes along and offers him a better deal—and a title. Okay. I'm willing to go that far right now, Thatch. What you say about adding another partner. Hell, the pie's big enough. How about it, Fred?" He turned to the bond partner at his side.

"Not a bad idea," said Fred Lincoln. "What do you say, Seth?"

Voorhees hesitated. Then he gave a short nod. "As long as he stays off the floor," he said.

"What I had in mind was bringing in a producer, some man from this office," said Thatcher. "And I'd like to pick him before the end of December. That way he can start off the new year sitting right here."

He knew what the others were doing: they were offering him a partial victory. Accept the new partner but stall the incorporation plan. It was not what he had wanted but his instincts told him to tread carefully. It was like a safety play in bridge; you had to be willing to lose a trick in order to win the game.

"That all right by everybody?" asked Thatcher. The men around the table nodded their approval. "Good," said Thatcher. "I'll work that out myself and tell you which customers' man I come up with."

"Sure," said Everly. "We're all going to be around for a while longer. There's no galloping rush about that other matter." He gave a forced laugh.

"No galloping rush," Thatcher repeated softly. "But two weeks from now I intend to reopen the discussion on incorporation."

A new voice spoke up on the other side of the room. *Chook-chook-a-chook*, it said. Beside Thatcher's desk the stock ticker had come alive. The ticker began running test patterns. Thatcher inclined his head, unable to resist the sound.

"Oh, my goodness!" exclaimed Ursula Leone.

She was pointing to the ticker. The tape spilling out of the machine was stained blood red; the spool of paper inside the ticker was about to run out.

"I'll change the roll, Mr. Kimbridge," Ursula said, rising heavily from her chair.

"No," the managing partner said. "Not until this meeting is over." The girl sat down obediently.

Thatcher Kimbridge looked around the table at his partners. Then he pushed back his chair. "Gentlemen," he said, "let's go to work and see if we can't make some money today for our clients."

"*And* ourselves," added Seth Voorhees.

Yes, thought Thatcher, the battle has been joined again.

3

The seven general partners of Kimbridge & Co. were bound together by ties and loyalties as real as any marriage contract. At its core was a single overriding relationship: unlimited liability. This meant that each man was liable for the business acts of his fellow partners down to the final penny of his personal fortune. A lapse of judgment by one man could send the heavens tumbling down upon their collective heads. The firm bonded its employees; it carried insurance to cover securities in transit as well as to protect against fraud, theft, fire, and a dozen lesser contingencies; but there was no insurance policy for faulty judgment.

The partners shared their profits in direct ratio to the amount of capital invested in Kimbridge & Co. Thatcher Kimbridge, as managing partner, held the largest single investment. The other capital positions, as stipulated every year in a new partnership agreement, ranged downward in size from that of Seth

Voorhees, who assumed command of the firm in Thatcher's absence, to Andy Kraft.

The firm also had ten limited partners who were mainly widows or heirs of Jared Kimbridge's early associates. Their capital was invested in multiples of one hundred thousand dollars, in return for which they were guaranteed an annual return of 7 per cent plus a share of the firm's profits. Any income derived by the limited partners above 7 per cent depended not only upon the course of the stock market, the bond market, commodity straddles, and underwriting participations by Kimbridge & Co. but also upon the success of private deals. The latter might include such investments as oil-drilling ventures, the development of timberlands, or leasing a fleet of tankers.

There was one other limited partner: the Estate of Jared Kimbridge. The founder had managed to cheat the grave with a finesse that evaded his deceased fellow partners. Upward of one million dollars of his money remained at work in the firm. Also contained in the Estate was the seat he had purchased on the Stock Exchange, a transaction that by this time represented a sizable capital gain, as if to signify that Jared Kimbridge still held one profitable trade up his sleeve.

Seth Voorhees, a product of Lawrenceville and Princeton, was easily the most debonair of the partners. He had a long whip of a body, a taut, bony face with restless eyes, and the habit of smoking cigarettes —he disdained filter brands—down to the final half inch, as if he meant to get the most out of anything he touched.

He owned perhaps the finest wardrobe of any member of the Stock Exchange. On the trading floor he wore gray slacks that were pressed daily before the market opening and one of several tweed jackets, side vented and flawlessly tailored, with a fresh chrys-anthemum in the lapel. Voorhees' shoes were imported from England and he wore the waxed laces British style, tied along the sides of the tongue rather than criss-crossed. There were standing instructions with attendants for shining these shoes; he insisted that the laces be removed each time and wiped separately with the shine cloth.

But he was by no means a dandy. He had the knack of making a specialist take on a large block of stock sometimes to clean up a Kimbridge & Co. order, whereas with some commission brokers a specialist might seem quite incapable of reading the figures in his book. There were ways, too, in which a specialist could tip off a broker on the shape of the market for a stock if the broker had an important query. Voorhees understood the men who handled these books and he could judge instantly how much of a trade he could afford to give up to the specialist. He seemed to have eyes in the back of his head; he always knew what the bellwether stocks were doing on the huge tapes around the floor.

On receiving a telephone call from his wife at the Kimbridge & Co. booth beside the floor, Voorhees always began by demanding impatiently, "Helen, *where are you?*" It was as though he were asking for the quote on a stock.

In addition to his other abilities, Seth Voorhees possessed a remarkable attribute. He had trained himself to function the entire day, if necessary, without going to the members' washroom until after the market closed.

Howard Merriam, as the research partner of Kimbridge & Co., was a man whose success depended upon his ability to evaluate random data. "The real secret of investment analysis," he once explained to his wife, "is to extrapolate. Extrapolate from a crumb. You take a crumb and you build it up into a cake."

In his approach to the stock market Howard Merriam was a technician. This meant that he laid greater stress on factors arising within the market itself, such as changes in the short interest or the movements of the advance-decline line, rather than the fundamental economic and political forces at work outside of the market. He plotted his own stock charts, taking them home each night to pencil in the lines with delicate care.

Several years earlier he had turned unaccountably bearish at a time when other chartists on Wall Street were predicting new highs in the Dow-Jones industrial average. By midsummer, however, Merriam's judgment was vindicated. The stock market was jolted by the heaviest selling wave in decades.

"It's what I *couldn't* see on the charts that scared me at first," he later said to Thatcher. "So I hedged. I decided to disregard my charts completely for the first time in my life. I kept watching the shipments of corrugated-paper boxes. Shipments were falling contraseasonally. I got the statistics straight from the paper companies, before the government tabulations were published." His pencil paused on a chart and then he drew the outline of a bear. "I wouldn't say it to anybody else in the world but, Thatch, I was scared stiff. . . ."

After Merriam's coup, Thatcher insisted that he and his wife go abroad for three months. "That's an order," Thatcher had said as gruffly as he could. "You damn well deserve a vacation."

The managing partner knew that Arlene Merriam had set her heart on such a trip for years but never dared mention it to her husband for fear it would take him away from the office and his beloved charts.

44

Finally, everything was in readiness for their departure. Arlene had worked out the final problem—the hotel where they would stay at a town in the Moselle Valley in Germany. There were only two hotels and she selected the one with the higher ratio of baths to rooms, reasoning that was the better hotel. "Extrapolate from a crumb," she had thought with amusement upon making her decision. But two days before the sailing date, something occurred that no one had predicted. As she was packing the teak-handled clothes brush she had bought as a surprise for her husband, Arlene Merriam was stricken with a massive cerebral hemorrhage. When Howard returned home that night, he found his wife lying face downward in the open suitcase, the clothes brush clutched in her stiff fingers.

The partners shared in sickness as well as death. When one of them cut a finger it was as if the others dripped blood. Each of them knew, for example, that when Andy Kraft took his last physical examination, a yearly ritual like drawing up the partnership agreement, the doctors had recommended the removal of the mole on his left shoulder. Until the mole was cut away, and the laboratory tests had proved negative, every partner in the firm carried an extra invisible load of anxiety.

The previous winter Thatcher Kimbridge had contracted pneumonia. He was forced to spend five weeks in bed and during part of this time he lost his voice. Toward the end of his convalescence he noticed small ridges growing on his thumbnails. His physician assured him that this often happened after a serious illness, but the thumbnails became a symbol to Thatcher of his own vulnerability. It was during his enforced stay in bed that he decided to set into motion the incorporation of Kimbridge & Co.

The Kimbridge & Co. partners sympathized with Fred Lincoln, the bond partner, when his wife went through a particularly severe menopause. Those terrible years did a lot to Janet Lincoln and one thing, somewhat akin to a religious experience, was that her snobbery vanished. It became an office joke after she once declared at a harpsichord recital: "But how *do* the Democrats keep winning elections? Why, I don't even *know* any Democrats." To everyone's amazement, with menopause behind her, Janet Lincoln took up flying at the age of forty-nine. She soloed within a spectacularly short time, learned happily that her instructor was a fourth-generation Democrat, and even purchased an airplane.

The wife most ridiculed in private was Priscilla Hooker. Her husband had a massive bald head with reddish lumps where the eyebrows should have been and when he squinted he looked like a Japanese wrestler. Hooker's first job after finishing agricultural college was as a county agent in Missouri. In time he grew tired of testing overly acid soils and advising farmers who didn't want to listen on the techniques of planting cover crops. Thereupon he came to Wall Street and got a job with a brokerage firm specializing in cotton and other commodities.

But even Jared had not bargained for Priscilla Hooker. Shortly after her husband had transferred to Kimbridge & Co. she appeared on the scene. She proceeded to inspect the partner offices ringing the outside of the bull pen and was disappointed to find them partitioned off into quite ordinary quarters, not at all as she had imagined with mahogany paneling and plush leather chairs. She found that her husband's office had the poorest window view and furthermore that it was narrower than any of the others. She lodged her complaint in person with Jared Kimbridge. His reaction was explosive; at the next meeting of the partners he instituted a rule forbidding any wife to venture past the reception room.

Julian Everly was a stocky, rather nervous man with champagne corks for cheeks. He was the only partner with a mustache and also the only one with a mistress. The latter was a dividend for him, in a sense, from an ill-fated musical to which the partners once had played angel. The mistress, a statuesque brunette whose endowments were clearly displayed in a bikini in a mating dance scene on a volcanic island, consulted her astrologist before entering into the liaison. The astrologist thought that the signs were favorable (she had also been right about the musical, cautioning the brunette, "Do not take part in any new undertaking") and that clinched it for her. She wore her hair in a ponytail which would bounce when she walked down the street humming Cole Porter tunes.

The other partners dutifully avoided comment about Everly's mistress. Once she tried to make Everly jealous by reporting to him that Andy Kraft, whom she had seen only at a distance, had made an indecent proposition to her. After the matter was straightened out—Julian blackened her left eye when he learned the truth—she had no contact, either real or imagined, with any of the other partners. As for the partners, their unexpressed consensus was to sympathize with Julian because of his wife. She was a strident sparrow of a woman who was always urging some new diet upon her husband.

In a sense, the partnership facilitated Everly's liaison with the brunette. At least one evening a week Wall Street strategy required that Kimbridge & Co. be represented at some black-tie function in Manhattan. It might be a dinner meeting for the Boy Scouts or a political gathering or even a cocktail party involving the charity of an important client. His fellow partners gladly stood aside to let Everly perform the honors—and have his night on the town.

One thing the partners did not know was that Everly had been a virgin when he married. This information had astounded his father who learned it from Julian's elder brother a week before the wedding. The father went immediately to Julian and offered to help him find "a convenient lady who can show you the ropes," a suggestion that horrified the bridegroom-to-be. There was something about a funeral that appealed in later years to Julian Everly; he was always willing to represent the firm and he had a gentle way with new widows. "You know the first funeral I ever enjoyed?" he said once to Thatcher Kimbridge. "My own father's funeral."

Fred Lincoln kept a set of clubs with a blue leather cover zipped over the top of the bag in one corner of his office. When he left New York, on business or vacation, the golf clubs always went along. His burning ambition was to score a hole in one before he died.

He was one of three partners in the *Social Register* —Thatcher and Seth Voorhees were the others—and a copy rested on the bottom shelf of his office bookcase. It was simply a convenience in drumming up golf matches on some new course outside of New York City. The book that really mattered to Fred Lincoln was a slim, leather-bound volume with tissue-thin pages that resembled *The Book of Common Prayer*. This book contained tables of bond values. Its pages were filled with columns of figures showing the net return on bonds and other redeemable securities at different interest periods. Fred Lincoln, even when his bursitis was bothering him, could determine the yield on a thirty-year refunding Triple-A utility bond in less time than it took the average man to blow his nose.

At Christmas, when the partners sent out cards to business acquaintances, his was the most distinctive. It consisted of a logarithmic scale done in the design of a Christmas tree; the cards bore cheerful red and green lines depicting interest-rate trends for the past year.

There was a coolness about Andy Kraft, an astringent quality that was communicated in his long face and rimless glasses, in his cool, detached way of shaking hands, and in his imported lime cologne that cost three dollars an ounce. People who met him for the first time could remember the scent of lime cologne after they had forgotten his face.

In a sense he was less of a Wall Street man than any of his fellow partners. The prospect of an underwriting failed completely to excite him, yet to Julian Everly the tombstone ads represented a form of literature with which Homer could not compare. "This is the deal," the ads in effect proclaimed in the financial pages of newspapers and magazines, "and here are the firms that did it."

Yet Andy Kraft's importance to Kimbridge & Co. grew steadily because of the endless battle against rising costs. As the back-office partner he was responsible for a vast range of operations—among them, the Cashier's Department, the Proxy Department, the Margin Department, the Computer Department—and nearly half of the firm's employees came under his direct supervision. He also functioned as the housekeeper, watching over supplies, mailing, stenciling, and the pay roll. The customers' men were made constantly aware of his existence. The memo pads on their desks bore the imprint of his slogan: "Write it down—verbal instructions can multiply errors!"

He was above all things a numbers man. Upon entering a taxi he would automatically memorize the number of the driver on the dashboard. Every afternoon when he left the office it was his custom to change into a sweat suit at the Downtown Athletic Club where he played ping-pong for relaxation. Before entering the club he memorized the license plates from three vehicles and then repeated them aloud as he swung his paddle; one result of this was that few members cared to play with him.

He had gone to work for Kimbridge & Co. in June, 1929, as a clerk in the cashier's cage. In those days the cage lived up to its name. It was fronted from floor to ceiling by woven steel wire into which an adventurous employee—but never Andy Kraft—might occasionally stick a picture postcard in order to break the jail-like expanse. His first job was to slit all envelopes containing stock certificates along three sides, thus making certain that nothing was left inside the envelope. Two months later he received a promotion after devising the scheme of placing covers over the wastebaskets with a small hole in the center, so that certificates could not slide accidentally into the baskets. This practice, which came to be known irreverently among junior clerks as "the Kraft hole," was still used by the firm.

At night Arlene Kraft and her husband read aloud to each other. They had started with Thackeray but eventually concentrated upon English spy stories. Every night they would read thirty-five pages. The reading session began as Arlene took her bath, with Andy perched on a bathroom scale, book in hand, and ended in their twin beds. The Krafts read exactly thirty-five pages, not one line more, even if it meant leaving a secret agent in distress with a gun muzzle pressing against his temple.

In a sense, the partners were like a tight band of aging warriors, chipped and battered but somehow still agile. As young men in the Street, in the days before they achieved partner status, they had watched Radio and Woolworth and Anaconda and Electric Bond & Share collapse before their unbelieving eyes, so that the Crash and what had followed became submerged in the darkest layer of their memories. Like almost everyone else, they had lost money then. But something far more precious drained away, at least for a long time. They had lost faith in what they stood for.

In the cage of Kimbridge & Co. young Andy Kraft was getting only three hours' sleep a night in late October of 1929. Standing before a row of adding machines with the other clerks, he would work frenziedly long past midnight figuring out the day's trades and wallowing in a sea of stock transfer papers. Then the clerks would fall exhausted onto cots installed in the office. In the early morning, before the cots were picked up, the board room had the appearance of an army field hospital. On the twenty-ninth of October the terror suddenly got to Andy Kraft. Leaning against the counter of the cage with a certificate for five hundred shares of Steel in his hand, he was seized by an uncontrollable trembling. Thereupon his sphincter muscles failed him and a smell that was unmistakable rose in the crowded working area. It was the most horrible moment of his life for Andy Kraft.

The partners' meeting every Monday morning could be compared to a reunion of old comrades in arms. None of them ever expressed the relationship in these terms, partly because it would be in poor taste but also for another reason: an unspoken fear that the shelling might start again without warning and this time they would be too old to survive the ordeal.

It was, somehow, their final dread. But the fact remained that the partners of Kimbridge & Co. did enjoy a common badge of honor. They had been *there*. And within their hearts lurked a silent scorn for the young men who had trooped down to Wall Street in those ensuing years, the jaunty, fresh-faced youths who had known only the Peace.

4

The board room, a few minutes before ten o'clock, breathed slowly and deliberately through its air-conditioning vents. The center of the room, brightly lit now, was dominated by steel desks with blue formica tops. Each desk occupied a small cubicle that gave the illusion of privacy although the glass partitions were only as high as a man's chest. The desks were arranged six across and five deep; a low hinged door provided entry to each cubicle. Placed on a common platform, the desks had the appearance of being lashed together and floating through the board room on a barge.

The front wall was covered by the quotations board that gave the room its name. This board, dull black in the fashion of nonreflecting military paint, remained still and expectant. It was flecked with white plastic symbols denoting stocks and commodities. Cut high into its center was a blank horizontal screen.

Just inside the entrance to the board room the door to a large storage closet stood ajar. The closet held a king's ransom in paper. Message pads, spools of ticker tape with the hardness of slate, order forms for the customers' men. Stack upon stack of new account forms, margin agreements, signature cards, releases for discretionary accounts, and a dozen other forms offering mute testimony that although a broker's word might be his bond there was nothing like getting it down on paper when it came to the customer. The mass of neatly boxed and stacked paper combined somehow to produce the faintly sour smell of a Chinese laundry.

The wall clock said nine fifty-nine. The second hand swept around the face of the clock. A bell rang stridently from behind the board. The market was open.

Seconds later, the board gave off a clacking sound. The opening stock prices whirred in their slots, displaying the whole numbers in white and the fractions in orange. A clack, then a number spinning into view. The board seemed to stretch and shake itself. It was like some strange animal slowly coming awake. The clacking numbers rippled along its hide.

Now there was a faint oily smell emanating from the board, the odor of some black metallic beast.

The movement of the board had bestirred the entire room, enervating it, twitching the occupants into motion. The telephones were jangling, each one pitched to a distinctive ring, summoning the customers' men. They hunched over their desks like artillery spotters, speaking in curt tones.

Voices raced from cubicle to cubicle. ". . . bid eight to a half . . . heard of this guy who ran up five thousand into . . . don't like it at this high level . . . check your portfolio for. . . . So, you've never bought

Treasury bills? . . . Shouldn't have sold it, I told her . . . twenty-eight, that's a good price . . . call you right back. . . " And a voice, incredulous, rising above the murmur: "You gonna sell out *here*? Why, you were talking telephone numbers for that stock just last month!"

The board room had come alive, pulsing, spitting, wondering, scheming, softly laughing.

And in the middle of the room a man's voice, triumphant, clinching the argument:

"So I said to him, let's be honest. For once, let's be honest. The stock market is just like a woman driver. A hand sticks out the window. Everybody figures out what it's gonna do, what it oughta do. So what happens? It takes its own sweet time and then it does the opposite, the unexpected."

Stock-market talk rippled across the room like a field of ripe wheat bending with the wind.

At a desk in the front row, across the aisle from the storage closet, sat a man with closely cropped blond hair and the watchful blue eyes of a hunter. His eyes were set deep under thick, sloping eyebrows and there were squint wrinkles above his prominent cheekbones. Across the desk his hands moved swiftly; it was as if he timed every movement with a stop watch. His face was set now in a serious mask but when he smiled a dimple would surface in the right cheek. "Where the angel poked you to see if you were done," his mother had said thirty-five years ago in a Georgia hospital. She had touched the dimple ever so gently and a name was born. Poke.

His telephone was ringing.

"Poke Jef-fers!" he said crisply, his voice rising on the final syllable.

"Where *have* you been? Pinching girls in the subway?" There followed a low, rumbling chuckle. It was Marion Parker, the chief telephone operator.

"Marion," he replied, brushing aside her question. "Tell me, what do you think of the market?" His voice had dropped, the tone suddenly confidential.

"Oh, go on with you!" She was laughing now and he could picture the crowded telephone room, switchboard and all, shaking around her.

"Mrs. Witherspoon has called twice already this morning. It was all I could do to keep her from phoning you at home.'" Marion loosed a giggle. "She must be specially lonely this morning. Here, I'll give you a line."

Poke hurriedly checked the market action of IBM for last Friday on the quotation board. High, low, close, net change.

"Yes-s-s?"

"Hi there, Mrs. Witherspoon. This is Poke Jeffers. It was up two and a half points on Friday. Notice that?"

What a joke, he thought. She dispatched a bellhop every weekday afternoon for a closing market edition so that she could feast on the final price for IBM. Her husband had owned a hat manufacturing plant in Danbury, Connecticut. In the years when the hat business had prospered, he put the proceeds into IBM stock rather than expand his factory. Thanks to his foresight—and stubbornness—his widow now owned 18,840 shares at a cost basis of slightly less than three dollars a share. She was a frail woman with large ears and after her husband's death she had become a Christian Scientist. Her bank account substituted for her personality. The bellhop was tipped generously to clip all of the bad news out of the evening paper before delivering it.

"Yes-s-s. It's holding up nicely, isn't it? Think positive thoughts, I always say, and a person's stocks will

56

hold up. But, Poke, I've got to let a little more go, I'm afraid. Some cruise clothes that I saw . . . I hope you're not going to scold me for selling three shares, just three teensie shares?"

"Why, no, ma'am! Sell three IBM," he repeated, his pencil chasing across the order form. "At the market." He dropped the slip onto the moving conveyor belt beside his desk. The paper rattled off toward the order cage in the rear of the board room.

He paid the homage that was expected of him. Although the commissions generated by her market activity were meager, she had referred a number of her friends to him. One of these, a practitioner, had developed into a trading account with a debit balance in six figures. That's how you got 90 per cent of your customers—referrals.

Only once had he lost control of himself and Mrs. Witherspoon knew nothing of the incident. Shortly after he had returned from the hospital, he received a present from her. He unwrapped the package while standing by the door on one leg and found himself staring down at a book by Mary Baker Eddy. Without thinking, he pivoted instantly in a shot-putting motion and heaved the book at the living-room window which, fortunately, was open. He never said anything to her about the book and later, when invitations to Christian Science lectures began to arrive in his mail, he ignored those, too.

"You just behave yourself aboard that cruise ship," he admonished. "Else you'll have to get a parade permit with all those men following you around the deck."

"Oh-h-h! Now, Poke. Shame on you!" She was highly pleased. "Well, ta, ta," she said.

He began to go through his mail, first culling out the checks and placing them in a brown manila enve-

57

lope that would be picked up shortly by a clerk. Finally, Poke had mastered the trick of detaching his mind while he was in the office. His very sanity had come to depend upon this. It was as though, by some maximum effort, he had succeeded in applying chloroform to that part of his consciousness screaming out that his left leg the previous winter had been amputated five inches below the knee. His reality narrowed down to a tight compartment: the board room, the market, the customers.

He had a reputation in the firm as a man who could move merchandise. Soon after he had started to work for Kimbridge & Co. in the Atlanta office, he demonstrated the ability to relate instantly to the needs of his customers. He was like some finely attuned scientific instrument that adjusted automatically to changes in pressure and temperature. This talent, plus boundless energy and the willingness to suffocate clients with service if necessary, had become his hallmark. In each account it was as if he himself became the customer, losing his identity in the needs and quirks of other people. He could still remember, the way a pitcher remembers years later the entire sequence of pitches in a crucial ball game, the portfolios of his first dozen clients and the prices they paid for their securities. His transfer to the Wall Street office six years ago was a symbol of recognition by the partners.

He skimmed through the interoffice memos and set aside a summary from Research on utility stocks paying dividends that were partially tax free. This was something that might appeal to some of his older clients. He would make the telephone calls later in the morning.

"So? The stock moved from 34 to 39 and that doesn't impress? Suppose it went from 340 to 390, what would you say? Well, all right. Same thing. What? No, you hold it! You don't sell, not today, not tomorrow—"

The sharp voice in the cubicle behind him, less excited now, lapsed into a conversational tone. That was Izzy Padawer, on the horn with some customer.

The magnified stock tape was moving now. The tape, almost the color of human flesh, fled across the screen.

Poke Jeffers watched the tape and marveled. It was crammed with power, stronger than any human muscle, and up there on the board the tape seemed to flaunt its strength. He could hear the steady thump of a stock ticker pulsing in the background. It was pounding like a runner's heart and the rhythm sank into the board room, a relentless downbeat to the hundred other sounds.

Poke closed his eyes for a few moments, nodding gently to the hypnotic beat. When you weren't looking at the tape, that beat was like the sound of jungle drums. Very few things really got to him any more. But the stock tape had a way of crawling under his skin.

The telephone rang, and his eyes flew open. He lifted the receiver and a voice instantly crackled, "Jeffers." It was a statement of fact. "Scovill here. How're they opening?"

Percy Scovill was the vice president of a large mutual fund that seldom took a position in a stock for less than one million dollars. He could command Poke's attention for a very good reason that neither of them ever mentioned: the possibility that the fund might divert commission business to Kimbridge & Co. for the first time.

Poke began to call out prices. He knew the fund's

59

portfolio by heart; he had memorized it a month ago after Scovill's first surprise call.

"Your Johnson & Johnson is up a quarter." It was always best to start out with a gainer, even when you were talking to another pro. "Jersey unchanged. Boeing down an eighth. Kodak up three-eighths. Good volume there. No, Monkey Ward hasn't opened yet. . . ."

He went on reciting, playing Scovill's little game without batting an eyelash. The vice president could get this same information from his fund's own trading department. But if he told Scovill to go whistle, a hundred other salesmen in the Street would turn cartwheels for a shot at the magic words: "Buy a thousand Steel. And, let's see, put a stop on that order at five-eighths." However, Scovill was not going to give his business away for nothing. He needed the right kind of investment idea—something special, not canned out of Research—and the right reasons for it. That's what Scovill's calls meant; Poke never asked where the man had obtained his name.

"Got it," snapped Scovill, ready to ring off. "Oh, say, call me when Monkey Ward opens." It was a flat statement, not a request.

Rebellion surged within Poke but he held it down, like volcano lava bubbling beneath the crust.

Hek-ek-clack. Hek-ek-ek-ek-clack. The price disks twirled in their slots. When the stock market was dropping, the board could sound like a mechanical Bronx cheer. Today it was simply stuttering, marking time. *Hek-ek-ek.* The Dow-Jones industrials, up zero point twenty.

Montgomery Ward crossed the tape. Poke dialed a number, heard Scovill's bored voice say, "Yes?" He talked fast. "Jeffers here. Your Ward, up a half."

The morning wore on. Poke made more than a

dozen calls. On the tax-free utilities he did not get a buyer until the fourth call. You had to bounce back every time you got a refusal; he had learned that long ago. It was no place for a philosopher, or somebody with butterflies in his stomach.

He called a customer who had paid for a transaction with a corporation check. The man had to be handled just right, or he might get indignant. But there was a policy at Kimbridge & Co.—debits on a personal account had to be paid with a check carrying the same name. The firm had gotten burned once on a trade and it took a fifteen-thousand-dollar loss. The customer was in a good humor. "Okay," he said to Poke. "Send back the check. I was just too lazy to deposit it in my own account. Say, will you charge me interest if I'm a day or two late?"

"Not on your life," Poke promised.

He took a call from the treasurer of an investment club, a group of housewives in Mineola, Long Island, and promised to send out seventeen Standard & Poor's yellow sheets on Safeway Stores. Investment clubs, frankly, were a pain in the neck. For every order he got from this source, he sent out a hundred pieces of literature. But housewives, even in Mineola, had husbands, uncles, friends, and—God knows—maybe even lovers who might need a stock broker someday.

There was a call from a squeaky wheel, a man who bought an odd lot every year or so and invariably complained about the execution. The man was convinced that Poke was pocketing a half point on every trade. "Excuse me," Poke said, "but I've got to take a long-distance call." He pushed the "hold" button and let the man stew for six minutes. When he came back on the line, the man had hung up.

That's what could kill you in the brokerage business if you didn't watch out. Chewing up time without producing commissions. You had to keep running, to give service until it hurt, but you couldn't afford to get trapped by the squeaky wheels. You wasted enough time making up for the errors that clerks made in the back office. Dividend checks were delayed, a stock transfer slip was lost, or the owner's name for a stock certificate in a joint account had been typed out incorrectly.

A customer telephoned for a quotation on an over-the-counter stock. Nothing doing, just curious. The man didn't have to say it; Poke knew by the tone of his voice. If the man had really wanted to buy the stock—something he may have heard about the night before—there would be a certain urgency in his voice. It took nearly a minute to relay the quote.

And then bam! An order to buy 600 shares of General Dynamics. Just like that. Executing the commission order took less time than handing the call for the over-the-counter quotation.

An amber button was blinking on his phone; he had another call waiting.

"Poke Jef-fers!"

"Good morning to you."

"Hi, Mr. Mulcahey."

"You always remember my voice. That's smart. You got anything for me this morning?"

"Not yet, Mr. Mulcahey, but I'm keeping my eyes open."

"You'll keep in touch then?"

"Yes, sir! Have a good day, Mr. Mulcahey. And my regards to the family."

Mr. Mulcahey had devised his own method of making money on the stock market. He would automatically buy any company listed on the Big Board if the stock was selling at less than four times cash flow.

A friend of Mrs. Witherspoon's telephoned to announce that Kimbridge & Co. was honest, after all. She had found her lost stock certificate and she apologized for accusing the Transfer Department of never sending it to her.

"Where was it?" Poke asked.

"Under the carpet. I was talking to Henry about how maybe we should buy a new broadloom for the study. And there it was, the certificate, right under the carpet where I had put it for safekeeping."

At eleven-twenty Poke took a call from another customer, a chemical engineer. This man had the theory that the market always showed its trend for the day at precisely that time. Every Monday morning he would go long or short of the market on a day trade.

"How are they?"

"Down a point twenty-two at eleven o'clock. And right now they haven't firmed up any."

"Xerox. Short thirty shares."

"Sell thirty Xerox at the market. Short!"

"—will do it, Frank, buddy! Sure appreciate this little order. See you 'round the campus!" The exultant voice belonged to Noel Bigelow at the adjoining desk across the conveyor belt.

Noel swung around in his chair. His eyes were gleaming like bright pennies. "Jeffers," he called out, "I feel great, just great! Buy you lunch. What do you say?"

"I'd be crazy to say no to something that happens once in a lifetime. Five minutes?"

"Five minutes it is."

He was no fan of Noel Bigelow, but he was curious to know what had occurred. "Frank, buddy," he knew, could mean only one person. A cousin of Noel who supervised the pension fund for a large textile company. The pension fund paid a downtown bank for its portfolio recommendations, and, to the bank's dismay, always directed the commission orders to Noel.

Noel stood up. "Let's weigh anchor," he said. "Alberto's suit you?"

"Sold," said Poke.

He glanced back at Izzy Padawer who took his calls when he went out of the office. It was the buddy system used by Boy Scouts in a swimming hole, but nobody called it that at Kimbridge & Co.

Izzy had a telephone wedged under his cheek and he was gesturing excitedly as he talked. He paused a moment to hold up a pencil. It was a signal to show that he knew Poke was leaving for lunch.

Israel Padawer was short and slight of build. The most distinctive thing about him as he sat in the cubicle was his face. He had large ears and a long, sloping face that stretched down across squint eyes, a quivering nose, flat lips, and a long iron-gray chin. The structure of his face, it seemed, had been decided upon only after the designing of the telephone, so as to afford him minimum efficiency as he talked with his customers.

"So long, Max," Noel said breezily. That was how he always addressed Israel Padawer.

The other man stared back at Noel, then nodded in embarrassment.

After completing this call, Israel Padawer would remove from his desk drawer a stout white bag. Inside the bag was a fare that never varied: one kosher pastrami sandwich and one kosher sour pickle wrapped in separate pieces of wax paper by his wife who also would have included a bottle of celery soda if there were any way to keep it cold. The bags came free; they were airsickness containers that his wife obtained from a cousin married to an airline steward.

"Yah," he rasped into the telephone. "Keep your

shirt on again. So your friend thinks his electronics company is such a genius bargain, let *him* buy the stock."

He watched Noel slap Poke on the back as the two men passed through the door to the reception room. A look of envy crossed his face.

"You're my customer," Izzy Padawer said into the telephone, "so again I say it, *no!* The Sears, Roebuck you hold. So maybe your wife, maybe your white Cadillac, you sell, the Sears, Roebuck you hold!" He listened impatiently, realizing that no matter how hard he tried he always fell into Yiddish speech rhythms when he became excited. Finally he lost control of himself. "Money is blood," he half shouted, "and you do not appreciate! So do me a favor, Sidney. Go to the bank this afternoon and take out two thousand dollars from your savings account. Small bills, nothing over a ten. Take it home, the money, and to-night you count it. Look at two thousand dollars, see how much it is, and then maybe you appreciate a lit-tle. What? Then Tuesday morning you take the money back to the bank. Yes, Sidney, good-by."

He reached into his desk for a small plastic bottle. He shook out one tranquilizer pill, put the pill in his mouth and chewed it down. He shuddered slightly as he always did when he ate the pill. But it gave Israel Padawer an odd satisfaction: the tranquilizer pill was the only part of his lunch that was not kosher.

5

Alberto's was located three blocks away on a short, curving street little wider than a lane. The street, which now housed mostly insurance companies and shipping firms, preserved the cowpath pattern of the early Dutch settlement. Half-timbered buildings with stucco walls and slanting roofs were holdovers from the real estate boom of the twenties.

The restaurant consisted of a single spacious room sunk partially below street level. Squat arches of brown glazed brick gave it the appearance of a cheerful catacomb. Alberto's was famous for its fast service, fresh sea food, inflated prices, and a Spanish bartender who served an extra portion to martini drinkers in a chilled carafe. To brokerage house employees who ate there, this carafe was known as Alberto's "SD," for special dividend. It was rumored that the bartender had made enough money—not in the stock market but in convertible bonds—to retire but that he stayed on because he could not resist the atmosphere of the place.

The restaurant offered large glazed menus, also in a brown brick color, with an italicized line at the bottom, "Fresh Horse-Radish Prepared on Premises." This was no rumor. Every weekday morning, in a storeroom off the kitchen, the lowest ranking cook donned a World War II gas mask and dutifully ground up horse-radish roots.

There were days, Poke was thinking, when you walked out of the board room all charged up. The market could do that to you. It was as if the electric current feeding the quotations board snaked out to pass through your own body. And it was obvious that Noel Bigelow felt that current today. His eyes were gleaming and he bounced up and down beside Poke as they stood in the line of people waiting for tables.

Noel was just past forty, a man with thinning blond hair and the glint of oil on his scalp. His compact frame was acquiring a layer of stomach fat but nevertheless he possessed the stamina of a dray horse. Fellow crew members on one Bermuda race told about the time he went twenty-six hours without sleep.

Noel took a cigarette from a silver case and lighted it. He looked about impatiently.

"Hey, simmer down," Poke said. "What happened back at the office, anyway? You win a sloop on some raffle?"

"Frank really delivered, that ole buddy! Ka-pow!" Noel smacked an open palm with his fist and exhaled smoke for emphasis. "My biggest order in months! Oh, baby, I can already see that bonus check in December!" He bounced up and down some more, then executed an impromptu jig without giving up his place in the line.

"What's his pension fund buying?"

"Kodak. A bundle. We're working out the order on the floor with the specialist. It's that big. I called Voorhees about it just before I spoke to my jeweler. I'm buying, too. Set of sapphire cuff links." Noel shook his head restlessly. "Say! I need a drink. Don't you need a drink?"

"Sure. But take it easy. We're in for a wait."

Ahead of them, standing near the cash register, the hostess held up a sheaf of menus. Beside the cash register was a stock ticker and the tape was ballooning softly into its tall basket. "Three or four?" the hostess called out.

No one replied. It was a waiting line of singles and doubles.

Noel glanced back toward the entrance. "Now just a minute, lad," he said softly to Poke. "We're enlarging this party. Miss, oh, Miss! Three here!" he was shouting at the hostess. Then Noel darted to the rear of the line and grabbed a girl by the arm. "Honey!" he exclaimed, "what took you so long? Come on. We're down here."

The girl was leafing through a copy of *The Oil and Gas Journal*. "Oh," she said, quite startled by the exuberant greeting. "Why—hello there, Noel."

"Hello, hello, hello," he fired back. He propelled the girl toward the hostess, gesturing for Poke to follow. "Here we are, Miss," he announced triumphantly. "The eternal triangle. We'll take that table."

They were led to an alcove along the far wall and sat down.

"I—I don't understand what's going on here," the girl stammered.

"What's going on," Noel said, "is that I'm inviting

68

you to lunch. Okay?" He beamed at the other two. "Great, I call this just great. Lad," he said to Poke, "I want you to meet a very special situation. The smartest analyst in Wall Street. Carol Tracey."

"Hi-yuh," Poke said. A woman analyst, he thought, an apron wringer.

"Turn off that Southern charm," commanded Noel. He faced the girl. "Carol, this is Poke Jeffers. Heaven's gift to women with money to invest. All those lonely old widows in the Bronx, crying themselves to sleep every night. Who do they turn to? Poke Jeffers. Oh, waiter! What'll it be, Carol? An SD?"

"Well—" She hesitated. "Usually I don't drink at lunch." She glanced quickly at Poke, then placed her magazine out of sight on the empty chair.

"A pair of SD's," Noel said to the waiter. "Jeffers?"

"Bourbon, please. On the rocks."

They settled back in their chairs and Carol took a sip of water. Noel was grinning now, enjoying his role of the gallant host.

"Usually I don't drink at lunch." It was Carol's voice—coming from Noel. The girl was so startled that she spilled water on the tablecloth.

"You'll have to forgive Noel for his manners," Poke said. "He went to Princeton and he never got over that part in a Triangle Club production. He mimicked the voices of the girls in the chorus."

"That's true," said Noel, grinning wider than ever. "I almost made a pass at my own roommate backstage, he looked that good. You know, lad, this girl is money in the bank for her firm. Hillyer & Hunt. They refuse to take an investment account with less than a quarter million. That's what I like about a special-situation house. Classy clients. We met—when was it, Carol?—oh, I'd say six or seven years ago. Dedication of a chemical plant down in Kentucky.

69

The chartered plane was supposed to be carrying only analysts. A nice, dignified way to generate sponsorship for your stock, of course. But our research guy got sick and I went along at the last minute for the ride." Noel shuddered. "What a trip! I almost fell into a vat of nitric acid. But Carol"—there was honest admiration in his voice—"knew more about the company's balance sheet than the board chairman."

"Oh, Noel," she protested. "What a speech. Really. You sound as though you were building me up for a public offering." She hesitated and then she said, "I'm going on another trip tomorrow night. To Pittsburgh."

Her cheeks were flushed. The pink improves her appearance, Poke thought. She wore her brown hair quite short. It was curled slightly at the edges and brushed against her cheeks. She had very white skin and a strong nose that was pinched at the tip like biscuit dough. She had lowered her head so that, listening to Noel, she seemed to be peering at him through her eyebrows. It gave her an air of severity under her tight helmet of hair. She was attractive in an angular sort of way, he decided. And there was something intensely feminine about the way she nodded and said, very quietly, "Yes, ah, yes," to Noel. The tip of her nose wiggled faintly when she spoke.

The waiter brought their drinks.

Noel raised his glass in a toast. "To my newly-departed wife," he said. "Off to Reno for a divorce."

"Oh, I'm so sorry," Carol said to Noel.

"You needn't be," he replied. "You should meet my mother-in-law." He took a long drink, then emptied the contents of the carafe into his glass.

"Cheers," Poke said with a brusque nod to Carol.

"Yes," she said. "Cheers." She tasted her martini. "Wow! That's strong!"

"It gets weaker as you drink it," Noel advised. "Say,

you two, I just heard the damnedest thing. About two outfits on the Street that use electronic computers for evaluating stocks. Bam! This morning they both put out bulletins on Jersey Standard. Know what? One firm calculated Jersey as a strong sell and the other one tagged it as the buy of the month. How about that?"

"G. I., G. O. That's what!" Carol said heatedly.

Poke looked at her in surprise. "What do you mean?" he asked.

"Garbage in, garbage out!" she snapped. "That's what I mean. A computer is no better than the information you feed into it. And that's what these houses do—pump garbage into the computer."

So that's it, Poke thought. You have a fierce sense of pride, Carol Tracey. It was something he respected in a person.

"Say, Carol," Noel said, "how about giving Hillyer & Hunt the old heave-ho? Come on over to Kimbridge & Co. Our computer doesn't give out advice on the stock market. No, sir. It's too busy fouling up the record system. Last spring the computer sent out duplicate dividend checks for every company beginning with a D or an E. Our Du Pont stockholders were very impressed until we wrote them a letter for lower prices in leather. Inflation wins again."

Carol had recovered from her outburst. She regarded Noel with an amused expression. "What about Howard Merriam?" she asked. "How would he react? He's a chartist and I'm not."

"Ba-lo-ney," snorted Noel. "He's a chartist, all right. But right now he's as nervous as a pregnant nun. You should see the stuff our Research Department is feeding us. The most speculative stock on their list of suggested buys is American Telephone. And Merriam's got all the research guys in his department singing

71

the same tune. The only decent lead I've had in the past week is an electronics stock. Know who gave it to me? Our utilities man."

"Well, you really can't blame Mr. Merriam," she said. "A lot of other houses are just as cautious with all this uncertainty about the market."

"Nuts!" said Noel. "So what happens? We customers' men are left with our hands tied, that's what. How can we produce if our Research doesn't hand us the merchandise?"

Poke stirred the round lumps of ice with a forefinger. He watched the Bourbon eddy downward in dark, swirling pennants.

"Tell me, Carol"—Noel flicked the stem of his martini glass—"what do you think of the market now?" He was elaborately casual.

Uh-huh, Poke thought, here it comes. The payoff for a free lunch. You didn't work next to Noel Bigelow without learning that he seldom did anything without putting a hook in it. It was always a good idea to count your fingers after shaking hands with him. Poke remembered something that Noel's wife once told him at a cocktail party. She had had a little too much to drink and, looking across the crowded room at her husband, she had said: "Noel went duck shooting this morning down in Southampton. He doesn't bring the ducks home for me to clean, thank God. But I'd prefer even that. He donates them to a local hospital for the patients to eat and he takes an income-tax deduction."

Carol took a sip from her glass and laughed nervously. "Well, the last thing I heard before leaving the office didn't sound too encouraging. One of our biggest customers told Mr. Hillyer that he wants to move out of stocks completely and go into corporate bonds. He says the market is in for a long decline. He thinks trading volume will dry up, too, and that—"

"Jesus! Don't talk like that!" Noel was indignant. "Who is this guy? Some Communist infiltrator? Why, the commissions in bonds are nothing." Noel reached over for Carol's carafe. "Thanks," he said and began to study her face. "Do *you* think it makes any sense? What this guy is claiming?"

She smiled and shook her head. "Oh, I don't know," she said.

"We'd better order lunch," Poke said, "before we all talk ourselves out of a job." But it was true, he reflected, the way your stomach could tighten when somebody tossed out some bearish theory on the market and it lay there right in front of you like a big firecracker with its fuse sputtering.

They gave their orders and then Poke found his attention drifting. Noel was telling Carol some story about a customer.

"—so when I told her Procter & Gamble planned to split, or anyway that was the rumor going around, you know what she said to me?" Noel proceeded to mimic a proper Bostonian voice. "'Oh, heavens, what a shame! And they've been together such a long time.'"

Poke heard Carol laughing appreciatively. Something made him look up. She was watching him over the edge of her glass.

He ignored her for a few moments. He swallowed the remainder of his drink and felt the Bourbon warmth seeping inside him.

"Did you know," he said to her, interrupting Noel on the brink of another story, "that your left earring is missing?"

"Oh, no!" Her hand shot up. "But I remember *now*. I did a lot of telephoning this morning and I forgot to put my earring back on." She rubbed the bare ear lobe gently.

"Anything interesting?" Poke inquired politely. It wasn't only Noel, he had to admit to himself, it was any customers' man. There was always this intense curiosity, no matter how well you tried to hide it, about what the research people were pushing at other firms.

"Hah," she said. "Wild-goose chase. I had the idea that shoe companies might be a good buy. Since cattle prices are so low. And I've never used the shoe stocks really. So-o-o, I checked into it this morning. Talked to Chicago and Omaha and even Kansas City. Turns out the *hide* market is booming. That's quite unusual in the face of record cattle slaughters." She shrugged and her clavicle—slim and white—showed under the momentary bulge of her seersucker suit.

"What gives?" asked Poke.

"There's a strong demand for hides in Europe. And I suspect also there's a speculative play in hide futures going on in the commodities market. Anyway," she said with a wan smile, "it sure ruins my theory for lower prices in leather. Inflation wins again."

"I have one customer who trades in nothing but meat-packing stocks," Poke said. "He takes a position every year in late September and he sells out before the spring thaw. That gives him long-term gains. He has a saying about the meat-packing stocks. Sell 'em or smell 'em. He called me up last week. Says this year he's going to sit on the side lines. Sort of like *your* man."

"Yes-s-s." She bent her helmet of hair toward Poke. But he had nothing more to say and she became self-conscious. "I—I don't usually come here for lunch," she said. "It's really too expensive. A Cádiz melon, they say on the menu, instead of a Spanish melon, and they charge a quarter extra. Only today I got so

74

depressed about the hide futures that I decided to splurge. If I worked around Fifth Avenue I probably would have gone out and bought a new blouse." She sat back. "Here comes our food," she said.

Carol was an appreciative audience for Noel right through the coffee. She played it just as politely, Poke was thinking, as an interview with some company official. And Noel. His eyes narrowed to slits in his round face when he got to the punch line in a story; he was really his own best audience because no one laughed quite as hard as Noel Bigelow.

After Noel had called for the check, he placed some bills on the tray. The bills were all new and they crackled like celluloid in his hands. Noel made a notation on a slip of paper and placed the paper inside his wallet.

So that was it! Poke recognized the gesture. Noel wasn't picking up the tab, after all. This lunch would go on his expense account, thanks to the chance meeting with Carol Tracey. She would be disguised as a client.

Carol picked up her magazine on the chair. "Thanks ever so much for lunch, Noel," she said. "It was fun."

"Think nothing of it," Noel responded gallantly. "I'm only sorry we can't entice you into the Kimbridge fold. Think it over. You could even give Jeffers here an idea now and then."

She led the way through the restaurant, cradling *The Oil and Gas Journal* in her arms. She was nearly a head taller than Noel and she walked with an awkward elegance.

They filed past the stock ticker. *Chook-chook-a-chook*, it chattered. Poke saw the tape falling from the ticker in languid coils, slowly, lovingly, like the emptying cartridge belt of a machine gun.

He glanced down at the tape and a print caught his eye. Kodak. Seven thousand shares. Only a quarter point higher than the opening price that morning. That was Noel's block, he sensed. Yes, Seth Voorhees had done a good job.

Dammit! His leg was beginning to throb. He walked behind the other two, trying to catch his reflection in the glass door so that he could adjust his gait properly.

His pace was off, he knew that, because he was compensating for the left leg. He knew it and he couldn't help himself. As he passed through the door, he could feel the perspiration oozing through the stump sock.

6

Carol Tracey arrived at Pennsylvania Station half an hour ahead of departure time. The call to Columbus was put through quickly.

"Yes, Mother, I'm fine. I'll be back in New York day after tomorrow." She hesitated. "Is everything all right at home? How is Dad?"

She could not hear clearly. Her mother, when responding to a long-distance call, would start out in a whisper and gradually pick up momentum like a runaway steam locomotive. "Mother!" she said sharply, feeling a fine toothcomb of terror along her spine.

"You don't have to shout, Caroline. I'm not deaf, you know." There was an offended pause.

"Yes, Mother. I'm sorry."

She listened impatiently as her mother rattled on about a neighbor who had died last week and, to the amazement of the entire block, had left his widow $315,000 in life insurance.

She remembered that when she first came to New

York her mother had sewn a chamois bag for money into her best brassière.

"—you feeling all right, dear?" Her mother finally buried the neighbor with all the life insurance.

"Yes, Mother, I'm fine. I take my combination vitamin pill every morning and I'm just fine. How—how are your hands, Mother?"

"Oh, well, dear . . ." The tone of voice told Carol that her mother was staring down at her fingers. Her mother's knuckles reminded Carol of scallop shells and she had looked at them in recent years with a growing sense of horror, knowing that someday her own knuckles would look just that way. "Growing old is no joy for—"

"How is Dad?" Carol interrupted. Her poor father, she thought, even the hairs inside his nose were turning white. "His back still bothering him?" She had a recurring nightmare: her father would die, white hairs sprouting like asparagus spears one midnight over his entire body, and she would have to return to Columbus and live with her mother. In her dream, after the funeral, her mother walked around the house wearing a glazed straw hat that was in fashion thirty years ago, one of those hats that looked like a berry-picking basket turned upside down.

"A little, yes," her mother conceded. "But Dr. Henderson had a look at it and he says it's nothing serious at all. And Mrs. Owens across the street agrees. She says what your father should do is drink cinnamon tea and take long walks. Ruth Templeton's doctor doesn't believe in shots *or* therapy. Pills, he says, pills . . ." There was a pause. "I do believe my fingers are getting worse—"

"Mo-*ther*. I'm sorry But I've got to run. Really. You give my love to Dad. Okay? And, Mother . . . I'm going to send a little something extra in this month's check. By, by."

Carol stood stiffly in the telephone booth staring down at her white knuckles. Suddenly she drew her hand away from the telephone as if it had touched a hot kettle.

The train hurtled through the grade crossing of a New Jersey town and the hooting of its diesel horn floated behind in the gathering dusk. The darkness softened the jagged edges of the town—ancient loft buildings, garages murky with neon, tin shanties huddled beside the track—all flashing by in a flattering instant of dignity. It might have been any small town in Ohio, thought Carol.

Alone in her compartment, she squinted into the fading light, her profile dark against the window. She was the only woman in the two special cars carrying stock-market analysts and investment bankers to Pittsburgh as guests of the steel company. Tomorrow morning the visitors would inspect a new continuous-casting installation.

In the taxi, with the black overnight bag on the seat beside her, she had felt the first pleasurable tingle of excitement. Slowly she had allowed herself to drift into the rootless splendor of the traveler. The people on the streets seemed already to belong to another world.

She rested her head gratefully against the clean white antimacassar. She had finally gotten her hair cut short. The bun was gone and now she could actually put her head back without turning to one side so that the pins would not jab. She had walked out of the hairdresser's and felt the wind play sensually upon the back of her neck. What was that old saying? That when a girl cuts off her hair it meant the end of

79

a poor romance. Well, not in her case. There was no romance, good or bad. It was simply that tomorrow was her thirtieth birthday and not knowing what else to do about it she had gone uptown to Saks where a little Frenchman with a sad face and incredibly long fingers had snipped away.

The train wheels mocked her: thirty years old, thirty years old, thirty years old. Then the wheel clicks were muffled in a new rhythm. Carol is thirty, Carol is thirty, Carol is thirty . . .

"I'm going to corner that first pot," a voice drifted into the compartment, "just you wait and see." Then the crisp sound of cards being shuffled, the rap of a deck against the table.

Carol recognized the voice. Joe Temple. Metals analyst for one of the large wire houses on Wall Street. He was sixty years old and his chief distinction was that he had visited every steel plant in the United States and all but two in Canada. He cannibalized the stock manuals, he knew many executives on a first-name basis, he played cards, and he drank free whisky on junkets. His chief contribution to securities research had been, two years ago, to prepare a report on a steel company that included photographs of the rolling mill in color. He was, in short, a hack, and Carol particularly detested the man because she happened to know that he made $7,000 a year more than she did.

Yet she felt a fierce attachment to her work; it was a little like being a spy. She never took notes and that impressed the executives. It also encouraged them to say things they might not otherwise have volunteered about their companies. She had a habit, when she wanted to fix some fact in her mind, of rephrasing the information aloud. The man would nod and, click, the fact was registered in her mind. She developed the tactic, after the dessert was ordered, of excusing herself and darting into the ladies' room. Here she would scribble down the information fixed neatly in her brain: profit ratios, sales projections, plans for capital spending, automation possibilities. And tag words such as "Joplin" for a new plant location that had not been announced, or "one-man show" to signify that management was weak below the top echelon. That was a bad sign for any institutional investor. Once, when she had forgotten to place notepaper in her purse, she committed the five-year expansion program of a major sulphur producer to pink toilet tissue.

She found that she had an instinct for security analysis the way some people possess an innate talent for music. In school, mathematics had held no fascination for her and, moreover, she was a poor speller. But the talent she had within her somehow flowered on Wall Street where the final question always became, "Is this stock a good buy—or a good sell?" She related to certain industries better than others; she avoided real estate stocks completely and she also shied away from motion-picture companies because it was difficult to extricate the press agentry and the bombast from the balance sheet. Somehow she could never trust what motion-picture executives told her and there was an added element of uncertainty beclouding investment judgment; nobody could tell whether or not a big-budget film was going to fall on its face.

Yet she could not help wondering if the whole process were not simply some horrible trick. Was she living on borrowed time? If you were a woman in Wall Street you could never escape the realization that you were intruding upon the private preserve of the male.

It was darker suddenly. The rushing trees were solid patches of black, no longer laced with sky between their branches. The landscape hurtled at her and fell away. Now she began to think about the next few hours. For her the nights were always the worst time on a trip.

A shadow fell across the train window.

"May I have the pleasure to sit down?" There was something strange about the voice. It had a foreign lilt.

She turned around quickly. A tall man—she judged him to be in his late thirties—was smiling down at her. A stranger with thick brown hair.

"Why, yes," she replied. "Yes, of course."

Carol crossed her legs in a scissors-like movement and pulled the skirt down over her knees.

He took the seat opposite her. He wore a blue double-breasted suit with wide lapels and a narrow waist.

He took a card from a small leather case and, leaning forward with a grave air, handed it to her.

The name on the card was in script. Frans Vanden Heuvel. And in the lower right corner, Amsterdam. So he is Dutch, she thought. In the opposite corner was the name of a banking house with the address. Something "straat," followed by hyphenated numbers. The tip of her thumb brushed automatically over the card; it was engraved.

He kept looking expectantly at her. And then she understood.

"My—my firm doesn't give calling cards," she said. "That is, not to its women employees. But my name is Carol Tracey. I'm an analyst in New York for Hillyer & Hunt."

"Ah," he said, nodding politely. He pointed to the window. "But you will hurt your eyes. It is not so good to stare outside after it comes night."

Those first minutes of conversation later remained a blank to Carol. Her finely trained memory simply deserted her. But somehow she had the feeling that the two of them were communicating on some mysterious channel while they were chatting about—whatever it was. He said something that made her laugh so hard that tears came to her eyes, she remembered that.

Frans lounged back in his seat. His jacket was unbuttoned now and he was smoking a cork-tipped cigarette. He seemed to have relaxed all at once. His black shoes bore a high gloss and when he stretched one leg across the aisle and rested it elegantly on the seat six inches away from her—an act that would have seemed boorish for any American—she did not mind at all. She noticed the indentation of a garter snap under his worsted trouser.

"—in Holland we are pessimistic always about our business," he was saying. "That is the Dutch way, I suppose. You see it even in our annual reports. A company never tells you"—he puffed out his chest—"this was the best year in history. No, no." His chest sagged. "The results were not unsatisfactory, that is how the company would say it."

"Yes," she said. "I see what you mean." His hair needs a trim, she thought.

"In the reports," Frans continued, "you read about the rising costs of labor and raw materials, so high they are, and the export problem and how necessary it is for lower taxes." Horizontal lines played under his eyes. "Finally, when you are thinking maybe this company will die tomorrow you see a little sentence saying that, oh, by the way, earnings are up 45 per cent over last year. It always comes just after—"

"I know," she broke in, sharing his smile now, "the results were not unsatisfactory."

He reached over and patted her on the hand. "Perfect," he said.

He swung his leg from the seat and stood up. "Come," he said. "Shall we go now into dinner?"

"That sounds fine, just fine." She stretched out her arms and shivered.

He reached down for her hand. Carol heard the diesel horn again. It seemed warm and filled with promise.

The green window shades were drawn in the dining car. They sat at a table for two. Just like newlyweds, she could not help thinking.

"I feel rather the intruder going to your Pittsburgh," he said. "After the war it was you Americans who built new steel facilities out of the rubble in Europe. And you even paid for them. Everything." He flung out his strong fingers expressively. "The buildings. Equipment. The engineering. Continuous casting we have already."

"Well, what's wrong with that?" she demanded. "We stood to prosper by a strong Europe. It wasn't completely unselfish, you know."

"Ah, yes. But now what happens? I am on this train for one good reason. Your steel company hopes that I will recommend the purchase of its stock to the clients of my firm in Amsterdam, no? But today"—his fingers closed into fists—"these same companies in Europe are competing with American steel. It does not seem quite fair. I feel—you must understand what I say—that I owe some sort of debt here."

The water swayed gently in their glasses and there was the clinking of ice. Like waltz music, thought Carol. She had to bite her tongue to keep from humming.

During dinner Frans told her about night life in Amsterdam and about his favorite salad made with bleu cheese and about the fake Rembrandt hanging in the Municipal Museum and about his cousin who made a handsome living by fishing out the motorcars that toppled daily into the city's canals.

They were sipping coffee and she kept expecting him to take out pictures of his family and show them to her. He was married, she felt sure of that. The photograph of his wife would be quite provocative; she was wearing a white bikini and walking away from the camera, one thumb hooked in the trunks.

But Frans offered no photographs and that made her intensely grateful. He *was* married, but somehow it did not stand between them.

"How long have you been away from home?" she asked.

"Three weeks it is now almost. From Pittsburgh I leave tomorrow afternoon for Detroit. But that is life, eh? No resting for what you call the wicked?"

He was smiling again, and she was glad. They went into the lounge car for liqueurs. The steel company was picking up all the checks; they moved grandly through the train signing their names.

The only liqueurs she had ever tasted were brandy and crème de menthe frappé. When she first came to New York she thought frappé was the brand name.

He ordered kümmel for them both. It was the best for digesting a fine meal, he said to her.

Carol twirled luxuriously in her lounge chair. She had the feeling that time had stopped. But right now the train must be about—no! All she wanted to think about this evening was Frans.

"You look like a bear," she said finally. "A big, contented bear."

They were alone at one end of the lounge car and even the waiter treated them with a special deference. As though he knew . . .

She savored the taste of the kümmel; it was like caraway seed. She had the sensation of being in some fine European hotel. The hotel ballroom was swaying ever so gently and this wonderful, ridiculous thought was ambling through her brain . . . Ah-h-h, yes.

And then she was shaking her head, startled by something she could not explain. Frans was leaning forward, one hand on her knee, and in the middle of the lounge car a magazine slid off a chair.

"You are all right? No?" His face was quite grave.

"Oh . . . yes." She felt so stupid. The spell was broken. "It's just that I can hardly keep my eyes open. All of a sudden." What made her say that? "I—well, I suppose I'd better go to bed."

She stood up unsteadily. She wondered—would he try to follow her? Suddenly the thought terrified her.

"You want me to come with you?" he asked.

"No, oh, no. It's just that I'm sleepy, that's all." She squeezed his hand and said hurriedly, "Good night, Frans. It's been lovely, just lovely. No—please stay here. I can make it back all right to my compartment. You stay here and have another drink."

Then she moved through the car, trying to judge the train sway so that she would not bump into the upright steel ash trays that were set into the floor like an obstacle course.

In the compartment she undressed slowly and crept into the narrow bed. The sheets were cool against her feet.

And now she was no longer sleepy. She could hear the clicking of the train wheels and she thought to herself, you are a perfect god-damned fool. You are thirty years old and you have never gone to bed with a man. Always, there was always some excuse. And what had she done this time? She had walked away—staggered away, really—from the perfect situation. A handsome foreigner, a chance meeting on the train, the striking of some brief, wonderful spark. My God, she thought, what could be more ideal? And she began to cry.

Carol is thirty, the train wheels sang, Carol is thirty.

There was the hoot of the diesel horn lashing about as it tried in vain to enter her compartment. After a while she drifted into sleep, remembering how Frans' hair grew down his neck in thickly bunched curls.

When she awoke the train was standing in the station. She dressed in a desperate hurry—somehow the thought crossed her mind that the train would pull away before she could leave—and when she yanked open the door to summon the porter there was Frans, leaning against the outside of the compartment with his arms crossed. He seemed remarkably fit and rested and he was smiling at her.

"Aha," he said. "You slept the good sleep, I trust?"

"Yes. Yes, I slept fine, thank you." Last night she had told herself, he will never speak to me again.

He took her bag and helped her down the steps of the train. The other analysts were milling about grousing good-naturedly.

Frans was as attentive as a suitor. Carol had never seen a person look so cheerful on a railroad platform at seven-fifteen in the morning.

He sat beside Carol in the chartered bus that carried the group to a hotel. Here they would check into rooms and eat breakfast before the bus transported them to the mill.

In the bus Frans kept twisting his head and peering out at the buildings. "Really," he said, turning to her. "What a pity to waste such a day inside a steel plant. These tours they should give only on rainy days." His eyes were shining. "Why don't we play"—he groped for the right word, then shrugged in defeat—"how do you call it?"

"Hooky!" she burst out.

At that instant she felt their line of secret communication spring alive again.

"Yes, that is it. Hooky." He made it sound like "hocky."

"All right," she said. The skin on her scalp tightened and, quite suddenly, it was difficult for her to breathe. She smoothed her linen skirt carefully. "I know what," she said. "I'll develop stomach cramps. After all, that's a woman's prerogative. But Frans"— she became terrified that some unseen obstacle would spoil their venture—"what about you?"

"Do not worry." He snapped his fingers. "At the hotel—so unexpected it is—I run into an old friend from Amsterdam. So what else? We must celebrate this great occasion, my friend and me. The steel company will say nothing if I miss their little tour. Remember, with me they are wearing the kid gloves."

From her room in the hotel Carol telephoned the community-relations man in charge of their tour and told him about the stomach cramps.

"Oh, I understand, I understand," he said nervously. It was all she could do to restrain him from telephoning the house physician.

A few minutes later her telephone rang. What a cheerful ring, she thought, like a warbler in the spring.

It was Frans. "Make ready for the hooky," he said. "Perhaps we will go to the zoo. In Pittsburgh they must have a zoo. We will talk about it."

"Yes, let's talk about it."

"Five minutes," he said. "I see you then."

She went over to the bureau and put on fresh lipstick. Suddenly she felt despondent. Why, the whole thing was ridiculous! I've known this man for less than one day, she scolded herself. Strangers meeting

on a train. How cornball! What had she been thinking?

She walked around the room and absently adjusted
a pillow on the couch. The bed was only a few steps
away and even in this large room it seemed embar-
rassingly near.

Carol is thirty. . . .

She knew nothing about making love other than
what she had read in books, starting with the well-
thumbed copies in the stacks of the library at home.
She remembered something about crushed ice; how it
was supposed to stimulate the male when placed
around his—the words always struck her as ludicrous
—private parts. Wasn't a man's hip, say, just as private
to him? My God, she thought, this whole thing is too
silly. We *will* go to the zoo. Yes, she decided. Nothing
was going to happen in this room. She practiced an
imaginary toss. Popcorn to the monkeys.

She heard the knock, three light taps, and her heart
skipped.

"Just a second," she called out.

She went over to the window and pulled the drapes
together. And suddenly she felt splendid, absolutely
splendid. "Light as a feather." She said the words
aloud.

Carol walked across the carpet and as she reached
out for the doorknob there was a tiny shock—she actually saw the spark fly toward her finger—and she
knew this was a sign.

She opened the door and twirled back into the
room, feeling her skirt fly up around her thighs. She
stopped with a mock curtsy.

"Welcome to the Municipal Zoo," she announced.

Frans came inside quietly and stood by a chair. His
head was tilted to one side and he was watching her.

The hotel room had turned dark as wine. A long

wedge of light from the bathroom lay across the carpet like a sword.

He walked slowly over to her. He seemed to be emerging from a dense fog. He stopped a foot from Carol. She saw the shaft of light cutting across his freshly shaven chin and it shone like gunmetal.

He moved closer. "And this," he said gently, "is the prize tigress of our zoo."

She laughed delightedly. "Yes," she said. She did not draw back; it was all so strange. The books had said nothing at all about what she was feeling at this moment. There was no shame and, quite oddly, almost an absence of passion. Only this great magnet-like pull and a tremendous curiosity.

Frans kissed her tenderly on the cheek. Then he undid the top button of her blouse and nodded toward the bathroom. There was not a sound in the entire world. "You must get ready in there, my sweet," he said finally. "Here I will be waiting."

She obeyed without saying a word. When she came out, hugging her arms together, she saw that he was in bed smoking a cigarette which he immediately proceeded to stub out.

She thought about the ancient Greek statues of Diana surprised at her bath and she realized then that the statues were a fraud. Diana's arms shielded her breasts, true enough, but the mouth was always *closed*.

Her knee touched the side of the bed. Frans reached out and the fresh sheet slid down, revealing his body naked to the hips. . . .

Later, she kept thinking about it. But no one *talked*; neither of us said anything, only a muffled sentence from Frans. It sounded like Dutch, and she did not need to understand the language to sense his pleasure.

The whole thing had proceeded more quickly, too, than she had imagined. Her ribs were aching where he had held tightly to her.

Frans, almost immediately afterward, had gone to sleep at her side. The ticking of his wrist watch filled the room.

She lay there reassembling the fragments. So that's the way it is, she kept thinking in wonderment, so that's the way it *feels*. She suppressed an idiotic desire to get out of bed and send her mother a telegram.

Later, after they had dressed, she turned to him.

"Frans," she said. "That debt you mentioned last night. About your owing this country something for all those continuous casting units we financed?"

"Yes?"

"Well, consider it paid. The slate is clean now."

She took his arm and they rode down in the elevator with Carol hugging him close. They marched arm in arm through the lobby to the coffee shop. She thought of the other analysts picking their way through the mill at this moment in their helmets.

"My God," she said in wonderment and hugged his arm. "Pittsburgh, Pennsylvania. Of all places!"

That afternoon Frans took a plane to Detroit and Carol interviewed the mill superintendent. The perfect incident was over.

But on her return to New York there remained one thing for her to do. She wrote an institutional memorandum for several of Hillyer & Hunt's clients. She recommended the purchase of the steel company's stock, both the common stock and the convertible preferred. "We firmly believe," ran the concluding sentence, "that results for patient investors will be not unsatisfactory."

7

The news was simply too much for Ursula Leone. So Kimbridge & Co. was going to take in a new partner! Why, nothing like that had happened in twenty years around here.

This was not something she could hold inside like the baby kicking in her belly. She simply had to tell *some*body. But who was the right person? This was very important. It had to be somebody she respected and it had to be somebody in the office. After the partners' meeting, Mr. Merriam had cautioned her again of the need for secrecy. Mr. Kimbridge's secretary, he told her, never breathed a word of what went on in these meetings. Ursula had nodded docilely at the research partner even as she was trying desperately to decide who should share her news. Besides— what could they do to her? In a few more weeks she would be gone for good from Kimbridge & Co. Her husband had made it quite plain; he wanted five children. After the first baby came, she knew, her world would revolve around diapers and formulas, no more stocks and bonds.

Ursula Leone, struggling mightily, held the secret inside her for three whole days. For lunch on Thursday she ate a plate of ripe olives and two scoops of peppermint-stick ice cream. By two-thirty in the afternoon she was so excited that it was all she could do to keep from wetting her pants.

She made up her mind: Poke Jeffers.

Yes, definitely Poke Jeffers. Of all the men in the office he was definitely the most appealing. And ever since that accident . . . well, he reminded her of all those stories of young men getting hideously wounded in the war.

Yes, Ursula thought, it had to be Poke Jeffers even though she had never said more than a dozen words to him aside from "My, isn't this some weather we're having?" And now her moment had come. Mr. Merriam had just gone out to the reception room to talk to a man from the printer's about proofs for a new portfolio review form. That discussion should be good for a half hour; Mr. Merriam was fascinated by anything that had to do with paper. Ursula Leone arose and went to the door. Moving majestically down the aisle, she felt the importance of her mission swelling inside her.

Poke sat very still in his chair. A lull had settled over the board room. It was like a battlefield with an artillery barrage suddenly suspended. Normally, he would have been on the telephone calling his customers and trying to drum up trade. There was a secondary distribution in Chrysler this afternoon and he ought to be down for at least a thousand shares. But he did not move.

Robertson had just called and Poke said, no, he was

very sorry but he wouldn't be able to make the trip this year. Maybe Robertson had understood what he really meant—but what the hell difference did it make?

Every October a half-dozen men, including Robertson and Poke, had made it a practice to take a week off from their jobs to go hunting. They would hunt in the Adirondacks not far below the Canadian border. It was wild country that suited Poke's taste: mountains, ravines, swamps, and thick woods. The land abounded with game. There were deer and black bear and if you happened to see a grouse all you had to do was slip some bird shot into your 12-gauge automatic shotgun. Once, while Poke was standing alone in the woods, a mink—a pure white mink—had slid over his left shoe, quite casually, as though the shoe were a tree root bulging above the ground. It gave him a splendid feeling, making him a part of the wilderness. In the morning you could hear the squirrels chattering and the *ka-pow!* sound of trees exploding—it was a sharper crack than a rifle made—as the sun began to warm them, those huge hardwood trees, after the cold night.

Black bear was his favorite target because it put a premium on the skill of the hunter; if you missed, things could get rough. The black bear weighed five or six hundred pounds and they loved chestnuts. You got your bear more often than not by chance, by running into it unexpectedly. But sometimes Poke would stand at the base of a chestnut tree with lead slugs in his shotgun, hoping for a bear to show his nose. A black bear had a hide an inch thick and when he showed, on your lucky days, you had to aim high, aim for his heart or shoulder. You wanted to break a shoulder so that the bear couldn't move fast. If you missed his heart, you still might hit a shoulder, or maybe even get him in the belly, and this could be very effective, too, but one thing you didn't do was to aim low. . . .

He would never go hunting again, not that Robertson and the others didn't want him but because he knew he could no longer carry his share of the load. The roads were really rugged in that wilderness. They used a fully equipped oil company truck—one of the men was a vice president of an oil company—to drive into the woods. The truck had a four-wheel drive and it carried axes and a winch. They had to pull away the logs that had fallen across the roads. They would cut away some of the branches and then pull the logs out with a winch. And he knew now that the other men would insist on his staying in the truck.

He watched an orange bulb light up on the far end of the quotations board. Some commodity had just touched a new contract low. A green light was the signal for a new high. Either light meant money on the run for some commodity trader, depending on whether he was long or short. But right now Poke Jeffers couldn't care less about the whole god-damned thing.

What he could do now was to sit in a chair in his apartment and lift a woman's pocketbook containing seventy pounds of lead weights with the stump of his left leg. It was one of his prescribed exercises, hooking a long-handled pocketbook over the stump and lifting it up and down, up and down, endlessly, in order to strengthen the leg muscles. There had been offers from eight different girls after he came home from the hospital, but he had spurned them all while saying things he should not have said. The ballad singer had wanted to send him a sixty-dollar model from Gucci. Finally, he accepted a castoff handbag from the wife of the building superintendent, a tired, surly woman with three of her front teeth missing.

By the time he came home from the hospital he already had mastered the proper technique for wrapping the stump. The wrapping was done with an elastic bandage that extended nine feet in length. The tan-colored wrap went over the bottom of the stump first and, when the job was finished, it covered what was left of his leg. The technique was to apply pressure gradually as you circled the wrap up your thigh —the big danger was to apply it too tightly, so that it had the effect of a tourniquet—and the wrapping had to be done eight or ten times a day at first. The pressure would gradually pull the wrap down so that it wrinkled around the bottom of his stump. "You have a fine conical stump," one of the doctors said to him admiringly when he went for a checkup. Then, a little while later, he overheard the doctor talking to a nurse —thanks to his alert god-damned hunter ears—in the corridor. "That fellow in there," the doctor had said. "This injury is going to do one of two things to him. Either motivate him or sink him." You might have thought the god-damned doctor was talking about the stock market. What the hell did he know anyway, this doctor? He still had two good legs and in his younger days racing had never been his whole life.

"Mr. Jeffers? I mean, Poke? Oh, I hope I'm not disturbing you. Is something wrong?" Ursula Leone stood uncertainly outside the cubicle.

"Uh?" He shook his head quickly. "Not at all, Ursula." He got up and held open the swinging door. She sat down carefully in the chair beside Poke's desk and folded her hands in her lap.

"Well," he said, "how are you, anyway?"

"Oh, fine, thanks," she replied. "Just fine. I saw my doctor yesterday. He has the date all picked out for my baby to arrive. Then in the next breath my doctor tells me you can never be sure in timing the first baby. So why is he so specific, I'd like to know."

"I suppose you'll be plenty relieved when your baby arrives."

"Gosh, no. Why, when you're pregnant you don't even have to wait in line at Radio City. They shoo you right up to the ticket office, no matter if the line is all the way around the block, and they practically follow you inside to your seat holding a pillow in case you fall—or something." She sighed wistfully. "You know something? I'd like to carry my baby for a couple of years. Honest. Everybody is so sweet when I'm like this. Even on Wall Street the traffic stops for me."

Poke nodded understandingly and glanced up at the stock tape.

She could tell that he was puzzled by her visit. After all, he had never bet in the office pool, unlike many of the other customers' men. Yes, thought Ursula, she would miss running the office pool on the daily Stock Exchange volume. She made her rounds in the morning before the market opened and collected a quarter from each participant. The person guessing the nearest figure to the volume was the winner; you automatically lost if your estimate exceeded the day's volume, even if you came closer than the best low figure.

"Why do you suppose it is," she said, as though she were including Poke in a matter she had long pondered, "that Mr. Kimbridge works so hard? I mean, well, he's here practically all the time. Now if he were a priest, I could see him hoping maybe someday he could become promoted to a monseignor. But with all that *money!* Why, the Kimbridges must have *zillions!*"

"Well, Ursula, after all, this is his family's business."

"Uh-huh," she said and blinked her eyes in a manner that she hoped was mysterious. "I heard something that might interest you . . ." She let her voice trail away.

"Yes?" he inquired politely.

She leaned forward. "Kimbridge & Co. may *incorporate*"—she uttered the word very slowly—"only nobody is supposed to know it yet."

"Really? You're sure of this?"

"Cross my heart," she said emphatically. She had his full attention now. "I heard it with my own ears at the dawn-patrol meeting. Miss Donahue was out sick and I took her place." Now suddenly Ursula was frightened. She remembered that Mr. Kimbridge always gave ten shares of American Telephone to any employee who had a baby. But if the managing partner found out she had babbled, she might not get her stock. "Listen," she pleaded, "you promise you won't tell anyone about this? I mean, until some announcement is made?"

"Cross my heart," Poke said.

She seemed reluctant to leave. "I don't know," she said vaguely, "I think there's bad blood somewhere among the partners. Mr. Kimbridge is going to have a real fight on his hands. You know, it's like one of those old Westerns you see on television. Anyway, I think there's trouble ahead.

"Well," she said, collecting herself, "I ought to be going." She stood up and glanced back at the Research Department. "All that glass," she said, half aloud, "it sort of reminds you of a nursery in a hospital, doesn't it?"

Poke held the door open again and Ursula Leone passed regally out into the aisle. It was simply amazing, she thought, how he could move so nimbly with only one real leg.

"I almost forgot," she said, turning around very

slowly, the way she imagined a stage actress might have done in a dramatic moment. "There is something else . . . Mr. Kimbridge has decided to take a younger man into the firm as a partner. He said something about picking one of the customers' men in this office. There's some opposition to his wanting to incorporate the firm. But he's got the green light to pick a new partner." She paused and tilted her head. "Now wouldn't that be something? A partner of Kimbridge & Co."

Poke had begun to ski only three years ago. But he possessed a natural affinity for sports and by the end of his second season he could push the instructor, a tall Swiss with a face like leather, in a downhill race.

The accident happened on a Friday night in December. He had parked the Jaguar downtown and left straight from the office after posting the day's trades in his account books.

Ahead of him stretched the blissful prospect of the first skiing weekend of the winter. And, of course, the new girl. The ballad singer who was giving a performance that week in Buffalo. She would fly over to Vermont and be waiting when he got to the lodge; he never knew ballad singers made that kind of money.

He rolled down the window after reaching the parkway. He could hear the skis whistling on the roof rack. The onrushing headlights, forming almost solid beams in the opposite lanes, kept beckoning him northward.

"Happy," he said softly and began thinking about a new body crouch that might shave a split second in the hip-turn swing. Skiing was like running, a solitary sport. In a race, above all things, there was this supreme sense of being alone, of complete independence, of a performance that came only from your own muscles and stamina and instincts. "Happy," he said again and felt the cold air whipping his face. He twisted his hips experimentally.

He thought about the girl then. Her letter was in his pocket. "Listen," she wrote, and he could almost hear her voice pulsing above the guitar moans, "you might never recognize me, so let me tell you about this outfit. There was this ski shop and I went wild. I bought Riviera sunglasses with pink frames to match the stretch pants. And the parka—well, you said you liked bright blue, remember? Anyhow, it's nylon on one side and imitation seal on the other. It's imported from Sweden and I said to myself, those people must know what they're doing with a parka."

He smiled. The letter sparkled just like the girl. He touched the accelerator a bit harder.

Finally, he was within twenty minutes of the lodge. He was thinking about the Jag now and the pleasure it gave him. It was like "getting wheels" when he was a kid—the same surge of excitement that came with his first bicycle. That excitement was rekindled with every new car he bought in New York. There had been a procession of cars—the Alfa-Romeo, the red Triumph, the Porsche, the Austin-Healey with its sprinter's start—and with each new automobile there had been a new girl. He remembered the girls that way sometimes: the blonde with the Triumph and the kindergarten teacher with the Alfa-Romeo. And now there was the ballad singer with the Jag.

What a sweet-running car! The burled walnut dashboard was bathed in a purple glow by a pair of tiny lights, and the smell of rich leather filled the car like perfume. The gasoline gauge winked at him and he listened to the fine hum, the running sound. He could put this car up to ninety without the slightest vibration on a straight road; it was as if the Jaguar were crouched perfectly motionless. It cost him eighty-five dollars a month to keep the car in top running form, but he did not mind the expense. He smiled again. When the car was not properly tuned, it refused even to start—he liked that. Now he leaned forward slightly and cocked an ear for any rattles in the huge hurtling car. But there was only the fine, solitary running sound.

Poke checked his speed. The road had been plowed for snow, but it might get icy. The Jag had a low center of gravity for such a big car. That made it perfect for these Vermont roads; the car could hug the winding, tilting roads like a skier twisting expertly down a slope.

The headlights picked up the gnarled maple trees set among the pines and the gooseberry bushes huddled in the slumped snow. In the distance, the ski trails cutting down the side of a mountain shone like silver rivers in the moonlight.

The car fled humming past a crumpled stone wall, the telltale sign of a farm that might have disappeared a century ago. The deer season had just ended and he wondered idly how many whitetails had survived. The least alert animals would have been killed off early. But most of the deer up this way were lazy; in the off season they made no effort to stick to the underbrush. You could spot their tracks leading right down the middle of the old logging roads and you could feel the indentations of their hoofs through your shoes as you walked. A wild animal, to his way of thinking, should remain wild the year round.

There was a movement off to his left and he wondered if it might have been the rack of a deer. In these woods, during the warm weather, you could recognize the *chouf-chouf-chouf* sound made by the deer. The sound would stop sometimes and that told you the deer were feeding nearby. Now, with the hunters gone, the bolder ones even came down to the roads. They loved to lick the salt put out by the highway department to melt the snow.

Poke flexed his shoulder muscles to ease the stiffness in his neck. He had been driving steadily since leaving New York.

He guided the purring car into a hairpin turn. He sensed some kind of movement again, but there was nothing in sight.

Another sharp turn—there! Dead ahead, in the path of the car! A deer with its head glued to the road. Suddenly he could see the eyes. They glowed like emeralds and grew enormous in a single onrushing second. Instinctively, he touched the wheel to the left. The deer should have moved back to the right, into the woods. But no! It bounded in the opposite direction!

There was a blur of white. Poke twisted desperately at the wheel. The luminous emerald eyes seemed to fill the windshield and just before losing consciousness he thought he heard the skis splintering on the roof rack. . . .

Ursula Leone's parting words echoed hollowly in his mind. "Now wouldn't that be something? A partner of Kimbridge & Co."

Poke pressed angrily through the late-afternoon crowds. He moved past the subway entrance. He would walk a few blocks and then maybe take the bus home for a change.

The tissue tightened about the scar on his left leg. He knew what that meant: rain within twenty-four hours. There was a milky tint to the blue sky, a hot summer sky with no trace of clouds.

All right, he told himself savagely, so Kimbridge &

Co. was going to admit a new partner. Would that bring back his leg? He increased his pace, skirting past the other pedestrians as though they were standing still.

After the accident, he had felt this intense desire—a desire to become invisible. He was a zombie, he lashed at himself, no better than a walking dead man.

Those first weeks, when he was learning to walk again, he had prowled the cold, deserted streets of midtown until late at night. Perfecting his stride had become a fetish with him. And when the hallway of his apartment building was empty, he would practice jogging up and down the steps dozens of times. His stump would turn to fire and he felt a fierce joy in the pain.

He experienced alternating periods of gloom and elation. At times he did strange things. One evening he took a box of pencils from the storage closet and, back in his apartment, whittled them right down to the eraser with quick, savage strokes of his hunting knife. Another day, fighting his way out of a black mood, he had taken three weeks of dirty clothes to the laundry and then stalked out, tearing up the ticket; he went to a store and bought an entire new supply of shirts, undershorts, and socks—stump socks for his left leg.

He remembered one morning as he walked toward the subway at Grand Central. The small sycamore trees were bending over the curb like slingshots as they strained to catch the sun. A girl in yellow slacks went sailing past on a bicycle. At her side, held by a chain attached to the handle bar, loped a Great Dane. There was something innately graceful about the girl and her dog. Poke watched until they were swallowed up by the traffic as all about him the morning crowds of Murray Hill hurried along, jockeying for

103

position like a pack of distance runners fresh from the starter's gun. A sudden hatred for this girl and her dog flared within him.

And now he kept walking, driving himself ever faster. There had been a nurse at the hospital; during an alcohol massage he had recognized the pressure of her fingers. She offered, quite casually, to come back to his room that night. He had wanted to shout blasphemies at her, instead, he shook his head, his eyes fixed on the strange cone of his amputated leg under the sheet.

He walked all the way home, telling himself over and over again that Kimbridge & Co. could go whistle. When he removed the stump sock, the tip of his thigh was red and swollen by the punishment.

8

Fred Lincoln stepped from the elevator on the seventh floor of the Stock Exchange building and glanced around. He had not been inside the luncheon club for more than a year. Above the elevators a row of massive mounted heads remained stolidly on guard. The bull moose, the buffalo, the reindeer with antlers the color of beeswax, all managing to convey the impression that they had been stampeded into the building only to become impaled in the wall.

He walked past the cigar counter where, under a glass top, the bull and the bear were locked in eternal conflict upon the ties of the luncheon club.

At breakfast only the tables in the front of the dining room, the section nearest the kitchen, were open for service. The tables were comfortably filled at nine-fifteen this morning; there was the pleasant clink of cutlery upon china.

Something crossed Fred Lincoln's mind. For all its stodginess, the club had never listed a thirteenth entree under its ready dishes. He glanced at the luncheon menu tacked up on a small wooden stand like a teacher's lectern. He read: "Number 12, mixed green salad with sea food, French dressing; Number 14, assorted cold cuts with cheese, potato salad."

Then he saw Seth Voorhees gesturing to him from the third table by the windows. This was the table reserved by tradition for the floor partner of Kimbridge & Co. Jared Kimbridge customarily had eaten at this table and the napkin ring, as it were, had passed on to Voorhees after his death. There had been an incident once involving a two-dollar broker, a newcomer to the club, who sat drinking his morning coffee at the table when Voorhees entered the dining room. Voorhees marched up and snapped abruptly, "You're in the wrong place, I believe," then sat down to read a newspaper while the two-dollar broker, realizing he had committed some unknown sacrilege, bolted from the dining room. In the process the broker managed to spill a pot of coffee over his trousers; Voorhees did not so much as glance up from his paper while the attendants hurried after the victim, flailing at him with napkins. Fred Lincoln was thinking about the incident as he sat down opposite his partner. He was a large man with the solidity of an andiron and when he leaned forward the table creaked under his weight. "Now that I'm here," rumbled Lincoln, "maybe you can explain all this mystery. Why couldn't we meet at the office?"

"Why, Fred," said Voorhees in a chiding voice, "I simply wanted to chat, that's all. What will you have?"

"Oh, clam juice, I guess. Still trying to reduce."

Voorhees wrote out the order and handed it to a waiter who had appeared instantly at his side.

In a few moments the waiter glided quickly up to

the table, setting down the clam juice before Lincoln and a plate of fried eggs and Irish bacon for Voorhees.

"This kitchen," said Lincoln with admiration, "still has the fastest draw in the East."

Voorhees nodded absently. He fingered the small white carnation in his lapel until the waiter filled the water glasses and went away. Then he wasted no time in preliminaries. "Fred," he said, "how do you stand on Thatch's damn-fool plan to incorporate the firm? We've got to prevent him from ruining Kimbridge & Co.! Don't you agree?"

"A-ha. I thought *that* was on your mind." Lincoln took a sip of clam juice and when he put down the glass his big square face was troubled. "To tell you the absolute truth, I'm still undecided. But I know one thing. I owe Thatch a great debt of gratitude for the way he backed me on those Spokane bonds. We get the deal, then the market turns sour on us. I've still got half the bonds on the shelf. What a bath! But not a peep out of Thatch. Hell, if Jared were still running the firm, he'd have my head on a platter." He rattled golf tees in his pocket and regarded his partner thoughtfully. "You know, Seth, You'd have made a good specialist. You've got the requirements. An arrogance for people and an arrogance for money."

Voorhees ignored this remark. He plunged his fork into an egg. "Listen," he said earnestly, "you have a son finishing Swarthmore in less than a year. You want him to come into Kimbridge & Co. That's fine. But tell me, do you want him to be a partner or a *vice president*? There's a whole world between those two things. Corporations are companies whose stock you sell. A brokerage house should be a partnership. With unlimited liability and a sense of the past."

Lincoln shook his head slowly. "Seth," he said,

"you're just like old Jared. You keep living in the past while the whole environment is changing around you. Sure, I know. A dozen years ago one partner could wear several hats. He could manage the back office and run Personnel. He could handle the real estate end of the business and, if he was really energetic, he could operate a small-loan business without charging interest for the employees who always run out of money before payday and he could keep the chits in his desk. But not any longer, Seth." He paused. "Why, I'll bet you that ten years from now practically every brokerage house doing a public business will be a corporation."

"I'm not talking about the dim and distant future," snapped Voorhees. "I'm talking about *now!* And what Thatch wants to do to the firm!"

"Well, sure, I admit I like the idea of Hobie becoming a partner. But I'm not certain that he would care so much about the title. Youngsters have a way of dreaming up their own dilemmas. They don't necessarily settle for the problems that you or I can point out to them. Maybe if a man has never been a partner it doesn't make so much difference. Why, the thing that bugged my boy his freshman year was the fact that people kept asking him at debutante parties whether Swarthmore was coed or not. Whew! I'll say it's coed. Now *last* year his main problem was motels."

"Motels?"

"That's right. It seems a college girl is insulted nowadays if you don't take her to a motel—a good motel—to shack up. You might as well try to lay her in a cave as on the front seat of an automobile. Or so Hobie, who is majoring in philosophy, informs me."

A man walked past their table, clapping Voorhees

on the shoulder. "'Morning, Seth," the man said cheerfully.

Voorhees acknowledged the greeting with a curt nod and watched the man pass out of the dining room. "That bastard!" he said vehemently. "That greedy bastard of a specialist! When you get a sell order in size for any one of his stocks, you've got to work it out of your palm. Show him something and it's plain murder. He'll drop the stock two points, that greedy bastard!"

Lincoln was silent as Voorhees resumed his attack on the eggs and the Irish bacon curling in thick slices on his plate.

The bond partner leaned forward. "Seth," he asked softly, "tell me something. Are you planning a palace revolution?"

Voorhees gave a thin, cold smile by way of reply.

"Well," said Lincoln, "I suppose you know the opposition is stacked against you. Why, the clerks in the Credit Department are already running a pool. On the new partner. Next thing they'll be running a pool on the date the partners approve incorporation."

"Really? Who's the favorite? For the new partner?"

"Search me. One of the producers in the corner, I'd guess. Either Bigelow, Jeffers, or Padawer—"

"Padawer!" Voorhees snorted in disgust. "I'd die first! Next thing you know the firm would be going under the name of Kimbridgestein & Co.!"

They knew it was only by chance that the three leading producers worked in the same corner of the board room. When Poke was transferred from the Atlanta office, the cubicle nearest the reception room had been the only space vacant. The production records of the salesmen were confidential information. But part of the secret inadvertently had leaked out a year ago when the partners circulated a study in the board room. This study showed a breakdown of clients by geographical location and, surprisingly enough, 22 per cent of all home-office customers lived outside of the commuting radius of New York City. A list of the salesmen's names appeared on the attached sheet. "INITIAL AND PASS ON," the instructions said. "RETURN TO MISS DONAHUE." The order of names appeared to follow no logical pattern; the names were not arranged alphabetically, or by desk position, or even by length of service. But the sheet might as well have been constructed in flashing neon lights for an office alert to the nuances of a memo. Here, set to-tem-pole fashion from the top man down to the bottom man, was the production ranking of the home office. Miss Donahue, worried at the time by her mother's health, had in a lapse of her customary watchfulness used a secret file to type out the names. Only the actual income figures were missing. The name of Israel Padawer led the list. It was followed by Noel Bigelow and in third place was Poke Jeffers. They led the field: Win, Place, and Show.

"Remember the old days?" Lincoln said softly. "Hell, we were certainly a lot more carefree back then. On warm days in the spring I'd visit the zoo in Central Park. Forty years ago a bond salesman never had to work in the afternoon if he could retail a few bonds in the morning. If it was raining, then we'd play bridge in some club around midtown. Phone the office at 4 P.M. and ask if any calls had come in—"

"Now who's living in the past?" Voorhees demanded. "Come on, Fred. Quit stalling. Are you with me on this—or not?"

Lincoln lifted the top from a marmalade jar on the table and inspected it carefully. After a long moment he looked across the table at his partner. "Don't you see what Thatch is trying to do? I can understand because of Hobie. He's determined to produce a substitute for Brit. Why should we bring in only one new partner? We could use a half-dozen more, a firm of our size. But that's not the way Thatch wants it. And in his mind the two things are tied together, I can see that. A new partner to substitute for his son and a new structure to keep Kimbridge & Co. alive forever." He replaced the top of the marmalade jar gently. "Even when we're gone, Seth. You, me, Thatch, the whole shooting match—"

"Poppycock! I know Thatch as well as my own brother. And I know when he can be made to back down. Now tell me, Fred. When he wanted to bring out an annual report for Kimbridge & Co., didn't we convince him that would be a bad move? What the hell, why should the whole world see what we're doing? And when he tried to stop me from trading for the firm's own account, you remember what happened. We changed his mind for him."

"He changed his own mind, Seth. And only for one reason. He thought you might consider him jealous of your own trading ability on the floor. But no, you don't grant that at all, do you?" Finally he asked, "Have you spoken to any of the others?"

"No. You're the first."

"It's a funny thing how people react to the prospect of our incorporating. Even Janet. Hell, you know perfectly well my wife has never been interested in things like that. She'll buy some fly-by-night stock now and then but she doesn't even use Kimbridge & Co. as a broker. She realizes that I wouldn't approve of her speculations. But when I mentioned this matter to Janet she amazed me. She's with you, you'll be pleased to learn. She said that we've worked hard for our money as partners and that it would be a sin to change Kimbridge & Co. in any form or fashion."

"Good girl!" Voorhees exclaimed. "But that still doesn't tell me your decision."

Lincoln took a deep breath. "Sorry, Seth," he said. "No sale. I'm lining up beside Thatch. I know what this whole thing really means to him. I keep thinking of the way I'd feel if something happened to Hobie . . . this way Thatch may not have a son but he will—"

"Fred, you're dead wrong. I wish to hell you could see things my way. Thatch is going to ruin Kimbridge & Co. if we let him go ahead."

Lincoln shifted unhappily in his chair. He looked down the far end of the dining room at the huge black-faced clock with gold numerals. It was nine-thirty-eight and the breakfast crowd had thinned out. He made a decision. "There's one way," he said slowly, "of putting an extra club in your bag. That is, if you're really determined to go ahead."

"What's that?" the floor partner asked quickly.

"Go to Edith Kimbridge and—"

Voorhees' coffee cup clattered onto his saucer. Lincoln looked at him in surprise and for a fleeting moment he saw something strange in the cold gray eyes. Some hidden nerve had been touched.

"Edith! Now what's *she* got to do with this?" said Voorhees. "Why, I haven't seen her since that circus of a housewarming party thrown by Priscilla Hooker."

"Well, Edith might be your answer. Win her over to your side and you'd have two of the three trustees of Jared's estate." Lincoln hesitated, as if loath to explain his strategy further. "If you get the Estate on the record as opposing incorporation, I'm sure of one thing. Thatch would not go through with it. As much as this means to him, he would give up the idea."

"You're sure?"

"Hell, yes, I'm sure! My God, what do you want?

You want Thatch to bleed in public for you just because you can't stand the idea of working for a member firm that's a corporation?" Lincoln suddenly lost his temper. "You remind me of Jared, do you know that? The two of you really think the public shouldn't be allowed to buy securities without a blood test and that the S.E.C. is contrary to the Bill of Rights!" Lincoln stood up and flung his napkin on the table.

"Calm down, Fred, now calm down." Voorhees' eyes narrowed as he turned the idea over in his mind. "Yes-s-s," he said, as if he were speaking to himself. "By Jesus, it just might do the trick. . . ."

Lincoln strode from the dining room and Voorhees followed.

"Wait a minute, Fred," Voorhees called out. "I'll just change my shoes and we can go down together."

"All right," said Lincoln in a tight voice. He was raging at himself now for having made the suggestion to Voorhees.

The cloakroom was situated on the other side of the elevator bank. Voorhees accepted the shoes that the attendant lifted from the rack as he was approaching.

"What are those made of!" asked Lincoln, indicating the shoes. But he said it in a way that signified to Voorhees that their conversation inside had ended.

"Lizard," said Voorhees. "Black lizard. Had my man in England send them over a couple of weeks ago. You should see those damn space shoes with ridged rubber soles that some of the men are wearing on the floor! It hurts me to do a trade with anybody wearing shoes like that."

Voorhees sat down on the chair and bent over to untie the laces of his street shoes. Suddenly he teetered forward and pitched onto the rug, managing to break the fall with his hands.

"Seth!" Lincoln cried out in alarm. "Seth, are you all right?"

Voorhees scrambled quickly to his feet and, spurning Lincoln's offer of assistance, began dusting off his trousers. "Yes, yes," Voorhees said. His face had flushed scarlet. "It's just—well, I get a fainting spell every now and then. But it's nothing." He glanced at his watch. "Hell," he exclaimed, "it's late. I think I'll just wear these shoes on the floor today. Be right with you," he said to Lincoln and stepped into the lavatory.

When Voorhees returned, Lincoln said, "Look. You ought to see a doctor—"

"I'm fine!" Voorhees declared. "Now, Fred, do me a favor. Forget it."

Voorhees' collar was damp, a sign to Lincoln that he had splashed cold water on his face. His skin was now quite gray, the color of wet dough.

"The pool that they're running in the Credit Department on the next partner," Voorhees said, "how do they program the odds?"

Fred Lincoln shook his head. "Frankly," he said, "their system is too complicated for me to understand. There are a couple of guys in that department who're in the wrong business. They ought to be horserace handicappers." He was peering anxiously at his floor partner as the elevator door snapped open.

9

The 50 Wall building and several neighboring sky-scrapers that first had reared their heads during the nineteen twenties were not unlike the Kimbridge & Co. partners themselves: venerable and craggy, scarred by disaster, secretly amazed by a resurgence in fortune, watching fretfully now their new challengers. These were the upstart buildings that demanded —and received—fanciful rental prices by the square foot, sleek and unmarked shafts with glass and metal skins that glistened in the sunlight like bathers on the French Riviera.

Fifty Wall was situated midway between Trinity Church and the East River. Its bell tower had been modeled after the campanile of St. Mark's Cathedral in Venice and at the base of the tower crouched four huge lions, one to a corner. The lions had been chiseled out of pink Tennessee marble by craftsmen imported from Tuscany. But the ravages of soot and weather had faded their once-proud coats to a dingy gray that almost matched the blackened smooth brick surface of the building itself. Deep cracks had appeared in the majestic heads and the flowing manes of the lions; their lair became the property of pigeons.

The building seemingly had the power to give life and to take it away. In 1926 a steel rigger was killed when he lost his footing and plunged to the pavement, narrowly missing an investment banker who thereafter went to mass every morning—until October, 1929. Twenty years later, when a leather strap supporting a window washer suddenly broke, the man was hauled to safety on the thirtieth floor by two margin clerks of Kimbridge & Co. who had seen his feet kicking frantically in the air.

The original financing for 50 Wall was arranged in England and the British interests circumspectly took what they considered to be an ingenious form of insurance against any reversal in the American economy. The architect, who was knighted in 1928, had designed the building so that it could be converted with a minimum of effort into a commercial hotel. As a result, the elevator and service facilities formed the central core and wide tile corridors corseted this area. Office suites opened onto either the main corridors or narrower ones that cut away at odd angles. Every suite was outfitted originally with plumbing facilities. Years later, with the installation of a central air-conditioning system, these fixtures were removed. However, in the cashier's cage of Kimbridge & Co. there still remained a solitary washstand with a sign above the bowl warning: "Caution! The Hot Water Is Very Hot." Upon discovering their oversight, the building authorities offered to remove the washstand. But Jared Kimbridge found that its absurdity appealed to him and so the washstand remained. As for the British, they had been guilty of a massive miscalculation;

they failed to realize that a prolonged economic slump would find hotels as well as office buildings begging for occupants.

By 1934 the building faced disaster. A sickening number of its tenants had gone into bankruptcy and less than half of the structure was occupied. The ranking partner of one law firm in the building discharged a young clerk for circulating rumors to the effect that "the lions up on top are getting set to jump." Eventually the combination of slashed rentals and empty suites proved too great a burden for the continuation of interest payments. The mortgage trustees foreclosed, the debentures sold as low as nine cents on the dollar, and the financial control of 50 Wall passed from the hands of the British to a small band of venturesome Americans captained by Jared Kimbridge. In the first year of the Korean War there was a move afoot to rename the building Kimbridge Tower in honor of its most successful speculator. By then the common stock had been detached from the debentures and split twenty-five for one. "No, thanks," said Jared to the offer. "If you want to put my name on this building, then it's time to sell." And he sold, realizing a profit of 2,800 per cent on his investment.

Postwar prosperity transformed 50 Wall into a prestige structure for the second time in its history. The present roster of tenants included four brokerage houses in addition to Kimbridge & Co. One of these, a firm that specialized in foreign securities, transported its clientele skyward in a private elevator from the lobby; there was a carved marble umbrella stand in the elevator. Other tenants included large corporations, eminent law firms, private foundations, a travel agency, shipping concerns, and the complaint office of a leading manufacturer of cosmetics.

One entire floor was occupied by dentists' offices.

During the Depression several young dentists, attracted by the low rents and the unparalleled plumbing facilities, had launched their practices at 50 Wall. A dental school migration subsequently set in, and along the corridors of this floor the aroma of cinnamon mouthwash continually lingered. One orthodontist who was an active trader in the stock market offered a 5 per cent discount to all patients who paid in full upon receiving an estimate for dental repair.

But 50 Wall, by and large, was dedicated to the realm of money on a more ambitious scale. Its corporations and stockbrokers and lawyers massaged this money along various stages of the distribution process and what was left over went occasionally to one of the foundations. The building itself did all that was possible to ward off financial adversity. There was no thirteenth floor so numbered, and in the high-domed lobby could be found a variety of hex signs, ranging from stars and divining rods to horseshoes and patches of clover, along the frieze. There were limestone angels with wings spread wide in protection and heroic figures from mythology. Placed between Hercules and Mercury, as the parting gesture of a disgruntled Tuscany sculptor, was a small statue of the architect. He was garbed in a toga and had the ears of an ass.

The lobby elevators carried a decorative scheme that invariably caused young visitors to point and giggle whenever they ventured inside 50 Wall. A pair of chubby angels, carved in Tennessee marble that had remained pink, supported the tablet above each elevator blinking "Up" or "Down." Every cherub, as the youngsters were quick to perceive, had suffered its penis to be chipped away.

Two floors below street level reposed the vault. Behind the stainless-steel face of the vault door was an intricate construction of nickel steel armor, cast steel, concrete, and jail rods, sections to protect against oxy-acetylene torches, a layer of copper and, on the inside, shatterproof glass. The door, complete with locking mechanism and boltwork and hinges, weighed fifty tons. But it was so delicately balanced that it could be swung with a single finger. It had been designed by an American craftsman, a resident of Chicago, and before accepting the commission he had made a brief statement of his philosophy to the British financiers. "First," he said, "you've got to hang a door this size perfectly. You can't have it run at the start or at the end of a swing. Otherwise, you chop off a hand." At this comment one Englishman dropped his monocle. "Second, you want to remember this," the designer continued. "Give me four days without being disturbed and I can get through any door ever made—even my own. Don't kid yourselves. With a vault like you want, you're not trying to guard against some guy tunneling into a bank. No, sir. What you're really buying, in case you don't know it, is protection against a mob of citizens, if New York City happens to go haywire someday."

The vault was used by a savings bank on the lobby floor and by the brokerage firms for the safekeeping of customer securities. Security measures included an alarm system operated by sonar. But in all the years no attempt had been made to assail the treasures of the vault, which included two postage-stamp collections and a food manufacturer's secret recipe for mustard. An alarm was tripped once by accident when a clerk moved his desk inside the vault; a cordon of city police and protection agency guards surrounded 50 Wall with drawn pistols.

Kimbridge & Co. rented one of the inner recesses of the vault, a space that resembled the torpedo room of

119

a submarine. This compartment contained a Muzak system—polkas and classical jazz music were played in the morning, more restrained tunes in the afternoon—and it was ablaze with fluorescent lamps as if to make up for the perpetual lack of sunlight. Securities were sent down from the firm's offices by pneumatic tubes and stored in gray filing cabinets lining the walls.

Six men from the Cashier's Department manned the Kimbridge & Co. compartment which, for purposes of added safety, was sealed off from the rest of the vault by its private five-ton door. Promptly at eight-thirty each workday morning two men from this department would come down in the freight elevator, pass through the entrance to the main vault, and proceed to twirl the dials on the inner door. The six men were divided into two rotating groups. Half of each group knew the top combination and the other half knew the bottom combination.

Once a month teams of coupon clippers would descend from the upstairs offices and snip coupons by hand for the bondholder clients of Kimbridge & Co. They worked with the swift expertise of cigar wrappers, wielding small metal T-squares, and during coupon-snipping time the rustle of parchment would provide background accompaniment for the piped-in polkas and waltzes. The most worthless securities kept in the vault—Czarist bonds and obligations of certain South American governments—bore ironically the most impressive engraving and coloring. Once a year, during the surprise audit of Kimbridge & Co., a team of auditors would enter the compartment to count and check every single certificate. Thatcher Kimbridge always knew when the auditors were coming. Three or four days in advance of their visit he would receive a call from the auditing firm. "We'll need a lot of tables and chairs," a man would say. "And please contact that restaurant around the corner. We'll need sandwiches and coffee at midnight."

Fifty Wall became at times the arena for pitched battles among its tenants. When the management decided to replace the original elevators with an automated system, the dentists staged a rebellion. The elevators had bronze grilles and rear benches upholstered in leather. But the dentists were not concerned with esthetics; a number of dentists had women patients who were fearful of traveling in unattended elevators. After a brief but fierce battle the management prevailed, upon agreeing to certain rent concessions. The elevators were transformed into automatic units whose stainless-steel doors shut just as silently and efficiently as the main vault door in the subbasement. But the cherubs remained in place above the elevator entrances, symbolizing both the casualties of a silent war and the awareness of tradition that abided in the building.

10

The heat spell broke on Friday of the following week. Municipal bond dealers wore their vests to work and on Wall Street at noontime the tourists moved in swarms, resplendent in sports shirts with wild poppy colors, their cameras clicking at the imposing buildings and at stout mothers posed beside skinny children. A man with a sign that said "Almost Blind" threaded through the crowd, shaking his tin cup only at tourists. In the street the manhole covers gleamed like old polished coins. A drowsy machine-gun stutter drifted down from above, the signal of a riveter bending unseen to his task.

Poke Jeffers was part of the sidewalk crowd, yet he held himself aloof from it. He did not search for familiar faces as he walked. Instead, he watched the flash of feet and gauged openings between the splendor of wild poppies.

In the winter a man could crisscross the financial district, passing through tunnels unknown to the tourists and through side entrances and bank lobbies and lower levels without so much as sticking his nose out-doors. Poke was thinking how Wall Street's tunnels were like the connecting trenches behind the bunkers in Korea. He passed by a revolving door, slicing along the side of a building, and he heard the door sighing, *whumpa, whumpa-whup-whum*PAAH! It was the sound of artillery shells caressing a distant ridge at dawn. He felt a sudden flash of pain and despair. He shook his head furiously; the feeling left him.

Walking ahead of him was a tall girl in a yellow dress. There was something familiar about her stride.

He drew alongside and, on an impulse, touched her arm. The girl stumbled in surprise.

"Hi," he said. "Carol Tracey, I presume."

"Why, hello . . . Poke."

She glanced at him uncertainly and he smiled. They had stopped. He took her elbow and drew her up on the broad, uncluttered steps of Federal Hall. Above them the bronze statue of George Washington gazed impassively at the Stock Exchange.

Right here, at the corner of Broad Street, he knew that he would be able to smell roasting coffee if rain were heading in from the southeast. A few blocks away in that direction was Front Street where a few remaining coffee merchants still roasted their samples.

"Honestly," he said, "you ought to do something about these salesmen at Kimbridge & Co. Always grabbing you by the elbow. How was Pittsburgh?"

"Oh, it was—lovely. Just lovely!"

"Then what's the trouble? You look unhappy. The market got you down?"

"No, not that." She hesitated. "It's just that—well, I've been playing errand boy and I don't like it."

She looked prettier than he had remembered her.

Whatever was troubling her had lent a subtle animation to her face.

"They turn you into a runner at Hillyer & Hunt?" He made a pretense of inspecting her handbag. "I don't see any securities bag."

A grateful smile fled across her face. "No," she said, "but Mr. Hillyer sent me chasing around to every bookstore south of Chambers Street on my lunch hour. He's just written a book. *Your Church and Its Bonds*. That's the title, honest. It's a pitch to the institutional church market. And today he sent me around to the bookstores to see if I could get him a better deal than the author's discount that the publisher is offering him."

"No luck?" he asked sympathetically.

"None at all," she replied, and there was an edge to her voice. "Why, no bookstore will come within 5 per cent of the author's discount. 'Try using a little leverage,' Mr. Hillyer told me. 'Tell the store I might give them some of my book business if they cooperate.'"

"And now you're hopping mad."

"Yes. And you know why? Not just this foolishness about a discount. What really hurts is that *I* practically wrote the damn book for him. He just added a few quotes from the Bible at the start of every chapter, that was *his* contribution. I'm in the foreword. He acknowledges his thanks to me, right in between *The Bond Buyer* and a Unitarian minister from Chicago." She paused. "There's a big market for religious bonds, you know. Especially out in the Far West and the Middle West. But it's all so dull. You should read the bulletin for an issue of first-mortgage serial bonds. 'Abner Heath was called two years ago as pastor'—she wrinkled her nose in disdain—'and upward of nine hundred children and adults are now enrolled in the Sunday school.'"

"Well, what the hell! You've got a nice weekend coming up tomorrow." He glanced up at the sky. "Take my advice. Get out to some beach this weekend and relax. You do like the beach?"

"Oh, yes, but I don't have any plans at all for this weekend."

A pigeon fluttered past them and bounced down on the steps. The pigeon began to pace cockily on a level with George Washington's head.

She was staring at her feet when she spoke again. "You really didn't approve of me that first day we met, did you? Please don't lie to me."

He shrugged. "Nothing personal," he said. "I just think women get in the way around Wall Street. The ones that get ahead—well, they become too much like the men around here."

"That's hardly a flattering comment."

"You asked me to be honest."

"Yes, that's true. I'm sorry."

Above them on the steps the pigeon pecked experimentally at a scrap of ticker tape.

Poke nodded at the bird. "I think it wants to build a nest," he said.

Carol was looking at the bird, too. "Have you ever been to France?" she asked. She clutched her purse tightly with both hands.

"Afraid not."

"Well, one Sunday morning when I was in Paris I put on my white gloves to go to church. I felt wonderful that morning, very dressed up in my white gloves. Then when I was walking under the trees along the Rue de Royale toward Notre Dame Cathedral I heard this bump. A man started cursing. I saw a car drive away and right there"—she turned and pointed to the traffic—"was a little white pigeon fluttering around in the street. I ran out and picked it up.

125

Golly," she said, shivering, "I almost got hit by another car—"

"Yes?" said Poke gently.

"The pigeon's body was as soft as pillow down," she said, almost in a whisper. "I tried to smooth down the feathers and I could feel its heart beating like a trip hammer. Just as I got back to the sidewalk, the pulse stopped. A drop of blood swelled in its beak and fell on my white glove. There was a Frenchman standing there watching me. 'Is it really dead?' I said to him. '*Oui, mademoiselle*,' he said, and then he touched a finger to his beret and walked away. Oh, I felt so sad and so silly standing there holding a dead pigeon. You've never tried to dispose of a dead pigeon on the way to Notre Dame?"

He shook his head.

"Well, believe me, it isn't easy. There aren't any litter baskets on the street like the ones here in New York. An old woman with white hair was walking by. 'What does one do?' I begged her. And you know what? She started to giggle and she said, 'Why, *chérie*, one takes the bird home and plucks it and roasts it with *petit pois*.' That horrid old woman actually smacked her lips and then she said, '*C'est delicieuse*.' Why, I could have choked her!"

"What did you do?"

"I handed her the pigeon. And then I ran sobbing like a child all the way to the cathedral. I even prayed a little for the pigeon, but that didn't make me feel any better."

Her eyes had grown darker. She seemed very vulnerable now and her sadness touched a chord within Poke.

Carol glanced away toward the street. A procession of taxis and automobiles and delivery trucks moved past at a slow, angry pace. There was a red armored car and then a truck with a huge pane of glass tilted at an angle on its rack. The reflection of Federal Hall and its squat columns wavered for a few moments on the glass and then vanished.

Poke coughed. "I've got a customer," he said, "who's figured out the solution to the traffic problem here. Outlaw all left turns. If you want to make a left turn, you take three right turns instead. Think it would work?"

"I don't know," she said and bit her lip.

Poke could sense the expectancy in the Wall Street crowd parading below them. On Friday afternoons there was always that extra tingle in the air.

He kicked the base of the statue and the pigeon fluttered away. "Say," he said abruptly, "if you're not busy this weekend, would you mind if I came by? Sunday night, say?"

She pressed down a pleat in her skirt. "Yes," she said quietly, her eyes still turned away from him, "that would be lovely."

"Nine o'clock okay?" He paused. "Say, I don't even know your address."

"Brooklyn Heights. I live in Brooklyn Heights. Here. I'll write it out for you."

She handed him the scrap of paper and suddenly he was anxious to be on his way.

But Carol seemed reluctant to leave. "Did you know," she said, "that the north side of Wall Street is straighter than the south side?"

"Never noticed the difference."

"Well, it's true. The Dutch built their wooden wall along this side and that's why it runs so—"

"Sunday night," he said impatiently, "we'll drink to the Dutch." For a research analyst, he thought, she talks too damn much.

"Yes," she said. "I'll be waiting."

The last time Poke had done any running was nearly a year ago. It was only a long, easy jog along the edge of the ocean but he could remember the feeling of power pounding through his body and the acute pleasure that running always gave to him. This was the thing he did best; it came to him naturally and he exulted in it with the soaring sense of freedom that a glider pilot might feel. But running was more personal because your own body became the perfectly controlled instrument. He remembered the rhythmic padding of his shoes on the damp, packed sand and the smell of the ocean and the feeling that he was the master of his universe. It was the kind of feeling that a youth knows at seventeen but he was twice as old then and he still felt it.

They drove out to Long Island, the girl and he, one Saturday morning in late September. The red Mercedes roadster glided along the asphalt road that skirted the beaches. Its chrome wire wheels became twirling flashes of silver in the sun. The beaches were deserted except for a few surf fishermen. They were casting their lines, with a peaceful, slow-motion movement, just beyond the whitecaps.

He had promised the girl a brunch of oyster stew. "This place I know," he told her in the apartment earlier that morning, "they fix the stew with pepper and chopped parsley floating in heavy cream. You've never tasted anything like this, they even heat the bowls first. But after we drive out I'd like to run a little before chow time. You pick out a book you can read in the car."

"That's the easiest sale you'll ever make in your life," the girl said.

The girl was wearing his tennis sweater with red and blue piping and despite its bulk the sweater made her look very feminine. She had tied a silk scarf over her head to keep her hair from blowing and the corners of the scarf kept snapping in the wind.

He braked the roadster to a stop in the shade, its tires resting on a bed of pine needles.

She was staring at him. "You know," she said, "even after you quit smiling, that dimple manages to stay on your cheek a few more seconds."

He swiveled his legs out from under the wheel and, bracing his arms, vaulted out of the front seat. He walked quickly toward the beach. Already the girl was slipping from his mind.

The shore line was hidden by low dunes covered with goldenrod and clumps of coarse grass. Fifty yards away there was a steep path that led down to the water.

He was wearing clean khaki pants and a plaid wool shirt. At the bottom of the path he removed his brown loafers and Argyle socks. The Argyles were a present from another girl—she was English and her first name was Nemesia, that was all he could recall at the moment except that she had exceptionally white skin—and he folded them carefully. He had the athlete's reverence for clean socks; he tucked the Argyles inside his loafers to keep them free of sand.

Poke knelt down and drew the laces tight on his tennis shoes. Then he stood up and began walking. Through the soles he could feel the gritty mounds of sand caving in gently with each step.

It was pleasantly warm on the sand. He swung his arms in wide, lazy arcs and looked about him. There was not a human being in sight.

He began taking deep breaths. The salt smell of the ocean was strong and moist. He closed his eyes and walked blind for a few paces. His eyelids became solid patches of bright pink when he held his head up to the sky. The desolate sensation of the beach seeped inside him, warming him with the sun.

Poke tested the sand some yards away from the water. The sand was packed and tinted and it had the color of caramel. He jogged in place for a few moments, letting his arms hang loose and shaking his limp fingers, the way he used to do before a race, and then he did a dozen deep knee bends, his sneakers sinking into the sand under the prolonged pressure.

"Man," he said happily. And then louder, "Man alive!"

On a shelf not far from shore the low waves were breaking. Nearby the foam rushed toward his feet and retreated reluctantly, hissing and frothing, to leave little white lines etched in the caramel sand.

Poke began to run in long, easy strides. He flexed his shoulders the first hundred yards and then settled into a steady jog, his hands reaching out to cup the air.

Clumps of seaweed had washed ashore and the raw smell was exhilarating to him. Sea gulls had left their tracks shaped like arrowheads on the sand but there were no gulls in sight. He jogged past a rusted oil drum that was half submerged in the sand. He looked out to sea. On the horizon a freighter was barely visible.

He slowed to a walk, taking deep breaths again, and then began to run at a slightly faster pace. On the sand his foreshortened shadow matched him stride for stride, mimicking each fluid leg sweep with a curiously dwarf-like gait.

He turned his head from side to side, like a spectator at a tennis match, and smiled then at an old memory.

In college his coach had broken Poke's mannerism of twisting his head during a race. "Waste of energy," the coach had barked. "Nausea, too. You keep on running like that and someday you'll puke right in the middle of the track. Probably in a meet against Tech." Poke was willing to listen to anything that would improve his time; racing had become a passion with him, and his entire life was geared to shaving split seconds from the 880-yard run. "Yes, *suh*," he said to the coach, and he meant it. Before the end of his sophomore year his style was perfected. A fast start and then a lap and a half of long, low strides skimming above the cinders with a slight rolling motion to his hips.

But it was the kick that became his trade-mark. It was customary strategy for a half-miler to wait until rounding the last turn before starting to kick. But Poke's kick erupted with half a lap remaining. It was an explosion that transformed his graceful stride into an odd hobbyhorse motion, his head bobbing on the stiff neck and the roll, accentuated now, moving down to the tips of his spiked shoes. In the final meet, when he broke his own Southeastern Conference record, a photographer for *The Atlanta Constitution* caught him at the tape: eyes glaring in their sockets and cheeks puffed with the final gulp of air. His aunt shuddered when she saw the picture. "I had no idea it was like *that*," she said. He smiled at her. It was all right that she didn't understand. He never liked to talk about racing. Besides, he had left his mark in the book; that was what counted.

His shoe crushed a scallop shell on the sand and he felt it snap away to rubble. He was beginning to perspire now and it was a marvelous feeling.

It was time to turn back. He slowed to a walk and, bending down, picked up a small black stone. He wiped the wet sand from the stone and felt its cool, smooth surface between his palms. Specks of quartz gleamed in the stone and a white band circled the larger end. Tossing the stone into the air and catching it as he ran, he began to jog again. A light breeze was blowing from the sea and he could feel the damp undershirt clinging to his back.

"Queep, queep!"

A lone sea gull came from behind Poke and wheeled away to the left over the water. He tracked the bird as it moved forward along his line of vision. He admired its sheer grace. Soaring on the breeze, its wings stretched wide, the gull floated effortlessly. Once it actually turned its head and, gazing along a curved yellow bill, looked back at Poke. The bird seemed to be pacing him at a distance as he ran.

But soon the gull moved swiftly ahead, without so much as a wing flutter, as if it had tired of this foolish game. "Queep." The cry became fainter.

The bird wheeled and coasted toward the beach. It glided down, some thirty yards ahead of Poke, and skipped along the wet sand before arching its wings briefly and folding them against its body. Standing there on matchstick legs with its heavy neckless head looking out to sea, the gull was transformed. It had become incredibly ugly.

Poke felt a sudden anger at the bird. He veered toward the gull, running faster now, and began to shout. "Get going! Get moving!"

The gull stared at him, offended by the boorish outburst. Grudgingly, as Poke approached within a few yards, the gull hitched up its wings and, skipping along the sand again, launched itself into the air with a final indignant "Queep!" When Poke came to the spot where the gull had stood there were only deep gouges in the sand. The gull was soaring again, its beauty restored.

Poke felt as though he could run forever without

tiring. He ran several wind sprints of fifty yards and that made him feel even better. "What the hell," he said. "Open up, Jeffers. Let's see what you can do." And there along the packed sand he kicked for a distance he judged to be the equivalent of half a lap.

A few minutes later he was taking off his tennis shoes and carefully unfolding the Argyle socks. He picked out bits of tar that were imbedded in the soles of the tennis shoes and then he vaulted up the path.

The girl was reading when he arrived at the car. She looked up at him and her face was shining. "Glory be to God for dappled things," she said and snapped the book shut.

"That's Hopkins," he said. "Ole Gerard Manley himself."

She nodded gravely. "I have a confession," she said. "I sneaked out to make sure you hadn't forgotten me. I was afraid you might have taken up with a mermaid or something." She tilted her head. "I watched you there at the end," she said softly. "When you cut out all the stops. My God, Poke! You were like a flash of gold against the ocean."

"Come on," he said. "Knock it off." She made him feel uncomfortable talking like that. "Present for you," he said and handed her the stone.

"Oh!" she cried delightedly. "It's a good-luck piece!" She traced a finger along the white line. "That means good luck. Here." She held out her hand. "You keep it."

"Unh-uh," he replied. "It's yours." He opened the door and climbed quickly into the car. "I make my own luck."

11

Noel Bigelow had settled into his reclining chair with the latest issue of *Yachting* when his wife walked softly into the living room. Then she said his name in the low, deliberate voice he had come to recognize in their two years of marriage; it meant she had been thinking for a long time about what she was about to say.

"Noel."

"Ummh?"

"Noel, look at me. Please."

"Okay, I'm looking. What is it?"

"I'm leaving you. Noel. And this time it's for good. None of this hiding for a weekend at the Plaza Hotel and hoping you'd go crazy worrying about me. We've both been kidding ourselves about this marriage. I don't know exactly when it began to go wrong, Noel, but I do know one thing. Our marriage isn't going to work. So I want to leave you before we have children and find ourselves chained together for life and grow-

ing to hate each other. I couldn't"—her voice faltered
—"take that, Noel."

He brought his chair forward as gingerly as he
might have eased his forty-foot yawl, *Sweet Gambol
II*, up to the dock and he said, "No, Avis, I don't believe you *are* kidding." He placed the magazine on
one arm of the chair. He had a sailor's careful way of
handling himself about the house. "Tell me something," he said. "Exactly what brought this on?"

Avis was standing a dozen feet from him, her arms
crossed as if she were very cold. He remembered
what he thought the first time he had seen her: a girl
with good sailing eyes. Her eyes were clear and blue
and they never blinked when she was concentrating.
She was standing there, tapping her fingers against
her elbows, the only indication of her nervousness,
and he knew she was right about their marriage and
that he was not going to try to hold her. He felt a
rush of affection for her at that instant, for this earnest rich girl who hid green mints in her riding boots
and who would not permit him to get a maid for their
house in Darien and who became terribly upset
when, as she had done on two occasions while washing the dishes as he sat in the living room, she broke
a dinner plate in their wedding pattern. "What the
hell," he had said. "So we buy a few more plates. It's
not going to bankrupt us." And she had replied, "No,
it's not that at all. These first plates"—she moved
her shoulders helplessly—"just mean something very
dear to me, that's all." She had given him this maroon
leather chair on the first Christmas after their marriage and later she confessed to making half-a-dozen
forays into Manhattan before deciding finally upon
the chair she thought would please him most.

Shortly after they were married, they had ex-
changed lists detailing their various clothes, hat, belt,

135

and glove sizes. Each list was to be a guideline to future presents. But one evening on the commuter train, when he opened his wallet to pay for the martinis, the list Avis had given to him dropped out. He had just conducted a test and found that a stand-up martini was a better buy in the club car than a martini on the rocks because the bartender cheated on the gin when he could pop ice into the glass. And now she was walking out and he knew that he was not going to lift a hand to stop her, just as he had made no effort to retrieve the typewritten list when it dropped beside his shoe in the club car.

"Avis . . ." he said. He knew that if he tried he could hold her, that she wanted him desperately to try.

Her fingers kept playing on her elbows. At night when she bathed she would sit in the tub with her arms crossed the same way. She used only a few inches of water, scalding hot, so as not to be wasteful, and when she stood up in the tub there would be a long, red rim down her buttocks and along the back of her legs.

"Oh, Noel!" she burst out, "perhaps we were never really married! That's what I've been thinking . . . I mean, we've lived together as man and wife but maybe we were never *really* married to each other. My God, Noel"—tears were brimming now in her eyes, clouding their blueness—"you don't know how happy I was. At the wedding, and later, at the reception, I felt—I don't know how to say it exactly—but I felt *outside* of myself. Maybe it was being the center of attention." She blinked her eyes as if to conjure up the memory. "It's a funny thing," she said, talking very rapidly, "but nobody talks to the bride just before the ceremony. I was so lonely all of a sudden and nobody would talk to me. Everybody thought I wanted those final moments to myself. But then when I walked down the aisle and you were standing there that made everything *right* for me. You stuck your tongue out at me but you were smiling. Do you remember, Noel?" Her voice trailed off and he realized the effort these words had cost her.

"But something has happened," he insisted. "What is it?"

"Oh, Noel, you actually don't know, do you?" Instead of answering him, Avis lapsed into a reverie again. "I never will forget how you fooled me about the honeymoon. . . . You kept saying Clearwater, Florida, and I was in such a daze after all the champagne and just being with you that I didn't realize it was Nassau until we got off the plane and there weren't orange trees around—"

"Your mother made it quite clear when we got back that it was a pretty thoughtless thing for me to do. She said you weren't carrying the right clothes for the Bahamas. My God, are clothes so damned important on a honeymoon?" He remembered how earnest Avis had been about the thank-you notes. She began writing them, three notes every morning before breakfast, during their honeymoon.

"Don't be angry with Mother, Noel. You know how thrilled I was over Nassau. You could have taken me to Coney Island. I wouldn't have cared."

"Yes," he said, momentarily humbled by her honesty. "You're right about that."

There was a quality about Avis that he had perceived soon after their marriage. For the outside world she adorned herself with a sort of polite, protective armor, just short of coquetry, and at parties when she met someone she had not seen in a long while she would bend her knees and say, "Hi!" She had a tremulous way of drawing out the word like a

137

bowstring and it was sure death to the stag line at a dance. But the core of her being, he came to know, was a radiant goodness. It was a quality he had never known before in a person, and he thought at first that because he was so different this quality would form a permanent magnet. But he had turned away from it and he did not understand why. Perhaps, he told himself, it was only because he knew he possessed the power to accept or to reject her.

"Do you know, Noel, what it is that most women want?"

"Tell me. What?"

"Just to be loved. It's really that simple, Noel. Just to be loved." She spoke slowly now, like a child caressing the face of a doll. "I suppose every new wife feels unsure of herself for some reason. Perhaps she's not sure that her husband genuinely approves of her friends or the clothes she wears or she simply may be afraid she makes bad coffee in the morning. But, Noel, it's the funniest thing, this feeling I've had about us. . . . I've never mentioned it to you but"— she raised her fingers helplessly—"it's as though somebody else always kept passing between you and me so that we couldn't make contact. I felt as though I never really got the wrapping paper off you. This other person was always there, wrapped around you like so many layers of tissue paper." She stopped talking and smiled forlornly. "Oh, Noel, don't you realize how useless this is? If you really cared about my leaving, you wouldn't just sit there like a district attorney with a witness. You'd jump up and throw things or you'd kiss me or . . . do something. If you really cared."

"Something *did* happen," he insisted.

"Yes! Something happened, all right!" She was shouting. "One week ago something *did* happen. It

138

was the night of our anniversary and when we were in bed, right at *that* moment, do you know what? You shouted 'Deirdre!' Right in my ear, you shouted Deirdre's name. Oh, Noel, I felt like dying right then. I didn't even have the will to be jealous. I just felt like dying." She paused. "I guess it was what people call a Freudian slip. Funny, I'd never known exactly *what* a Freudian slip was before. Well, I know now."

"Avis, don't be ridiculous! Why in the world would I mention Deirdre Kimbridge at a time like that? My God, I haven't even seen her in five years."

"You don't have to see a person in order to keep thinking about her."

"Yes, but—"

"Noel, please let's not argue. There is only one thing for us to settle. Are you going to give me a divorce? A nice, civilized divorce without any sackcloth and ashes? We're both adults and we can afford it. So, please, Noel, let's not fight about it and spoil everything. I—well—I still love you too much, I guess . . ."

He stared at her and he thought she was going to start crying again. But he was wrong. He could hear the katydids outside and somewhere the barking of a dog.

At that moment the telephone rang.

He started up from his chair but Avis was already hurrying across the room. "Hello," she said quickly. Then, "Yes, Mother, how are you? Are you all packed for your trip?" Her voice was perfectly normal now.

Noel arose. He did not even want to be in the same room while Avis was talking with her mother. He could see his mother-in-law's face all too vividly. Mrs. Lomax had an oddly wrinkled face that reminded him of the shells of English walnuts; the same color and texture and, yes, the same hardness. She did not look at all like Avis, except that both mother and daughter had the same clear blue eyes. It was the damnedest thing! Mrs. Lomax was one of the few people in the world he felt incapable of besting and he was certain she had disliked him thoroughly from their first meeting. Mrs. Lomax was one of those persons, Noel reflected grimly, who still managed to live by a set of principles that would have humbled Cotton Mather on his best day. What a hard old witch she was! She even insisted on inspecting taxi drivers in New York City before deciding whether or not to enter the cab.

And now Mrs. Lomax, a widow with little but time and money on her hands, was preparing to leave for Europe again. She was going with a friend who also collected brass rubbings. He could see his mother-in-law now, kneeling on the floor of some parish church in England with a black piece of cobbler's wax in her hand as she rubbed the tracing paper. He shuddered. The fact that beneath those brass figures the dead lay in their burial vaults did not deter Mrs. Lomax.

"Yes, Mother, I think a rubbing would go wonderfully over the umbrella stand in your front hallway," Avis said. She had turned her back to Noel. "Yes, yes. Flannel dusters would be *fine* for cleaning the brass first."

To hell with Avis and her mother, Noel thought savagely as he walked out of the room. He went down the hallway and, ducking his head under the low beam, entered the "Fo'c's'le."

He lighted a cigarette and glanced with satisfaction about the low-ceilinged room. Originally, the room had served as a library. But when they bought this house, primarily so that Noel could be near his boat, he had set to work transforming it. He had done much of the remodeling with his own hands. The refurbishing energy of the sailor was ingrained in him; every spring, before putting his boat in water, he inspected and repaired the sails himself. It was Avis who had provided the name "Fo'c'sle" and he went along with her suggestion. In a sense, this room was more a part of him than his own wife. The floor was teak, just like the deck of *Sweet Gambol II* and the library shelves had been replaced with wide planks of Honduras mahogany.

A flotilla of pictures and framed photographs sailed upon the walls. There was a photograph of Noel as a youngster hiking on a small boat—the first boat he ever owned—with a floppy hat on his head and his bottom scooting just above the whitecaps. The photographs traced out his developing manhood and his increasingly expensive tastes. There was a color shot, taken during his junior year at Princeton, of Noel crouching on the deck of a twelve-meter owned by a classmate. He was preparing to jibe the spinnaker and a can of beer was tucked pirate-like inside his belt. Another photograph of Noel storing sail below decks of another boat and a shot of him on deck, flashing a victory grin and sporting a scraggly beard, that year he made the Bermuda race on a sloop owned by one of his customers at Kimbridge & Co.

There was a large etching of yachtsman's knots with a bowline, a fisherman's bend, a buntline hitch, a half bowknot, and a rolling hitch arrayed in rather surrealistic fashion. And, finally, in the far corner there hung an old photograph, now badly faded and with the creases showing plainly along one edge, of a long, low, beautiful schooner that was built for his father in 1928. His father had sailed the schooner for a single season and then the stock market crash had wiped it away as effectively as a typhoon. The name of that schooner was barely visible in the photograph

141

—*Sweet Gambol I*—and Noel Bigelow had waited half a lifetime before he owned a boat that he considered worthy to be its successor.

In the center of the room was a large cocktail table with a ship's wheel under the round glass top. Noel had scoured antique shops in New England for chart chests after the house was purchased and these chests provided the only seating area in the room. Six chart chests, each slightly more than a foot high, were arranged along the walls beneath the pictures and three other chests formed an open-ended triangle around the cocktail table. The chests were made of mahogany and he had rubbed them down and then polished them to a fine gloss. They were a real find, those chests; a seaman's chest was commonplace, but a chart chest was special because there was only one to a sailing ship and it belonged to the captain.

Noel adjusted a picture on the wall.

Why the hell did Avis have to bring up that business about Deirdre? Of course, she was right, by God, but then how many men got to marry the one woman in their lives who really infatuated them? He stared across the room at his father's schooner and realized that the reason he had married Avis was because she fitted so readily into the world of Deirdre Kimbridge.

Avis was still standing by the telephone when Noel came back into the living room.

"Did you tell your mother . . . about us?" he asked.

"No. That's something we haven't settled yet. Have we, Noel?"

He ignored the question. "What's your mother got to say?"

"Oh," replied Avis lightly, "her next big ambition after this trip is to rub brasses in the Soviet bloc countries. Now isn't that something for a woman of sixty-four?"

142

"Umm." He knew this was Avis's way of pleading for him to say she was crazy to ask for a divorce.

"Well, Noel?"

He smiled crookedly at her. Then he said in a low voice, "Act perfectly natural. I just saw an Indian go by the window. War paint on his face. Sioux, I think. You know what *they* do to white women."

She began to move toward him, a radiant look upon her face. "Oh, my darling," she said, "if you only knew—"

And he stopped Avis in her tracks, wanting fiercely to hurt her. "How do you want to arrange it?" he said. "You want to go to Reno? Or shall I do it? That would take me away from the office, you realize."

She put a hand to her face.

"Oh, no, Noel. I wouldn't *dream* of taking you away from your office. After all, the brokerage business is so *important*." Her words were like the frost on a pond in winter.

"What about your mother?" he said.

"What about her? You mean, will I ask her to cancel her trip abroad? The answer is no. Reno takes six weeks. Isn't that correct? It will all be over when Mother gets back. I'll tell her then. I don't want to spoil her trip."

"Then what about her account? Will I get to keep her brokerage account until—well, until we've finished this business?"

"Oh, my God!" She steadied herself then and said, "Yes, Noel. By all means, keep the account."

He stared at Avis. There may as well have been an ocean between them.

"All right, then," he said with a shrug. "Consider it settled. Of course, we'll need different lawyers. You can use Frank. At least, he can recommend a good man for you. I'll find somebody else."

"All right," she said. "That's fine with me." She hesitated a moment and then she said, "I'd better put away the dishes."

"Bigelow, you shyster! I hear everything's about to collapse! Stocks, bonds, convertible bonds, the works! Bigelow, you better run for the rowboat, boy!"

It was Tim McVay, his roommate at college, on the office phone. Tim telephoned occasionally to relate a new set of jokes. When elephant jokes had been popular around New York, Tim had seventy-eight of them filed on index cards. Now the becalmed stock market had put a damper on new jokes along Wall Street but it failed to deter Tim.

"Greetings, Tim. How is life among the toiling class?"

Tim lived on a twenty-acre estate in Litchfield inherited from his father. His wife set aside an egg-shaped room simply for wrapping gifts. Every summer he threw a party for a hundred guests and servants in colonial costumes served roast suckling pig on pewter plates bearing the McVay seal. He had never worked a day in his life but the galling thing to Noel was that Tim McVay had yet to give him a dime's worth of business.

"Say, fella, we've got something new, Nicole and me. Raising Newfoundland dogs! Really great. You have to be mighty careful though about the people who want to buy the pups. Nicole and I insist on two interviews with the prospective owner."

"You give them away?" asked Noel. He detested dogs—and cats, too—and Avis said once it was because they sometimes made such poor sailers.

Noel held the telephone away from his ear. Tim McVay's delighted bellow could be heard halfway across the board room. "Bigelow, you take the cake!

Hell, no. We get two hundred apiece for the males and two seventy-five for the bitches. If I don't watch out, I'm going to show a profit. How about that?" Without waiting for a reply, Tim rattled on. "Ran into somebody at Bergdorf's the other day. I was looking for a jeweled dog collar." Tim's voice became secretive. "Old friend of yours, Bigelow."

"I know. Mrs. Lomax. Except she's in Europe."

"No . . . but you're on the right track. It was Deirdre Kimbridge. She just blew in from Paris."

There was a coppery taste in Noel's mouth. "You're not kidding me?" he said harshly. "Tim, if this is your idea of a joke—"

But, no, not even Tim would be joking about Deirdre Kimbridge. By God, if he were, he'd have a broken leg to show for it.

Noel took a deep breath. "Is she—is she still single?" he said.

"Appears to be free as the air. You know Deirdre. She's always too busy saving somebody or launching some fool project to get tied down. Damn shame, too. She's the sexiest looking Vassar girl I ever saw."

"Where's she staying?"

"Didn't ask. And it wouldn't be safe for me to know either. If I did find out, I'd probably beat down the door and try to lay her. And Nicole wouldn't like that. She's French but not that French."

"No," said Noel. "I guess she wouldn't. Wives can be funny that way." He was anxious to be rid of Tim McVay. "See you, Tim."

"Sure. Maybe we can get you up to God's country for a weekend. Your new apartment in Greenwich Village must cramp you after Darien. I'm committee chairman for Founders' Day at the club. Say, Bigelow, what do you think of this idea? I get some show girl, maybe size forty, from the Latin Quarter, for

145

Sunday afternoon. This babe strips to the waist, see, and a helicopter shoots her around the golf course. She drops down on every putting green. Exhibition only, of course. How about that?"

"It should impress your membership," Noel said. " 'By, Tim."

So Deirdre Kimbridge was back in town. . . . The phrase kept drumming through his mind. Deirdre had sunk into the core of his being like a drill bit boring into a deck. He had succeeded in sweeping away the shavings but that was all. So Deirdre Kimbridge was back in town. . . .

In times of emotional stress Noel Bigelow believed in taking direct action. On the first occasion he did not even realize what he was doing. It was the afternoon of his father's suicide and finally he had sneaked out of the house to sit alone in the back yard. He saw ants scurrying about their anthill, like slaves building a pyramid. Their precision had infuriated Noel. He rolled up a newspaper, set it afire, and then thrust the torch into the anthill.

And now, cool and detached on the surface as he sat in the board room, Noel felt a tremendous compulsion to *do* something. Yes, a symbolic act to celebrate Deirdre's return, that was it precisely.

The time had come, he decided, to put his little plan into action.

He wrote out the order slips for the discretionary account with a look of glee. Within a few minutes, thanks to the speed of order executions on which Kimbridge & Co. prided itself, it was all done. He had sold $612,000 worth of stocks in his mother-in-law's account. Two-thirds of the proceeds went into growth-oriented mutual funds; the remainder he had put into tax-free municipals. Mrs. Lomax, he was certain, would remain silent when she learned in time of the trades. On the outside chance that she might protest to the partners, Noel was prepared to defend his investment judgment. He was going to lose the account, anyway, as soon as the divorce became final. Noel had calculated his commissions to the dollar; the commissions would cover the entire cost of the divorce, plus the decorator's fee on his new apartment.

12

He had met Deirdre one warm night in late spring. Noel was on his way to a cocktail party being given by one of the men at the bank where he worked, a municipal bond trader whose family was White Russian. Walking slowly down Third Avenue, he faced the truth that he had become bored with his job at the bank and somehow the prospect of a noisy room filled with people hoisting their glasses to undulating interest rates did not appeal to him.

He glanced idly into an old saloon and saw the long, decklike sweep of the bar. He decided suddenly that this neighborhood saloon suited his mood and he went inside. The place smelled agreeably of beer and old wood. Noel thought about ordering a beer but he asked instead for a martini.

Noel took a sip from his drink—too much vermouth, dammit!—but he did not have the spirit to complain to the bartender. What could you expect for fifty cents?

He stood apart from a knot of men at the bar and stared at a vase of wax daffodils. Morosely he considered his future at the Wall Street bank where he was employed as a loan officer.

It was one of the few banks in the city that had preserved its main banking room in the grand style, and for Noel Bigelow this fact was entered on the credit side of the ledger. This enormous room might have been lifted straight out of the Vatican. Its floor was covered with maroon carpeting and the massive columns were faced with burled walnut. Crystal chandeliers sprinkled their light softly, and in the middle of the ornate gilt ceiling was a painting attributed to a student of Tiepolo. The guards wore their shoulder holsters under blue business suits. It was a tradition at the bank to hire only former Marines as guards because the honorary board chairman was a retired Marine colonel.

From the bank's point of view, Noel reflected, he was well on the way to a successful career—if he only hung on long enough. The previous year he had been elevated to the platform, a ledge raised some eight inches from the main floor, and he now had the authority to authorize personal loans up to $3,000 without the signature of another officer. On the day of his promotion the colonel himself had appeared to offer his congratulations. And a word of advice—"No bow ties, my boy, on the platform." The colonel was not even a Republican; he was a Whig.

The bank always announced promotions on the final business day before Christmas and Noel knew that his ascendancy to assistant vice president—due in five and a half years—would qualify him to patronize the officers' barbershop on the eighteenth floor.

"Nuts," said Noel Bigelow to the wax daffodils. Patience had never been one of his strong points.

149

Once you had worked inside the bank for a while you saw some of the ridiculous things that went on. For example, a dozen men had devoted their full time to a project that involved changing the design of the passbook. Finally, after four months, the decision was made not to adopt the enlarged design for passbooks because it would require the installation of new machines at the teller windows.

One thing alone held him at the bank. That was the way money—*real* money, not the childish amounts with which he dealt—could be created as if from thin air. One telephone call, a few pieces of paper, one man saying the magic words, "We'll do it," and presto! The borrower suddenly had a debit balance of $5,000,000. It was tantalizing to work in surroundings where such miracles were performed.

Noel was staring down at his drink and debating whether to order another one when he heard a girl's voice behind him.

"Why, that *bas*tard!" the voice murmured, as if confirming a suspicion. "Pardon me," the girl said to the bartender, "but have you seen a man wearing a white dinner jacket in here within the past twenty minutes or so? A blond man about six feet two?"

"No, Miss," the bartender said. "Nobody's been in here all spring in a white dinner jacket. I'd sure have noticed him."

Noel glanced at the bartender. A change seemed to have come over him. He was a sloppy man with rheumy eyes and a large red nose; he needed a shave badly and his apron appeared not to have been washed since St. Patrick's Day. But now the bartender drew himself erect and actually straightened his tie. He asked respectfully, "Anything I can get for you, Miss?"

The girl did not reply. Instead, she muttered once

more, "That cheap bastard," biting off the words. "It's my date," Noel heard her say to the bartender. "I can't find him anywhere. We were around the corner at El Morocco and he said he was going to the john." She spoke matter-of-factly and the bartender, standing at something akin to attention, gave an understanding nod. "It's an old trick of his," the girl said. "He can't *stand* to tip a john attendant. So he always runs around the corner to some cheap bar—oops, excuse me—I didn't mean it that way." The bartender gave a magnanimous shrug. "So he goes to the john free and then picks up a shot for the price of the tip," the girl said. "That way he figures he's ahead of the game." Noel could hear a shoe tapping behind him on the tile floor. "Oh, what the hell!" the girl said. "You've been very nice. Give me a gin, please. Straight gin. In a glass of ice."

A hush had settled over the entire bar. Most of the men were in shirt sleeves or shabby work clothes and now they all seemed to be staring at the new arrival over their beer glasses. Noel noticed one of the men who was standing near the bend of the bar take off his cap and stuff it into a pants pocket.

The girl put her foot on the bar rail beside Noel. "Thank you," she said to the bartender as he set down her drink. He handled the glass as if it were heirloom crystal.

Noel was still absorbed in his own thoughts. So some girl had lost track of her date. That was her tough luck. And then an odd thing happened to him. He actually began to *feel* the magnetism—it was exactly as if someone were hauling in a rowboat with a line—of this person. He turned to look at the girl for the first time.

She gave him a glance, then a curt nod that said unmistakably that she wanted to be left alone. She was a girl who could take care of herself without reaching for the long hat pin; that was his initial assessment.

He began to smell the perfume. It was sharp and direct, like the girl herself, but somehow provocatively feminine. He frowned over the scent and then it came to him. It was like the tart fragrance of apples in a bin.

Noel decided to have another drink. He pointed to his empty glass and the bartender nodded. "Go easy on the vermouth this time," Noel said.

Under the pretense of watching the bartender mix his martini, Noel inspected the girl out of the corner of his eye. She was quite short and she appeared to be about twenty-two or twenty-three. She had dark hair and a strong, neat profile. But the most arresting thing about the girl was her deeply tanned skin. It had a sheen like heated silk. Noel had the curious sensation that if he were to reach out and touch this girl her skin would give off a more intense apple scent. The girl climbed up on a bar stool.

She was wearing a simple black dress, cut squarely in the front and held up by two ridiculously thin cords across her rounded shoulders. Noel prided himself as an expert on women's clothes and he mentally put down this dress as the simple-looking type that cost $200. The girl sat stiff-backed on the shabby, imitation-leather stool with her hands clasping the glass as though she were holding the reins of a show horse.

Noel took a swallow from his martini. He made a wry face. Smart girl, to order straight gin.

He heard a hiccup beside him. Not a demure hiccup but one that was operatic in its delivery. He tensed slightly, wondering if the girl would hiccup again. Thereupon, she emitted a string of hiccups, loud and full, the last one accompanied by an exasperated, "Goddamit—'up!"

The girl twisted around toward Noel. "Would you mind giving me a whack?" she said. "There may be small children sleeping in the neighborhood."

Upon issuing this request, she spun around and presented Noel with her back. He hit her smartly with the flat of his hand. She gave a little snap with her head and then hiccuped again. "Once more, if you don't mind," she said. He obliged her, and this time he noticed that the clasp on her string of pearls was fashioned with tiny rubies and diamonds. The clasp was in the shape of a sea horse.

"It doesn't seem to do the trick," he said and, as if to confirm his statement, the girl gave another hiccup. "Maybe we ought to let the bull elephant out of the back room," he said, "and see if that scares you."

"Goddamit," was all she said, and then the girl hiccuped so violently that her entire body shook.

Along the length of the bar the other men leaned forward to watch, their faces filled with genuine concern.

"I've got an idea," said Noel. "Try drinking from your glass backward." She gave him a cold look. "No, seriously," he insisted. "That works sometimes. It's the concentration that does it. Look, I'll show you how."

Noel set the martini glass on the bar and stretched his head forward. Then he tilted the glass away from him and sipped the drink from the far side, catching the liquid inside his upper lip. He straightened up. "See?" he said. "That's all there is to it."

Like an obedient child, she followed his example. Every man in the bar seemed to be holding his breath. The bartender had placed a glass of water on the bar and he now was anxiously gripping his cloth.

After about a minute the girl straightened up and

sat back on the stool. Her face was flushed under the curiously warm skin. "By God," she announced finally, "it works." She gave Noel a grateful smile. "You're a genius, Dr. Mayo. Whew! For a little while there I thought I was going to make medical history. The first girl ever to die of hiccups in a Third Avenue bar."

"You'd better have another gin," said Noel. "Just for insurance."

The bartender immediately fetched drinks for the two of them. "On the house," he announced proudly.

"By God," Noel said to the girl, "you *are* making history."

They began talking over their drinks. He learned she had graduated from Vassar the year before and was working as a secretary—"I've developed filing-cabinet knees," she said ruefully—at the Ford Foundation.

Her eyebrows were full and dark, curving slightly over eyes that were almost coal black. He noticed the ripples like baby fat at her armpits. The ripples of flesh were powdered white and they appeared inordinately sensuous to Noel.

"What do you do?" she asked.

"I work at a bank."

She puckered up her face. "Banks," she said. "Ugh. I never can balance my checkbook. So I just trust the bank to do it for me."

He was horrified. "But you might get cheated doing that!"

"Cheated? By a bank?" Her dark eyes opened wide in wonder. "But aren't they supposed to be honest?"

"Of course. But even a bank can make mistakes." He took a deep swallow from the martini. He felt protective toward this girl for some strange reason, in addition to the tremendous physical pull that was like an undertow. "Look," he said, "it's really very simple to balance a checkbook. You just total up your checks that are still outstanding. Then you deduct that figure from the balance on your last stub, as of the date you get the statement from the bank. That way your checkbook and the bank's statement should agree—"

"But they never *do*." She shook her head. "I've tried that and they never agree. So you know how I've solved the problem?"

"How?"

"I write very few checks. I try to pay as many bills as possible with cash. But there are some things you can't handle very conveniently that way. Like Con Edison, for instance. *Their* office is way to hell and gone. But I should have done it. I should have gone down there and handed them the four dollars and sixteen cents like a good girl. So what happened? What happened is that this morning I woke up and my radio wouldn't work. Those bastards shut off my electricity! I don't care about myself. Personally, I love candles. Candles and firewood. But you can't build a fire this time of the year. And, besides, I don't have a fireplace in my apartment. But it's the goldfish I'm worried about. Somebody told me it's bad for their nerves to use candles."

She had a way of talking quite fast and chopping up her phrases with short bursts of laughter so that the words came squirting out, as though greased by her laughter, and when she finished talking she was a bit breathless. Also, she was the first person Noel ever had heard who could say "bastard" and make it sound almost dignified.

The girl spun around on her stool. Leaning with her back against the edge of the bar, she began to appraise the saloon through half-closed eyes.

"With no trouble at all," she said, nodding her head

155

for emphasis, "they could turn this spot into another P. J. Clarke's. No trouble at all. . . ." She pointed to the travel posters of Ireland pasted on a wall that was the color of mustard. "What they do first is knock down that wall and open up the other side for serving food. There's an abandoned butcher shop next door and it's got the most wonderful old meat lockers. I know because I noticed it when I passed by. I thought my date might have wandered in *there* looking for a free leg of lamb or something. Anyway, they just rub down those meat lockers and the hardwood would be lovely." The excitement was building up in her voice again, making her breathless and causing her eyes to shine. "They keep this area as the bar," she went on, "and partition off the other side. In place of tablecloths with red-and-white checks, they use stripes. They buy a couple of Tiffany lamps and hang them from the ceiling—my God!" She was inspecting the ceiling. "Have you ever seen so much dirt! They sprinkle sawdust—green sawdust to preserve the Irish flavor—on the floor. And Irish coffee . . . that could be the specialty of the house." She glanced about. "Over there they hang up a slate board for the menu. And outside they put up an old pub sign. I could find a genuine one for them easy. I practically haunt antique shops." She leaned over and clutched Noel by the arm. "Oh," she implored, "can't you just *see* it?"

He smelled the rich, warm scent of her body and nodded dumbly.

"People would *jam* into here," the girl cried. "But no reservations. Rule of the house. First come, first served."

He decided to humor the girl for fear she might launch her project immediately with the bartender. Yes, he thought, she's just screwy enough to do that.

"Say," Noel said, putting down his empty glass, "as

156

long as your date has disappeared, can I take you home? My car's parked a couple blocks down the street."

"All right," she said with a little shrug. "That's damn nice of you." She held out her hand. "But I suppose you ought to know my name. Deirdre Kimbridge. But please don't call me Deedee. If you do that I'm apt to slash your tires."

"My name is—"

"Wait," she commanded. "I'd like to guess. Let's see . . . your first name—is it Boyd?"

"No."

"Bristol? Are you a Bristol?"

"Two strikes on you."

"Ummnn." Her dark brows knit in concentration. Suddenly she smiled. "Then you're Burgess!" she burst out. "God, that's a nice name, Burgess."

"Sorry," he said. "Three strikes and you're out. My name's Noel." The girl looked so downcast that he felt slightly foolish. "But you got a lot closer with my last name," he said encouragingly. "It's Bigelow. Noel Bigelow."

"Well, that's something, isn't it?" she said. But she seemed oddly disappointed.

Noel paid the check and the bartender said to Deirdre, "Come again, Miss." Noel thought for a moment the bartender was going to shake her hand.

They walked to his car and Noel held the door open for her.

"Oh, God!" she cried. "You've got a ticket!"

The car was parked three feet from a fire hydrant. Noel closed the door after Deirdre climbed inside. Then he calmly walked around to the windshield, untied the green ticket from the wiper, and struck it in his pocket. "Don't worry about it," he said, getting in beside her.

"Well, I must say. You're certainly cool enough. I'd be mad as a hornet if *I* got a parking ticket."

"I put it there myself," he said. "Before I went into the bar."

"Say, maybe you could patent this idea. Did you think it up yourself?"

"No. One of the guards at the bank told me about it. He joined the police force after his hitch in the Marines. Now he's one of New York's finest. Bank guards, that is."

"You sound quite democratic. None of my friends know any bank guards."

Noel shrugged. "Oh, I gave him some advice once on how to go about arranging a loan. At another bank. Who knows? Someday he may be able to return the favor." He started the engine.

Deirdre lived on 10th Street, in the block west of Fifth Avenue. "Come on up," she said, "and I'll give you a nightcap. That's the least you deserve."

Her apartment was on the third floor. She led the way upstairs and, following close behind her, Noel observed the smooth, pumping motion of her legs. The calves winked in and out. She wore no stockings and her ankles were quite thin.

"That is it," she announced. She swung open the door and flicked the wall switch. "Damn! I forgot about the lights. You wait there in the hallway until I find the candles." In a few moments she called out, "The coast is clear!"

He stepped inside and, in the swaying candlelight, surveyed the apartment. The living room was small and surprisingly drab. It reminded him of the saloon they had just left. Noel felt cheated somehow.

Deirdre had disappeared behind a screen. "Brandy all right with you?" he heard her say.

"That's fine."

She emerged with a bottle of Calvados and two expensive-looking liqueur glasses. She blew at the Calvados bottle. "Honestly," she exclaimed, "this town is so *dusty*. Tell me, they don't have any suggestions for beating the dust down at your bank?"

"No, that's a bit out of our line."

"By the way, what is your bank?"

He gave her the name, and she nodded.

She handed him a glass and promptly sat down on the floor, tucking her feet under her. Noel looked about uncertainly and decided finally upon the small couch. The slip cover, he noticed, had a long rip.

"What shall we drink to?" he asked.

"Oh, I don't know." She tossed her head. "To all wonderful men whose names begin with B," she said and raised her glass.

"Yes," he said and sipped the Calvados. When she raised her arm her face fell into darkness.

He watched the candlelight—the candles were two squat red ones, placed in china saucers—play over her smooth, dark shoulders and throw up tiny shadows along her collar bone. He looked at her firm round breasts thrusting above the square neckline and he thought, she's wearing a half bra.

They remained that way for perhaps five minutes, neither one of them saying a word.

She looked up at him suddenly. "Your job at the bank," she said. "Are you happy with it?"

"Well, no. As a matter of fact. Personally, I prefer a little more action. I've thought of selling but . . ."

"What about the brokerage business?" she asked. "Selling securities. Would you like that?"

He looked at her in puzzlement. Over Deirdre's left shoulder he saw a goldfish bowl on the table. There were two fish in the bowl and they glided slowly into view now, their eyes bulbous and unblinking, refracted through the thick glass bowl with a kind of deep-ocean depth. Their mouths were slowly opening and closing. He stared at the goldfish, thinking about this strange girl sitting on the floor, and then he said, "Sure. Why not? If the right opportunity came along."

"Good," she said, clapping her hands. "As a matter of fact, there's a brokerage firm in our family. Kimbridge & Co."

"I know about it. A good house. Our Trust Department does some business with them."

"That figures," she said. She was smiling now. "Your bank happens to manage my trust."

He wondered if she were playing with him. She acted like a rich girl all right, but this apartment was completely out of character. He decided suddenly to call her bluff. "I'm at your service," he said. "What do I do? Show up Monday morning for an interview?" He said it mockingly.

"That would be wonderful," she said. "I'll set it up with my father. He insists on hiring the salesmen at the home office himself."

The goldfish swam out of sight behind a submerged castle and beyond the table he could see the curtains rising heavily with the breeze. What an odd girl, he thought. A real take-charge girl. First the saloon and now himself. She had the direct manner of a cookbook: place sausages in skillet; add water to cover; bring to a boil. Tear out the wall; remodel rundown saloon; get new job for Noel Bigelow.

She had turned and was looking over her shoulder at the goldfish. "I know a psychiatrist," she said, "who keeps a bowl of fish in his office. It's supposed to encourage patients to be more communicative."

Noel coughed, and she looked back at him. He raised his empty glass meaningfully.

Deirdre sprang up from the floor. "Do you mind?"

she said. "I've got a bit of a headache. And tomorrow's a school day, dammit."

"Sure," he said roughly. He got to his feet, feeling angry and helpless. No telling what might have developed if he had sat down on the floor beside her. He felt an intense desire to touch her bare arms.

He went to the door and turned around. Something on a chair caught his eye and he squinted. It was the Kiplinger Letter. God-damit, he thought, that takes the cake!

She opened the door and held out her hand. She was much shorter now. Then he saw that she had kicked off her shoes. He smelled the sharp apple scent again and nodded like an idiot as she said, "Thanks so much, Noel. I'll call you at the bank after I set up a meeting with Daddy. Who knows? The brokerage business might be just what you're looking for."

Her manner made it obvious that she did not want to be kissed.

Noel saluted her with a forefinger. "Aye, aye, sir," he said.

Going down the stairs, he was still so mad at the way she had kept him at a distance that he nearly stumbled over the bottom step.

13

The amazing thing to Noel was that he took the job.

He sat across the desk from Thatcher Kimbridge and he kept thinking to himself, this man is the girl's father. He realized then how much Deirdre had begun to tantalize him. He *had* to see her, and he sensed that if he did not go to work for Kimbridge & Co. she would be terribly disappointed. She might not even talk to him again.

"Don't let your age bother you," Thatcher Kimbridge said, "You've had a crack at another field and now you probably know better what it is you wanted to do. We've got a salesman in our mid-town office who started out as a lawyer. And down in Baltimore our best producer is a man who spent five years as a radio announcer—"

Yes, thought Noel, I know what it is I want.

He started to ask a question, then thought better of

it. Suppose Thatcher Kimbridge had known his father, what of it?

The next day Noel returned to meet several of the other partners and to take some aptitude tests. The brief talks with the partners came off with surprising smoothness. Like a calm run through Gardiner's Bay, thought Noel. He learned later from the girl administering the tests that he had scored exceptionally high in the acquisitive category. "That's very promising," she told him.

Before departing from the bank, Noel engaged in a bit of research. From a friend in the Trust Department he found the bank indeed did administer a trust for Deirdre Kimbridge. The trust had been established upon the death of her grandfather. Noel could not suppress a smile when his friend told him the size of the trust: four million eight. "Damnedest thing, though," the friend had said. "She used the first fifty thousand of her income from the trust to start a foundation. The proceeds go into rheumatic-fever work. Seems she had a brother who came down with rheumatic fever once in college."

In his first months as a trainee at Kimbridge & Co. Noel saw a great deal of Deirdre. She was not batty, he decided, but beyond this assessment he did not know what to make of her. Deirdre was like the weather at sea: she was simply unpredictable.

On the night they went out to celebrate his new job —she had been so genuinely pleased at the news that she presented him with a leather case from Mark Cross engraved, "For Your Parking Ticket"—she turned to him suddenly at the table, interrupting a story he was telling. "It is the human's natural instinct to kill," she said. "Do you believe that, Noel? In war this is easy because society accepts it. But the same instinct runs through our everyday lives. The instinct is stronger in some people than in others. We hide it or we sublimate it in a thousand different ways. But it's always there, this terrible instinct to kill. Noel, do you believe that?"

"I suppose so," he stammered. Her bare arms with their fine white hairs mocked him and he stared at the pulse moving in her slim brown neck.

A particular weakness of Deirdre's was watching Errol Flynn movies. "It's cutlasses now, men!" the hero would shout to his crew as he swung over the side of the ship and there was Deirdre, breathless on the edge of her seat. "Be*hind* you!" she cried out one night, thereby causing several rows of film patrons to duck in alarm while Errol Flynn wheeled about in time to miss a flashing sword. Later, after Olivia de Havilland had been saved and they emerged from the theater, there were tears staining Deirdre's cheeks. She squeezed Noel's hand as if to apologize and slipped on a pair of dark glasses. Like so many incidents with Deirdre, he found it froze in a tiny locker of his memory. He did not have the heart to tell her the Spanish galleons had been sitting ducks because they were over-canvased. They turned down Fifth Avenue, walking slowly, and he remembered the buildings bending upon her dark glasses.

Certain of her habits maddened Noel. He did not carry a watch and whenever he asked Deirdre for the time she would count up the minutes aloud. "It's ten-twenty . . . one, two, three, four. Ten-twenty-four." She laughed at him for always carrying new bills. "Don't they stick together?" she asked, and he replied, "Not if you're careful." He made a point of getting new bills because a teller at the bank once had miscounted in Noel's favor while stripping a packet of currency. But she listened attentively when he described the proper technique for forging a signature.

"You don't simply trace over the signature," he said, "because a person never signs his name the same way twice. Besides, if you trace over the check heavily and then follow the grooves with a pen, a good teller can spot it instantly. The pressure shows up on the back of the check. Like this. See? The best way to forge a signature is to turn the original upside down and then copy it slowly in free hand." He laughed and said, "No, I've never forged a check."

That was the night she startled him with her interpretation of George Washington. "No," she cried, shaking her head, "he wasn't a good president at all! How do I know? Because he spent so much time posing for all those portraits. On horseback or in an artist's studio or the drawing room at Mount Vernon. A good president wouldn't have wasted all that time simply on posing! Noel, do you believe that?"

There was something all too convincing about Deirdre Kimbridge. If she told him Whistler's mother had been a notorious bank robber, he would have believed her.

He did not alter one original impression: she was hell on wheels when it came to causes. Noel took to crossing the streets when he saw a panhandler approaching them. One autumn night Deirdre had delivered a brief but inspiring lecture to a bearded bum whose tongue kept slipping in and out of his mouth. "You're a-*live!*" she had exhorted him. "That's what counts! Oh, don't you see?" Noel had stood to one side in embarrassment and the astonished bum stumbled away.

A few minutes later she said in a soft voice, "The good die young. Do you believe that, Noel?"

"I—don't know."

"But you're alive, Noel. That's important."

"Perhaps I'm not so good, that's why."

165

She shrugged helplessly. "Perhaps. But you are alive." Then, "I have a life wish. I guess you could call it the opposite of a death wish. I believe in life—for people, for everything!" The words came out in a rush.

"Even for Kimbridge & Co.?"

"Oh, yes! For Kimbridge & Co. especially!"

She had a habit of roaming the city at night by herself, often in deserted neighborhoods, and the thought terrified Noel. "You don't know who you'll run into," he scolded her. "It's not safe for a girl to be alone. Don't you read the papers?"

She was touched by his concern. "All right, Noel," she said. "Tell you what I'll do. I'll carry a razor in my handbag. An old-fashioned straight razor. How's that? I've got one that Grandfather left. I use it to shave my legs when I take a bath— Is something the matter, Noel? You look pale."

"No, nothing's the matter," he said quickly, and he thought about that Sunday morning in the winter of 1929 when as a small boy he had wandered into his father's bathroom . . . the water was running in the tub and there was his father floating on his back . . . his arm was thrown over the side of the tub and there was a razor held in the stiffened fingers . . . the water was pink and bubbly . . . Noel was too young to realize what his father had done but he knew that something was terribly wrong. "Mommy, Mommy!" he had screamed and then ran down the stairs.

"Well," said Deirdre. "It's just that I've never seen you look that way before."

"Did you ever hear of Bigelow, Quigg?"

She shook her head.

"It used to be a big underwriting house. Then one sunny day an underwriting turned sour and another

166

firm had to bail them out. There was a merger and that was the end of Bigelow, Quigg."

"Any relation to you?" she asked.

"Yes," he said. "The Bigelow was my father."

Deirdre was left-handed and Noel noticed that she always wore a gold signet ring on the little finger of her right hand. Sometimes while she was talking she would twist the ring absently around her finger. There was a chip on the face of the ring, and a set of worn initials: a B and an L with a large K in the center. Noel learned in time that the initials stood for Brittin Lansdell Kimbridge and that the ring had been fitted for Deirdre's finger after the death of her brother. He learned other things as well. Her brother had called her Deedee and once, when Noel used the same name affectionately, she snapped at him: "Don't you call me that . . . *ever* again." And so it was that Bridge—that was her pet name for Brittin—became part of the mystery that was Deirdre Kimbridge.

One night they went to listen to jazz music at Eddie Condon's. During an intermission the drummer, a Negro, came over to sit at their table. He told Deirdre that his great ambition was to become the prime minister of Nigeria. Thereupon, Deirdre spent the rest of the evening, when the drummer was off the bandstand and drinking white crème de menthe at Noel's expense, trying to convince him that he should return home and go into politics.

It was raining when Noel drove Deirdre to her apartment that night and his fingers drummed on the steering wheel. What a girl, Noel was thinking, she has the ability to figure out the solution to everybody's life but her own.

"Did you know," Deirdre said on the seat beside him, "the Marines always bring in their own dead?" Her voice was so low that he had to strain his ears in

167

order to hear her. She kept looking straight ahead. "It's a matter of special pride with the Marine Corps," she said. "A Marine will risk his life just to bring in the body of a dead Marine."

In the silence that followed he was conscious of her sitting stiffly at his side. The only sound in the car was the *clunk, clunk* of the windshield wipers. In an endless dance, the wipers slowly swept away the surging neon along the street and then painstakingly resurrected the signs.

He remembered one nght shortly after the war had ended in Europe. He was on a train and it was raining. The Army was shuttling dead American soldiers to French ports and so it was that Noel, newly transferred to grave registration duty, found himself shepherding a lone coffin from Düsseldorf to Le Havre. The train was so crowded that he had curled up on top of the wooden coffin in order to sleep. The train kept shaking as though it had a fever. Suddenly he awoke. He had fallen through the coffin and the warm, sweet death inside was embracing him. . . .

"Noel," said Deirdre, breaking the silence in the car, "what did you do during the war?"

That old ridiculous question, he thought. What did it ever prove? But he had the strange sensation that Deirdre might have been reading his mind.

"Oh," he said, watching the traffic carefully through the nodding windshield wipers, "I was in the M.P.'s mostly. That is, except for a couple months on the Continent after the war was over."

"The M.P.'s," she repeated softly. "Was it . . . rough?"

He slowed the car as a pedestrian ran across the street against the slanting rain. "Not so bad really," he replied. "My unit was assigned most of the time to prisoner-of-war camps in England."

He remembered the last dreary mill town where he had been stationed. The D-Day attack had been launched and the first German prisoners were being brought back to England. All the arrangements were makeshift at first; it was as though the capturing of German soldiers had taken the Allied high command by surprise. They had herded the prisoners into an old cotton mill that had warped wooden floors reeking of linseed oil. The women of the mill town were more pitiful than the German prisoners. They had been deprived of their own men for as many as a half-dozen years; most of them were wives of mill workers and their husbands were either off fighting somewhere or else they were dead. The memory sent a pleasant shiver through Noel. At the local pub, after the second glass of warm beer, the women actually reached out for your fly. . . .

"Finally I shipped across the Channel," he said gruffly.

Deirdre's respectful silence told him that she understood about such matters. He had been in the war and that seemed to give him a passing mark in her book.

Her body was driving Noel mad with desire. He would sit close to her in a restaurant or the theater or in her apartment and be seized with a wild impulse to push that rounded tan body under him and kiss the baby fat of her armpits. But he never got beyond the affectionate embraces and the light kisses of Deirdre. He might as well have tried to crack into the gold vault at the Federal Reserve Building two blocks from 50 Wall.

"I'm sorry, Noel," she told him the night he brought her home from Eddie Condon's, "but I don't feel anything *chemical* between us. That is, not yet, anyway. So until then . . . well, it's no use without that, is it?"

He watched the goldfish make obscene faces in their bowl and he felt utterly foolish.

So he dated other girls. He flirted with them and slept with them while he waited for some chemical reaction to occur within Deirdre Kimbridge.

He gave up seeing her for two months and then he passed his examination and officially became a registered representative for Kimbridge & Co.

Deidre was so proud—she called him and he responded like a love-struck schoolboy—that he realized how foolish he was for trying to avoid her.

She began to confide increasingly in him and Noel became a willing listener. "After I learned about Bridge's death," she said, "I wore his pajamas to bed. I did that, Noel, for two whole years."

Noel pictured her body under the bed sheet. He could see the nipples pouting under the sheet and the firm, rounded outline of her thighs. It flashed across his mind that the sidewalk of Wall Street, across from the Stock Exchange, had a slight bulge, just like the bulge that Deirdre's belly would make under the sheet—

"Bridge was a real cutup. He was always pulling the most outlandish jokes. At the Junior Prom he got his date to paint eyeballs on her eyelids and when he described it all to me later, why I split my sides laughing! Can't you just see that girl dancing along dreamily with her eyes closed and a pair of bright brown eyes staring out?"

She looked at Noel imploringly now, and what he saw was not a girl at a college prom but the personality of her brother gradually claiming his flesh anew. The truth was simply that Brittin Kimbridge had never died as far as Deirdre was concerned. Noel was competing for her against a living ghost. He began to despise Brittin Kimbridge.

One Saturday afternoon they were strolling north on Park Avenue in the Sixties. It was a clear, pleasant day in late spring and far ahead of them Park Avenue formed a crest where the taxis with their bright yellow and red and green tops dropped suddenly from sight. The trees were beginning to bud and high above, on the terrace of a penthouse, a birdhouse on stilts was visible.

Deirdre and Noel passed a uniformed doorman. The doorman was basking in the sun and rolling an unlighted cigar between his fingers.

"I know him," Deirdre said, nodding in the direction of the apartment building.

"Who? You know that doorman?"

"No, silly. The doctor." She pointed to a brass nameplate. "He's a psychiatrist actually. A lot of these M.D. plates on the East Side are really covers for psychiatrists."

"Oh?" said Noel, and they walked on. He knew that Deirdre went to a psychiatrist but then every second girl he met in New York seemed to be going through analysis, or else thinking about it. Deirdre had an annoying habit of darting away at times to "keep an appointment" and she once shocked Noel by saying her psychiatrist's bill came to $200 a week.

"The doctor has the strangest theory," Deirdre said as they paused at the corner. "He thinks most people in the stock market actually want to lose money. He says this satisfies their guilt feelings."

"Why, that's absurd," said Noel. "I haven't met any customer yet who wants to buy a stock that's sure to go down."

"Oh, they never admit it. That's part of the masochistic pattern. In fact, the customers themselves often don't recognize this inner drive. It stems from something locked deep inside them." Her voice had at

171

times the quality of a mournful clarinet. Noel even began to mimic her voice, striking up imaginary conversations with Deirdre when they were apart.

But suddenly he became angry. The trouble with Deirdre was that she accepted the notion of money, lots of money, as naturally as the air about her. She had never experienced the fear of losing a job; no, her wealth was simply a sort of cotton padding against reality. And now, on this bright spring afternoon, he felt a fierce desire to shock her somehow.

"We had a fellow at the bank, a trust officer," he said. "Now there was somebody who really needed a psychiatrist. He was a little guy, not more than five feet two. He used to tell me about his nightmares. Big feet stomping all around him, trying to squash him. And balls"—Noel began to imitate the man's voice—"balls up above me! Huge swinging balls!"

Deirdre did not shock easily, however. They crossed the street and she said calmly, "What ever happened to him, this poor man?"

"Don't waste your pity. He made out very nicely. The bank has a rule against any trust officer becoming the sole beneficiary to an estate he is handling. Well, there was this old widow and she was loaded with dough. He kept playing up to the old gal—she didn't have any close relatives—and fixed it so that he became the only beneficiary."

"And the bank fired him?"

"Yes, the bank fired him. But by that time he had the money. Very conveniently for him the old gal kicked off before the bank tumbled to what was going on. Poor management controls, that's what some people at the bank said later. But personally I thought it was the neatest bit of imaginative thinking I ever saw in all the time I worked there."

Then the day came when Deirdre told him she had decided to go abroad.

"The Ford Foundation will have to struggle along without me," she said. "Oh, Noel, it's all so sad. Yesterday morning a man came into our office. He was wearing a funny little white suit with dirty cuffs. He told the receptionist he was God and he just wanted to have a look at how we were running things for him. You know, he seemed quite pleased." Her stomach gurgled at that moment. "It was just the final straw, I guess," she said, and then she reached over and touched Noel's Oxford cloth shirt just above his heart. "You're the only man I know," she said, "who wears a shirt with a button on the pocket, too." The goldfish stared opaquely at Noel through the bowl and he felt an insane desire to destroy them.

The chemical reaction never took place. Instead, Deirdre went off to Europe and Noel improved his production at Kimbridge & Co. For the first few months he received postcards from St. Moritz and Florence and Venice. The messages were printed in boarding-school script and the final postcard, which arrived without a return address, said simply: "Have decided to live in France for a while. Other night got hiccups again. Brandy and soda works, too." The following summer he met Avis at a dance in Easthampton.

14

At four o'clock Seth Voorhees rang the bell of the Kimbridge town house. The door opened and a man in his shirt sleeves, a polishing cloth in one hand, said respectfully, "Yes, sir?"

"Is Mrs. Kimbridge in? I'm Seth Voorhees. I should like to see Mrs. Kimbridge."

"Won't you please come in, sir," said Pinckney, stepping aside. "She's out in the garden. I'll tell her you are waiting if—"

"No, that's quite all right. I'll see her in the garden."

"Very good, sir." Pinckney led the way through the dim, cool hallway, past the library, the dining room, and a spacious kitchen with copper pots and skillets hanging from cast-iron hooks. A cook was slicing carrots and Voorhees heard the soft *thock-thock-thock* of the knife on a wooden board.

The far end of the hallway was ablaze with colors; it was as if a rainbow had drifted into the house. The colors flung out from a collection of Sandwich glass arranged in tiers against the rear window to catch the sunlight. Voorhees noted that not a speck of dust seemed to cling to any of the delicately wrought perfume flasks, paperweights, and apothecary jars. Then an object caught his eye and he paused for a moment. A lone salt dish, ruby red in color, was placed prominently on the center shelf. He remembered the salt dish; he had given it to Edith very long ago when he decided she was the girl he wanted to marry. She had kept it all these years!

"This way, sir."

Pinckney was holding open the rear door.

Voorhees ducked instinctively as he passed under a hanging basket filled with anemones, soft impish blossoms resting among ferns. He stepped down onto a flagstone walk and the door closed behind him. He stood alone in the garden.

What struck him instantly was the complete tranquillity. There was not a single sound, not even the beep of an automobile horn. Terraced banks of white and purple fuchsia in full bloom adorned the wall of old bricks to his left; the flowers seemed as immaculate as the Sandwich glass inside the house. Tall willow trees shaded the opposite end of the garden, and the flagstone walk traced out leisurely curves among the flowerbeds. Voorhees was grateful for the silence, a sensation that lasted for perhaps ten seconds, and then he called out, "Edith?"

"Yoo-hoo!" a voice answered. "Over here! By the magnolia tree!"

Voorhees strode past a high boxwood hedge and there, kneeling beside a mound of loam with a trowel in her hand and a wide-brimmed straw hat on her head, was Edith Kimbridge.

"Seth! Why, *Seth!*" She scrambled to her feet and

175

then gripped the trowel with both hands. "There's nothing wrong? Thatch—"

He shook his head restlessly.

"Why, then," she said with a rush of relief that stirred in Voorhees a muted chord of jealousy. "Why, shame on you for surprising a woman in such a state." She looked down in despair at her tattered smock and flat muddy shoes and then back at Voorhees who had moved toward her after hanging back momentarily. "You don't give a person much warning, do you?" she said, and then she laughed. "Why, *Seth*. It's been such a long, long time."

"Hello, Edith. You look quite lovely." He stared at her intently, as if drinking in her appearance. "I'm flying a false flag, really. I called just before the market got busy at three o'clock to find out if you would be home. I'm afraid I told your man"—he nodded toward the closed door—"to expect a package from Cartier after I found out this was your afternoon for gardening. That was my ruse. I grabbed a cab right after the closing and, well, here I am."

"Oh, you devil," she said in a mock reprimand. "And I thought it was going to be a present from Thatch. Tomorrow is our anniversary." She slipped off the heavy cotton work gloves and took his right hand warmly. "Well, well," she said, tilting her head to one side. "Yes, a long time."

"Yes." He coughed. "It has been. My God, Edith! You always did have lovely hands. White as milk. And not a wrinkle. You look just as pretty as the time —" He shrugged brusquely but then he went on. The memory was too powerful for him to dismiss so easily. "I can remember the first time I saw you. I remember how impressed I felt. You were the only girl I knew whose doll house in Newport had a real fireplace. On a damp summer day you could smell the old ashes. Only it wasn't the fireplace that impressed me."

"Seth, Seth. You always were such a flatterer." She laughed again, showing her pleasure. "Wouldn't you like something cool to drink? Honestly, this weather. Hot, cool, now hot again. Lemonade? Or perhaps something a bit stronger?"

"No. Nothing, thanks." He lit a cigarette and then scowled at the match, uncertain as to where he should place it. "Let's sit down, shall we? I'm actually here on a business matter—well, sort of."

"Oh, business, pooh! That's all a partner of Kimbridge & Co. ever thinks of. Business. Seth, I'm not going to talk about a thing until you tell me about yourself. And I want to hear about the children." She took the match from his fingers and plunged it into the soft loam as though she were planting a shoot. They sat down on a white stone bench set on a tiny round island of marble chips. "Oh, Seth," she said, removing her hat and shaking loose her hair, "you're so lucky to have so many children—to have so much *life* throbbing all around you. But tell me . . . do you find it difficult to communicate with them?"

"No trouble at all with the ones who are away. I just communicate by check."

"Well, perhaps it's less of a problem when you have —how many is it, Seth? Nine? No. Oh, *eleven.* How wonderful for you! Now, you take Deirdre. There is a daughter. She's so independent. She's back in New York now and you know what? She lets us see her all of once a month."

"Like an alimony check."

"Well, hardly *that*," exclaimed Edith Kimbridge. She stared at him for a few moments. "Seth, you look tired. And you always did smoke too much," she said, leaning over to pat his hand. "But no lectures. I promise. You never were one for lectures. Not even from the most well-intentioned of young ladies."

"You're right," he agreed. "I remember one night you called me a snob. I suppose for every person in the world like myself there is somebody who can call him a snob and get away with it. For me, Edith, you were that one person. The only one."

"That's not the most pleasant of memories, is it? Let's talk about something else." She clapped her hands. "Now I have a perfectly delightful memory for you. That time on the Cape. That wonderful resort hotel that closed down during the Depression. Remember? When we went inside you handed the captain a twenty-dollar bill and you asked him to send the wine steward over to our table. You picked out a burgundy—"

"Château Lafite-Rothschild. The 1890."

"Yes, yes," she said delightedly. "Then you told the wine steward to present the bottle to the chef with our compliments. You requested the chef to order for us. Oh, Seth, I've never eaten such a glorious meal! Course after course and everything simply perfection! It was one of those magic nights. I remember a man with white whiskers three tables away—he looked just like an old sea captain—who actually *waved* at us while I was chewing the most divine mussel with that sauce . . . then as we were finishing who comes up but the chef himself! With that huge, floppy white hat and your bottle of burgundy under his arm. There was just enough wine for two glasses. I can imagine his drinking the wine out in the kitchen while he was preparing our courses—"

"And singing, too."

"Yes—and singing, too. Remember? He poured out a glass for you and then a glass for himself. It came out perfectly. To the last drop. Then the two of you

178

drank a toast to me—that was the first time I'd ever been toasted, Seth, and I remember wishing somehow it would be the last, it was so perfect—and the chef raised his glass and said one word. 'Voilà!' And with that he drank down his wine, turned on his heel, and marched out of the dining room like a conquering general."

"I remember that," said Voorhees slowly. "I remember telling you the wine was superb. That it tasted like gold dust."

He took a final puff on the cigarette. It had begun to scorch his fingertips. He ground out the cigarette carefully against his shoe and tore apart the paper.

The two of them were caught suddenly in a tight, embarrassed silence. Edith watched with fierce concentration as the brown tobacco shreds blew across a bed of powdery blue asters nodding primly in the breeze. Without uttering a word they shared the same thoughts: how close they had come and how irrevocably it had ended. . . .

Edith Kimbridge touched the brim of the hat which lay upon her lap like a huge straw flower. "Seth," she said, "are you *sure* you wouldn't like some lemonade? I make it a special way. With a little grape juice added for color. And a sprig of mint. So you can make believe it's a mint julep if you like."

"No, no," Seth Voorhees said in a burst of impatience. "Look here, Edith"—he flicked away a ladybug perched on the cuff of his trouser—"I meant it when I told you I came here on business." He looked at her carefully and then dropped his eyes. "Well . . . I'm worried about what Thatch wants to do with the firm. I'll be honest with you He's going to ruin what Kimbridge & Co. stands for if he incorporates the firm." Voorhees stared at the straw hat in her lap. "Even Janet Lincoln thinks so—"

"Oh, pooh, Seth. When did you men start consulting your wives about Kimbridge & Co.? That's just ammunition, what you're saying about Janet. Besides —I don't see why you're telling *me* all this."

"It's very simple, Edith. You're one of the three trustees of Jared's estate. If you and I vote against the plan, that would mean the Estate formally registers its disapproval." He drew a deep breath. "I think, by God, that would be enough for Thatch to see the light of day, to give up once and forever this fool notion."

She nodded slowly. "Oh, I understand now," she said. For a few moments she was silent, letting her gaze travel over the garden. Then she gave a shiver and turned to face Voorhees. "My, my," she said. "Good old Jared. Even the grave can't keep him silent, can it? Isn't that what you came here for? A voice from the grave?" She shivered again. "He was really such a horrid man—"

"Edith!" Voorhees said sharply. "You don't mean that!"

"Oh, don't I? He *was* horrid. I spent half a lifetime watching him make Thatch go through agony. Oh, Seth, if you only knew! Why, you were more of a son to him than Thatch ever could be. You had the same kind of mind—the stock-market mind—and that's all my father-in-law ever cared about. The market! A week after our engagement was announced he took me to lunch at the Colony. I was impressed because he came uptown in the middle of the day just to see me. Then you know what he did? Just before we went inside he called the office. He bought a thousand shares of American Telephone. 'I've been watching that stock this morning,' he said to me. 'I think I can make a turn on it that will pay for this lunch.'

180

Well, I had to force my food down. It was like eating gravel—"

"What happened?"

"Oh, I was all right. No stomach problems or anything."

"No, the stock. What did Telephone do?"

She smiled wanly at Seth Voorhees. "He was correct, of course. The stock was half a point higher when we came out. He called the office again before he got his coat. He sold the thousand shares and he was chuckling—I might as well have been on Mars— all the time he was putting on his coat. That luncheon is not my loveliest memory. Did you know that I hated him so much"—her voice was shaking—"I voted for Roosevelt? I knew that would make him furious. But then, of course, I never had the nerve to tell him what I had done."

"You were afraid of him?"

"No, not really. I was afraid he would take it out on Thatch." She stroked the straw hat gently. "There are nights when I still wake up in this house and think I hear Jared walking around . . . and Thatch!" She lifted her hands helplessly. "Thatch would have died for his father." Edith stood up. "Oh, the whole thing is so useless!"

Then she said something very softly, "The bullet that killed Brit," she said, looking off into the distance, "it really killed Jared, too. He had such plans for Brit in the firm—"

Voorhees arose and straightened his cuffs. "If I ask you to do this, well, as a favor to me—if I ask you to vote against incorporation would you do it, Edith?"

"Don't ask me that. I wouldn't want you to ask me that. Do you understand?"

He coughed. "Then your answer, I take it, is no?"

"I'm sorry, Seth. But that's the way it's got to be.

I'm an old-fashioned girl. I love my husband too much to do anything that would hurt him. I know why he wants to incorporate the firm. He wants to give life everlasting to Kimbridge & Co. It would be like a plant that lives forever."

He was looking at her with an odd expression. "It's an old story, isn't it?" he said. "When I ask you something—something really important—the answer always seems to be no." He shrugged. "I guess that's that. Do me a favor, though. I'd appreciate your not mentioning my errand to Thatch."

"All right, Seth. For old time's sake." She reached up and took the wilted chrysanthemum from his lapel. "Wait just a moment," she said and ran over to a small bed of flowers. She came back with a bachelor's button and placed it in the lapel. "There," she said, stepping back and attempting to inject gaiety into her voice. "Compliments of the house. Blue was Brit's favorite color. You can't know what a temptation it is for me not to plant everything here"—her hand swept about the garden—"in blue."

"I know, Edith," he said softly. "Don't think I don't know why we have desks with blue formica tops in our board rooms. And why the Kimbridge & Co. checks are blue." He glanced at the bachelor's button. "Thanks for this," he said and then blurted, as though making a confession, "Dammit, I just wish my wife had your knack with flowers. She's the only woman I know in River House whose philodendron keeps dying on her. Philodendron, for God's sake!"

"Well, Seth, she's given you children. That's more than I can do now for Thatch." She pointed to a stunted magnolia tree a dozen feet away. "See that tree? It's a Southern magnolia. A variety that's not supposed to grow in this climate. But I'm determined to make it live. That's what I can do, Seth. It's not

182

really very much, is it? I face challenges in my garden. With Deirdre it's animals and unwed mothers."

When Voorhees turned to leave, she took his arm. She looked up at him and blinked her eyes. "Thatch told me once," she said, "that the best floor brokers are lady killers. Is that true? Is it a tradition at the Stock Exchange?"

"Hardly," he said. He started to say something else but instead he held the door for her. Before entering the house Edith Kimbridge took off the muddy shoes.

They walked through the dim hallway, Edith padding behind him in stockinged feet, and suddenly Voorhees stopped.

"That's a nice painting," he said gruffly. Somehow he seemed loath to leave.

"Why, aren't you sweet to notice! It's a Guardi. The last one I had sent over from England." She moved to his side and they stared at the canvas that glistened under the pencil spotlight in the ceiling. "A man from the Metropolitan called me a few days ago," she said. "They're doing a Guardi show and he said these three paintings are among the finest examples of Guardi's work in the United States. They want the paintings for their show. The man said many of the Guardis in this country are fake."

"You're going to lend them out?"

"No," she said with a wan smile. "Thatch doesn't really approve of my tastes in art. I'm afraid to let him find out they're such good paintings—"

"My God, Edith! You're not a wife. You're an angel." He strode abruptly toward the front door.

"Seth," she called, and he turned around. She came up to him and, stretching high on her toes, adjusted the flower. "You're not—you won't stop fighting Thatch on this incorporation thing, will you? Not even if I ask?"

183

"No, Edith. Not even if you ask. I'll find some way—"

"Something happened yesterday, didn't it? Something bad."

"At our Monday-morning meeting?" Voorhees nodded grimly. "Thatch brought up the incorporation again and I—well, I lost my temper. Miss Donahue dropped her dictation pad, it was that tense for a couple minutes. Then Howard got between me and Thatch and played peacemaker." Voorhees slapped his thigh, reliving the scene. "Christ! Andy Kraft is afraid we'll have a mandatory retirement age for the partners if we incorporate. But then that's the reaction you might expect from somebody who never asks how the market is doing. What's the volume?—that's all he wants to know."

"You've been gathering ammunition to fight Thatch. Oh, Seth, you needn't look so innocent! It doesn't become you. But don't forget. Thatch won't stop fighting either. You realize that, don't you?" She searched his face.

"Yes," he said quietly, "I know that."

"I'm so sorry," she said. "Well"—she held out her hand—"goodby, Seth."

"Edith," he said, with a sharp nod, and touched her hand for only an instant.

Seth Voorhees opened the door and stepped outside into the slanting afternoon sunlight. He lighted a cigarette before hailing a cab and gratefully drew in the first lungful of smoke. He noticed a slender plane tree in front of the house. It was green and tender, its foliage perfect despite the parched summer, a tree as full of promise as a girl he had known long ago. "Cab!" he called sharply.

15

At nine-thirty on Sunday evening Poke Jeffers mounted the steps of a small apartment building faced with stucco. Two iron pots filled with petunias stood guard at the entrance. The dark slits on the petunias bore a faintly sinister look, like Chinese soldiers in disguise.

He pressed the buzzer and Carol's voice answered instantly over the intercom. "Yes?"

"It's me," he said. "Sorry I'm a bit late."

"Oh, that's all right. That's quite all right. I'm on the ground floor. All the way to the rear."

His footsteps echoed in the hallway with its high ceiling. A door swung open as he approached.

"Well," Carol said, "it's certainly nice to see you. I was afraid you might be lost. You didn't wear a hat? I thought it looked like rain a little while ago."

She was wearing a blue silk dress with a bow at the waist and some instinct told him that she had bought the dress especially for this evening. He could see the pulse throbbing in her throat above the clavicle.

"No," he said. "I never wear a hat. Even when it rains."

He stepped inside the apartment and followed her into the living room. The room was long and narrow and the bulky furniture—a sofa, two stuffed armchairs, a heavy bookcase with a glass front—gave it the appearance of being off balance. The air was rather musty and he noticed a row of potted green plants along the window ledge.

My God, he thought suddenly, what am I doing here? He had circled the block ten times, like a distance runner worrying a cinder track, and five minutes earlier he had fought back the impulse to step into a telephone booth and announce to Carol Tracey that he was sick in bed with a cold.

"Won't you sit down, Poke? I think the sofa is the most comfortable. I had this furniture shipped out from Columbus." She pulled a carpenter's bench away from the sofa to make more room. "You know," she said. "A home away from home."

"Thanks," he said, "but I suppose we ought to get going."

"Oh, I hope you won't mind. But I had a brainstorm." Carol stood awkwardly before him, matching the clumsiness of the room. "I told myself, why should we bother going out for a drink? That's silly. So I bought something for us."

She hurried to the far end of the room where a counter divided off the kitchen area. She ducked out of sight behind the counter and he could hear the clinking of bottles.

Carol brought back a bottle with the seal unbroken and handed it to him. "Will this be all right?" she asked.

He looked at the bottle. It was bonded Bourbon, twelve years old.

"Yes," he said. "This is fine."

She gave a little laugh of relief. "It's really the nicest liquor store," she said. "The only place I've found in New York where they hold the door for you when you walk out. The salesmen are really very nice."

"They're not salesmen," he said irritably. "Not in a liquor store. They're just order takers. There's a difference." He thrust the bottle back in her hands.

"Oh, yes. I'm sorry. I didn't mean to— Isn't New York really the oddest place, though? When I came here the first thing I noticed was all the people walking down the street and talking to themselves." She shivered slightly. "At first I thought they were talking to me. Anyway, it's all very sad. What was the first thing that struck you about New York?"

"The girls," he said. "All the pretty girls." He nodded at the bottle. "Would you like me to do the honors?"

"Oh, would you? The ice cubes are all ready. They're in a bowl in the refrigerator. And the water—"

"I can find the water all right," he said.

He prepared the drinks and returned to the center of the living room where Carol was still standing, as if she were afraid he might decide suddenly to leave the apartment.

"When I was a little girl," she said, "I used to freeze ginger ale in ice cubes and chew them. My mother never approved of that." Then she said, "Honestly, I feel quite bad about tonight."

"What's the problem?"

"Well, really. I might have asked you over for dinner. But cooking isn't my strong point. Those recipe books, all their best dishes are for six servings. All

187

right, so I divide everything by three. But how in the world do you divide an egg into three? And marshmallows . . . one cup of marshmallows. How can you measure a cupful of marshmallows?"

"I wouldn't worry about it." He raised his glass. "Cheers."

"Yes. Cheers."

He tasted the Bourbon. It was excellent. He took another swallow before sitting down on the sofa.

Carol sat opposite him in an armchair. She crossed her legs and her stockings made a sound like the riffling of ticker tape. The skin of one knee was stretched white and shiny over the patella.

He glanced out the window and saw a small park with lampposts that led down to the East River. He could make out the faint outlines of the buildings of the financial district across the river; they seemed hazy and quite unreal in the night.

"How is Noel?" she said, breaking the silence.

"Oh, he's having a tough time. Like everybody else in this market. He's run clean out of gimmicks. For a while he was putting his customers into new issues—marina projects, mostly—but that's played out. Before that he had a pretty good thing going. He'd have clients load up on a stock as soon as a company was approved for listing on the Big Board. He had some contact over at the Stock Exchange and that meant he got hold of the official bulletin two days before it came out on Friday. The in-and-out trades were usually good for a couple points anyway."

He took a long drink, holding the Bourbon in his mouth and letting it trickle slowly down his throat. He was feeling better now.

"So ole Noel is up the creek without a paddle," Poke said. "In fact, he may be reduced to pushing mutual funds if the market doesn't perk up soon.

188

That's how he financed his honeymoon, by the way. One of the growth funds staged a sales contest. You sold $60,000 worth of the fund's shares and you got a free trip to the Bahamas. A hundred and twenty thousand, then you could take your wife for free." He rattled the ice in his glass. "Ole Noel swung it. He won himself a honeymoon to Nassau, all expenses paid."

Carol's eyes were wide with wonder. He watched her gulp down the last of her Bourbon. "Another drink?" he asked .

"Yes," she said. "I'd love that."

When he returned with their drinks he saw that Carol had taken off her shoes and tucked both feet under her.

She began to talk more easily now. About how hot the summer had been and about the difficulty of keeping plants watered properly in a New York apartment and about football—she *loved* college football games.

"—when I'm out some place and people hear that I work on Wall Street, they come up to me. They all want tips on the market." She smiled wanly. "I once had a roommate who never let me stay in the living room when her dates came by to pick her up. Her dates and I would always get to talking about the market—and that made her furious. Besides, what if you did give a tip to someone? That's only half the treasure map. There comes a time to sell a stock usually. But how can you call up everyone you've talked to and tell them to unload? Most of the time you don't even know their names. So-o-o, I never give tips."

"But you invest in the market?"

"Oh, heavens, no! I've never owned a single stock."

"You're kidding."

"No, it's true. The only time I ever did anything

189

like that was to give some advice to my brother. He wanted the money to buy a house and I got so tired of his badgering me—you know, he thought I had little secrets all locked up in an office safe or something —that I finally gave in."

"What happened?"

She looked down into her glass. "I told him to hock everything he had and to take out a bank loan. I put him into convertible debentures and had him margin himself up to the hilt. Oh, my God," she said softly, "I went through hell . . . he tripled his money and six months and one day later I telephoned him at three o'clock in the morning. 'Sell out today,' that's what I yelled at him, and then I hung up."

"Well, anyway, he must have appreciated it. Your help, I mean."

She shrugged. "That's the funny part of it. I never see him. He's an engineer out in Seattle and we've never really been close. But after they bought the house I had the feeling my sister-in-law was getting cooler and cooler toward me." She looked up at him suddenly. "I've never mentioned this before to anyone," she said, "but all the time I kept waiting for the stock to move up and for the debentures to do even better than the common stock I had this wonderful feeling right along with the terror. You probably think I'm silly, but I saw my brother for what he is. A nice guy with no drive. But this was his one big chance! He took a chance and it worked! I've never forgotten that feeling." She made a sweeping motion with one arm. "The house, that part of it isn't important. It's just that wonderful thrill of taking a chance!"

"But you do that all the time in your work, don't you?"

"It's not the same thing. I mean, sure, the institutional clients do very well for themselves, but it's not the same thing for me personally. At Hillyer & Hunt you know what I feel like sometimes?"

"What?"

"You know when you're at a play and the curtain opens for the next act, how all the scenery has been changed?"

He nodded.

"Well, that's exactly what I feel like. I'm one of those people you never see on the stage. I move the scenery but you never, never see me." She paused, and then she said, "Goodness, I don't know what's making me carry on like this. I sound like a real blabbermouth. Do you know, Poke, that you have a certain quality? No"—she put out her hand toward him —"it's true, really true. You have the quality of making people want to confide in you. I'll bet anything that you're a very good salesman."

"Sure," he said, "I'm terrific."

"What about your family? Lots and lots of relatives?"

He shook his head. "My mother died when I was a little kid and my father, he had a heart attack and died while I was away in the Army."

"Oh, Poke, how sad. I'm terribly sorry."

"So I have an aunt at home," he said impatiently. "She once sent me a blanket all the way to Korea. Now she worries about my not going to church. I know because she scribbles notes on the church bulletin." Carol was watching him silently. "My aunt's big on bird watching. Stuffs the bird feeder with sunflower seeds. She keeps hoping for her idea of a double miracle—my going to church and whistling swans stopping over during the spring migration someday."

Carol nodded slowly. He rose from the sofa.

"You're not going?" she cried, leaning forward in alarm. "It's so early yet."

"No, just stretching. This leg gets stiff sometimes."
He was sorry as soon as he said that. He walked over
to the bookcase and scanned the titles.

"Would you like a cigar?" Carol asked. She jumped
up from her chair and came across the room.

Something in her manner touched him. It seemed
very important to her that he should want to smoke a
cigar.

"Do you keep them around the apartment?" he
asked. "I hear Amy Lowell did that. You have any of
her poems here?"

Carol shook her head. "Oh, no," she said, "I don't
think so. But I went to a meeting for institutional analysts last week. At Toots Shor's. They'll let me in
there. But when these private meetings are held at
the Links Club or the Lotos Club"—she drew a flat
hand across her neck—"then I'm dead. They won't let
a woman attend. You'd think I was planning to crash
the steam room or something."

"All right," he said. "You get the cigar. I'll fix us another drink."

She ran into another room. He heard a drawer open
and then close. He went behind the counter and
reached for the bottle of Bourbon. What the hell, he
wondered, am I doing here? He shrugged and when
Carol reappeared he was standing beside the sofa.

"It took me a minute," she said, "to find some
matches."

She handed him a dark-leafed cigar wrapped in
cellophane. My God, he thought, we should go into
vaudeville.

"It's really a very good cigar," she said, pausing to
sip the drink. "Ummh. But the company president
made one mistake. He passed around these cigars *before* the meeting got under way. Somehow that made
me lose faith in what he said afterward. He seemed a

little too anxious to make an impression upon us. He should have passed the cigars *later*, don't you agree?"

"Definitely. Mark him down as a poor strategist. By the way, do you always take a cigar?"

"No, not really. It's just that this fellow from Bache teased me about it. 'Why don't you have a cigar, Carol?' he said, and so I did. Just to show him."

Poke removed the cellophane and the paper band. He squeezed the blunt end of the cigar between his fingers and the tip broke gently open.

"If you dip the end of the cigar in brandy," Carol said, "it tastes even better."

"Who told you that? The man from Bache?"

"Unh-uh. It was somebody from Smith, Barney."

"That sounds more like Smith, Barney."

"Can I light it for you?" she said.

"Be my guest."

She stood very close to him, holding the lighted match carefully as he inhaled. He turned the cigar slowly so as to light it evenly, and the rich gray smoke rose luxuriously above their heads. There was a smell, almost like incense, in the room.

"It's really a fine cigar," he said.

She picked up the paper band and slipped it over a finger absently.

"Can I—would you mind if I took a puff?" she said. He looked down at her. Her eyes were dark and shining. "Not at all," he said.

Carol held the cigar gingerly, as though afraid it might explode. Then she placed it between her lips and inhaled.

"Yes, it's—" she began, and suddenly she was coughing. A few moments later she shook her head and when she looked up at him again there were tears in her eyes. But she was smiling. "Thank you," she said and handed him the cigar with an air of ceremony. "It *is* a fine cigar," she said.

Poke noticed a faint stain of lipstick on the moist tip of the cigar. He had the odd sensation that the two of them somehow had passed into a new relationship. The smoking of the cigar, almost like a tribal rite, seemed to have sealed their pact.

The smoke drifted toward a lampshade. The lampshade created a funnel for the smoke and as it was drawn upward through the shade the smoke changed color from grayish blue to a thin white cloud.

Carol's eyes were closed. She rose on her toes and tilted toward him ever so slightly. He took the cigar from his mouth and kissed her on the lips There was not much else he could do under the circumstances.

She uttered a little cry. He felt her arms encircling his waist and he held the cigar out so that it would not brush against her. He kissed her again and she opened her eyes, blinking away the last of the cough tears.

"Why did you ask me for a date?" she said. "I mean —if you didn't like me and all?"

She's like a child, he thought. She says the first thing that pops into her mind. Heaven help the institutional clients of Hillyer & Hunt.

"I never said I didn't like you," he replied.

"Then you *do* like me?" She made it sound almost like a dare.

"Sure. Sure, I like you."

Since the moment he had entered this room he had the feeling the two of them were sparring. Lord knows about what. Certainly not *that*, he thought. The last thing he wanted to do in the world was to make love to somebody, to let a girl see that grotesque stump, perhaps fondle it. . . . He swelled with helpless rage.

194

"Well, then," she said and gave a nervous laugh, "why don't we sit down?"

He let her guide him to the sofa and they sat down. She tucked his hand under her arm and he saw that a tiny cigar ash was clinging to her silk dress. The bit of ash waved delicately on her thigh.

"Am I too forward?" she said. "Do you think I'm too forward?"

"No. As a matter of fact, I think you're a very appealing girl." There's no use hurting her, he thought. She had given him good Bourbon and a good cigar and now he had the decidedly uncomfortable sensation that she was willing to give him a lot more. He shifted into her tactics, the rat-tat-tat questions, in order to hold her off. "I suppose," he said, retrieving the cigar and puffing on it vigorously, "there's a special knack to being an institutional analyst. Thatcher Kimbridge has the theory that every customer deserves the same break. Whether he's ready to invest a thousand dollars or half a million. An analyst is an analyst—"

"—is an analyst," she broke in gaily. Carol blew away the cloud of smoke that had formed between them. His hand was still pinioned under her arm.

When she moved he could feel the swelling of her breast. The faint dampness in the room seemed to be closing in on him.

"It's very interesting work," he said desperately. "I'm sure of that."

"Well," she said, "we conduct longer interviews and it takes us quite a while to prepare reports. At Hillyer & Hunt we copyright our reports to prevent the competition from reproducing them. The trouble is that we take so long—the company gets a chance to check over our facts, too—a stock can get away from us. A stock may be selling at 40 and by the time we've finished the report it may have gotten up into the 50's."

The cigar had gone out. Poke dropped it into an ash tray on the carpenter's bench. "You never make any mistakes?" he asked.

"Goodness, yes. The California savings-and-loans fooled me once." She leaned her head on his shoulder. "But I was lucky. I got our clients out and they even made a small profit. It was simply a much shorter ride than I had expected." Her breast was pressing against him. "We have a policy of never making an outright sell recommendation," she said. "If the management finds out, well, that company never speaks to you again, that's all. But our clients get so they can read between the lines. We may say something like this: 'Prospects for the near term are not considered as encouraging as we had projected.' We say that in the follow-up recommendation Do you know something? I'm a terrible speller, just terrible The proofreader has a field day with my reports." She paused. "I understand," she said slowly, "that Kimbridge & Co. is going to pick a new partner."

He sat upright, moving so quickly that his hand fell free from Carol's arm.

"Who told you that?" he demanded.

"Noel Bigelow. He called me up the other day and from the way he was sniffling around I suspected something. He's like all the people I used to meet at parties. He wanted a stock tip. Anyhow, he told me what was going on."

"Did you say anything?"

"No. I didn't tell him a thing. Somehow I don't quite trust Noel."

He had no warning of what came next.

She turned upon him savagely and he heard a seam pop in her dress. Her mouth was pressed against his and then he could feel the wild exploring of her tongue. Her tongue ran under his lips and then across the edges of his front teeth.

"Poke, Poke," she moaned and she began rocking gently. "Poke, Poke . . ."

She drew back for a moment and then her hands were clasping and unclasping on his face. There was a clean smell, almost like starch, to her body, as if she had been delivered to him fresh from a laundry.

The shoulder nearer him was bare and a red flush had spread across the skin. He drew away with a sudden motion and lost his balance; the Monster had not been prepared for Carol's onslaught. She was kneeling on the sofa now, her knees pressing against him. The room had tilted crazily.

His stump began to throb. He grasped her hands and held them tightly. "Stop that, dammit!" he shouted and heaved himself back to a sitting position. Now he could feel the dampness on his stump sock.

She drew back, still kneeling beside him on the couch, as if he had struck her.

"What's the matter?" she demanded. "What sort of man are you, anyway?"

"Look," he said, "let's just take it a little easy."

She scrambled to her feet and ran into the small hallway. She turned to face him when he caught up with her. "I think the time has come for you to leave, *Mister* Jeffers. It was so nice,"—she was choking the words from her throat—"of you to take the time to drop by—"

"Carol! Stop that!"

He reached out and pulled the dress back over her shoulder. Her body was trembling.

They stood there facing each other and finally she said in a faint voice, "You're not angry? I—I just don't know what came over me all of a sudden . . . I—it's never been like this for me before. Oh, you must think I'm terrible."

"Now listen. Don't be ridiculous. It's just that—well, I think we ought to slow down a bit. That's all. Now don't start crying, for God's sake!"

"I'm not—not crying," she said and her voice shook.

He put his hand out to touch her cheek and she drew back against the wall.

"No, please," she said.

"All right," he said softly and turned toward the door.

Then he heard her moving behind him. She grasped his arm and twisted him around.

"Please," she said. "Please stay with me. Just tonight, stay with me. I won't cause you any trouble or demand anything. I promise you." She tore the cigar band from her finger and let it flutter to the carpet. "After all," she said, "a little risk taking. That's what it's all about anyway, isn't it? Why shouldn't we"—she gave a helpless shrug—"well, live a little? After all, we're adults. Oh, Poke . . ."

He started to say something and she pressed her fingers over his mouth.

The Monster was like lead. The thought of unbuckling the strap and removing the Monster in front of a girl . . .

"I can help you, Poke," she was saying. "I've got some ideas about stocks. Even in this market you can find the movers." Her voice was barely audible; it was as if she were murmuring a prayer. "That is, if you know where to look."

"What do you mean?" he said harshly. But he knew exactly what she was offering to him. She could not have been more explicit if she had put it all down in a prospectus.

Her face was in shadow but he could feel her eyes

upon him. Her eyes were wide and dark, like the eyes of a doe.

"You don't know what you're saying," he said angrily. "What the hell do you take me for?"

"Just try me," she murmured. "That's all I ask. Just try me."

Her eyes grew larger until they seemed to fill her entire face. They stood in the hallway as if they were carved from stone.

"What would you like for breakfast?" she asked, coming slowly toward him.

16

His left foot was caught in a hole!

Poke had been walking across the floor and suddenly his foot had plunged through this hole. He tried desperately to draw free but it was as if a bear trap had snapped upon his foot.

He pulled again and he could feel the pain running up and down his leg.

He came awake then and heard the pain rattle dying in his throat. He lay on his back and felt the perspiration rising along his entire body. For a few moments he did not realize where he was. The nightmare had been far more real than this room with its odd ceiling fixture that seemed like a glass coolie hat turned upside down. The bathroom door stood ajar and an all-night bulb cast a pale yellow glow through the door.

Poke heard the girl turn on the bed beside him and then he remembered . . . he could tell from Carol's deep breathing that she was fast asleep.

God! It hadn't happened for weeks, the nightmare about his foot wedged in a hole.

"You may feel something known as phantom pain," the doctor had said at the hospital. "Usually this phantom pain is present in the immediate postoperative period and then recurs indefinitely. But it may not appear for as long as six weeks after surgery." The doctor's voice was calm, almost germicidal. He paused to remove a speck of lint from his white jacket. "You see, the nerves in the leg are like a telephone cable," the doctor went on. "They are bound tightly together but they splay out at the end. What the patient *feels* is the bruised nerve ends of the main cable, you might say. The nerve ends for your toes, your heel, your ankle are all right there at the amputation site and they can continue to convey sensations. Furthermore"—it seemed almost an afterthought—"there isn't anything that can be done about it. Phantom pain, you may be interested to know, often occurs in patients with an abnormal proprioceptive sense."

Listening to the cool little discourse, Poke had felt only a vicious hatred for the doctor. Everything about him, the antiseptic voice and the white jacket and the mole below his nose, every last god-damned detail.

Moving carefully so that he would not awaken Carol, he reached down and touched the scar. There were times when he could not bring himself to believe the accident actually had happened. The illusion was strongest at night when he lay in bed. He remembered hearing somewhere that welders often see flashes at night while they dream. But it was different with a welder; when he woke up in the morning he was whole.

Carol stirred beside him. "Poke," she whispered. "Poke . . ."

He looked at her. Her eyes were still closed. The sheet was thrown back across her stomach and he could see the deep crease made by her pear-shaped breast as it fell to one side. Tiny blue veins coursed toward the nipple. A lustrous black hair, long and glossy, teased the nipple.

He lay perfectly still. There was a faint buzzing sound in the room. He decided finally that it came from an electric clock he had seen on the dresser last night. He had propped the Monster beside the dresser and then pulled a chair in front of it as camouflage. But a sliver of pumpkin flesh from the Monster seemed to be grinning at him now in the half darkness. He could not be sure.

Carol had not mentioned the leg.

She had been so eager to please him that Poke felt thoroughly cheapened. There was no lust in his body, only a strange numbness. He had rubbed her back gently and then placed his hand against the small of her back. He remembered how she gave a little shiver and he could sense the ecstasy rippling softly through her body. "Aaa-aah," she had said and a few moments later she was kissing his fingers. "You have such lovely hands, Poke. So strong and lovely."

He remembered the sharp, angular bone of her hip and the hollow just below it. Her thighs were very warm, in contrast to the small of her back which was cold to his touch.

Later, there had been one terrible instant when he almost lost his balance. He could feel the stump mocking him in the act of love. But then it was all over and Carol was bubbling—there was no other word for it—with happiness. God! She rambled all over the lot, talking about her childhood and his hands and how she was going to learn to cook, until finally he had been forced to smother her mouth with kisses in order to silence her. After what seemed an eternity to Poke she had gone to sleep and then he had not dared to remove his hand from her thigh for fear of awakening her.

He lay awake, staring at the inverted coolie hat on the ceiling, and he remembered how the pupils of a soldier, newly killed, can be fixed and dilated. He thought then about Korea and he marveled at how neatly the filth and boredom and mud and shellfire had been buried in the inner recesses of his mind. He had always felt a curious sort of apology about the war; the premonition of death or dismemberment supposedly universal among fighting men in every war had simply never touched him. He had felt fear, of course, but never that other thing. Christ, he thought now without humor, he had been such a god-damned Christian Scientist in Korea.

He had always loved guns and his father had taken him hunting in the backwoods of Georgia before he was as tall as a shotgun. He could remember the shiver of delight at shooting his first squirrel and then slicing off a forepaw and tossing it to his dog. In Korea, leaning forward against the sandbags of the combat bunker, he had felt the same hunter's joy as he gauged the wind and adjusted the telescope on his '03 Springfield. Here were desperate gray hills with their scrubby little pines denuded by shellfire; his target had simply shifted from forest game to Chinese soldiers in odd quilted uniforms. With his hand still on Carol's thigh, he remembered now seeing a string of Chink prisoners walking past an American tank knocked over on its side with a muddy track frozen against the sky. The prisoners had been stripped naked and as they moved away, hands clasped on their heads, their shockingly white buttocks made

203

them appear like schoolboys caught in a swimming hole by a truant officer.

His thoughts shifted to his boyhood, as if in search of some soothing ointment.

His father had been a lawyer in a county seat not far from Atlanta and while Poke was still a youngster there was no doubt in his mind about his future calling. It seemed as natural as rain. He would go to college and law school and then he would come back home to practice with his father. Jeffers and Jeffers, Attorneys at Law, he could visualize the black lettering on the glass door. His father's office was located across the street from the courthouse and that proud domed building with its dusty red bricks became as familiar to young Poke Jeffers as the Georgia woods.

The courthouse stood in the center of the square, indisputable as a rock cliff, smelling of glue and yellowed notices and washed-away spit, jealously guarding the unfolding of countless crimes, the hub of the town's architecture and its grief and its gossip, and yet somehow managing to possess frailties that were almost human: the four sides of the clock faces adorning the dome were never quite synchronized. The chancery clerk kept a pet deer in the courthouse and one election eve the deer jumped out of a second-floor window, smashing through the glass and landing unhurt. Nobody ever saw the deer again, and the chancery clerk, after six straight terms in office, after passing out as usual the little name cards adorned with courteous-reliable-experienced-appreciative-sober-sincere along the edges was defeated at the polls the following day. The townspeople took the disappearance of the deer as a sign but then again the town was full of little mysteries like that.

He loved to squat in the dust around the courthouse benches and listen to the old men talk. There

204

was a dignity about their canes and white straw hats and suspenders and starched shirts that he never forgot. These men taught him how to whittle cedar branches; they had fought in old wars and they talked interminably about politics and cotton and what the sheriff was doing about whisky stills. One of the men took great pride in being a designer of stills and he once told Poke, very gravely, "Watch out when you grow up, young feller. Bonded Bourbon can kill you." The old men sat and talked under the linden trees and there were window shades stretched between the branches to protect the men from pigeon splatter. What they had, these old men, was a dignity that went as deep as bone marrow.

His father had been a trial lawyer. He would steal silently into the courthouse when his father was defending a case—his father always wore a tattered seersucker jacket for trying his toughest cases—and listen spellbound to the fine, sonorous words that wheeled out as the big wooden-bladed fans twirled overhead. "Gentlemen of the jury . . ." he could hear his father saying with a hand stuck in one torn pocket of the seersucker jacket. At home at night his father would tell Poke, "You know why I wear that old jacket, boy? It's so the men on the jury will know I don't believe I'm any better than they are, that's why." Whenever his father had a defendant who was a fox hunter, he would make a point to get a fox hunter on the jury. "No man with foxhounds," his father would say, "is gonna convict a fox hunter. You harken to my word, boy."

His father was right, of course. But there was an old grief that his father could never soften, the grief of losing Poke's mother. That grief hung about the large house with its wide porch as real as the gray paint that peeled slowly away from the walls. His father never mentioned the grief to Poke but as the boy grew older he could isolate the grief for himself and wonder about it. His aunt—his father's sister—came to live with them after the death of his mother and she was like an old bird fluttering about the house, a kind and attentive and fussy sparrow of a woman tolerated by the two men who did not really belong to her in their inner hearts.

He dozed into a fitful sleep, his mind trailing softly into the green Georgia woods and then shifting the scene to Vermont where the snow curled on tree branches like huge white cats. . . .

Suddenly he jackknifed into a sitting position. Perspiration was dripping from his face and the smell of the hospital, the stench of disinfectant and medicine, was clogging his nostrils.

Carol moved on the bed beside him, propping herself up sleepily on one arm.

"Poke?" she said tentatively. She moved close to him and then she said, "What's the matter, darling? Oh, Poke, you look so forlorn!" She took his hand and placed it on her breast and when he drew his hand away she seemed to be gripped with terror. "Tell me, tell me!" she implored. "What have I done? Why are you looking like that?" Her voice was higher now.

"Oh, Carol, shut up!"

He had not meant to say it but the words just came out. "Leave me alone!" He was half shouting now. "Why in God's name can't you leave me *alone!*"

She did not say anything. He lay back in the bed and closed his eyes. He could hear her moving about the bedroom and then there was the sound of the bedroom door being shut gently.

He lay in bed but sleep was impossible. After a while he got up and hopped over to the dresser. The luminous dial told him it was twelve minutes past six.

The sibilant hiss from the electric clock seemed to jeer at him. Poke was alone in the bedroom.

He had to take a shower—as though that might cleanse him for what he had done in this room.

A few minutes later he was balancing carefully on his right foot; the hard, lean muscles quivered along his calf and thigh.

Once he had pulled a hamstring muscle just before a meet at college. His eyes were shut as he lay stomach down on the rubbing table, smelling the strong, rich liniment while down the corridor of the field house he could hear a shower dripping. . . .

The warm shower water riddled his back. Finally he bent over, with an air of ceremony, to lather the left leg.

The stump had become noticeably pointed within the last month. This meant normal muscle atrophy in his case. Lathering the stump, he could feel the beveled edge of the fibula, the flat outer bone of the lower leg, where it had been cut off shorter than the tibia during the operation.

"You're lucky," the surgeon had said. "If the knee joint is lost, every problem is compounded. Postoperative recovery, getting the stump into condition, fitting the prosthesis. The whole works." The surgeon smiled; he seemed very pleased with the whole business. That was the first time Poke had heard the word. Prosthesis. The artificial limb. The Monster.

He stood erect on his right leg and watched the shower water sweep away the thick lather laid over the stump. He had a perfect scar. It was no bigger than a crease in his palm. The scar was positioned on the bottom of the stump and even the hair, short and blond and tightly curled, had grown back here. It felt smooth and conical, the stump, not unlike the end of his elbow when he flexed his arm.

For a few moments he stared down at the ugly shriveled cone of a leg and he remembered when he had first seen it, all puffed up under a bed sheet in the hospital. At first he could not believe what had happened. And after he did believe it, the other feeling kept living inside: his own body had betrayed him. Abruptly his hand reached out for the cold-water spigot. "Ha-*whoosh!*" he snorted, his stomach suddenly all ice.

He flung back the shower curtain. Now he got a firm grip on the washbasin and, tensing carefully against the slippery film of soap under his right foot, vaulted out of the tub. Tiny steam tornadoes were bouncing on the tile floor. He dug his toes into the cotton mat to keep his balance and began to towel himself furiously.

"You're a hopper," the prosthetics man had announced when Poke was ready for his fitting. "Okay, so you hop around a little. But if you want to keep on taking showers, do it sitting on a stool. Find yourself a milking stool, so's it won't tip over. And crutches—always keep a pair of crutches beside your bed. You know, in case you have to get up during the night." The prosthetics man could not have been more than forty, but already he had an old man's face. "Of course," he said, "there's always the *tiny* danger of some accident. Why, I had one fellow whose foot broke when he stepped down too hard from the curb. It was the steel bolt inside that gave way. This fellow fell and skinned himself up a bit. But we fixed up that limb good as new."

He dried his face and hopped into the bedroom. He moved with floor-thumping leaps, like a man pressing his luck in a poker game.

The artificial limb, pale pumpkin in color, waited in

208

its black shined shoe and drooping black sock and open garter.

"Hello, Monster," he said softly.

He vaulted over to the chair, sliding as he landed on a scatter rug.

He would have given a thousand dollars at that moment for a clean stump sock. At his apartment, inside the top dresser drawer, meticulously clean and rolled into tight wads, lay a dozen of the finest stump socks available, five-ply white wool socks.

The plastic surface of the Monster reminded him of the skin of a snake when he touched it. He eased the stump into its leather socket, buckled the straps tightly around his knee, pulled up the black outer sock, and snapped the garter. Now he could put on his shorts. That was the damnedest thing; you couldn't slip on a pair of shorts standing up if you had only one leg. Then, quite unconsciously, he hooked his thumbs along the top of his shorts and ran them back and forth, a habit from his racing days.

A squeaking noise came from beyond the bedroom door. He went over to the door and pulled it open. Across the counter top he saw Carol. She was dressed in a pink nightgown and she was running a sweeper over the carpet.

"What the hell are you doing?" he demanded. "Don't you know you can catch cold that way?"

She straightened up. The handle of the carpet sweeper was pressed against the side of her face. He noticed her feet. They were long and white and narrow.

"Oh," she said, swallowing with an effort. "I didn't mean to disturb you. I thought I was being very quiet—"

"Put something on before you catch cold, dammit!"

She made no effort to move. "It's funny about

girls," she said. "Some of them love to cook and sew and iron and others are no good at all about those things." She did not look at him but kept her eyes fixed on the carpet as she spoke. "Now you take me, for instance. I like to sweep rugs. But I hate to iron. I suppose that's because the moment you put on a blouse you know it's getting creased." She waved the handle of the carpet sweeper aimlessly.

The next forty minutes was a cold disaster for both of them.

"Oh, but you *must* eat something," she insisted. "I just won't let you go out without eating breakfast."

"All right," he said. He felt suddenly drained of energy and there was not even the will to fight her.

They sat stiffly on high stools on opposite sides of the counter. The windows were open but a cigar odor lingered stubbornly in the room.

"What did you do with the blanket?" she asked.

He did not understand for a moment what she meant. She avoided his eyes and he knew that she had been crying.

"What blanket?"

"The one your aunt sent you in Korea."

"Oh. I gave it to some Korean kid."

"I had an aunt once," she said in a hollow voice. "She had a favorite recipe for crumb cake. But she would never give it to anyone in the family. After she died, we found the recipe in her things. She mixed the butter and sugar and used half of it at first and then she used the rest of it later on the crumbs."

My God, he thought, now we're cooking crumb cake. He started to say that the last note from his own aunt, scribbled on the church bulletin between the organ prelude and the call to worship, had said: "Stay out of Harlem." But he remained silent, unwilling to talk any longer about himself. Carol seemed to sweep together bits of his life like crumbs and he wanted fiercely to remain free of her.

He forced down a mouthful of toast and drank the coffee. It had the taste of gunmetal in his mouth.

She was wearing a pumpkin-colored dress. The collar was buttoned tight around her neck and she wore a pearl choker. The color of her dress was almost the exact shade of the Monster.

When he pushed back his chair and stood up, she busied herself with the dishes.

"I'd better get started," he said awkwardly.

"Yes, yes. I suppose you had."

"I want to stop by a barbershop for a shave before I go to the office."

"*Wait.*"

He had moved into the living room and was standing in front of the sofa. She came toward him. There was a dust rag on the carpenter's bench and she bent over to pick up the rag.

He waited for her to speak, but she said nothing. "Carol—" he began.

"I haven't told you about any stocks."

"I don't want to hear about any stocks. You don't owe me anything."

She nodded stiffly and twisted the rag around a forearm. "Oh, yes, I do," she said. "Don't you know that a person's word is his bond on Wall Street?"

He fought back an impulse to slap her. Beyond her face, off to one side, he could see the buildings of the financial district. The sky was blue and the buildings stood out so clearly that the view framed by the window seemed like a picture postcard.

"This stock . . ." she said, and then she hesitated for a split second.

For some reason he felt powerless to stop her. He realized than how much he really wanted her to keep

211

talking. Did he give an imperceptible nod of encouragement? Or was he imagining things?

". . . is one I've been working on for an institutional study. Emerson Coal. It's an important producer of steam coal for generating electric power." Her voice was devoid of emotion. "I think the stock can double within the next year. Maybe do even better than that. The earnings ought to be up to forty, forty-two cents a share this year. The company has a price-earnings ratio that's lower than the industry average. That means it can go up to a more liberal earnings multiple at the same time it's showing higher profits." A note of desperation entered her voice. "Oh, Poke, won't you let me help you? Please, please." She looked down at the rag. "People used to buy electric utility stocks as a hedge against uncertainty in the stock market. Well, today I think Emerson is a much better bargain than any utility stock." She looked up at him and smiled thinly. "You know something? Electric utility presidents are walking zombies, the ones I've met, anyway. You have to get into natural gas companies before the top brass has any life."

"Thanks, Carol," he said quietly. "I'm going now." He opened the hallway door and turned around. She remained standing inside the apartment, a dozen steps away. He sensed that her pride had taken over at last. The next move—if there was any next move—would be up to him. "So long," he said and closed the door.

The pull of her face was so powerful that he could almost feel it through the door. He walked stiffly through the hallway and outside into the bright sun. The grinning petunias with their slit eyes bade him farewell.

17

Poke shifted restlessly in his swivel chair. The bracing odor of bay rum lingered on his smoothly shaven face. But it served only to remind him that his shirt, though still presentable, was a day old. He felt an itching sense of uncleanliness that had become steadily more oppressive after he left the barbershop.

It was ten minutes before the market opening. He had read the newspapers and attended to the paper work on his desk. But the first thing he had done upon entering the office was to look up Emerson Coal in the stock manuals. Just for the hell of it, he kept telling himself as he turned the pages. He did not want any help from Carol; he ran his own races.

A clerk passed down the aisle and dropped something into the "in" box. Poke slit open the envelope.

It was another crank letter.

"Dere Mister Stockbroker," the scrawl began, "you and your kind are the scum of the earth. You take money from the poor people and you get rich so's you can run around in limozines and spend half your time in niteclubs." The letter was written in a small cramped script in black ink. Angry little streaks edged down from some of the words, giving the letter the erratic appearance of a road sign that had been put up before the paint had dried. "I hate all you bastards," the letter continued, "and so does every decent peace-loving Americun."

The letter was unsigned, of course. Poke looked at the envelope. It bore a Bayonne, New Jersey, postmark.

The telephone rang.

"Poke Jef-fers!"

It was Mrs. Hendricks, calling to complain about a dividend check. The check had arrived a day later than usual. "Why?" Mrs. Hendricks wailed. "Why is it always me?" She was eighty-three years old, nearly blind, very cantankerous, and not too bright. She was a lonely widow who lived on Riverside Drive and Poke suspected that her running gun battle with Kimbridge & Co. was probably the sustaining factor in Mrs. Hendricks' existence. She was one of those customers for whom you never could do anything right. She complained about every execution, whether she was buying or selling, and she could whine away for five minutes or better about the "hokey mokie," as she termed it, conducted on the floor of the American Stock Exchange. Satisfaction was the last thing on earth that Mrs. Hendricks wanted. What was life with satisfaction?

Poke listened to her harangue, nodding his head soothingly and saying to himself, "Don't turn around, Mrs. Hendricks. For God's sake! Keep still. They didn't get King Kong in that movie, after all. He somehow staged a miraculous escape from the Empire State Building. And Mrs. Hendricks . . . this-very-instant-his-big-black-eyes-are-shining-right-into-your-window. . . . Good God! The hairy arm, Mrs. Hendricks! It-is-coming-right-through-your-open-window. . . ."

"Yes, yes, I'll take care of it personally, Mrs. Hendricks. I'll call up our Dividend Department and have them make a special note of it for next time. Not at all, Mrs. Hendricks, not at all. Good-by, ma'am."

Service, Poke thought, you've got to kill them with service.

And all the time there was one thing you did not forget: the customer was the enemy. The cubicle was your fighting bunker and the customer waited somewhere out there on the other side. Few of them were willing to face up to the fact that investing was a business of mistakes—that somebody was selling too low or buying too high on every trade. And the toughest customer to deal with was the mad winner; he never forgave you for selling him out too soon with a profit.

Ten o'clock. The board room quivered and shook.

"Go whistle," muttered Poke to the world at large. The stump was itching fiercely now and the sensation of uncleanliness spread through his body like venom.

Last week three of his customers switched their accounts. The same thing was happening at other firms all over Wall Street. It was this crazy market that put everybody on edge. But when a customer took his account away, he never called you. You learned about it when the Accounting Department asked you if the customer had any open orders.

Even when you weren't talking about the market to a customer, you had to be careful what you said. Some of them tried to trap you into committing yourself on politics. What you did was to sidestep the leading question and succumb to a brief, inspired lecture on national, state, or local politics. But always you were very polite.

"There it is!" cried out a tape watcher sitting a dozen feet from Poke's cubicle. "I win, I win!" The man spelled out, "BELLY BUTTON."

"It's a misprint," protested the tape watcher beside him.

Poke regarded the men with contempt. There they sat, a row of gobblers with wrinkled necks, staring spellbound up at the tape. The tape watchers in the board room had invented a new game. They played imaginary bets of $1,000,000 and the man who, in an allotted span of five minutes, picked out the longest phrase formed by the random stock symbols was the winner.

Tape watchers and runners. Runners—what a laugh! A bunch of burned-out men, retired policemen and Sanitation Department workers and subway conductors. Maybe these men ran in the old days around the financial district, carrying checks and certificates in their leather bags. But now they moved as slow as cold molasses. Their specialty, from what Poke could observe, was sitting on the gravestones beside Trinity Church to rest their feet.

Dammit, *he* had been running ever since he hit Wall Street. The transfer from Atlanta simply meant racing on another track. He had started out fast in New York and the technique was simple: contacting potential clients in person. In the mornings before coming to the office and in the evenings after the stock market closed. The Jeffers radar had worked its magic. On Easterners, on ex-Southerners, on anybody with money to invest. And his energy had been boundless. During his first year at 50 Wall Poke developed another technique. He persuaded the Proxy Department of Kimbridge & Co. to give him all the

216

Street-name proxies he could lay his hands on. "I'm going that way," he would tell the clerk with a smile. "Save the firm some postage." Even the board chairman of a corporation didn't dare refuse admittance to a stranger bearing proxies for 30,000 shares—all signed and sealed for management, of course—to vote at the annual meeting. Eventually he received the personal investment accounts of some of these company executives. The other type of business was just as good. Persuading the corporation to invest idle funds—in commercial paper, Treasury bills, short-term governments—through Kimbridge & Co. And occasionally the big plums, a piece of the company's pension fund, would fall into his lap. It just took a hell of a lot of running. And he was very good at that.

The telephone rang again. "Scovill here. How're they opening?"

Percy Scovill. The mutual fund vice president. The man who always sounded as if he were talking through a layer of dry ice. But this morning Poke thought he could detect something else in that voice. A hint of worry. The market was getting to the mutual funds, too; the funds didn't know whether to go ahead and plunge or to sit back and wait awhile longer for the market to show its hand. It was agony for a mutual fund to sit with cash; its shareholders wanted performance the way a prize-fight audience cries for blood. So Scovill was worried . . .

Poke ran through the opening prices.

"United Air Lines is up five-eighths this morning," he added.

"We haven't owned that stock since February," Scovill said testily.

"That's right, you haven't," Poke agreed. He knew damn well the fund had cleaned out United Air Lines only to watch the stock gain 30 points in the next few months. But it was one way to get back at Scovill, to chip away at that layer of dry ice.

Poke knew something else. Scovill's fund was starting to get hit by redemptions. That could rock a fund; its management had less money to play with—and less confidence.

Scovill was in no hurry. "If your people ever come up with some ideas," he said, "I think we might be in a position to listen."

Poke was staring at the quotations board. For a fleeting instant he thought he saw Carol Tracey's face imploring him. He caught his breath. He was concious of her glistening mouth and of the stump sock rubbing into his flesh like sandpaper. Suddenly his temper snapped.

"It just so happens," he heard himself saying, "that I *do* have an idea."

He had a sensation of teetering at the brink, of going against his promise to himself. Goddamit! What was he doing? And the girl—Why should he trust her? But he was angry; he felt this tremendous anger surging inside his chest, struggling to get free. He was angry at having to cater to people such as Scovill and he was angry at his customers such as stupid old Mrs. Hendricks who could still take her shoes off and squint at her own two feet. He was angry at the whole goddam world and most of all he was angry at himself.

"*Yes?*" Scovill's tone had changed abruptly. If the stock market was doing nothing, even if it was falling to pieces, there was always this thirst for an idea, a real winner. When that thirst no longer existed, Wall Street could close up shop.

"Actually, it's quite hush-hush," Poke said slowly. "Something I ran across myself. It didn't come from our own research people. In fact, I get the impression they've turned conservative, very conservative, for the time—"

"*What is it?*"

Crawl, you cocky bastard, Poke said to himself, crawl.

"Oh, some stock you've probably never even looked at seriously," he said aloud to Scovill. He hesitated— and then he made the plunge. "Emerson Coal," he said.

"Emerson Coal? Why?"

"My information—and it comes straight from the in- side—is that the company's earnings will be up forty cents or better this year. The P-E ratio is lower than any of the other big coal producers. Your portfolio is loaded with electric utility stocks. You could achieve the same results with Emerson Coal, protect yourself against down-side risk, and get a better yield in the bargain. There's also—"

"What do you see for that stock?"

"I was just coming to that. A doubler. A doubler within a year. And one thing more—some institutions ought to be looking it over shortly."

"But none of them have moved in yet?"

"No," said Poke, "not yet. You'd be the first aboard. That is, except for Emerson Coal's own pension fund."

The symbol for Emerson Coal jogged across the magnified tape. The stock was 25¼. Down a half point from its close on Friday.

"There it is now on the tape," Poke said. "Two hun- dred shares just crossed. Stock is 25¼. No interest showing there yet. You know something? I always find it's good luck when you're talking about a stock and there it is on the tape right in front of your eyes."

"Yes, yes," Scovill said impatiently. "Tell you what, Jeffers. I may be getting back to you."

He rang off, and Poke sat very still in his chair. He

219

was staring at the tape. Had Carol Tracey led him into a trap? He did not know, and that was the plain truth. But there were times when success and failure hung in the balance and a man had to act. For Poke the compulsion had always been to act, to move. . . .

The morning wore on. The market was drifting lower. But there was no selling pressure. The market was like a man who watches the blood leave his body drop by drop.

At ten minutes before noon, while Poke was talking with a customer, the plastic button on his other line began to blink urgently. When the light went on in that button, it became almost the color of the Monster.

Poke finished his call and Scovill came on the line.

"I've been talking to our Trading Department, Jeffers. They're cleaning up the sale of fifteen thousand CBS. Got nine hundred shares left. I'd like you to handle that. Put in an order a quarter point above the present market. Tell your floor man that if he can't get off the sale at that price to go ahead and feed out the nine hundred before the close today. At the best prices he can get."

"Right," Poke said, jotting down the instructions.

"And Jeffers—"

"Yes?"

"About that Emerson Coal. I've mentioned it to some of our people here. I think they're interested. But you understand we've got to look it over ourselves. Our investment committee meets on Wednesday. Can you get me a little more information from your source? Anything you can find out will be welcome. Then we'll check it out from our end before we decide to do anything."

"I'll do my best. I'll let you know what I find out."

Scovill, probably, was bluffing. If Poke were convincing enough with the information he obtained, the fund might well go ahead and act. Scovill was simply providing a little window dressing for the way his fund operated. But that was all right with Poke.

He made the next call before he had a chance to hesitate.

"Yes?" the voice was guarded.

"Hi," said Poke. "It's me. The Wall Street man for the FBI. Where were you at eleven o'clock last night?"

"Oh, Poke . . . Poke." He knew then that she was crying. "Oh, my darling," she said.

"Hey," he said, trying to sound jovial. "Take it easy. This line may be tapped. Just one question. When can I see you?"

"Tonight? Would tonight be all right?"

"Yes," he said. "That would be fine. I'll buy you dinner. How are you on steak?"

"I've been known . . . to be very good on steak, thank you."

"Seven-thirty, then? I'll pick you up at your apartment."

"All right, Poke. I'll be waiting."

He put down the telephone and he thought, well, that is *that*.

Suddenly he longed to do something violent, like breaking a chair. Instead, he telephoned six of his customers. Four of them were interested. "Well, if you *say* so. You sound so enthusiastic about this stock." Their orders for Emerson Coal ranged from 250 shares to 700 shares.

He ran his thumbs unconsciously along his belt.

"Hey, Max!"

It was Noel Bigelow calling over his shoulder to Izzy. Poke glanced at Noel and then he heard Izzy's voice behind him. "What is it?" Izzy asked anxiously.

221

"Max, you know something?" Noel said, winking at Poke. Noel did not even favor Izzy by turning his head. "If you don't eat matzoth—a friend of mine just called me with this one and I think it's terrific—in bed, Max, you know what?"

"No, what is it?" He sounded as eager to please as a puppy.

"Then you won't sleep with crumbs, Max!" Noel whacked his desk with a palm and Poke watched his round face break into a circus-clown grin.

There was a pained silence in the cubicle behind Poke, silence and heavy breathing.

Noel got up from his chair, whistling softly, and went over to the drinking fountain under the clock. Not once had he so much as looked at Izzy.

You no-good bastard, Poke thought, watching Noel bend his head over the fountain. There had been a similar exchange on Friday. Noel told Izzy he had a new stock—a company that bottled both kosher tonic water and non-kosher tonic water.

Poke swung around now to face Izzy. "Listen," he said quietly, "it's none of my business. But you don't have to take this from Bigelow. Why the hell don't you stand up to him? Call his bluff just once—take a swing at him, for God's sake—and he'll never bother you again. The worst that can happen is maybe you'll break your glasses. What's the matter with you? His kind is no better than the people who write those damned crank letters. Don't you realize that, Izzy?"

Israel Padawer was shaking his head. "No," he said miserably, "no. It is nothing, it is nothing. But thank you. I appreciate."

A few moments later there was a call from a woman. She had heard about Poke from a friend in the investment club at Mineola—the Hetty Green Club—and she wanted to open an account.

"I'm bad luck," the woman said. "I probably shouldn't tell you this, but my last broker died a week ago. That's happened to me twice in the past year. So I thought I'd better try another firm. You know, to ease my conscience."

Poke took down the pertinent information. "I won't ask your age," he said, "as long as you're old enough to vote," and they both laughed. He gave the woman instructions on transferring her securities. "I'll mail you a signature card," he said. "Just sign it and send it back in the return envelope."

"I understand," she said. "Don't think I'm nosy, but —you're sure you feel all right?"

"Yes, ma'am. I feel just fine. Good-by and many thanks."

In a week or so, if he had not heard from the woman, he would give her a ring and talk in a general way about investments. There would be no pressure, no suggestions to buy any stocks with his first call.

You had to play it by ear with a new client. But in time you learned the damnedest things about some of them. They discussed their marital problems (he had talked one joint account out of seeking a legal separation) and they asked for all kinds of advice. Where to go on vacation, where to send their children to college, what to give for Christmas presents. Poke had one Negro customer, a postman in the Bronx who had called a month ago asking where he might take his wife to celebrate their twenty-fifth wedding anniversary. "A nice place," the man had said. and Poke knew what he meant, a place where there would be no embarrassment. He had recommended a good restaurant in Manhattan and then he called the owner, who also happened to be a customer, and gave instructions to send a bottle of champagne to the table.

"Put it on my bill," Poke said. The anniversary dinner had been a great success.

Poke tilted back his chair and regarded the lazily jogging tape.

Well, Jeffers, he thought, you've done it. Now you're running on Carol Tracey's legs. And not merely to boost your production. No, fella, you're in there running for the partnership of Kimbridge & Co. First place. You signed the entry blank a little while ago.

His stump felt numb; the itching had stopped.

He had responded to the challenge like an old fire-wagon horse answering the bell. He shook his head. The tape, the tumble and spurt of prices in the market, could do that to a man. The lust to compete rose up out of the board-room floor the way hot sulphur fumes ooze from a spring. To sit here and not compete—well, that was no better than being a soldier and not firing your rifle in battle.

Goddamit!

He twisted a knob on his desk drawer until he heard the splintering of wood. It was all so damn *polite*. He glanced around at the other customers' men in the room. Everybody was racing but the whole thing was under cover. Nobody ever mentioned the race. And nobody would take a swing at another man when the going got rough. Noel would bait Izzy and Izzy would take it lying down. It was such cozy little tea party.

So this is how the race begins. Easy, easy, easy.

In the Research Department Thatcher Kimbridge bent over the clattering teletype. He could feel the heat of the machine on his palms as he read the message.

224

TO ALL BRANCH MANAGERS:

IN MARKETS SUCH AS WE HAVE BEEN EXPERIENCING WE KNOW FROM PAST HISTORY THAT REGISTERED REPRESENTATIVES ALL TOO OFTEN FAIL TO MAINTAIN CONTACT WITH THEIR CUSTOMERS. ALERT REPRESENTATIVES SHOULD BE ABLE TO GENERATE SUBSTANTIAL BUSINESS BY STUDYING CUSTOMER PORTFOLIOS, MAKING APPROPRIATE RECOMMENDATIONS FOR UPGRADING ACCOUNTS AND THEN SUGGESTING THE PROPER SWITCHES.

REMEMBER THAT INVESTORS WANT ADVICE EVEN DURING PERIODS OF STOCK MARKET UNCERTAINTY—

This message, like the others, was sighed JD. Not WS for Wall Street, not even HOME OFFICE. Simply JD, for JARED'S DEPARTMENT. These two initials had served as the shorthand method of designating the office at 50 Wall when Kimbridge & Co. installed its first message wire—a loop to Philadelphia and Baltimore—and long ago they had become part of the terse language of the teletype machines. The Philadelphia office was PH and Baltimore answered to BT.

Thatcher smiled inwardly; Howard was exhibiting the old college try, all right. He lifted the glass and ran the yellow paper through his hands, scanning the other messages.

There were over-the-counter quotations, a summary of the market's action that morning, a query from the Atlanta office asking what Research considered the most attractive cement stock for capital-gains potential, weather reports from the Middle West, the announcement of a stock split, a dividend reduction by another company, and the latest bulletin, taken from the wires of The Associated Press, on the hurricane raking the coast of Florida.

Thatcher riffled the yellow paper.

THIS MORNING'S RALLY IN EGG FUTURES APPEARS MAINLY TECHNICAL AND IN PART MAY REFLECT A STEADIER UNDERTONE FOR FRESH EGGS. DOMINANT FACTOR HOWEVER REMAINS THE LARGE SUPPLY OF EGGS IN STORAGE AT CHICAGO SUBSTANTIAL PART OF WHICH APPEARS IN A POSITION FOR DELIVERY VS NEARBY CONTRACTS. THIS SUGGESTS ADDITIONAL FIRMNESS IN EGG FUTURES SHOULD BE TEMPORARY—

Nothing is certain, the managing partner reflected wryly, even eggs which have yet to be laid.

"There," exclaimed Howard Merriam in triumph. "I'm done." He pulled the sheet from his typewriter. "It's hellish to write a monthly investment letter in a market like this." He turned toward Thatcher, a look of professorial jollity now lighting his gaunt face, and said, "Well, well. And what's on your mind?"

"All I want to know is what you think of the market."

Merriam tilted his head back and roared with laughter. "Is *that* all? he said finally, wiping the tears from his eyes. "Well, I'll tell you something." He leaned across the typewriter. "Had a call a little while ago from a friend of mine. This man's strictly a fundamentalist. He wouldn't believe a chart if it pointed to the Second Coming. Well, he'd been interviewed recently by two news magazines. He told them both the same thing—even wrote it down for the reporters—in order to play it perfectly safe. What happened? Both magazines were on the stands this morning. In one he's quoted as being bearish. In the other he sounds like the biggest bull in Wall Street." Merriam rang the bell on his typewriter. "And now his partners are on his neck. They say a thing like this—if enough readers spot the discrepancy—can ruin the firm's reputation for being research oriented."

Thatcher nodded with a smile. Then his face clouded up. "Labor Day is past," he said. "By now the market should be showing some new direction. But the Dow-Jones industrials just keep making that damn straight line. I don't understand it. What about that economist at Harvard we keep on a retainer? What does he say about business prospects?"

"Oh, he's quite pessimistic," replied Merriam. "But that's no surprise for an economist. The world will forgive an economist if he's not optimistic enough. But let him miss a real downturn in the economy and that's something else again! It's the one thing he can't afford to show on his record. So a lot of economists—like our graybeard in Cambridge—like to hedge by issuing the standard gloomy forecast every now and then."

At the desks near the partners a dozen research analysts of Kimbridge & Co. bent to their tasks.

"Howard, I think you really want to turn bullish."

"Yes, I do," Merriam replied carefully. "I've got that feeling in my bones. But I'm not sure I trust my bones. I'd rather wait for the cold figures to tell me the story. Remember cardboard containers? Even that indicator is on the fence. Thought I saw it going ahead last month. But now it's gone flat again. Thatch, I'm going to make a confession to you. After all these years, you know what? I think I'm turning into a fundamentalist. No—don't smile. It's like losing my religion. This market has played hob with the chartists."

Yes, Thatcher said to himself, we are getting old. Old and cautious. He felt it in himself the way a man feels a fever and he recognized the symptoms now in Howard Merriam.

"What's that you're mumbling?" asked Merriam.

"I was just thinking how even the auditors appear

to be getting younger every year, that's all." The managing partner turned to leave. "Duty calls," he said. "It's my day to sign the checks."

As Thatcher walked toward the bull pen, his mind shifted from the uncertain course of the stock market to a more immediate worry. What was Seth up to? Something was brewing, he felt certain, to throw a roadblock in the path of incorporation. Yesterday, when he had walked into the floor partner's office late in the afternoon, Seth abruptly ended a telephone call. There was something in his manner that conveyed a warning to Thatcher. But what did Seth have up his sleeve? The clamor of the board room grew fainter in Thatcher's ears.

Under the glass top of Thatcher Kimbridge's desk were affixed two pieces of paper. One was a snapshot of Brit taken in the exhibition pool at Yale. It showed a handsome young man with cropped hair smiling—it was a characteristic smile of his, impish and slightly bemused—directly into the camera. In black trunks he struck a mock pose of resting against the Yale fence. The photograph had been taken on the day Brit was elected captain of the swimming team.

The other piece of paper was much larger—a map of the eastern half of the United States with black crosses marking the location of each of the twenty-one offices of Kimbridge & Co. When linked together by an imaginary line, these offices assumed the form of a crescent with Boston as one tip and St. Louis as the other tip. The similarity had not been lost upon the managing partner. "We are either the new moon or the old moon," Thatcher once remarked to Fred Lincoln, gesturing toward the map. "As a brokerage firm we are either waxing or waning. Only time will give us the answer." The bond partner nodded. "Make a good sand trap," he said. "Tricky."

A handle was appended to the convex side of the crescent by the state of Florida where there were five black crosses. The cumulative effect was not unlike an Olympic torch held aloft by an unseen hand in the vicinity of the Caribbean.

The home office at 50 Wall was the nerve center of the entire firm. But without its branch offices Kimbridge & Co. was powerless to survive. It was as if an army had dispatched troops to far-flung outposts while maintaining its top command and a unit of elite troops at headquarters.

The branch offices were knit together by a common command and a common tradition but they differed in many respects. All three offices in New England—Boston, Hartford, and Providence—were the result of an expansion program by Kimbridge & Co. in the years following World War I. Later, when larger quarters became necessary in Boston, it had been Jared Kimbridge's decision to establish the new office near the public library. He believed that such a location would impress favorably the residents of that particular city and his judgment was borne out in time by a substantial increase in the volume of business.

A subsequent wave of expansion southward along the Atlantic seaboard had resulted in offices at Washington, Richmond, and Charleston. The economies inherent in a message wire system were a guiding factor in this leapfrog growth. Each new office along the way could be tied into the same trunk. In Charlotte, stock quotations were still posted by hand on green chalk boards. Atlanta, a considerably larger installation, paid the price for more modern equipment one New Year's Eve when its electric board developed a short circuit. The electric gong used to signal the start of trading every morning had rung at ten-second intervals until the police forced their way inside shortly after midnight.

The Florida offices, quite by accident, carried out the crescent motif on a smaller and more angular scale. Jacksonville formed the eastern tip while Palm Beach, Fort Lauderdale, and Miami continued the bend that came to an end with St. Petersburg on the West Coast. Each of the offices in Florida was located on the street level to afford easy access. The St. Petersburg branch, in addition, was outfitted with sturdy handrails and a ramp for wheel chairs. Situated in a community composed largely of retired persons, this office generated more mutual-fund volume than any other unit for Kimbridge & Co. The offices in Miami and Palm Beach catered partly to tourists, many of whom seasoned their vacation by speculating in stocks and commodities. Their attitude toward mutual funds was best summed up by a dress manufacturer from Seventh Avenue who declared to his companion, a buxom girl in a bathing suit: "I should buy a mutual fund? To me that's like finding a Band-Aid in my potato salad, a mutual fund." These board rooms on the Florida East Coast were the only ones that provided a tiled area for tape watchers in their bathing suits.

Kimbridge & Co. had acquired its Florida offices by the simple expedient in 1933 of assuming the liabilities—and customers—of a financially beleaguered member firm of the Stock Exchange. Several years later it added offices in Baltimore and Philadelphia by the same process. Jared Kimbridge had discovered a tell-tale sign when a brokerage house fell into such difficulties; it began to delay sending out account statements to clients. In Baltimore and Philadelphia the partners of the acquired local firms (one house had an underwriting history that stretched all the way back to the Civil War) became limited partners of Kimbridge & Co., a step that removed them gracefully from the sphere of management. The other employees kept their jobs.

The Baltimore office of Kimbridge & Co. was located in what originally had been a bank enjoying a carriage-trade clientele. The bank left these premises upon its merger with a larger bank. Later, as its own volume increased, Kimbridge & Co. elected to remain in the same location. A suspended balcony was placed in what had been the main banking room to provide additional desk space for customers' men and velvet curtains were hung across the high, cathedral-like windows. The bank president's private office, an impressive arena of carved oak, was sealed off from the rest of the establishment and rented out as a chemist's shop. The president's pornography collection, reputed to be the finest in Baltimore and to be secreted in his office, was never found. He had died shortly before the bank merger took effect.

In the midst of this restrained opulence, the Baltimore office of Kimbridge & Co. also became the setting for a succession of resident managers. One man was lured away by a partnership offer in another brokerage firm and the next two managers decided in time that institutional sales offered greener pastures. Kimbridge & Co. had a policy of not permitting its office managers to service customer accounts. This was the sole province of the customers' men.

A self-imposed duty of Thatcher Kimbridge was to act in the capacity of branch manager for the home office. This meant that each morning he scanned the production sheets, printed out by the computer, denoting every transaction that had taken place at 50

231

Wall the previous day. He was acutely conscious of the parade of office managers that had left Kimbridge & Co. over the years for other houses. In the eyes of Thatcher Kimbridge, one of the most convincing arguments for incorporation was that it would permit every one of the twenty resident managers to become overnight an assistant vice president. What so many of the men wanted, he knew, was a title. In the brokerage business, a title sometimes meant more than money. Possibly, he often reflected, this would help the resident managers to forget something else, namely, that they made less money than the top producers in the firm.

The office in Philadelphia, which was almost forced to close during World War II for lack of competent personnel, was notable for several reasons. It was the only branch with as many as two women in the Sales Department. Somehow they managed to contradict the general conviction among Kimbridge & Co. partners that a man did not want advice from a woman on three things—politics, sports, and the stock market. The office in Philadelphia also achieved a certain distinction when, several years earlier, a wealthy client insisted on a remarkable request. This was a good-till-canceled order to purchase 5,000 shares of General Motors at a price of one dollar a share. Seth Voorhees actually blushed when he placed the order with the specialist on the floor of the Stock Exchange; later that same day the specialist, a hearty man who had not missed work in twenty years, became ill and left early for his home.

In Memphis one resident manager had been the son of a Methodist bishop who met his wife on a Mississippi River excursion boat. When his wife went to the hospital for the arrival of their third child, her sister came to tend house for the husband. When the wife arrived home with a eight-pound girl she found a note from her husband; he had run away with her sister. There was a small but explosive local scandal and Thatcher Kimbridge had to spend a week in Memphis to smooth things over with Kimbridge & Co. clients and to select another manager. He chose a salesman whose wife had no sisters.

The Washington office had blossomed into existence when nine customers' men from other firms, disenchanted with their employers for various reasons, had come to Thatcher Kimbridge with a simple proposition: open an office and he would have a ready-made sales force who knew the territory. The move was swiftly approved at a meeting of the dawn patrol. Several congressmen and two Cabinet members were among the customers of the Washington office but for some reason nobody could fathom this office also received a steady stream of requests for brokerage literature from penitentiaries in half-a-dozen states.

Kimbridge & Co. had a single office in New Jersey —at a shopping center in Newark—and years ago the firm had operated branches on a temporary basis at summer resorts in New York State and at various county fairs in the East.

But the most unlikely outpost the firm ever had was in Srevart, a small town in the Poconos founded shortly before the Mexican War by a merchant named Travers. In addition to a genius for running country stores at a profit, the merchant possessed a sense of humor and accordingly the post-office address he bestowed upon the hamlet was his own name spelled backward. In time there resided in Srevart a Dane by the name of Jorgeson who had married into the Travers family and who ultimately became one of the richest landowners in Pennsylvania. He owned several thousand rolling green acres in Bucks County but, much to the consternation of the gentry in that area, preferred to make his home in Srevart. Mr. Jorgeson became interested in the stock market shortly before Repeal. Mortgaging his land holdings, he invested heavily in the shares of liquor companies and, when Wall Street professionals suddenly discovered the distillery stocks and sent prices skyward, the largest obliging seller was the Dane who lived in Pennsylvania.

A member firm of the Stock Exchange kept open an office above the Travers hardware store for the sole purpose of servicing Mr. Jorgeson's account. He was in the stock market to stay after his experience with Repeal. In 1948 there occurred a dispute when Mr. Jorgeson refused to pay nineteen dollars in federal transfer taxes on a transaction and, before the firm's management had realized a crisis was at hand, he told the customers' man to go to hell and, in the next breath, withdrew his account. Jared Kimbridge heard the story on the trading floor and he swung immediately into action. The other firm, which saw no reason to maintain an office in such a forsaken place without the business of its only customer, agreed to let Kimbridge & Co. take over the location. Jared Kimbridge promptly visited Mr. Jorgeson and agreed to pay the transfer taxes out of his own pocket. This impressed the Dane and he agreed to deliver his account to Kimbridge & Co.

A curious kinship sprang up between the two men; they were like two dinosaurs who recognized each other as allies in a hostile modern age. The office above the hardware store consisted of a small room that managed to give forth year round the acrid odor of leaky radiators. There was no stock ticker in the office, not even a chalk board or a teletype machine. The office was staffed by an obliging local dairy worker who somehow had managed to pass his registration test with the Stock Exchange and became duly registered—a term that afforded him great private amusement. The only equipment, aside from the bare furniture on which the salesman played checkers with Mr. Jorgeson, was a telephone. But that was sufficient. This telephone generated the largest business from any single customer, including institutions in New York, in Kimbridge & Co.

Mr. Jorgeson was given carte blanche by Jared Kimbridge to call the Research Department at 50 Wall if the spirit ever moved him and to speak directly with Howard Merriam. But Mr. Jorgeson exercised this privilege only three times; on each occasion he asked for theater tickets for nieces who planned to visit New York City. When he died, every partner of Kimbridge & Co. attended the funeral; the last thing they did before leaving town was to close up for good the Kimbridge & Co. office in Srevart.

St. Louis provided the firm with its only office in a hotel. This had proved a strategic spot inasmuch as the most exclusive barbershop in the city was located nearby off the main lobby. Patrons of the barbershop developed the habit of watching the tape in the Kimbridge & Co. office until time for their haircut appointments. This office also generated some business from guests staying at the hotel; when a customer from another office in the firm executed a trade in St. Louis, it was customary for the two branches to split the commission.

In terms of total production, the office on Park Avenue ran second only to 50 Wall. Thus, while Kimbridge & Co. competed with every other brokerage house, its own offices operated with a keen sense of competition among themselves. Monthly rankings of production, office by office, were dispatched over the message wire.

Another office in Metropolitan New York was in White Plains. This branch shared a common grudge with Park Avenue against the home office, namely, that the customers' men at 50 Wall received the lion's share of institutional business parceled out to the firm. For their part, the home-office salesmen displayed a somewhat scornful attitude toward all branch offices. They referred to White Plains, where the resident manager the previous Christmas had presented each producer with a black tie initialed WP in red silk thread, as "We Pee."

Kimbridge & Co. had neither offices nor representatives stationed overseas. It was the judgment of the firm's founder—and on this count Thatcher Kimbridge completely agreed with his father—that too many brokerage offices abroad existed for one essential reason: to offer a convenient cover to partners who wanted to write off a vacation in Europe as a business expense. All overseas business was handled out of 50 Wall. The firm included a cable address on its stationery, Kimco, that was identical with its designation used on order pads at the New York Stock Exchange and the other principal stock and commodity exchanges in the United States.

The typical overseas account was institutional while in Atlanta the largest institutional customer was a Negro life-insurance company. Poke Jeffers had snared this account after ten personal calls. "You jes' won't take no for an answer," the insurance company president finally said, with a flash of ivory teeth. "No," agreed Poke and smiled in response. This insurance company, which had evolved from a burial society, was a buyer mainly of corporate bonds and Treasury bills. When Poke was transferred to Wall Street, the president asked that he retain the account. Thatcher Kimbridge agreed to the request; if the account were big enough and if the customer made the request, a producer could retain certain accounts, no matter where he went in the organization.

For the most part, of course, the clients were simply people who wanted to make money in the market. But the identities and fixations and minor quirks of many customers ultimately rubbed off on the customers' men in varying degrees. One Kimbridge & Co. client in Boston insisted she was the reincarnation of Lizzie Borden, a belief in which her salesman humored her to the extent of sending duplicate sets of research literature addressed to Miss L. Borden, in care of the customer. In Hartford one client was a retired insurance executive who had a stock ticker installed in the bedroom of his home. He telephoned the Kimbridge & Co. office daily but had not made a purchase in four months; he studied the tape and he was convinced that a repeat of the 1937 market decline was imminent. His caution spread to certain Hartford salesmen whose production thereupon plummeted.

There existed a Mecca-like orientation of the branches toward the main office at 50 Wall but the partners had learned that in certain communities—particularly in Richmond and in Charlotte—it was often wise to convey the impression that the local office was all-important. There were still a surprising number of Kimbridge & Co. customers who considered Wall Street the land of goblins. In order to foster regional loyalties—and to preserve a more personal touch—the firm had a policy of mailing out confirmations from the office where the orders originated. After the stock market closed each day, a battery of teletypes began chattering at 50 Wall. Perforated tapes fed these machines, and across the Kimbridge & Co. crescent the confirmation forms inserted in the receiving teletype machines were imprinted with the proper data, sealed into envelopes, and dispatched for mailing before nightfall.

All envelopes were franked with the identical slogan: "Kimbridge & Co., Service to Customers since 1907."

18

"Sixty-nine . . . seventy . . . seventy-one . . . seven-ty-two."

Israel Padawer, seated in his cubicle at eight-thirty in the morning, prayerfully was counting his pulse. Good, the pulse was normal, a normal beat and no skipping. During the market break several years ago, his pulse unaccountably had taken to skipping beats, once or twice every twenty seconds, and he had been terrified. Izzy Padawer had his own theory about medical science; as long as your pulse was normal you enjoyed good health. Izzy was very careful about his health. He never gave blood to the Red Cross because he had heard this terrible story about a needle.

" 'Morning, Izzy."

"Good morning, Mr. Kimbridge."

Izzy turned to watch Thatcher Kimbridge walk down the aisle toward the bull pen. Good again. His little plan had worked perfectly. He was the first customers' man in the office this morning and Mr. Kimbridge must certainly have noticed. Every morning, Izzy promised himself, he would be the first arrival.

Yesterday afternoon Izzy had heard the news, that the firm planned to take in a younger partner. The prospect made him feel actually dizzy. A partner in Kimbridge & Co.! Such an opportunity!

Shortly after Ursula Leone had confided her secret to Poke Jeffers, the dam had burst. Ursula next informed the chief telephone operator and then in turn all of the Catholic girls in the office, followed by Miss Grissom, Noel Bigelow, and finally the Puerto Rican delivery boy who brought up sandwiches for Mr. Merriam. Marion Parker ranked especially high in the order of persons to be told because she had arranged the bridal shower given for Ursula by the office girls. The shower took place at Fraunces Tavern, where George Washington had said farewell to his officers, and Ursula Leone was a person who appreciated the distinction between a Revolutionary landmark and a Schrafft's, say, that featured half portions for children.

In his first job as a customers' man Izzy had been employed by a small brokerage house owned by a Jewish family that made its fortune a generation earlier with a matzoth factory. Izzy's great fear in his first job had been that he would be fired. If it happens, he kept telling himself, I know the reason already. Produce or get out.

The firm had its main office not on Wall Street but nearby on Pearl Street where the rent was cheaper. There was a branch office uptown in the garment district where the family was always fighting with the landlord. The firm was not allowed even to paint its name on the windows because the building was owned by Arabs.

The main office was a cramped dirty place with the

brown worm tracks of burnt-out cigarettes on the wooden floor. In the men's room water bugs were always holding a convention. The main office was located on the second floor of a loft building, directly above a printing shop, and when the presses downstairs were running at maximum speed, the entire building would shake slightly. Izzy could feel the tremors pushing through the legs of his wooden chair and jarring into his body. On days when the stock market was dropping, the effect could be terrifying.

The quotations board in the office was quite small and there was no magnified stock ticker in the front of the room. In one corner near the entrance to the board room stood six old chairs. Each chair had a sign pasted to its back that read "Reserved for Our Customers Only." The firm concentrated its business mostly in margin accounts and the head partner—the eldest son who had broken away from matzoth and bought a seat on the Stock Exchange—kept two sets of books, one for the SEC and the examiner from the Stock Exchange and the other in Yiddish. Whenever the firm mailed out securities it automatically added a twenty-cent surcharge to the cost of shipping.

There was an ancient electric fan on the column behind Izzy's desk and, turning slowly from side to side, it made a wheezing sound just like the head partner who suffered from asthma. Izzy never knew whether it was the fan or the head partner wheezing behind his back. He had started out as a trainee at forty dollars a week, too inexperienced in the ways of Wall Street to recognize his salary as insultingly low. The term trainee was a sham. Even before he was registered formally as a salesman, Izzy Padawer—young, frightened nearly out of his wits, newly married, and with an idle father to support—was expected to furnish ideas to the other producers. Finally, when he got his own desk and began to contact prospective clients, he also received an ultimatum. In one year, if his production did not reach a specified level, he would be out of a job.

But Izzy Padawer found something that ultimately proved to be his salvation. The United Jewish Appeal had been of assistance in bring Izzy and his father to the United States and now, desperately in need, he turned to it once again. One of the things that had amazed him when he came to America was the number of his relatives—an entire tribe of cousins, aunts, and uncles, it seemed—living around New York City. One of his cousins was a secretary who worked in the headquarters of the United Jewish Appeal. He prevailed upon her to smuggle out a list of the largest donors. At first she had balked at the idea but gave in finally after Izzy insisted, "For us the Passover must be every day."

The roster of donors became Izzy's prospect list for brokerage customers. And it had worked—oh, how it had worked! Izzy would telephone the donors, or call upon them in person after the market had closed, and begin by explaining how grateful he was to the UJA. It was quite flattering for these people to see the fruits of their charity translated into a living exhibit, and a surprising number of them in time diverted some commission business to Izzy. His investment advice evolved into a single maxim: "Buy the blue chips, buy and hold." He had a deep respect for any corporation that had proven itself successful over the years and he was able to communicate this feeling to his new clients. When he was alone he would say the wonderful names aloud, as if he were learning the English language. "Stan-dard Oil Company of New Jersey . . . Minn-e-sota Mining and Manufacturing

. . . Am-er-a-*da* Petroleum . . . Sears, Roebuck and Com-pa-*ny*."

As a result, his customers made profits and his commission volume bounded ahead. He refused to let clients speculate with stocks he called disparagingly "the catsy doggy ones" and, if they insisted, he asked them to take these transactions elsewhere, a gamble that seldom failed to impress customers. He lost his temper only once—and it cost him a customer. A man called up and put in an order for a German chemical stock. Izzy was white with anger. "You would buy *that?*" he hissed. "You would dare to buy a *German* company? With all the wonderful companies in America? Have you no pride in being a Jew? Maybe you should buy shares in some munitions company on the Rhine!" The man withdrew his account, but Izzy Padawer did not have to write out the order slip.

Izzy was becoming educated at his own expense. Early in his career he had agreed to share a loss, fifty-fifty, with a customer after the man cursed him over the telephone for recommending a stock that went down. Izzy did not realize at the time that he was being duped and, what was worse, that he was breaking the rules of the Stock Exchange. Izzy began to hate the cramped, ugly board room where the traders kept their hats and coats on and did not remove the cigars from their mouths when they talked. There was a loudspeaker system in the room and once, when a clerk announced a railroad ticket for Bay Shore had been found on the floor, one of the traders called out, "I'll bid five-eighths!"

But Izzy Padawer felt hopelessly trapped. Already he was developing the disease, Newyorkitis. Money, there was never enough money. The only solution was to expand his list of clients. Instead of contacting donors to the UJA's regular campaign, he began to concentrate on a more select group, contributors to the special fund. Beside the name of Thatcher Kimbridge he found a respectable sum. Ten thousand dollars.

And so he came to call. So intent was Izzy upon rehearsing his gratitude speech that he drew a blank as he entered the office. It was not until he spoke to the receptionist that he realized in panic that Thatcher Kimbridge was not a Jew who had changed his name for business reasons. He was a Kimbridge of Kimbridge & Co.! Suddenly Izzy felt like Daniel in the lion's den—only without the courage of a Daniel.

A few minutes later, in Mr. Kimbridge's private office, the honeyed words turned to ashes on his tongue. Izzy's only thought was to escape as quickly as possible. But Mr. Kimbridge seemed to have all the time in the world. And for him, Israel Padawer, a nobody. Mr. Kimbridge picked up the telephone and instructed his secretary, "Hold my calls, please." This man is a *presence,* Izzy thought. It was like being in the same room with a United States senator.

His ingrained respect for tradition, a tradition he could feel in almost a physical sense in the offices of Kimbridge & Co., virtually hypnotized Izzy. He began to talk about himself under the gentle prodding of this quiet man who sat behind the scarred old desk.

Izzy told about living with his parents in the town near Stuttgart. There were only seventeen Jewish families in the town and one morning as he was walking to school he saw the shopwindows of the Feigenbaum family smashed to bits. "The store dummies," Izzy said, "they were lying in the cobblestone street like so many dead people," and Thatcher Kimbridge nodded. The store, Izzy explained, had been looted by members of the Hitler youth movement. It was the first open sign of hate on the part of his German classmates. One week after the looting of the Feigenbaum store the Jewish families left town. They vanished at night like gypsies, some families bound for Denmark and the others going to Holland. The rabbi had arranged this exodus, and later Izzy learned of the rabbi's own escape. He had hidden in the bottom of a manure cart.

In Denmark arrangements for the proper papers cost Izzy's father, who had owned a bookshop, nearly all the money he possessed. But his father already had tasted the age-old fear, a taste like lox that was spoiled, and he had brought along only one suitcase for himself, a suitcase crammed with his most beloved books, the works of the Hebrew scholars.

One thing Izzy did not tell Thatcher Kimbridge. Two nights before they left the town, a German had walked into their house without knocking. Izzy was alone in the house with his mother when the man entered. He was the shoemaker, a man with a dill pickle of a nose whom they had known for years, but now he had become a Nazi. The man strode up to Izzy's mother and, without uttering a word, spat in her face. Not a little spit but a huge hocking one that clung to her cheek like an oyster. Izzy almost stopped breathing. He stood rooted with fear as his mother's imploring eyes bored into his very soul. His mother was by no means a violent woman but he knew what she was asking of him. In those terrible moments Israel Padawer realized he was a coward. His mother never mentioned the incident. Later, while the family was waiting in Copenhagen to board the ship, she suddenly became sick and died. . . .

A few minutes later, after he had completed the Padawer saga, Izzy said that he, too, was in the business, that he was a customers' man. "Are you free for lunch tomorrow by any chance?" Mr. Kimbridge had asked, and Izzy nodded dumbly.

Mr. Kimbridge took him to lunch at the Downtown Association. "I always bring our Boston clients here," Mr. Kimbridge said with a smile. "It reminds them of home." All through the meal Izzy kept hearing the voice of his cousin Alec, who was now a shoe salesman at a store in Times Square. "Eat but don't join," Alec kept saying.

Thatcher Kimbridge did most of the talking during lunch. He told Izzy about Kimbridge & Co. and he asked a few questions about Izzy's own work. In a way, Izzy thought, it was like being interviewed for a job. He knew about customers' men who went job hunting, carrying the W-2 form like a passport in order to display their production for the previous year. But Izzy realized he would never have the nerve to do such a thing. And then Thatcher Kimbridge, stirring sugar into his coffee, half a lump, had asked, "Would you by any chance be interested in coming to work with us?" Izzy was so dumfounded that all he could do was to nod his head. Suddenly lunch was over and they shook hands. Izzy went home that night and mailed his first donation since arriving in the United States, a check for $500, to the United Jewish Appeal.

Some time after he joined Kimbridge & Co. he learned something from Noel Bigelow. "Max," Noel had said, "you're the first Jew ever to be hired here as a salesman." Israel Padawer had never felt so important, not since he was *bar mitzvah*.

Izzy's telephone was ringing.

"Padawer," he answered. It was his first telephone call of the morning.

"Israel," said Rabbi Stern, "so what do you think of the market?"

"It is here, Rabbi, and I think it will stay."

246

"Yes," Rabbi Stern agreed. "The market knows everything and yet it says nothing."

Rabbi Stern was Reform and he carried the movement to its permissible limits. He enjoyed a salary of $23,000 a year, he wore suits from Abercrombie & Fitch, he played a fast game of tennis—and always he used fresh tennis balls—he drove a black Lincoln Continental given to him by his prosperous congregation, and when the time came to build a larger temple he had encouraged the hiring of a professional fund raiser. The fund raiser had his own formula for payments: 15 per cent off the top for synagogues, 12 per cent off the top for Protestant drives. His staff was divided neatly into a subsidiary of Jewish employees and another with only Gentiles.

Izzy felt immensely uncomfortable in the gleaming new synagogue. It had soft slide-back seats and its smell reminded him of the small plush movie theaters near Bloomingdale's. Rabbi Stern, as a crowning touch of ingenuity, had devised a special ceremony for officiating at the dedication of the Long Island estates owned by several members of his congregation; it was a pool warming. Once, after buying a cement stock recommended by the Research Department of Kimbridge & Co., Rabbi Stern had placed copies of the study on each synagogue seat.

Izzy's vision of a rabbi was a man with a long white beard and dirty fingernails and he secretly believed that Rabbi Stern, with cheeks like fuzzy new tennis balls, was a fraud. No, Rabbi Stern would never ride in the bottom of a manure cart, he thought, not if he could meet Moses face to face as his reward. Rabbi Gentile—Rabbi *Goy*—that was Izzy's secret name for him. But now, with the time approaching for his own son to be *bar mitzvah*, Izzy was eager to please the rabbi in any way possible.

247

Rabbi Stern coughed discreetly. "So, Israel," he said, "the stock market stands still and it does not speak. Like a youth afraid to tell his love for the girl he worships." His voice changed subtly. "So, Israel, when do you think my stocks will go up again?"

"Rabbi, who can read the future?"

And then Izzy realized this was his first telephone call of the morning. He felt the same compulsion as Aaron Kaplan, a distant relative on his mother's side. Aaron owned a haberdashery store in Brooklyn and he could not bear to see the first customer of the day leave his store without buying something, even a small button. It would be a bad sign for the entire day and who could afford that? "Wait!" Aaron would scream, snatching a tie or a shirt from the counter and running after the customer. "Here, take it! So I'll forget the sales tax! NO? Then a third off—my profit even—and forget the sales tax still!" By this time he would be holding the customer by the arm and blocking the door.

Izzy hesitated. "Rabbi," he said finally, "you own one hundred and ninety shares of General Motors. I think you should buy ten more shares. To make it an even two hundred. That way, when you sell, you sell in a round lot. You save the odd lot differential." He almost said it, "Forget the sales tax."

"All right, Israel. I respect your opinion. Buy for me ten shares of General Motors. Tell me something. You think it will go up soon?"

"I hope so, Rabbi." Izzy hesitated again. "Oh, Rabbi, you will remember please to send me the check within four business days? Like the rules say, by the settlement date? The last time—"

"Of course, Israel. Your own rabbi you do not trust? This is what Wall Street has done to you? Ach-ach."

"It is not that—" Izzy hated himself and he hated Rabbi Stern for what was happening. The last time there had been no check at all from the rabbi. Izzy had paid for the purchase with his own money. He paid in cash, not daring to sign his own name to a check. It was an infraction of the rules but Izzy had been ashamed to call the rabbi. A loan, he told himself, a loan it is. For his own father's sake he would not press the rabbi. His father was a very religious man.

"Ah, Israel, soon it will be time for your Abraham's *bar mitzvah*, no?"

"Yes, Rabbi, in January." Again Izzy held his tongue. The rabbi knew the exact date because he had been in the rabbi's office when he marked it on the calendar with a gold fountain pen.

"Such a *bar mitzvah* it should be," rhapsodized Rabbi Stern. "I am glad you agreed to the hotel I suggested, Israel. Instead of the one you had in mind. Here I know the manager."

"Of course, Rabbi." Yes, Israel Padawer vowed to himself, this would be a *bar mitzvah* not soon to be forgotten. He decided not to ask the rabbi for his money until after January.

Izzy's father had spoken only last night again of the *bar mitzvah* the Halperns had given for their son Solomon, whom Izzy considered a perfect 100 per cent idiot. The Halperns were the richest family that the Padawers knew socially and they had given an affair for six hundred guests with *three* orchestras. The master of ceremonies was a man who had played once in the Hollywood movies. Izzy recognized the man immediately even though his hair was dyed and the mustache was shaved off; he remembered the movie where this man was a gangster and tried to squeal on Al Capone only to be deposited in Lake

249

Michigan in a barrel of cement. But style, no. The *bar mitzvah* for the idiot Solomon had no style. Solomon they should put in a barrel.

So what to do? Izzy had a plan, a secret still from his father and the rabbi. His plan was to charter a fleet of Greyhound busses that would transport the entire party from the hotel to the Grand Central. There the guests would step inside a special train hired from the New York Central people and ride up Park Avenue to the siding, a *private* siding, at the Waldorf-Astoria. A ride for seven blocks underground, a ride worthy of royalty, and he, Israel Padawer, was arranging it for his son. Such a gesture—

"Well, Israel, I must go," Rabbi Stern said. "I have an appointment. Mr. Sharpenstein. That's *Leonard* Sharpenstein. He wants I should go with him to look at a place. On the Island, and he's thinking of buying it. He says the swimming pool is shaped almost like the Star of David. I think this is a sign he should buy. What do you think?"

"Yes, I agree. Good-by, Rabbi."

Izzy put the telephone in its cradle and stared at the stock tape. General Motors went past, down an eighth. How he hated Jews! Not just the rabbi and the idiot boy Solomon Halpern and now Mr. Sharpenstein who was considering the purchase of an estate on Long Island. But *all* Jews and most of all himself. There were times when Israel felt that his Jewishness was forming a huge pimple, a pimple that covered his face and squeezed his eyes almost shut, a ripened pimple proclaiming his Jewishness for all the world to behold. And now, with this feeling inside him, he could almost cry because he was so ashamed.

He could never quite conquer this feeling of helplessness over being a Jew. Oh, yes, he was the biggest producer in Kimbridge & Co. and this realization was the sweetest thing in his life, next to his son Abraham. But a Jew in Wall Street. . . . It had a way of pouncing on you when you least expected, like a tiger in a bakery shop. Only last week one of Izzy's uncles had walked into the board room. His uncle was a runner for another brokerage house and he had taken the job because it was the only firm that provided uniforms—fine green uniforms with matching caps—for its messengers. His uncle had just made a delivery of securities upstairs and he came into the board room to greet Israel. And what had his uncle done? Very solemnly, as Izzy stood up in his cubicle, his uncle had leaned over and kissed him on the forehead. Noel Bigelow had been watching, with God knows what kind of expression on his face, and Israel had wanted to sink right through the floor boards, so great was his shame.

His eyes ached. Whenever he watched the magnified tape for more than a few minutes and then glanced aside at the quotations board the board seemed to waver and buckle until his eyes adjusted. Noel Bigelow kept a pair of opera glasses on his desk for checking quotations on the far side of the board. But Izzy just kept squinting through his glasses; he was afraid Noel would laugh at him if he bought opera glasses. Izzy wore rimless glasses because that seemed to him somehow less Jewish, and now as he raged inwardly at himself the glasses were fogging up.

There were, of course, all types of Jews on Wall Street. For the very few, for the select, the investment bankers with a tradition of family and money behind them, the Jewishness had been covered over like a coat of glossy paint. Then there were the others, the Jewish hustlers and salesmen. Some of these made it to the top and they had a way of joking among themselves. They wore white silk ties and white-on-white shirts and tailored suits and they formed a secret little club all their own. Izzy could almost smell them, the slick and successful Jewish producers, always thin men with bright eyes, whose money bought them cars and boats and fine houses and expensive, beautiful wives who creamed their faces and laughed like silver knives striking crystal goblets. But he, Israel Padawer, was on the outside even among his own people. The rich, slick Jewish salesmen were as foreign to him as the Episcopalians who went to the right colleges and wore ties with regimental stripes. Take Noel Bigelow, for instance. He sometimes said, "No kid-*ding*," when he was talking on the telephone, and that expression, too, was like a foreign language. Izzy had tried to say it the same way but it never came out right. He might as well be speaking Yiddish. Last winter he had bought a Countess Mara tie, just because Noel had received one for Christmas and made a point of showing it around the office. The tie carried an embroidered monogram near the bottom. But on the day that Izzy finally summoned up enough courage to wear the tie to the office he had tucked the monogram inside his pants. Twenty dollars, hiding behind a belt buckle.

"You hear the news?" said Noel Bigelow. He had swung around in his chair, asking his question to Poke Jeffers in a loud voice that included Izzy on its perimeter.

"Sure," said Poke. "The Ford Foundation's planning another secondary and they want you to handle the entire offering personally. Congratulations."

"Quit kidding," Noel said. "You hear anything, Max?"

Izzy swallowed and shook his head. He was so delighted that Noel was including him in the conversa-

252

tion that his glasses became completely fogged over. He took off his glasses and rubbed them with a handkerchief, squinting at Noel to show he was listening.

"Ursula Leone," Noel announced. "They've just sacked her."

"What do you mean?" Poke said. "She was due to go on maternity leave in another month. She produce early?"

"Not that," Noel replied, "but she's sure as hell leaving early. Today, in fact."

"She did something bad?" asked Izzy.

"You hit it on the head, Max. She did something bad. She spilled the beans on what went on in the dawn-patrol meeting. And the word got back to the bull pen. I understand Mr. Kimbridge was furious when he learned what she had done. He had her on the carpet this morning."

"They're keeping her benefits, the firm?" asked Izzy. "They're not stopping her benefits?"

"Not on your life," replied Noel. "One thing about Thatcher Kimbridge, he plays by the rule book." Noel jiggled from side to side in his swivel chair. "Say," he said, "you suppose they'll post a formal notice soon about that incorporation plan?"

"You've got me," Poke said with a shrug.

We are walking now on dangerous ground, thought Izzy. He felt his pulse quicken.

"Friend of mine told me about the big blast the partners of his firm gave at the St. Regis the night before the incorporation took effect," said Noel. "He said it was hard to tell whether it was a wake or a celebration."

Izzy sucked in his breath. He had a premonition that Noel was about to say something about the selection of a new partner at Kimbridge & Co.

Poke stood up. "Think I'll get a drink of water," he

said, pointedly bringing the conversation to an end. Noel nodded with an amused look and he swung around to his desk.

Izzy began calculating the debts he would incur in the next few months. They would be staggering, he knew, what with sending his father to Florida and the new heating system for the house and the bill for his son's camp and the contribution he made to B'nai B'rith on the anniversary of his mother's death. He donated $2,000 more to B'nai B'rith than did Solomon Halpern's father, and this knowledge gave Izzy a fierce satisfaction. No, he was not willing to cut a penny from that donation. Newyorkitis, he thought, there was never enough money.

19

Israel Padawer had known Sarah for six weeks when he asked her to marry him. She was a quiet girl who seemed to spend a great deal of time with a sewing basket in her lap and she had reminded him with an aching sadness of his mother.

He sensed that in time she would evolve simply into an older version of what she was now: a quiet Jewish girl with an instinct for obedience and long suffering, with the curve at the end of her nose becoming slightly more pronounced with each passing year. That was fine, just fine, Israel Padawer told himself. Was he not himself a quiet man, a scholar almost, a man to whom romantic passion had never seemed important? In life there were other things.

From the beginning they had been painfully ignorant of each other's needs and desires. Israel kissed Sarah for the first time on the night he proposed. He had borrowed a car and then had trouble with the starter in front of the house where Sarah was staying with relatives. He had to push the car downhill to get it started. They drove to East End Avenue on a chilly spring night and he stopped the car and kissed Sarah while he kept the motor running. Israel could see the roof of the mayor's mansion beyond Sarah's head and he smelled the sour stench from the East River as he kissed her awkwardly, first on the forehead and then finally on the lips. "Oooo-oooh," she had murmured, and he could not tell whether she was pleased or frightened. He still remembered the way the car was shaking and after a few minutes she made him stop kissing her because she said the motion was making her dizzy. Somehow, during this brief and unsatisfactory encounter, it became known to both of them that they were engaged.

It was important for Israel—an act of honor, in fact —to buy a ring at Tiffany's, and the following day he skipped lunch and went uptown. He bought the least expensive diamond in the store; the ring was priced at $104 and that seemed a king's ransom to him at the time. Israel did not quibble; he paid the going price. But he thought of all the Jews he knew who would have tried to get the ring a little cheaper, Jews who would be quite undaunted by Tiffany's and the quiet man who stood pushing the revolving door and trying not to look like a store detective.

As he hovered before the counter, averting his eyes from huge winking jewels, Israel kept telling himself that a home and a family, and not sexual enjoyment, constituted the heart of a marriage. Several years passed before he would admit secretly that while he had gotten precisely what he had bargained for in this respect, he could not help feeling enormously cheated. He often wondered if he possessed the capacities of a daring and energetic lover; Sarah was content to submit to him in bed but without any visible relish for the sex act. There were times when he thought she was going to raise her head suddenly and ask him to stop rocking the bed so that she would not become dizzy. As a result, with the passing years, he retreated ultimately into a state of virtual continence. Meanwhile, Sarah grew into a devoted Jewish mother who kept sewing and mending everything in their house except the kitchen stove.

He sat now at his desk watching the stock tape. One of the Kimbridge & Co. operators had just rung him up to pass along a message and she had called him "Dear," quite automatically. She talked this way with every customers' man in the office but it never failed to send a sharp tingle through Israel Padawer.

The telephone rang again. This week he was trying something new. He was answering his calls by saying "Pada-werl" and making his voice ride on the last syllable the way Poke Jeffers did. The net effect, Israel hoped fervently, would be to impart an Anglo-Saxon ring to his voice.

"Pada-werl"

"So, Israel," a voice chided, "always minding the store. A fine day like this, the weather cool, I thought maybe you would be out at the races. So what's hot in the market today, Israel? What's your loss leader? A coffee stock, maybe?"

"Hello, Alec," said Israel Padawer wearily to his cousin the shoe salesman, the one who had loaned him the car that night he had kissed Sarah.

"I just heard something, Israel, and I'm just calling to check up," said Alec cheerfully. "What I heard is this. A brokerage house that a friend of mine uses, this customers' man guarantees practically a 30 per cent profit every year on bonds. *Bonds*, Israel. What this fellow does is buy corporate bonds before the company announces it is going to call them in. He has a pipe line. The bonds go up 25 per cent, sometimes 35 per cent after the news comes out—"

"Impossible! Nobody can do that. The guy's just trying to get your friend's business, is all."

"Israel, his office is on Madison Avenue. So maybe on Madison Avenue the brokers hear things that don't get down to Wall Street?"

"Maybe, maybe." Israel conceded the argument.

It was, after all, useless to try to get the better of his cousin, a person for whom Israel had little respect but tremendous envy. His cousin was one of the few people who could sail through life undeterred by the fact he was a Jew. For Irving Slotnick, the son of a cantor, the first step toward a solution had been the simple expedient of changing his name. Now he was Alec Sims and Israel had learned not to make the mistake, not ever, to call him Irving again. It was the only thing that still made Irving—Alec, that is—quite angry. After his cousin had changed his own name he began calling his English bulldog Winston and everybody had said how fine a thing that was, to name his dog after Winston Churchill, the hero who had saved England during the war. "Nonsense," his cousin had to explain repeatedly. "The dog's name was *Weinstein*. So when I changed my name I changed his, too. Winston Churchill had nothing to do with it." The confusion aroused in the dog's own mind evidently had been too much to withstand. A year later the dog, known to be a strong swimmer, stalked one day into the calm ocean and was drowned.

Alec, a slim man with black eyes and olive skin, was a carefree bachelor who went through life on a cut-rate basis. He saw the last two acts of every popular musical on Broadway without paying a penny, thanks to his technique of mingling with the intermission crowd on the street and then slipping into the theater and taking a select spot at the back with the other standees. He cried in the closing act of *My Fair Lady* and the girl standing next to him, a lingerie buyer at Altman's, was so touched that she took him out afterward and bought him a drink. Alec promptly ordered a Martin, his name for a martini. Even his drinks had become Anglicized. Alec's wallet was filled with teacher identification cards that he used for special admission rates whenever he took a date to the movies. And the strangest thing of all was that Alec, after changing his name, no longer even looked Jewish.

Alec's sister was the girl who had supplied Izzy years ago with the list of contributors to the United Jewish Appeal. She had gone on to marry a pharmacist—Israel sometimes wondered if he dispensed kosher Bromo Seltzer from a special container—and now lived with her husband and three small children, all under five years of age, in a sunless apartment in Sunnyside, Long Island.

Alec was one of the best shoe salesmen in Manhattan. Even Israel's father, in an unexplained lapse of devotion to the professional arts, was proud of Alec's record as a shoe salesman. His cousin had started out at Sears, Roebuck and, in time, he was fired for tickling a policewoman's feet between fittings. It was a source of particular agony to Israel that Sears, Roebuck, his favorite stock, was so badly treated by Alec.

As for Alec, he simply moved on to his present job; he worked in a shoe store for women. Alec would say softly, "Israel, you should see the one I had last night." Along with the shoes, Alec managed to sell himself with surprising frequency. "They are starved for love, so many of these women," he would tell Israel. "So what can I do to oblige? I am there, their feet are bare, the stockings like honey sometimes, and

259

I am rubbing their feet so gently . . . Ah, Israel, the times I end up in their beds as soon as the store closes. You are in the wrong business. Not only shoes. Buyers from Chicago, even. A smart man, a buyer in undergarments, he won't sign up an order until the model takes off her bra."

But Israel Padawer did not dare to offend his cousin. After all, it was Alec who only last month had agreed to talk to his son Abraham, explaining about sex. Israel could not bring himself to do this and Sarah kept wailing in his ear, "Some things the boy knows already from his friends. But he must have questions . . ." For the preliminary talk with Abraham—sex was something that had to be talked about in detail by Alec, not just a once-over-lightly—his cousin had taken the boy to Yankee Stadium, using two tickets he had won in a raffle at the shoe store. Alec always wore a manila jacket in the store and it struck Israel that it looked just like the jackets worn by clerks on the floor of the Stock Exchange.

"So, Israel. For the *bar mitzvah* you are all set?"

"Yes, I suppose. Rabbi Stern called again this morning. He has made the final arrangements. The entertainment will include his two nephews. They play the guitar and—"

"How much?"

"Well—to tell the truth, one hundred dollars."

"Each nephew, one hundred dollars?"

"Yes," said Israel with a sigh. "Each nephew."

"Ah, Israel, you *nudnick*. Stern, he is a rabbi. You are the rabbit."

"Alec, I am busy. There was something . . . ?"

"Your father, he is feeling better?" Alec the vagabond, the tickler of feet and the pursuer of women, he had the odd way of asking after Israel's father and it never failed to touch him.

"Much, much better. He is down in Florida. I was talking with Florida just two days ago. He loves the sun and it is good for him."

"That is good news. Give him my love. And, Israel . . . your son Abraham He is a fine boy. You should be proud. The New York Yankees, maybe a mascot they could make of him. The night we were at the Stadium, they won ten to nothing. So long, Israel. And take my advice. Find a loss leader you can push. Personally, I never invest but I hear the stock market is sleeping on its Dow-Jones. *Mazel tov.*"

"Good-by, Alec."

His next call was from Mr. Finkelman, the scrap dealer who had boasted of bribing the purser on his last ocean voyage so that he and Mrs. Finkelman could sit at the captain's table. Mr. Finkelman, who flew to Europe this year, wanted to tell Israel about his audience with the Pope. He listened politely and, twenty feet away, the quotations board clacked merrily—like twin guitars almost.

Mr. Finkelman was describing how he had filled his brief case with stock certificates so that the Pope could bless it.

"What looks good?" asked Mr. Finkelman.

"Sears, Roebuck," Israel said promptly. After all, was it not the biggest retail organization in the entire country? And *goys* in the top management. What could be safer?

"Okay. Buy me 400 shares. In my son's account put it. The rate his portfolio is building up, that kid, he won't ever have to work."

Writing out the order, Izzy was touched suddenly by the old awe, the way commissions could roll up on Wall Street. You pushed a pencil across the paper and it was just like printing money for yourself.

Another client called. She was a divorcée in

her middle thirties, a woman with two small children, and she was worried about the stock market.

"Why should you be so anxious?" Israel demanded.

She had come to him last year with a divorce settlement amounting to $650,000. He had put her into good stocks and then given her two words of advice: "Be patient."

This woman is bored, Israel told himself, that is it. She is bored and she wants attention from a man. So she called him. Was not this a part of his business, after all, to hold the hand of the customer? For a moment he wondered if the woman was trying to say something else to him. There was something in her voice . . . yes, yes. *No!* He thrust the thought from his mind. She is a *shiksa*, he said over and over to himself, a *shiksa*. What would a Gentile woman want with him?

He pretended that he was very busy—"please pardon, please pardon"—and his hand was shaking when he put down the telephone.

There was a call from a customer who would only talk business in a steam bath; he did not want any stranger to know what he was doing in the market and he did not trust telephone operators. So Israel Padawer, who was terrified of steam baths—all those vapors and God knows what else!—reluctantly made an appointment with his customer for the following Wednesday in the steam bath of his club.

Mr. Zeitlin telephoned from Maryland, collect, and Israel told the operator he would accept the call. Mr. Zeitlin had come to the United States from his native Hungary years ago, a refugee with $1,200 sewn inside his coat, and proceeded to make a fortune in the commodity markets. "No lead or copper futures for me," Mr. Zeitlin had said to Israel. "Once you starve, you never forget it. I only trade in commodities I can eat.

Corn, wheat, cocoa." Mr. Zeitlin was now a gentleman farmer. No, he was thinking about a stock investment, not commodities today. No, not Sears, Roebuck, thank you, Israel. Ah, that is an idea. A company that *supplies* Sears, Roebuck. Mr. Zeitlin put in a good-till-canceled order for 2,000 shares. A half-point below the market for the first 500 shares and then 500 shares on quarter-point scaledowns. Mr. Zeitlin could wait; he would not chase the market, even for a company that made merchandise for Sears, Roebuck.

A Jewish tailor telephoned to sell 50 shares; he only sold through Kimbridge & Co. The tailor used another broker for buying stock. Such secrecy, Israel thought to himself as he repeated the instructions on sending in the certificate. Maybe he should take along the tailor to the steam bath next Wednesday; his two customers should meet, they were both such lovers of secrecy—

Thatcher Kimbridge passed down the aisle and spoke a silent "hello" to Israel as he went by the cubicle.

There was another long-distance call. Yes, he would accept the charges. Yes, yes, Operator.

"Israel? That is you?" The voice spoke in Yiddish.

"Yes, Papa," he replied in Yiddish. "There's something wrong, Papa?" He became alarmed; his father had not telephoned him at the office five times in his life. On *Shabbos*, the Sabbath, his father would not even pick up the telephone in the house when it rang.

"It is raining," his father announced solemnly, ignoring the question. "I am sitting here in Miami Beach and it is raining. Ach, such is the fate of our people."

"Soon the rain should stop, Papa." Unconsciously, he had lowered his voice, as if fearful that the ghost of Jared Kimbridge might overhear him speaking in

Yiddish. "Maybe you could play a little backgammon with Mr. Stepanian until the rain stops."

"Ach, he is down in the lobby. Taking tango lessons. For twelve dollars an hour they should give you tango in a hotel. For twelve dollars a family could live for a week in the old country. Live and have in the relatives for dinner again."

"Yes, Papa."

He loved to spend money on his father. Israel had filled the shelves of his father's room in their house with works of the Hebrew scholars, all bound in the most expensive morocco. The first hundred dollars Israel earned as a customers' man—a time when he had only one suit to his name—he had given to his father who had promptly sent the money off to a charity that claimed to finance escapes through the Iron Curtain. His father was so religious that on *Shabbos* he would not step inside a bus, not even to ride from Riverdale in the Bronx to visit relatives in Manhattan. Every Rosh Hashanah his father received from Israel two hundred white cards with a blue border to send to his friends. The cards were purchased at Tiffany's. "All good wishes for your health and happiness through the coming year . . ." And his father had almost died from shame when Israel told him he was going to become a customers' man for a brokerage house.

When he was home, his father liked to spend the warm afternoons sitting on a park bench near their house. "So I heard Bernard Baruch would do this same thing, ach, ach." And there his father would sit with his cronies and rock gently back and forth on the park bench, a frayed black skullcap on his head and worn leather slippers on his feet. Israel's devotion was so strong that he even subsidized his father's friends, chief among them Levon Stepanian, the retired rug dealer who had confided to Israel: "There is no big money in oriental rugs. How can you tell, you ask? Because there are no Jews in the oriental rug business." Simply to please his father, Israel had bought several rugs from what Mr. Stepanian referred to as his "private collection." Mr. Stepanian would slice up cigars and smoke them in his foul-smelling pipe while he sat on the bench with Israel's father. He taught the elder Padawer how to play backgammon and there was something about the way Mr. Stepanian threw the dice and shouted in Armenian that made Israel suspect the man was cheating his father even though they played without stakes. Mr. Stepanian often appeared at the Padawer house just before dinnertime and he even got so that he knew the Jewish ceremonies. He would eat only the heart of the bread, leaving the crust on his plate like a calling card.

His father loved company as much as he loved the hot sun. So one week ago Israel had sent both his father and Mr. Stepanian to the most expensive hotel in Miami Beach. Suddenly Israel realized why his father was calling: he needed more money. He would call for one of two reasons: either somebody had died or he needed more money.

". . . is all around you in this place," his father was complaining now about the Muzak. "The lobby, the elevators, even when you go to the bathroom, you hear the music."

"Papa, did you find a nice synagogue?"

"Ach, yes. This morning there were present only nine men. It was a crisis. So we finally decided to count the Lord as the tenth man and went ahead with the service."

Every sunrise and every sundown, no matter where he was, his father attended services. When he first came to New York, he walked into a Con Edison generating station by mistake, thinking it was a synagogue.

"Papa, it is such a funny thing you are calling now. I was just wiring you some money. Perhaps there is a little something you can use . . . will $500 be enough, Papa?"

"Ach, money. Yes, yes. Maybe $800 you should make it. Just rounding out, as you say. Levon wants we should go to the horse races. Yesterday he met an Armenian jockey. A little shrimp of a fellow, Israel, shorter than you even."

"Fine, Papa. Eight hundred. It will be at the Western Union desk in your hotel inside two hours."

"Baskets of fruit we are sending North. Grapefruit and oranges. Ten dollars a basket. Levon has five brothers and they say the fruit here is like the old country. Very brave men. They all fought the Turks and ate mule meat."

"One thousand even I'd better make it, Papa. So take care of yourself now, Papa."

And then he was staring at the quotations board again and his father's voice was gone. He would have to go to the bank to get the money. So he would ask Poke to cover his telephone calls for fifteen minutes. He thought about his father in wonderment; the old man seemed to believe money flowed from a bottomless well on Wall Street. So if he wasn't a stockbroker, where was all this money going to come from? Even his son, Israel thought, even Abraham at his age had an acute consciousness of money. He had been horrified to learn that Abraham could recite, in order, the names of the ten richest boys in his class at school, a boarding school with a quota of 3 per cent for Jewish students who attended by day and went home at night.

Israel Padawer stood up. Life was so strange, but one could make plans. . . . His son, he already had decided, would become a doctor. Yes, that would please his father. There was one final thing: he himself was going to become the next partner of Kimbridge & Co. *That* even his father would have to respect. He walked out of his cubicle.

"Poke," he said, "I'm going out. Please take care of my calls."

He wanted to add, "If a rabbi calls, hang up," but Israel Padawer did not have the nerve. It was just the kind of joke Noel Bigelow would have made, he thought miserably.

20

So Deirdre Kimbridge was back in town. . . .

"How's the market?" asked the customer.

"It's up," replied Noel.

"What do you mean? I hear the Dow is down seven points. That's why I'm calling."

"I mean," said Noel hastily, "that *yields* are up."

"Very funny. What have you got for a fast turn?"

"There is this stock"—Noel's voice took on a confidential tone—"that I hear Lehman Brothers is buying. . . ."

"That's more like it."

So Deirdre Kimbridge was back in town. . . . Noel could hear her odd, breathless way of talking and smell the apple-bin scent of her body. The memory of Deirdre was so vivid that he could almost reach out and touch her. But what he touched was an order pad; this was a customer still on 50 per cent margin and Noel was arranging a same-day switch so that the customer would not lose any buying power.

Two weeks ago, after the call from Tim McVay, he had obtained Deirdre's new listing from Information. He dialed her number immediately, ignoring the blinking light that signaled an incoming call.

"Why, No-*el!*" she exclaimed, sending a shiver along his spine. She had seemed genuinely glad to hear from him. But no, she could not see him for a while. There were so many things she had to do. Finally, they had made a date for this evening. Six-thirty. At the 59th Street entrance to Central Park. "Don't bring your car," she had said. "I'd love to go walking in the Park."

There were so many unanswered questions. What were her plans? Had she changed at all?

But now his spirits were soaring. Three o'clock. Just three and a half more hours until he saw Deirdre.

Another call.

"Yes, yes," he said, his voice confident and full of good will, "there are one or two trading ideas I have. You know the old saying. 'Buy on Rosh Hashanah and sell on Yom Kippur.' With that sort of thing going for you, how can you lose?" He delivered a perfect imitation of a ram's horn and there was an appreciative chuckle from the customer.

She was already there, gazing up at the gold statue of General Sherman, when Noel arrived. A pigeon added a gray plume to the general's hat. She was wearing a sleeveless blue linen dress and her hair was tied in back with a small bow.

"Well, hello," he said, and she turned around.

She looked the way he remembered her except for the lipstick. She was wearing pink lipstick.

Then Deirdre said something quite strange; she had not lost that ability to surprise him. Instead of running up to him as he had pictured this reunion countless times, Deirdre stood there with her hands behind her and said, quite gravely, "Do you know there's a theory about statues? That you can tell how an officer died in battle by the stance of his horse?"

Noel shook his head. He restrained himself from kissing her. Then he slipped into her mood, nodding toward the statue and saying, "Anyway, it doesn't apply to Sherman. He didn't get killed in battle."

"That's true," she said with a little laugh and touched his coat sleeve lightly. "Hello, Noel," she said. "You're looking prosperous."

"Hello again," he said. There were the same little folds of baby fat under her armpits and the same round, smooth shoulders with their deep tan. He marveled again at this luminous quality of Deirdre's skin and suddenly he had the impression that she was not wearing anything beneath the linen dress. "Would you like a drink?" he asked.

"No, thanks. Let's just walk a little."

They crossed the street. It seemed to Noel that they had thrown a bridge across time, that he had seen Deirdre only the day before. Perhaps, he told himself as they strolled along the edge of the lake, it was because everything about her had been so riveted into his senses.

He took her arm and they walked in silence under the trees. They passed a small boy who was holding a water pistol. The boy pointed his pistol straight up and squeezed the trigger; he grinned at them madly with delight as the water came cascading down upon his head. They laughed, sharing the boy's pleasure, and Noel could feel the warmth of Deirdre's body.

Finally, when Deirdre spoke, she surprised him again.

"I had a letter from Avis the other day," she said. "I'm sorry"—she had stopped now and was looking at him solemnly—"that things didn't work out for you two. Noel, do you hear from her?"

"No," he said, feeling suddenly ill at ease. He did not want to talk about Avis. "Look," he said, "are you sure you don't want a drink?"

"No-o-o. Come on, silly. Exercise is good for you."

They turned onto a small incline. He felt a ring on her little finger and then he remembered—it was her brother's signet ring.

"Tell me about yourself," he said finally. "What are you doing?" He glanced sideways at her as they passed the bird sanctuary.

"Oh, there's not really much to tell. I simply grew tired of Paris, that's all. It's a June city, you know. When September comes everybody migrates to Venice. I woke up one morning and discovered everyone I knew had left Paris. So I packed my bags. Besides —Paris has changed so. The artists wear dinner jackets at Maxim's. Everyone is so prosperous."

Then she hadn't returned home to marry someone!

It was cool in the Park and the sun was a low red ball, resting like an apple on a thin plate of a cloud. The parched summer finally was over. He had never liked autumn in the past because it meant taking his boat out of water. That day was always the saddest one in the year for him. Now he did not care. Not so long as Deirdre was back in town. . . .

"You're smiling," she said.

"Yes," he agreed and aimed an imaginary water pistol into the air. They both laughed.

Noel looked toward Central Park South. The buildings were soft and gray in the fading light. The Park was slowly embracing the night.

"Oh, how I love this place," Deirdre said, locking her fingers together and stretching out her arms. "Father used to bring us here for walks when Bridge and

I were little. We'd pretend we were animals in the zoo. Bridge made the most wonderful camel"—her voice was suddenly filled with melancholy—"and you could practically see the humps on his back."

There were so many things he wanted to say to her and now the ghost of her brother had sprung up once again between them.

"What were you?" Noel asked.

"Me? Oh, I kept changing. One week a panther. Then a seal. For a while I was a leopard—that was the summer I had the measles. But the crowning glory was my chimpanzee week. I pretended to unlock all the cages and set the animals free."

Listening to her, Noel imagined that he could smell the zoo in the distance.

"I came here for a walk last night," she said.

"What? You shouldn't do that. This isn't Paris, for goodness sakes. Haven't you read about the muggings?"

"Oh, Noel, you're so sweet. You're always worrying about me." She patted her purse. "I'm perfectly safe. I still carry my grandfather's trusty straight razor. Remember?"

Her hand darted into the purse. Noel saw the bone handle and then the glint of a blade. Deirdre bent over, neatly clipping a weed.

"See?" she said.

There was something menacing about the way she used the razor. She dropped it back into the purse.

"It's dinnertime," he announced. "Where would you like to eat?"

"Noel, I *can't*. I've got to be at my job."

"Job? At this time of night? What are you talking about?"

"I do volunteer work. At a home for unwed mothers. I go there five nights a week. Oh, Noel, I feel genuinely useful for the first time in my life! Those poor girls, they're so young and so vulnerable. One of them is only fifteen years old. I met her at the bus terminal when she arrived from Alabama. She was carrying a catfish sandwich in a shopping bag with all the clothes to her name and she's going to have a baby in just seven weeks!" Deirdre looked off into the distance. "Many girls come to New York simply because they are pregnant. Their own families turn against them."

"Well, that's very noble of you," he said, fighting to control his temper. "But *five* nights a swek? Deirdre, why can't you work maybe one night a week and give a check to this place?"

"Oh, I've already done that."

"How much was it?" He could not resist asking.

"Ten thousand dol—"

"My God!"

"Oh, Noel, I wish you could come down to the shelter. You'd approve. It's really a very good address. In the Fifties and on the East Side. But men visitors aren't allowed."

"Well," he grumbled, "at least *that* makes sense."

"The poor girls from Harlem and from Bedford-Stuyvesant, they're the most pitiful ones. They're only teenagers and they're scared to death to go see a doctor when they become pregnant. They need vitamins and vegetables and proteins. But what do they live on? Potato chips and Coca-Cola. It's hard to imagine a worse diet. Salt is bad for them. Noel, what time is it?"

"Seven-thirty," he said stiffly. "I finally invested in a watch."

"Oops! I'm late!" She ran on ahead and Noel had a sudden fear that she was about to vanish from him forever. They reached a cobblestone walk.

"Here," he said, "I'll get you a cab. But when will I see you again?"

He held up an arm and miraculously a taxi coasted to a stop. "Wonderful!" cried Deirdre and leaped inside. She stuck her head out the window. "Brunch on Sunday? How's that? Come to my apartment. Just a second, driver." She scribbled down her address and handed Noel a scrap of paper. "Eleven o'clock," she sang out, and then the taxi disappeared into the night.

Noel stood under a street light. He had to smile; she was so concerned about being late that she had forgotten to offer him a lift. Slowly he began to walk toward Central Park South. There was the soft clop-clop of horse hoofs behind him and an open hansom passed by. The gathering darkness lent a certain dignity to the ancient horse, and as the hansom reached a crest in the road the top hat of the driver was silhouetted against the sky. In the back Noel could see the head of a man and a woman pressed close together; for a moment Noel imagined that he and Deirdre were riding in the hansom.

Well, he thought, this time I can afford to wait. . . .

He had lost Deirdre once but it would not happen again. Marriage had taught him an awareness he did not possess before. He felt confident now that he knew how to handle Deirdre. She was a girl you couldn't crowd; you had to allow her plenty of slack. The clop-clop-clop grew fainter in the distance. He could smell the urgent promise in the earth and trees about him. Yes, he exulted, it was going to be a wonderful autumn.

He began to hum a tune from the Triangle Club show his senior year, improvising a new set of lyrics. So Deirdre was back in town. . . .

Deirdre had taken an apartment on 72nd Street. Pausing in front of the door, Noel had recalled the drab place she had occupied when he first knew her. Yet that was why he had moved into the Village—because Deirdre once lived there. He adjusted his tie and pressed the buzzer.

"Come in!" he heard her call. "Door's unlocked!"

He opened the door and her voice was clearer. It came in short, breathless bursts. "Crucial moment—I'm turning the eggs and the coffee's just about to stop perking—thank God you've come on time!—Father says you're always one of the first salesmen in the board room—eight forty-five sharp, he says—make yourself at home, Noel!—but watch out for tacks—laid the carpet myself—couldn't wait for those fool union people—they hire one fellow to lay and three to watch —*my Lord but I'm starved!*—how about you?"

"Yes, me, too!" he called out. He swung the door shut and surveyed the apartment.

He was not prepared for the transformation. It was a large sunny room and the floor was covered with a textured gold carpet. The furniture was Danish—teakwood, he noted with approval—and the chairs and tables were obviously expensive. He pressed his toe into the carpet; it had a deep, springy pile. But the walls! They were adorned with old samplers—collector's items that he judged to be genuine—and with ancient tin weather vanes. There was a tin ram, almost life size, mounted on a wooden block and, on the opposite wall, a trotting horse with its tail flying. "I fell wildly in love with horses when I was twelve years old," Deirdre told him. "Frankly, I preferred horses to the human race for two whole years."

Noel had the sensation that he was still missing something important. Slowly he turned around.

Above the door, jutting out into the room by a full

four feet, was a ship's figurehead, a bosomed woman with flowing gold tresses that matched the color of the carpet perfectly. The figurehead was garbed in what he took to be a classical Greek robe.

Beside another door, which presumably led to the bedroom, was a marble mantel. Above the mantel, instead of a painting, there was mounted a Masonite panel with inlaid sections of cork. He had to smile; the room was so filled with crosscurrents that it seemed a perfect reflection of Deirdre.

Then she entered, carrying a large tray tilted against her stomach, and he forgot all about the room.

She was wearing blue jeans and a loose-fitting yellow sweater. The jeans, almost white with age, clung to her thighs.

"Here," he said, advancing toward her, "let me help you."

As she handed him the tray, it caught momentarily on her sweater. The sweater pulled tight, revealing the outline of a nipple.

Deirdre hurried back into the kitchen. "Hold it," she called over her shoulder and returned with a butcher's chopping block that was slightly hollowed in the center by white cleaver marks. "Put the tray here, please," she said. "It makes a wonderful brunch table, don't you think, Noel?"

She drew up two teakwood chairs and the big sunny room was rich now with her private scent.

Noel nodded dumbly. He did not trust himself to speak.

They began to eat, and he realized that never in his life had he felt so happily domesticated, not even with Avis.

There was fresh orange juice with shaved ice and fried eggs sprinkled lightly with herbs and fine black coffee and panettone shaped like the crown of a felt hat without the crease. He ate the light Italian cake with his fingers, savoring the plump raisins and the bits of glazed fruit.

Deirdre was eyeing him with immense satisfaction. "You're a wonderful guest," she said. "You'll have to come more often."

Being with her, he thought, was like walking through a street newly washed with rain at dawn and trailing a bunch of bobbing colored balloons on a string. He realized again—it cut through him as sharply as Deirdre's knife slicing the panettone—that she was the only girl who had truly bewitched him.

He swallowed a mouthful of cake and said, "If I were your psychiatrist, I'd say you were completely in charge of things."

"Poor Noel," she said, cocking her head to one side and regarding him fondly. "Remember how I used to go running off to my appointments at the strangest hours?"

"Yes, I do. You were sandwiched in between a federal court judge and a Roman Catholic priest at one stage."

"That was Dr. Donaldson, my third psychiatrist. When he found out I was decorating this apartment, he offered me the couch in his office. It's a beauty! Green leather and no button bumps. But his wife beat me to it. She said if he didn't let her have it for their country place she would leave him."

"Do you still go . . . to anyone?"

She gave him a thoughtful look. Her eyebrows, which she left unplucked, were thick and brown. There was a tiny vertical crease, almost like a dimple, that appeared between her eyebrows when she grew serious. "No," she said, brushing cake crumbs from her thigh onto the napkin. Noel saw that the jeans were beginning to split along one inner seam. "'That is, I still see a lot of psychiatrists. But only as friends now. I get invited to their parties. They're just like anybody else. They like to stand around with a drink in their hands and talk shop. Swap stories about their patients—goodness, you should *hear* some of the tales they tell! Only they don't use real names, of course."

Noel felt a rush of jealousy. He could picture Deirdre, warm and attentive and utterly desirable, in the midst of foggy old men with pointed beards. He decided to change the subject.

"I like your friend," he said, nodding at the figurehead.

She was obviously pleased; she possessed the childlike quality of showing pleasure without reservation. "Oh, yes!" she said. "Bridge bought that years ago. He was invited up to Greenwich for a weekend and he found it at an antique store. He thought it would make a perfect present for the hostess. Just a gag, of course. He said he had me in mind all the time. Oh, Noel, can't you just see the hostess when he handed her that thing? It weighs eighty pounds!"

Suddenly she seemed to have drifted far away, out of the room and beyond Noel's reach.

He stood up restlessly and lighted a cigarette. "You still don't smoke, I suppose?" he asked brusquely.

Deirdre shook her head; she was suspended in a trance.

"When the telegram came about Bridge," she said in a singsong voice, "I was still a student at Chapin. I had a plan for getting Father to speak at our commencement. I figured it was about time we got the word from Wall Street but"—she smiled sadly—"Sally Simpson beat me out. Her uncle was Secretary of State. . . . I came home that day and there was the telegram on the silver card tray in the front hall. Fa-

278

ther and Mother were both away. I opened the telegram and read it. . . . Oh, God! How I longed for
someone to put his arms around me at that instant
and crush me, crush me so I'd never breathe again!"
She stopped talking suddenly and began to rub her
eyes. "I'm sorry," she said. She picked up the napkin,
flinging bits of glazed fruit onto the carpet, and blew
her nose. Deirdre rose hurriedly and carried the tray
into the kitchen.

Noel, feeling quite helpless, remained in the living
room. He longed to hold her tightly and to whisper
that she no longer need fear anything. But some instinct told him this was not the time. It was the same
old routine, he told himself angrily, the Kimbridge
family embracing its ghosts. Then he heard water
rushing into the sink.

He found himself studying one of the samplers on
the wall. The numerals had been cross-stitched evidently by a child—perhaps some colonial ancestor of
Deirdre?—and several letters in the alphabet were
misplaced. The outline of a church spire rose in the
top of the sampler and in the churchyard two men
with tall black hats were carrying a coffin. The background was brown and so faded with age that it had
taken on the color of dirt.

A few minutes later he heard Deirdre's voice again.
It sounded quite affectionate, almost playful. "Come
on out," she was saying. "We have company."

Instantly a cat bounded into the room and stopped
at Noel's shoes. He could hear its claws digging into
the carpet. God, how he hated cats! So this was Deirdre's answer, he thought savagely, holing up with a
damned cat. That wondrous body, all that money, everything about her—it was all going to waste. She was
going to waste away into a spinster; he could foresee

her fate just as surely as if it were stitched into the sampler.

Noel retreated a few paces and sat down in a chair. The cat stalked slowly toward him. It was an immense gray cat with black rings around its body and tail and a broad black stripe down the middle of the back. The cat pressed against Noel's leg. He could hear the languorous purring rattle deep within the cat's throat and felt its ribs pressing against his leg. The cat moved with a slow and liquid motion, twisting its head toward the carpet. The long, curved tail was waving gently. Noel knew that in a few moments his nose would stop up and he would then start to sneeze.

"Mur-rur-row," went the cat, and Noel actually felt the forming of the sound against his calf.

"Oh, Noel! How wonderful! Joan of Arc *likes* you." Deirdre was regarding the cat with a rapt expression. "You should feel honored. It's very unusual for her to accept a stranger so readily. Why, she carried on a regular war with my concierge in Paris. And when I brought her through Customs she bit the quarantine officer. It's so sad, Noel. Do you realize that pets excluded from entry into the United States have to be destroyed? Either that or shipped back to where they came from. I'm thinking of starting up a special fund to change all that."

Deirdre was standing in the center of the room. She clapped her hands—"That's how I call her," she said—and the cat immediately drew away from Noel and darted to her mistress. "Joan of Arc," said Deirdre, looking down at the cat, "you've made a real conquest. You really like Noel, don't you?"

The cat sat on her haunches. Then, very deliberately, she revolved her head and paused for a moment; for the first time Noel saw that the cat was

280

blind in one eye. He had the distinct impression that Joan of Arc had shielded this infirmity until deciding that he could join the charmed circle of the apartment. He realized that he had been the object of a scrutiny—brief, intense, and quite eerie—that made his admission into the Cottage Club at college seem paltry by comparison.

"What happened to Joan's eye?" he asked.

"Oh, you mustn't call her Joan. She's very conscious of her full name. You've got to call her Joan of Arc if you want to keep her respect."

Noel took a deep breath and succeeded in swallowing a sneeze.

The cat remained frozen on her haunches, staring at Noel with her good right eye. The eye was a lustrous green, the size of an emerald in a king's crown, and it had a black upright slit in the center.

"What's wrong with Joan of Arc's eye?" Noel said finally.

"I don't know. She was that way when I found her three years ago. She was a tiny kitten then and the eye was already gone. I found her in an alley behind the place where I lived. Oh, Noel, I felt so sorry for her . . . I decided it was fate, finding an alley cat in an alley. So I adopted her." Deirdre tilted her head to regard the cat lovingly; it was the same motion of the head that Joan of Arc had used when she began staring at Noel. "She's quite Gallic," Deirdre added.

The cat seemed to understand that they were discussing her. She yawned contentedly and, taking her emerald eye away from Noel at last, she marched across the carpet. There was a bright rectangle of sunlight on the carpet near a couch and Joan of Arc chose to stretch out on this spot. Somehow the cat seemed almost human.

"When I brought her to New York," Deirdre said,

"she refused to eat out of her meal pan. I discovered that she would take food only when it was served to her on a copy of *Paris Match*."

Joan of Arc began to lick her thick gray coat. Noel shivered as the pink triangular tongue darted along the fur. The whiskers were white and gleaming in the sunlight.

"What's her favorite food?" asked Noel. He had no wish to learn about the cat's diet but it seemed a way to cement Deirdre's approval. Play from strength, he said to himself, that's what a person always should do, no matter whether it was the stock market or the discussion about a damned cat. How much like Deirdre it was to pick up an ordinary tabby cat, a crippled stray, instead of a blooded Siamese or a Manx in perfect condition.

"Bologna is her very favorite dish," Deirdre said. "I think that's because she knows I like bologna sandwiches. Oh, look, Noel. She is perfectly relaxed with you. I can tell when she feels that way. She always tucks her front paws under her head."

The cat had put her head down on the carpet and the good eye was closed. Noel watched the slow, even bellows movement of the cat's rib cage. Suddenly he gave a violent sneeze and the emerald eye flicked open to stare accusingly at him.

"Sorry," Noel said and reached for a handkerchief.

"Noel, you're not getting a cold?"

"No. It's just the coming of autumn." He sneezed again. "I always sneeze at this time of year." That god-damned cat, he thought, and smiled at Deirdre.

Joan of Arc evidently had her fill of sunlight. The cat arose, stretched languidly, and then bounded across the room. She leaped onto a table and then sprang with lightning grace up on the ship's figurehead. From this vantage point the cat alternately surveyed the two people in the room. Her pointed ears twitched.

Deirdre was laughing softly as she watched the cat. She murmured some unintelligible phrases and the cat stiffened with attention. The two of them seemed to Noel to have ventured onto some territory from which he was excluded.

"In my apartment in Paris," Deirdre said, not taking her eyes from the cat, "Joan of Arc liked to creep out on the window ledge and watch the couple in the apartment below make love. She would watch them for the *longest* time. They weren't married, this couple, and somehow I think Joan of Arc approved of that. After all, she *is* a French cat. I thought of rigging up a mirror on a long metal arm so that she could be safe and watch from inside my place. But then I decided a mirror would take the zest out of the situation for her. Do you think I was right, Noel?"

"Absolutely," he agreed, folding his handkerchief. He could feel the cold emerald eye staring at him now from above. But he refused to give the cat the satisfaction of returning her gaze.

Deirdre sat down on the patch of sunlight that the cat had vacated. She tucked one leg under her and the split widened along the seam. Noel had never seen anything so voluptuous as that sliver of tanned flesh. Does she know how desirable she is? he wondered. She must know. He was stricken by another thought. Did Deirdre herself take a lover in Paris? He felt certain that she had had affairs with men. There was something about her completely casual acceptance of him in the apartment that fortified his conviction.

Joan of Arc plunged downward from her watching place. She raced across the carpet, turned back to move slowly toward Noel and, after a brief purring rub of his leg, stalked over to Deirdre. She picked the cat up and held her above her head; she fell back upon the carpet, one knee weaving in the air, and shook the cat gently as she spoke. "Ah, precious one," she crooned. "You like your new friend, don't you, precious?" She placed the cat on her stomach and began to stroke her fur. "You should see her in bed with me, Noel . . ."

"Mur-r-r-r, mur-row."

That god-damned cat, he raged inwardly, we're going to spend the rest of eternity talking about that god-damned cat.

"She curls up behind my knees when I'm in bed," Deirdre said. "I sleep on my side. In the morning she's always there. I give her a whisk behind the ear and she stretches out"—Deirdre was writhing on the carpet by way of demonstration and Noel watched the superb breasts gliding under her sweater—"and then we're both ready to start another day."

He watched Deirdre sweep up Joan of Arc and rub the cat's head across her cheek. The cat's staring eye slowly closed; it became a dark, horizontal slit and the slit curved upward with the pressure against Deirdre's cheek.

Noel stood up. He could not bear to look at them any longer. He plucked a long gray hair from his trousers and cleared his throat. "I was thinking," he said, "what a great day this is for a ride in the country. The two of us. My car's outside. What do you say?"

"Oh, Noel, I'd love to, but Sunday afternoons are a bad time. When the weather is nice like this, I take a few of the girls at the shelter out for a walk. We go down to a little park beside the East River and we look at the boats and the barges going by—"

"But sometime," he insisted, "maybe some Saturday afternoon. How would that be?"

"Yes," she said. "That sounds wonderful." The eagerness in her voice excited him anew.

Deirdre jumped up nimbly, Joan of Arc still cradled in her arms, and walked toward the door. The cat opened her eye to stare briefly at Noel and then closed it again.

"Joan of Arc's a great one for going to sleep, isn't she?" said Deirdre. "And at the oddest moments."

"It must be her Gallic temperament," said Noel, his hand on the doorknob. He could not bring himself to kiss Deirdre with the cat between them.

Steady, boy, steady, he told himself. Take your time. Someday Deirdre will be yours, that wonderful body, all your own. . . . He knew it as surely as he was standing there.

There was something else: if he were not selected as the next partner of Kimbridge & Co. then Deirdre herself would become his hedge. Marry Deirdre and someday he would run the firm. Why not? He was in the business; what made better sense?

He had made a mistake with Avis, he was willing to admit that to himself. He simply had married a girl that he did not love. But with Deirdre it was different. And by some incredible stroke of luck the brokerage house also was going to fall into his lap. What a man had to do in this world was to set his plans carefully and, at last, he had learned how that even applied to marriage. A little imagination. . . .

Suddenly he felt something like wet sandpaper against his hand. Without opening her eye, Joan of Arc was licking his hand. Noel suppressed a desire to reach out and strangle the cat.

"I'll call you," he said to Deirdre, forcing a smile as he opened the door.

21

"Mind if I sit down for a moment?"

Thatcher Kimbridge was standing outside Poke's cubicle.

"No, sir. Please do, Mr. Kimbridge."

Poke half rose in his chair and the managing partner said, "No, no, don't let me disturb you." Thatcher Kimbridge took the chair beside the desk and began to watch the tape. Stock Exchange volume in the first hour was down sharply.

Poke also stared at the tape. It stumbled like a sleepwalker in slow motion; there was neither rhythm nor urgency to its movements. He hated days like this when the board room took on the appearance of a funeral parlor. But at the moment he was wondering about Thatcher Kimbridge. He knew that every salesman in the room must have taken note that the managing partner had entered his cubicle. Yes, Poke thought, it's a minor event.

Thatcher Kimbridge crossed his legs and, with a little laugh, he said, "You know, when my father ran the firm, he didn't really approve of customers looking at the tape." He rapped his chair. "These things were turned around so that they faced the back of the board room. My father's theory was that the producer should decide which stocks to buy and sell. The tape only distracted the average customer, that's what my father always said." He paused. "After he died, I waited one month and then I turned these chairs around. Besides—it used to give Howard Merriam an attack of hives every so often, having the customers staring straight through the glass at his department."

"Yes, sir."

The managing partner rested an elbow on the desk. "I just wanted to tell you," he said mildly, "that I noticed that new piece of business you brought in. The mutual fund. What was the size of the order?"

"Nineteen thousand shares."

"Yes. Nineteen thousand." The managing partner's fingers began to drum on the desk. "That was very nice, Poke. Especially in a market like this."

"Thank you, sir."

"What was that stock the fund picked up?"

Poke tensed slightly. "Emerson Coal," he said in a careful voice. "It was Emerson Coal."

"They go anywhere else for it, do you happen to know?"

"Yes, sir. The third market. And one other brokerage house. That was reciprocal business. They finished rounding out their position two days ago. The vice president of the fund called to tell me. I asked him that same question. He was quite frank about it."

"I see." The fingers kept drumming. "Do you like that stock?" Thatcher Kimbridge was looking at Poke with an odd expression.

"You bet I do. It's up from what the fund paid for

287

its block through us. I think it could be a doubler and—"

The palm lay flat on the desk. "Don't sell me," said Thatcher Kimbridge, and then he smiled to soften his remark. "I'll take your word for it. I think I'll pick up a thousand shares for my own account. On one condition—that you tell me when you think the stock is a good sale. All right?"

"Glad to, sir."

The managing partner gave a final glance at the tape and stood up.

The telephone rang but Poke did not answer it immediately. "Thanks again," Thatcher Kimbridge said with a nod and swung open the door of the cubicle.

The excursions to Brooklyn Heights had become a part of Poke's new life. Each time he passed the whitewashed pots with their grinning Chinese faces and walked down the hallway to Carol's door he felt the apartment house tightening about his body like a huge trap.

If he had a code in life, it was to be free, absolutely free. People could get just so close to him and then— bam!—the door leading to his inner self slammed shut.

And now—Carol Tracey.

The apartment door flew open and she was running her hand over the doorknob.

"Hello," he said.

"Hello, yourself, hello." And she was in his arms and he smelled her starched laundry scent.

"Here," he said, struggling to free an arm. "I brought you a present." He reached inside his pocket. "I thought you ought to see what the competition is saying. Here's the latest market letter from Kimbridge & Co. Hot off the press."

"Later," she said.

"No, wait. You ought to take a look at it. It's not even about the stock market. Merriam devotes the whole market letter to the time he saw Houdini perform at the Hippodrome. They put handcuffs and leg irons on Houdini and stuck him in a packing case. They nailed the packing case down and tied ropes around it. Hey!" he yelled. She was unbuttoning his shirt. "Don't you want to know how Houdini got out? That's the kicker in this market letter."

She shook her head. "Poke, oh, Poke . . ."

And then there was breakfast.

"I've come across something that's quite interesting," Carol said, breaking a piece of toast. "A metal stock I've been watching for a long time. The tipoff is the latest insider report. Last month the president of this company bought thirty-nine hundred shares and the treasurer picked up two thousand shares—"

"Stock options," Poke rasped, wanting to fight back at her, "that's all it means—"

She cut him off with an impatient wave of the toast. "No," she said, "it's much more than that. Oh, sure, they were exercising options, they weren't about to bid up the price of the shares in the open market. But it's something else." She leaned back, the collar of the robe falling away from her white neck, and she spoke as collectedly as if she were addressing an investment committee. "The important thing is that neither one of these men had exercised an outstanding option for *nine years*. And now they both do it simultaneously. It means something . . . can't you see that, Poke? I *know* something must be in the works. Something big is about to happen in that company."

"How can you be so sure?" he countered. But there was something in her manner that told him she was right. Right enough, that is, to play the percentages; that was all you could hope for in the stock market.

"Oh, it happens," she said. "If you keep watching a situation, you can spot the tiny point that other people overlook. Why, it's like the first split in Telephone. Remember that?"

He nodded. "I was in the Atlanta office then," he said.

"Well, an analyst who had been following Telephone for years, interviewing company officials and getting no more than the polite time of day, *he* suddenly spotted something. A big jump in retained earnings. That made this man willing to go out on a limb and predict an increase in Telephone's dividend —and its first stock split ever—when nobody else in Wall Street could see it."

He resisted the temptation to tell her that Thatcher Kimbridge had climbed aboard the bandwagon for Emerson Coal. If a person thought you were smart, let him have his way. That was Rule One on Wall Street. Rule Two was never call attention to your mistakes. Poke swore under his breath. How different it all was from running on an open track for all the world to see. Sometimes a breeze could spring up, slanting across the grass oval just enough to throw you off pace—

"The stock," he said abruptly. "That metal stock you mentioned."

"Oh, yes." She gave him the name.

That morning he put four customers into the stock. He waited several days and then encouraged more clients to buy it. He had to move with care. If he loaded up accounts heavily with a single stock, Thatcher Kimbridge might become suspicious. By the end of the week he had put a dozen customers into the new situation.

The following week the stock began to move. Soon it was up four points. He realized what was happening. After Carol gave him a new stock, she would wait awhile and then begin filtering the same information out to the institutions she serviced. The institutions, with cash piling up, were hungry for investment ideas with a story. Carol Tracey obliged the institutions. And Poke's customers were getting the finest sponsorship imaginable. She had smiled at Poke one morning at breakfast and said, "It's the strangest thing, but you know something? I feel, well, more creative these days. I've never been so full of ideas."

His initial skepticism about her ability had vanished. Carol possessed a knack for analyzing the market that was just as real as his own racing ability in college. And now he was running on her legs in Wall Street.

He came to understand other things about her. There was her consuming hatred for David Hillyer. "Oh, I can't stand that man!" she had said with a shiver. "He has his secretary write a letter to his mother every day and he signs it right after the market closing. Signs the letter without even reading it. And that's not all! He has a hatchet hanging in his private bathroom at the office"—a malicious smile crossed her face—"so that he can hack his way out if the door ever jams. That's been known to happen downtown when a building settles. Why, Mr. Hillyer even has a telephone installed in his bathroom. I mean, how can anyone trust a man whose own friends call him David? Never Dave. I'll make a confession. I got my job through a lie—and now I'm glad I did lie! Why, it was the most adventurous thing I'd ever done since eating a grasshopper on a dare at the age of twelve. During the interview Mr. Hillyer asked me if I knew how to use a slide rule.

Heavens! I'd never even *touched* a slide rule before. But I told him I was an expert. Do you know, Poke, what I did? I ran out of that interview and bought a slide rule at the first store I could find. Then I spent the entire weekend mastering that damned stick. Now I can calculate a stock yield in less time than it takes me to zip up a dress. Well, anyway, I got the job. My price was right, you see. For the first couple years I was an assistant analyst. I specialized in electric utilities, because Mr. Hillyer thinks some women have orderly minds and that's fine for utility stocks. Finally, I brought a couple of outside situations to his attention —I was scared to death I might be wrong!—and he got the message. *After* the stocks went up. He let me climb out of utilities. You know where? Portfolio analysis. That's what I did for three years. Advise rich clients on how to invest their money." She brushed a speck of bacon into her palm and dropped it into the empty coffee cup. "I came to hate all those people I never saw. All that money . . . why, it's perfectly unbelievable how much money some hardware store owner in Joliet, Illinois, has in the stock market! We won't take an individual account, you understand, unless we can tack on an advisory fee. The fee is tax deductible, that's what Mr. Hillyer always says, and people fall for it."

Her voice had a way of turning hard when she talked about the wealthy clients of the firm. But if she hated Mr. Hillyer and his rich clients, it became equally obvious to Poke how much she loved her father. One night that was all she had talked about. He was, Poke told himself, a regular A.A.U. champion of a listener.

"My father's never been a success at business," she said. "Oh, his prospects were very bright at first. He was the treasurer for a small chain of grocery stores before he was thirty-five"—her head tilted proudly— "and then came the Crash. He was out of work for the longest while and then finally he became a salesman for a beer company. Only his brand of beer never seemed to sell very well on that particular route. He'd walk into a bar and ask for a bottle of beer. His brand was always on the bottom. The bottles are interlaced in the ice but why were all the other brands on top? I'll tell you. Daddy wasn't paying off the icer like his competition did. The icer—he's the fellow who stacks the bottles in the ice—had his hand out for a payoff. But poor Daddy didn't think that was ethical." Her eyes held tiny pinpoints of light, like the eyes of a stage performer reflecting the gleam of the spotlight. "He's such a sweet, sweet man. But he never had a chance in the business world. Whenever we were all home for dinner, my brother and his family and my mother and myself, he would look around the table and he'd say, 'This is nice, this is very nice.' I had a dream once. Daddy was lying in his coffin and all of us were gathered around. He sat up in the coffin and gave us a long look. Finally, he said in a whisper, 'This is nice, this is very nice,' and then he fell back." She stood up and stroked the top of the coffeepot. "Daddy always crooks the coffee mug with his middle finger," she said softly. "His index finger was shot off in World War I."

She began giving him little presents. A black knit tie, expensive linen handkerchiefs, an Alfa-Romeo model to adorn his desk at the office. "Women buy 85 per cent of men's underwear," she said one day. "I'm a regular storehouse for random facts." She saw the expression on his face and never purchased any underwear for him. But one night there was a present in a long, flat box with a ribbon on it. A long-handled shoehorn. When Poke Jeffers accepted the shoehorn without a fight, he realized how far down the road he had traveled with Carol.

Once she gave him a green plant for his apartment; in turn he gave it to the superintendent's wife. He refused to let her visit the apartment, as if that permitted him a tiny vestige of freedom. But he came often to Brooklyn Heights and the Monster was hidden each night behind the chair in the bedroom.

One morning, a Saturday, she offered to wash his stump socks and she did not understand why he became so angry.

"Let's go for a walk," he said abruptly.

Then, in the reflection of a shopwindow two blocks from her apartment, he noticed something. Carol was limping, exactly the way he limped when he was tired.

He stalked on, correcting his gait as he went.

At the next street crossing they had to detour around an excavation set off by fluttering Con Edison flags. The rocks that had been removed from the pavement were piled neatly beside the curb and a generator was humming nearby. Poke looked down into the hole, with Carol a step behind him, and he saw the exposed pipes and cables, covered with a layer of white dust, running beneath the crust of the pavement. There was a surgical precision to the excavation; it was like an incision made upon a human body.

She began to ask him about his customers at Kimbridge & Co. He told her about Mrs. Gustavson who had just returned from a trip to Europe.

"She's writing a novel," Poke said. "A novel about Ireland. Some garage mechanic is the hero."

"What happens?" Carol asked.

"She has a flat tire."

"What does the mechanic do?"

"He takes care of her flat tire."

"Oh."

"I was reading a novel the other night while you were taking a shower," she said. "It was by some Russian author."

"You liked it?"

"It was very sad. It was about this man and woman. He was a count and she had met him at a dance. They were in love, I'm sure of that. But the saddest thing happened. They were out in the garden and he seemed about to propose to her. And then, all of a sudden, a bird flew out of a bush and frightened the girl. The spell was broken. Just by that silly little bird."

"Then what happened?"

"Oh, they drifted apart. I told you it was very sad."

22

The cab hurtled along the East River Drive. White-caps flecked the river, an oily gray in the cold rays of the morning sun.

Ralph Creek turned to Thatcher and spoke, a lawyer's voice, cautious and low. "What do you hear about David Hillyer?"

Thatcher grunted. "Nothing much," he said. "As a matter of fact, somebody told me the other day he's trying to steal a chef from some fancy Italian restaurant. For the private dining room of Hillyer & Hunt." He wrinkled his nose. It was Friday morning and he felt a hundred years old.

Creek ran his hands across the lid of his brief case. "There's another merger he also happens to have in mind," he said.

"Oh?"

"You haven't heard?"

"No, not a thing. Frankly, he's not my favorite human being."

"I know," said Creek. He inspected an iron fence

rail blurring beside the Drive. "Thatch," he said earnestly, "I'm going to tell you something. Something that would horrify my law partners if they knew what I was doing. Even if it means jeopardizing the interests of a client . . . you ever feel a conflict of interest in the brokerage business?" Creek's heavy lid was drooping low over his eye as he regarded Thatcher.

"Sure," replied Thatcher with a short laugh. "That's our specialty. Conflicts of interest. Why?"

"Well, Seth has been talking to David Hillyer. Talking merger. Your firm with Hillyer & Hunt. I don't happen to approve of their tactics."

"What?" Thatcher stared at Creek. "You're serious, aren't you?" he said finally.

"I'm very serious. One of my partners does some work for Hillyer & Hunt. Now you know why—the conflict of interest."

"Yes-s-s." Thatcher's breath blew a cone of frosted air inside the cab. The towers of Wall Street surfaced on the horizon. "Which firm," he said carefully, "would be the surviving one?" A pair of small clouds, dark and vicious, seemed to jeer at him like capers.

"One guess. Hillyer & Hunt. The plan is that Seth would be high up, too." Creek rapped his knuckles on the brief case. "That's all I've got," he said.

"I'm much obliged to you, Ralph," Thatcher said softly. The outline of 50 Wall drew nearer. So that was it, he thought, seeing Seth's plan now as clearly as the skyline before him. "He won't get away with this," Thatcher said.

"Seth?"

"Yes, Seth."

"Well, you'd better move fast. I don't have to tell you, that's the best way to head off a mutiny." The lawyer shook his head. "Lord!" he exclaimed. "Why would Seth want to do a thing like this!"

297

"David Hillyer has a genuine Sheraton table in the partners' dining room," said Thatcher, thinking aloud.

"I know, I know. There's already a little joke going. About how the table is round so that nobody will sit at the head after the deal is done—"

"*There will never be a deal!* Not with Kimbridge & Co. and David Hillyer's firm, dammit!"

"That's the way I like to hear you talk," Ralph Creek said. "But Thatch, don't waste any time."

"Don't worry. I won't." The managing partner of Kimbridge & Co. began to rub the side of his nose furiously.

"Miss Donahue. Get Mr. Voorhees on the floor, please. Tell him I want to see him this afternoon."

A few minutes later Miss Donahue reappeared. "I'm sorry, Mr. Kimbridge, but Mr. Voorhees says he's got an appointment this afternoon that he simply cannot break. And he's going away for the weekend. Will Monday morning be all right?"

Thatcher Kimbridge hesitated. What urgent appointment could Seth have set for this afternoon? Did it concern Hillyer & Hunt? Or was it something to do with a client? The managing partner glared at the chattering stock ticker. "All right," he said finally to his secretary, "Monday morning."

Ralph Creek was right, of course. He must move quickly. He must call Seth's hand. Monday, he reflected grimly, so Monday would become D-Day.

If Seth developed the proper momentum, he could take over Kimbridge & Co. as neatly as any mutiny at sea. Or he might destroy the firm in the process. Thatcher had known this to happen to another member firm only last spring. One morning a delegation had marched into the office of the senior partner and presented him with an ultimatum: move aside or we take out our capital. The senior partner, dazed and angry, had decided to make a fight of it. Two weeks later the best men in the Underwriting Department had departed for a large wire house. Then the commodity partner left, followed by a group of bond traders. Worst of all, large amounts of capital were withdrawn from the firm. Today the firm survived but it was only a skeleton. And in time the customers would begin to wonder and the firm would collapse like a house of cards. Already the talk was filtering beyond Wall Street.

Yes, the same thing could happen right here, despite his name and his money and the friendships of forty years. It was like an unexpected movement in some stock, random factors suddenly crystallizing to trigger a disastrous decline. Monday. He must deal with Seth on Monday.

Thatcher Kimbridge picked up a pencil and pressed its sharp point into the back of his hand. He inspected the small gray imprint with a sense of detachment, as though the hand and the prick of pain belonged to someone else.

He had his own private appraisal of the firm: Kimbridge & Co. was big enough to buy a computer but too small to hold a two-week seminar for its office managers at the Westchester Country Club. That was the size of it precisely.

The gap was steadily widening between the giant wire houses and the medium-sized firms such as Kimbridge & Co. that did a public business. These firms were the most expendable ones in the brokerage community; they had to compete with the biggest houses and their fixed costs would not permit them to concentrate, say, on institutional accounts such as some of the smaller specialty firms.

He rubbed the pencil mark morosely. The big

houses did so many things in this era of image building—how he hated the phrase!—that Kimbridge & Co. could not afford to do. They sponsored art shows for employees and when they opened a new office they served more champagne and hors d'oeuvres than a wedding reception. He knew one firm that had instituted a *Manual for Developing Production*—it was used on "problem" customers' men who generated less than $30,000 a year in commission business—and another wire house that kept a staff psychologist on its payroll.

In the old days how different it had been! The clerks were all men; they were invariably Irish and they preferred bonuses to salary increases in good years. You could always tell when times were flush on Wall Street because the first thing a clerk would do when he received his bonus—that is, after stopping off for a few drinks—was to go to a haberdashery store and buy a new hat. Even a dozen years ago nobody on the Street ever mentioned things like "scientific management." The truth was that the brokerage business was becoming every day more like any other form of business. It was becoming progressively departmentalized and computerized and organized—and there was nothing in the world he or anybody else could do about it.

After his father's death, Thatcher had begun emphasizing other sources of principal business—municipal bonds and underwriting, as well as mutual funds—while seeing to it that the firm steadily increased its share of Stock Exchange volume. It was simply part of the balanced approach that became necessary in an era of competing with the giants. Kimbridge & Co. had to fight the large wire houses on every front: research, service, speed of executions, over-the-counter markets, expanded benefits for employees. But it could not afford such niceties as a telephone-answering service to supply stock-market quotations to the public.

The answer, of course, was more money. That was the great advantage of incorporation. A brokerage firm could begin to budget against the future. Thatcher Kimbridge tapped the pencil on his desk.

Meanwhile, you had to coddle and to wheedle. He had divided the bank business of Kimbridge & Co. The pay-roll account in one bank, the commodities account in another bank, the cash balance some place else—and brokers' loans for carrying margin accounts at eight different banks. He permitted himself an ironic grunt. The surest source of profit for Kimbridge & Co. was not in outguessing the stock market but in putting the customers' own funds to use. Net debit balances meant a minimum of a half point of daylight —almost entirely pure profit—between the rates charged by the banks to Kimbridge & Co. and the interest charged in turn by the firm to its margin clients.

In his father's day, the firm used only one bank. "Simplifies the bookkeeping"—that had been Jared Kimbridge's reasoning. Such a procedure today simply would mean lost business to the firm.

There were ways, of course, to generate additional income. An investment advisory service on a fee basis was one possibility. Other houses did it and reaped a handsome profit. They took customer accounts with a minimum of $100,000 and applied a supervisory fee schedule. But Thatcher believed firmly that any customer of Kimbridge & Co., regardless of the size of the account, should not be required to pay such a fee. He agreed with Howard Merriam on another score: the smallest customer received research reports on the same day they were made available to institutional

301

clients. Some of his friends on the Street, when they commented on this policy of Kimbridge & Co., were distinctly uncomplimentary.

Merge, an inner voice spoke, why not merge?

Yes, there was that possibility for Kimbridge & Co. with some firm other than Hillyer & Hunt. But merger was a ticklish matter. It was like marriage: you never knew how it would work out until you tried it and then it was too late. He was committed, moreover, to the principle that any merger must leave Kimbridge & Co. as the surviving firm—both in name and in fact. Only last week he had received a nibble from a slightly smaller house based in California. The firm did not have its own man on the floor and it decided it no longer wished to remain a correspondent house. Thatcher had been flattered by the invitation—"Our registered reps get up early," the firm's senior partner had said to him with a chuckle. "They're on the job at six o'clock sharp so they can be ready when you boys open up in New York"—but his innate caution had prompted him to do some quiet investigating. There might be some other reason . . . the senior partner had seemed just a little too anxious to join forces. Thatcher's suspicion proved correct. The money partner, he found out from a college friend on the West Coast, had leukemia. It was only a matter of months before his capital—one-third of all the capital in the firm—would be withdrawn. So Thatcher had politely declined the invitation.

Money partners—he rubbed his nose again—were people he had never respected, anyway. A money partner never pulled his own oar. They were taken into brokerage firms—Thatcher knew of a dozen such cases on Wall Street—for one reason: they provided the capital. In turn the brokerage house provided a desk or, if enough money were involved, a private office with a secretary. The money partners never produced any business. They took long lunches and held interminable telephone conversations, talking for hours with other money partners or with the professional at the golf club or with their gardener. He knew one money partner on Pine Street who spent four hours a day listening to recordings provided by the John Birch Society.

The stock ticker beside his desk idled for a few moments. When he visited a branch office of the firm, the first thing he always did was to stand by a ticker and feel the tape upon his fingers as if to reassure himself that the market still existed. It was his reaffirmation of reality. He did not in his heart accept the new electronic quotation machines and, much to the disgust of the customers' men at 50 Wall, he would not permit any of these desk units to be installed in the board room.

The narcotic effect of the stock market was unescapable for him. Two years earlier he had taken Edith to London for a holiday and they had stayed at the Connaught. Quite unaccountably, at tea in the lounge, Thatcher got into a violent argument with an earl who had been boasting about the loopholes in England's death duties for the very rich. Edith understood the signs. The following morning she told him, "We're going home. You tell the desk downstairs and arrange for space on the plane. Tonight. I'll pack."

"But why?" he protested, half-heartedly, and she had simply kissed him and pushed him out of the bedroom.

Thatcher picked up the tape and stared absently at the prices. Yes, he thought, everything was changing so rapidly. The buildings on Wall Street always looked the same but that, too, was part of the deception. Suddenly a boyish grin crossed his face. There were still ways to fight; his mind hovered momentarily on the telegrapher who sat in one corner of the firm's order room. He was an old man who wore a green eyeshade and, to the casual observer, he would be regarded as an anachronism in this electronic age. Yet there was something remarkable about this old telegrapher. He maintained contact with the Boston office and he could work just as fast as the teletype machines. The telegrapher's fingers moved in a blur as he sat hunched over his sending key, and the empty can of pipe tobacco in the resonator box beside him sent up a steady raucous clacking that was like music to the ears of the managing partner. The day would come when a machine would replace the old telegrapher—Thatcher was resigned to this eventuality—but as long as he wanted the job it was his.

"Mr. Kimbridge . . ."

Miss Donahue was hovering just inside the door.

"Yes, what is it?"

"That man from the advertising agency. He's here again. He's out in the reception room. Said he was in the neighborhood and wondered if you might see him."

"Tell him I'm in conference. I don't want to see him."

She closed the door quietly.

Madison Avenue! The man was a vice president in a large agency uptown. He wanted to sell Thatcher on a campaign he had dreamed up. What rot! Kimbridge & Co. fashioned its own image. With every underwriting and with every telephone call by a customers' man. Furthermore, the firm had been served by the same downtown agency since its inception. In the winter of 1907 a young man had prevailed upon his father: "You've just started a brokerage house. Well, I've just opened my own advertising agency. I want your business. If you can't afford to pay me, I'll carry you on credit for a year." Jared Kimbridge had been unable to resist the bargain. Thereupon, he consented to running the first tombstone ad of Kimbridge & Co. Over the intervening years the two firms—the brokerage house and the advertising agency—had prospered together. "And nobody else," Thatcher now said aloud, "will ever get our business."

His eyes fell to the photograph of Brit on the desk. He thought again about Poke Jeffers. Yes, it was uncanny. Something about young Jeffers—a kind of defiance of spirit lurking behind his face—reminded Thatcher so acutely of his own son.

He remembered then about the government bonds he planned to buy for Edith. Bonds . . .

Three weeks before his father died he had bought half a million dollars' worth of Treasury bonds at an eight-point discount. For estate purposes these bonds later had been redeemed at par. It was his father's last trade and even from the grave Jared Kimbridge had managed to turn a profit.

23

Carol met him at the door on Saturday and said, "Close your eyes." She led him into the living room. "All right," she said, "you can open your eyes."

A color television set reposed on a gold stand opposite the sofa.

"Good Lord!" he said. "That's not for me?"

"No," she said, laughing. "I'd really love to give it to you. But I know you're too proud to take it. Besides—that would give me a legitimate reason for getting inside your apartment. No, sweetheart, it's not for you."

"You bought it?"

She shook her head. "It was sent to me on a, well, trial basis. By the manufacturer. It's the very latest model. But even the stores won't be stocking it for another couple months."

"What's the deal?"

She took his hands and, humming softly, waltzed him in front of the set. He kept his balance and the

Monster moved smoothly. She stopped after a few steps, smiling at him, and said, "The deal is that I happen to know the treasurer of the company. In a very genteel way he's asking me to take a look at his company's stock and—"

"And maybe suggest it as a purchase for the clients of Hillyer & Hunt," he finished. "You're not going to do it, are you?"

"Of course not. But I'm going to hang on to the set. For a while, anyhow." She kissed the dimple on his cheek. "You see, my sweet, I'm far more shameless than you."

"Don't say that!" he said sharply.

He saw then that he had hurt her. "Come here," he commanded. She came to him obediently and he kissed her. "There," he said, "that's better, isn't it?"

She gave a quick nod. "I thought we might watch a football game this afternoon," she said. "Just to christen the set. I was waiting until you got here before I turned it on. The game's already started."

A few minutes later they were settled on the sofa. Carol had hooked her hand under Poke's right knee.

Blue jerseys and gold helmets bobbing on the field, swelling into the television screen. Girls crouched in fur coats waving frantically at the camera as it panned across the crowd. The drone of an airplane passing overhead. And then a voice drifting into the microphone, "Hey-y-eh, who wants a hot dog he-e-e-ahh? *Hot dog!*"

The game throbbed into the living room.

". . . two evenly matched teams in this Ivy League classic, you have to admire their fighting spirit down there." The announcer's voice was smooth, almost patronizing.

"It's like a blossom opening!" cried Carol.

"What is?" asked Poke.

"Why, the huddle. When it breaks up."

"Yeah." Poke watched the quarterback, hands poised to take the ball from the center, and he tried to guess the play.

"Hut . . . hut." The voice of the quarterback, a spindly faraway cry, drifted into the room. His shoulders jerked downward with each call.

Poke had figured the play correctly: a sweep to the right. A line backer rushed up to plug the hole. Good for three yards.

The runner, still lying flat, waited until the tackler climbed off his chest. Then he flipped the ball to the referee standing above him in an immaculate white shirt with black stripes. The runner had been hit hard. When he got up from the ground he walked like an old man back to the huddle.

". . . on the forty-two-yard line," said the announcer in creamy tones. Poke began to hate the announcer.

Carol was sitting on the edge of the sofa, her mouth half open with excitement. "Oh, darn!" she exclaimed. "I keep losing the ball."

"Watch the guards. The ball carrier will follow them. There—see?"

"Yes, I see now."

"Watch his hand go to the ground. That kept his knee from touching."

It was a gang tackle, the kind of tackle that could snap a runner's neck if he were off balance just enough. Poke felt the weary anguish of the ball carrier; the ground was hard and cold to his touch and the perspiration glued the shoulder pads onto his skin.

"The line backers are blitzing," Poke said suddenly. "Dammit," he yelled out to the quarterback, "call a draw play!"

The camera swung toward the side lines. There was a cheer from the stands. The camera caught a girl waving her pennant, a Roman Catholic priest crossing himself and, for a moment behind the goal post, three paraplegics sitting in wheel chairs. Brilliant red blankets covered the laps of the paraplegics. High above their heads appeared the silver gleam of a tilted flask.

"I went to an Army-Navy game in Philadelphia once," Carol said. "A store buyer from Columbus took me. We had seats right behind the Cadet corps. But guess what. The Cadets stood up all through the game. So we had to stand, too, or we couldn't see the players."

"You had no business there," said Poke, his eyes remaining on the screen.

"Why? What do you mean?" Her face was puzzled. "We paid for our seats. Ten dollars a seat."

"It was their game," said Poke. And then, "Nothing. Forget it."

She was watching the television set again and it was as if she were part of the crowd. Poke could picture her sitting in the stands watching the Ohio State team, then after the game going on a hayride in the country. The country lanes would have only the moon for light.

". . . makes the score twenty-five to six in this brilliant duel with just three minutes to go until half time." The announcer gave the impression that the battle of the century was unfolding before the television audience—and that the final outcome was anybody's guess.

Poke snorted with disgust. The truth was that it was a terrible game. Five touchdowns and only a single extra point. The freshman team at Georgia, he thought, could lick these squads in the same afternoon. The thing that was real was the pain of the players, no matter how poorly they performed, no matter how badly they were coached.

"The set works fine, don't you think?" asked Carol.

"Yes."

Poke stood up. He kept passing an ash tray from hand to hand as he watched the screen. He winced as a defensive end got trapped; his knees bent as the man went down.

"Would you like a cigar?" asked Carol. "I got some special from Dunhill's. Just in case you ever felt like one. They're very good cigars, the salesman said. Each one comes in its own aluminum tube."

"No," he said. "No, I don't want a cigar."

It was half time. He went over to the set and lowered the volume so that he would not have to listen to the announcer's voice. A band marched onto the field, playing noiselessly, and strung out to form the initials of the visiting college.

"My," said Carol. "It looks just like a ticker symbol."

Poke put the ash tray on the table.

"Did you play football?" Carol said. "I had the feeling you were waiting for the coach to send you into the game."

"Not after my sophomore year in college. I gave up football so I wouldn't injure my legs for track."

"Were you good? At football, I mean."

He shrugged. "I was a tailback. I was always running the option play. But I didn't pass very much. I guess I liked to run too much."

"The crowd. Would you hear it cheering while you ran? In track, I mean."

He looked at her. Her eyes were round saucers staring at him. "No," he said slowly, "you don't hear it at all."

"Oh . . . well, I guess I was wrong about that."

The sun glinted on the silver buttons of the drum major. He led the band stiffly off the field, his white plume waving and the baton keeping time to the music they could not hear. The cheeks of a tuba player went in and out, in and out, in a close-up shot.

"It's almost like watching a silent movie," she said.

He sat down on the sofa. The stump was beginning to throb.

The teams were coming out on the field.

Carol jumped up. "I'll turn up the volume," she said.

In the third quarter the leading team quickly punched across two more touchdowns. The game had degenerated into a rout. Even the announcer had become subdued; he devoted the empty moments to recalling stirring battles of the past between the two teams.

"Look! They're clotheslining him!" shouted Poke. He half rose from the sofa.

"Who? What? I don't see any clothesline."

Poke turned to glare at her. "That substitute quarterback, the fellow who's thrown three bum passes in a row. That's who. He's starting to duck. No wonder he's so wild. One of the defensive tackles just caught him with an arm."

The team punted and Carol gave Poke a pleading look. "I . . . I don't understand what you mean," she said finally.

"Okay. I'll show you," he said. "A clothesline in football is this." He brought his stiffened forearm up under her chin. "The defensive man catches you smack in the neck. It's ten times worse than being tackled. Some linemen wrap cardboard around their arms and then cover it with tape. It's like getting hit with a plaster-of-Paris cast." He lowered his arm. "I

311

saw it happen to a back at Georgia. This fellow had
release time like nobody you ever saw. Eyes in the
back of his head. Perfect coordination. He'd start ped-
daling back with the ball and then he'd pivot like
this"—Poke's knee brushed against the carpenter's
bench—"and throw forty yards downfield. Bull's-eye.
And then in a game against Tech he got the clothesline treatment. That was the end of him. He started
ducking when the defense swarmed in. He was a
washout after that game." Poke slapped his thigh savagely. "Now do you see what I mean?" he demanded.

"I—I guess so. But what should he have done, this
back?"

He looked at her. "There's just one thing you do in
a case like that," he said slowly. "The next time the
clothesliner comes at you, you forget your receivers
for one play. You step back and give it to him. You
bullet the ball right square at his helmet with all your
might. It does the trick. I know. I did it once."

"What happened?"

"Hah! You should have seen that tackle. His eyes
puffed up like black balloons. They had to lead him
off the field. But nobody on that team ever tried to
clothesline me again."

"Oh . . . I see."

"No, you don't," he said hoarsely. "Not really. How
can you? You're just saying that." He stamped over to
the television set and glared down at it.

". . . goes the stretcher," crooned the announcer.
"And naturally our deepest sympathy goes to the
player. But just remember, fans, as soon as the team
doctor determines just how badly he's hurt we'll pass
on the word to you."

On the field a player was rocking in agony. His
teammates stood around him helplessly in a half circle. The player was covering his face with one arm

312

but Poke recognized him: it was the quarterback. For a moment Poke felt himself become the injured man.

"And now this message from our sponsor," the announcer said. On the screen appeared a young man and a girl leaning over the rail of a ferryboat. They were smiling at each other and smoking cigarettes and inhaling blissfully.

"Go to hell," Poke said to the television set. He switched it off.

Carol left the room quietly. When she returned a few minutes later he glanced at her. He saw that she had put on fresh lipstick.

"Hello," she said tentatively. She was frightened.

"Hello."

She made another try. "Will you take me on the Staten Island ferry sometime?" she asked.

"Sure," he said. "Any time." He looked out the window and counted the leaves on a tree.

"Oh, Poke, you really mustn't hate yourself. There's nothing you can do."

He turned his back to her. He placed his forehead on the window and felt the coolness of the glass.

Then, a little while later, he heard the rattle of pans across the room.

"Guess what," she said with forced gaiety. "I'm going to cook supper for you. Actually *cook*. Do you like wild rice?"

"I guess so."

"Well, I bought a special strainer the other day. One where the rice doesn't touch the water. That's the secret of wild rice, the cookbook says. It must steam for four hours and then break open slowly."

"That's great. Just great."

She busied herself with the preparations for dinner. Then she came over to him by the window.

She placed a hand on his chest. "Please," she said.

Her eyes were pleading with him. He let her loosen his black knit tie. She started toward the bedroom. "I'll pull the blinds," she said. "You'll see. It will be just like nighttime."

He followed her slowly. He could hear the water bubbling on the stove. Four hours, he thought, four hours.

On the bed lay her nightgown and beside it a pair of men's pajamas. Another present from Carol.

It seemed an eternity before she spoke to him again. . . .

"What is it about skiing," she asked softly, "that made you love it so much? I've always been too frightened to ski."

She turned toward him in the bed. Despite the darkness he could see her navel creasing into a soft V shape. The nightgown was rolled up around her ribs.

"Skiing?" he repeated. He was silent for a few moments. Then he said, "When you ski, you're all alone. . . ."

She drew his head down to her throat. He could feel the pulse throbbing against his lips.

"Ah, my sweet," she said. "You're not alone any longer. You have your Carol."

24

"Gentlemen, I don't think we have much choice in this matter," Thatcher Kimbridge declared with an air of finality. He glanced sourly at the ceiling of his office and for a moment he seemed to visualize the computer room directly overhead. "It comes under a new classification in our business. The care and feeding of electronic computers."

The dawn-patrol meeting was drawing to its close.

"The simple fact is," Thatcher continued, "that a clerk from Purchases and Sales happened to discover a reel of magnetic tape lying in the gutter on the Pine Street side of this building. Luckily for us, he saw the firm's name on the reel and picked it up. A single reel of magnetic tape containing our entire list of customers. Think what it would mean if another brokerage firm had access to that reel! It would be like breaking the enemy's secret code—"

"I still don't understand," interrupted Julian Everly,

"how that reel got there in the first place. We don't just toss those things out the window."

"My guess is that it fell off the truck that carts away our waste paper," replied Thatcher. "We dispose of our computer reels the same way. This was the run from last month's customer list. We have a new reel upstairs that is up to date."

"Christ," muttered Everly with a look at the ceiling. "It's like having your mother-in-law living right above you." He stroked his mustache gingerly.

"It's not that bad!" Andy Kraft sprang to the defense of his beloved computer. "Anything with a set of rules," he said proudly, "you can program on a computer."

"Too bad we haven't gotten to the point where we can program mothers-in-law," said Seth Voorhees, and an appreciative chuckle ran around the table. The floor partner was wearing a blue shirt with white cuffs and a white detachable collar. Over his shirt was a vest with lapels and the hair stripes of his shirt matched perfectly the stripes of his suit jacket. He was dressed with his characteristic flair that seemed more suited to the House of Lords than to Wall Street.

"I think our course is clear," Thatcher said, letting the murmur expire and then coming in forcibly like an actor determined that he would not be upstaged. "The thing to do is to buy a shredding machine and install it in the basement. That way there's no chance of anything of this sort happening again. We can dispose of our own waste material. Of course, there's the amortized cost of the machine and we'll need to hire two men to run it. But on the other hand we'll save something on our disposal bill." He looked quickly at the yellow pad before him. "My preliminary estimate is that the daylight between the new costs and what

316

we stand to save amounts to—ummh—about eight thousand a year."

"On the debit side?" asked Howard Merriam.

"What else?" replied the managing partner. He paused. "Are we all agreed, gentlemen, on the purchase of a shredding machine?"

The partners nodded their assent. Miss Donahue wrote busily on her pad.

If only the plan of incorporation could pass through this smoothly, Thatcher was thinking. By tacit agreement the partners seemed to understand that his plan would not come before the meeting this morning. That realization lent a certain note of jocularity to the session. Seth, in particular, appeared to be in good spirits. But Thatcher thought he detected turbulence beneath the outward calm: the ash tray in front of the floor partner was heaped with half-inch cigarette butts.

Fred Lincoln turned to Red Hooker and said, "I hear you're planning to sell your house."

Hooker winked and a wide grin split his face. "That's right," he said. "Got an offer I just can't afford to turn down. From a toy manufacturer who made it big with a new kind of doll. Damn dolls are rigged so that they can eat pablum. He's named a price that gives me a profit of a hundred ten thousand." Hooker rubbed a hand over his bald head. "Hell's bells, I couldn't sleep nights if I turned that down."

"What about Priscilla?" said Everly across the table. "She's more married to that house than to you. What're you going to tell her?"

"She'll go along," said Hooker confidently. "If she doesn't, I'll tell everybody in the neighborhood that she's four years older than I am. And *that* would make her leave."

"Oats will follow corn, that's it?" said Everly.

317

"You've got it," replied the commodity partner. "Besides, I've got a new place all picked out. A French country manor house. Complete with its own gymnasium and a sauna bath. Priscilla can have a field day doing that place over. She won't be able to resist the challenge."

"How's the sod at the new place?" The question came from Fred Lincoln. On his pad the bond partner had just landed a golf ball in a treacherous sand trap shielded by rolling embankments.

"Great!" exclaimed Hooker. "You can putt on the front lawn all the way out to the mailbox. It's a French Provincial mailbox."

"Buy it," said Lincoln.

Thatcher's thoughts shifted momentarily to the computer room upstairs. The second night crew would be finishing its work just about now and the computer, implacable and nerveless, almost flaunting its lack of concern about the stock market, actually would remain idle until early afternoon. Then the first transactions of the day would begin to be programmed into the machine and by nightfall, with Wall Street turning into a ghost city, the computer would settle down to its work in earnest. All through the night the colored reels would spin in the computer room. The computer tallied the free credit balance of every customer account in Kimbridge & Co.; it handled the bookkeeping chores and it figured buying power. It prepared dividend checks for printout and it assembled confirmations for each trade made during the day. The reels clicked and the computer worked with mystical speed.

Somehow Thatcher never had quite gotten used to the machine upstairs, a machine whose inner operations he did not pretend to understand. He realized, as the head of a brokerage house, how vital automa-

318

tion had become. Without access to a computer, Kimbridge & Co. could not compete; it was that simple. He remembered how his father would stalk into the Margin Department in the old days and peer about like a proud eagle. The margin accounts were posted by hand and his father could smell whether the stock market was going up or down simply by observing the activity of the margin clerks. It was an uncanny knack of his father's, something that could never be programmed into an unreceptive human brain in a million years. And now the computer, utilizing a single magnetic tape that outwardly resembled a reel of motion-picture film, could conduct the margin run for the entire firm in forty minutes. Untouched by human hand. If his father were to walk into the computer room this moment, the only scent he could detect would be that of a newly-cleaned Pullman car.

Thatcher brought his mind back to the battleground; the time was ripe to drop a shell.

"Gentlemen," he said, "there is another matter that I'm sure we've all been giving a lot of thought. The incorporation of Kimbridge & Co." Thatcher glanced at Voorhees and saw the floor partner's finger stiffen as he ground out a cigarette. "I want us to take a vote at our final meeting before Christmas. That would get us just under the wire. There will be no problem drawing up the papers." He paused and then said softly, "If we decide in favor of it, I'd like to start out the new year as a corporation. And by that time we'll have added a new man to our group here."

The stock ticker across the room was cheerfully running its test sequences. "EZEZEZ . . ." The ticker sound swelled and then died away as the partners scraped back their chairs.

"Oh, Seth," the managing partner called out, "would you mind staying a moment?"

319

Voorhees looked impatiently at his watch. "I've got a call coming in on my private line," he said. "It's quite urgent. Would you see me in my office, Thatch? Say, fifteen minutes?"

"All right. Your office. Fifteen minutes." It was like confirming a trade, Thatcher thought.

At Seth Voorhees' insistence the temperature of his corner office was maintained fifteen degrees cooler than all other offices in the bull pen. His partners told a story about Seth's squash-playing days at Princeton. He had seen to it that the university squash courts were kept at the approximate temperature of a meat locker, with the result that the squash ball had virtually no bounce early in a match. This procedure had given Princeton an excellent home record at squash.

The office was unusual in other respects. It contained no chairs—an arrangement which effectively discouraged visits—but in one corner stood an old-fashioned writing desk with a sloping top. Here Seth would glance through his morning mail and then set off immediately for the floor. There was a homey touch to the office that contrasted with its essential coldness: a glass bowl filled with candies wrapped in cellophane. "Gives you quick energy." That was Seth's explanation for the candy.

On a wall shelf were five photographs. One was an informal picture of Seth Voorhees, immaculate in captain's stripes, chatting with the Secretary of the Navy. Beside it stood a row of four identical silver frames, each depicting a pretty young blond mother surrounded by several children. These photographs had been taken by the same studio which, together with the matching frames, gave them a sort of timeless unity.

"'Lo, Thatch." Seth Voorhees, hanging up the telephone, crossed quickly to the candy bowl. He unwrapped a lemon drop and popped it into his mouth. "Well," he said, peering intently at the managing partner, "what can I do for you?"

Thatcher Kimbridge shifted uncomfortably. He was aware that Seth had gained a subtle advantage by bringing him to this office. For a few moments he hesitated; he felt reluctant to say what was on his mind. It was like launching a torpedo—chances were that afterward Kimbridge & Co. would never again be quite the same. Something far more important than money was in danger of being lost.

He took a devious tack. "My accountants have hit upon an ingenious plan," he said mildly. "Like to know what you think of it. If we incorporate, there'd be no cash dividends paid out on the common stock. But we could declare sizable stock dividends from time to time in the form of a senior preferred. Fully convertible into common. That would permit the younger stockholders we take into the firm to build up their equity without putting up a single additional penny for their shares—"

"*Thatch!* I'm not interested." Voorhees crunched the lemon drop. "What do you really want to see me about? You're not a very good bluffer, you know."

"All right, Seth"—Thatcher's voice became brittle—"I'll tell you. I understand you're talking merger without my authority. A merger with Hillyer & Hunt. Is that true, Seth?"

The eyes of the floor partner flicked coldly; there was no other perceptible reaction. His eyes were those of a trader, adjusting instantly to what he sees on the stock tape.

Watching Voorhees closely, the managing partner

321

thought: God, he looks tired. But perhaps Seth was only a mirror image of himself.

Voorhees tugged calmly at the corners of his vest. Without saying a word, he moved quickly to the desk and began shuffling the unopened envelopes.

Thatcher looked away and his eyes fell upon the set of framed photographs. He realized with a start how much the four women looked alike—and that each of them bore a striking resemblance to Edith when she was young.

"All right, you hit it on the head," Seth lashed out across the room. "Frankly, I don't know how you found out. The deal would have been set to spring inside of another week." He shrugged. "But I guess it's hard to keep any kind of secret on Wall Street. It's very simple, Thatch. I think you'll wreck Kimbridge & Co. and everything we stand for by incorporating. If we have to change, it should be in the form of a bigger partnership. So now the whole thing's out in the open. Just what do you propose to do?"

"I want you to stop this jockeying around with Hillyer & Hunt. We'll just forget it ever happened, you and I—"

Voorhees was shaking his head. "Never!" he snapped. "If Kimbridge & Co. incorporates, it will do so without me." He met Thatcher's searching gaze. "I'd leave the firm," Voorhees said very softly. "I mean that, Thatch."

"Then, goddamit, you can leave the firm!" The coldness of the room closed in on Thatcher. He felt terribly old. With an effort he said, "When do you want to go?"

"End of this year. That will be fine by me. Now, if you don't mind, I'm already late for the floor."

"Yes-s-s. I realize the amount of commission business Hillyer & Hunt has gotten this year from your bank. . . ." The telephone pressed against Carol Tracey's ear like a blunt instrument of torture. "All right," she said finally, "there *is* something we can do for you. We're putting out a new institutional report one week from today. I'll send you a draft this afternoon . . . yes, you'll be the first to see it."

"Thanks, Miss Tracey. We won't forget this little favor."

Carol hung up the telephone and rubbed her ear nervously. Oh, you stupid fool, she raged at herself.

The call had come from the vice president of a bank that administered several large pension plans as trustee. There had been no mistaking the man's suggestion. He wanted his bank to get the jump on the other institutional clients of Hillyer & Hunt. A polite little bit of Wall Street pressure. Don't play ball with me, the man had said in effect, and I won't direct commissions to your firm. She hated to be placed in this sort of position; she simply could not deal with it. So good old Carol had given in. Why, the bank vice president must be laughing right this moment at her gullibility. He knew perfectly well that she was taking a calculated risk, that she could not involve anyone else at Hillyer & Hunt. That was the rule of the game—and the name of the game was money. If she were caught, her head would roll.

Carol shuddered and looked out the window. She occupied a tiny space along the back corridor of the Hillyer & Hunt offices but it was her own private world.

The view from her window was sliced and slabbed with exotic shapes. At this lofty height the buildings burst into decorative mosques and pyramids and basilicas and miniature French châteaux. A hundred yards away a mighty eagle perched atop a white stone building. The wings of the eagle were upraised and it seemed about to lift itself in flight from the row of stately Doric columns that covered up the water tanks. A ladder led up the back of the eagle and once Carol had spent half an hour, in a curious spellbound pleasure, as she watched a repairman climb up the ladder and meticulously adjust the television aerial clutched in the claws of the eagle. And then the repairman had done a perfectly extraordinary thing: he unzipped his pants and, in an unmistakable motion, proceeded to pee down upon Wall Street.

The weather played strange tricks at her window. A cloud could pass overhead and suddenly the building tops would grow gray and ominous. Sometimes it grew so dark that she could not even see the eagle; then she would be enveloped in a cloud that gave her a formless sensation. And when it snowed, the air currents tossed the snow toward the sky.

She knew that if she rose now and peered down through her window she would be able to see a slice of Trinity Church graveyard far below. The tombstones would be like flower shoots poking up through the earth. The shoeshine boys would be lining the iron fence outside the churchyard and on rainy days the fruit vendors would be standing on empty Coca-Cola boxes in order to keep their feet dry.

She thought dreamily of the rain and she imagined it beating against the window. On rainy days the rear corridor would sprout with umbrellas and the umbrellas always reminded Carol of a field of wild colored flowers all anchored to the floor, huge and ribbed and flecked with dew, snapping now as they slowly dried and sending up the damp antiseptic smell of coated silk—

She walked slowly to the door. The corridor was empty. She could hear the wind whining up the shaft of the freight elevator.

Then she thought of the room next to her own office and she shuddered again. The Fort, that was her name for the large room that now housed the Civil War collection of Mr. Hillyer. Two weeks ago this space, formerly a locker room for employees, had been preempted. The walls were covered with frayed battle flags and muster rolls used for General McClellan's troops at Antietam. On the floor were arranged muskets and powder kegs and bedrolls and every afternoon, when the sun struck the windows, Mr. Hillyer's secretary marched inside to lower the awnings. In the center of the room, accorded the place of eminence, was an ugly squat cannon with a single ball on the floor beside it. The cannon was aimed directly at Carol's desk on the other side of the wall.

She closed the door. Was that story true, she wondered, about Mr. Hillyer's grandfather? The grandfather, according to this account, had smuggled Union cavalry horses across the line and sold them to the Confederates.

Carol looked about the office in despair. "Oh," she cried out, "how does a girl like you get into this business?" She had been asked that question a hundred times since coming to Wall Street but now, in this lonely room, it sounded like an accusation instead of a feeble attempt at humor.

In desperation she thought about Poke. She had made arrangements to have the television set sent back to the company. Yes, that should please him. Carol touched her ear again. "Oh, Poke," she cried, softly this time, "Poke, my darling . . ." When she

325

was away from him now, it was as if she were not a living person but only a shadow, or no more permanent than the snow when it tossed outside her office window.

25

Izzy Padawer walked past the entrance, glanced furtively through the iron grillwork into a dim recess, and then kept walking the half block to Park Avenue.

He felt out of place in this part of the city. It was an area where in the evening wealthy Jewish men strolled two by two, their white silk ties immaculate and their wives, carefully corseted and with each hair lacquered into place, walking a few paces in front like poodles fresh from the trimming shop.

Shortly after he arrived in the United States, he had gotten up early one morning to pay a visit to Park Avenue. Izzy had a premonition that if he appeared on Park Avenue in the middle of the day the doormen—or the police—would not permit him to walk down the street. So he had stolen there shortly after dawn one summer morning. The buildings were still asleep. Hose lines snaked across the sidewalk. Attendants were washing off the walks and the rich green canopies. That was his first view of Park Avenue: a hot summer morning and water dripping like rain from the canopies.

Now it was October and the weather was raw, even on Park Avenue. And Izzy Padawer was torn by indecision.

He had made an appointment to meet a man who had called him that morning at the office. The man's name was Saul Spiegelman and he had mentioned, by way of introduction, one of Izzy's most important customers. "It's in the cards we should meet," Saul Spiegelman had said. "Something could come of it, something to our mutual"—he had stretched the word like an accordion—"advantage."

So Izzy had agreed to meet him at five-thirty in the bar of one of the most expensive restaurants in Manhattan. Saul Spiegelman had made the selection. At first Izzy was under the impression that the man wanted to open a brokerage account. But later, as he reconsidered the brief conversation, he had the feeling that this meeting was for some other purpose. Something slightly sinister . . . he had not liked Saul Spiegelman's voice.

He stood beside a lamppost, beseeching Park Avenue for strength, and watched the late-afternoon traffic choking the lanes that led southward to Grand Central Terminal. Noel Bigelow and Poke Jeffers, he knew, each had sold 1,200 shares in a secondary offering that afternoon. Izzy calculated their commission credits, triple the normal rate on a secondary, and felt the coldness of the lamppost against his shoulder. Many customers were unable to resist the lure of a secondary when it was appropriately dangled; the customer paid no commissions but purchased the stock on a net basis. And what had he done in the afternoon? He had received a visit from his uncle the runner.

His uncle had kissed him gravely and then he had told Izzy of a Jew he had met. The Jew had no money and he was out of a job. During the war he had lived in Holland, hiding from the Nazis, and in the final three months before the Allied liberation the man had subsisted on tulip bulbs. Izzy had given his uncle a check for $600 to present to the man.

Abruptly he made his decision. He strode back to the restaurant and just as he was reaching for the wrought-iron handle the door slid noiselessly open to reveal an attendant in a bright uniform. He looked like a Cossack officer ready for a dress parade.

Once inside, Izzy hesitated a few moments, letting his eyes become accustomed to a dimness that gave the unmistakable impression of luxury. He found himself standing next to a serving cart. In its center was a crystal serving bowl containing scoops of meringue topped with chipped almonds and banana slices, all floating in a sea of heavy cream. The mixture jiggled slightly and it reminded Izzy of the rich breasts he had seen once on a chorus girl.

"Pada-wer! In here, in here!"

Through an alcove, a man was waving to him. Izzy walked into the small bar and sat down at a chair that the man, without rising, had pushed out from the table.

"Saul Spiegelman," the man said, extending a heavy, damp hand.

"Yes," Izzy responded. "How do you do." He had an intense dislike for shaking hands because the Germans were so fond of it. And at the office he tried desperately to control his habit—a Jewish habit, he kept telling himself—of gesturing with his hands while he talked over the telephone.

Saul Spiegelman was a short, squat man with an enormous head. He was quite bald. His skin had the

329

texture of an Irish potato that had been scrubbed meticulously.

"Captain!" Saul Spiegelman held his hand aloft and snapped his fingers. A waiter hurried forward.

Izzy glanced quickly around the bar and saw with relief that it was almost empty and that none of the other patrons, leaning forward at their tables in the intimate half darkness, was paying the slightest attention to them.

"What'll you have?" his host asked. Before Izzy could reply, he leveled a finger at his own glass and said, "'Nother one of these for me. A King Alphonse." The name seemed to give him pleasure.

"Yes, sir," the waiter said.

"I—uh, can I just have a ginger ale?" Izzy asked.

The other man leaned back in his chair and shook with laughter. "A g-g-gin-ginger *ale?*" he sputtered. "Listen, maybe you should have a celery soda. A celery soda with a pastrami sandwich yet!" He roared with hilarity. "Captain," he said finally to the waiter, "bring my friend here a Scotch with maybe a little water." He wiped his eyes with a white handkerchief almost as large as the tablecloth.

Izzy said nothing and the waiter went away. A small glass of Scotch appeared in front of Izzy, who sat quite still as Spiegelman tasted his second drink. The cream left a rim on Spiegelman's upper lip, a streak of white against the washed potato. How could Izzy tell this man that he had a Wall Street stomach? That the only way he could drink whisky was in Pepto Bismol?

"So you are wondering why I called you, huh?"

"I have the greatest respect for Mr. Ormont," Izzy replied guardedly. Mr. Ormont was the owner of Ormont Slumberwear. He added, as if by way of proof, "I even wear his pajamas."

"Not me," said Spiegelman. "Bare ass, that's the only way to sleep." He stuffed the handkerchief back into his breast pocket.

Izzy touched the glass in front of him and drew his hand away quickly. "What is it," he said, "that I can do for you?"

"Bare ass . . ." muttered Spiegelman again. His eyes, small and red like the eyes of a hippopotamus, focused tightly upon Izzy. "So maybe you have a tootsie waiting some place? You know what honest to God I'd really like to do? I'd like to be a bum. I'd like to live in the Village and screw every sixteen-year-old girl that came by. That's what I'd like." He smiled a hippopotamus smile. "Sure," he said, "why not get down to business?" He moved his shoulders expressively. Then he said, "I understand you are the only Indian selling stocks for Kimbridge & Co. down on Wall Street. You must be pretty good."

Izzy did not understand at first what the man meant. Israel Padawer—an Indian? The little red eyes, still fastened upon him, had narrowed into slits. "Yes," Izzy said, comprehending, "yes, that is so."

"All right. I'll put my cards smack on the table. I run a couple advisory services. Over in New Jersey. Princeton. One I call my *Ivy League Trader*—howzat for a classy name? The other, it's *The SS Theorist*. Heard of 'em?"

"Yes," said Izzy. "But I never read material from the advisory ser—"

"Ho-ho!" roared Spiegelman. "So when you get insomnia I'll send you a free subscription!" He spooned soft white cheese onto a cracker and tossed the cracker into his mouth. "I have what you might call a network," he said, chewing. "A network of, well, associates . . . people in various brokerage houses. Now and then they feed me the names of certain stocks

331

that are ready for a move and"—he swallowed with a grunting noise—"I recommend the stocks in my advisory services." The red eyes riveted on the knot in Izzy's tie. "How would you like to walk on a stepladder?" he asked suddenly.

"A stepladder? I don't understand. For acrobatics I am not much."

"Ho-ho! Oh, Pada-*wer!* You are going to kill me! *Ho!*" Spiegelman finally recovered his breath. "Here," he said, his voice still gurgling, "I'll explain it to you simple like." He took a silver pen from an inside pocket and, without turning the point, traced out the imprint of a ladder on the tablecloth. "Every point a stock goes up," he said, "my associate gets one hunnert bucks. Just for fingering the stock. Hunnert bucks for every point. Every smart customers' man has all sorts of contacts. So why not give him a goose up with my stepladder, I say." He reached again into his coat. "Here. Take a look. Canceled checks from last month. From my associates. Some of the best houses in the business, you'd be surprised maybe." He tossed the bundle of checks on the tablecloth and Izzy hesitated. "Go ahead," Spiegelman said. "They won't bite you. The teeth I took out already. The point is"—he was leaning forward and Izzy could smell the sour perspiration of the man—"everything is legal, very legal. Your firm needn't know a thing. This is a personal arrangement, you could say. Nobody gets hurt and everybody wins. Even Uncle Sam. I make out a W-2 form in your name, so's Uncle gets his cut legal like. No troubles on the income tax." Saul Spiegelman spread cheese on two crackers and tossed them both into his mouth. He chewed reflectively. "Well?" he said to Izzy.

"Suppose a stock goes down? Does your associate pay *you* a hundred dollars a point?"

"Oh-ho-ho! You kill me!" The handkerchief was stabbing again at the red eyes. "Of course *not!* Me, I take that risk. So all the associate can do is make money. Why, I got one guy at an investment banking house—one of the very best in the business—and all he gives me is lemons. So after a coupla times, you know what I did?"

"You kicked him out?"

"Nah. Think a little. I started using his stocks for short sales! He's hit seven in a row. But he never reads my services. Like you, unnerstand? So I'm not out one nickel on him so far. 'Don't worry,' I say when I call him up. 'You'll start hitting 'em one day yet.' So what happens? I don't pay him a nickel and he feels bad. Oh, does he feel bad. It's his pride—or somethin'. The worse he feels, the harder he tries. The harder he tries, the better short sales he gives me. Oh-ho! This guy I love!"

Izzy looked at his Scotch. He had not tasted the drink. Spiegelman disgusted him—everything about the man was the black side of being a Jew. "It doesn't sound quite honest to me," he said, "what you are doing." He placed his hand on the back of his chair. He was ready to leave, to leave Saul Spiegelman and his conniving and this dark place that made him nervous with its rich smells, to leave untouched the Scotch he wanted desperately but did not dare to sip even a little.

"Listen, *schlub.*"

The savagery in Spiegelman's voice lashed over Izzy like a whip. He was so startled that he slipped back into the chair, holding on to the seat with one hand.

"Who the goddam hell you think you're foolin', huh?" Spiegelman spat out. "One way you get ahead in this business and from me you should learn it? So."

333

He drew a line with his pen all the way across the tablecloth. This time the ball point was out; a black line lay upon the cloth. "I'll tell you what," Spiegelman said. "You're afraid to cross the *line!* But you don't know from nothin', *schlub.* You don't know *there is no line.* The first lesson and you ain't even learned it yet. So how does anybody get ahead on Wall Street? By showin' that extra bit of guts, that's how. Whatsa matter, kid? You got no guts?" Spiegelman put out a hand. "So keep your jock strap on. I'm not finished. What I'm tellin' you is better'n three years at the Harvard B School. In this business you got to cut a corner here, cut a corner there. Else what happens? You're boxed in good for life, that's what happens." Spiegelman snorted and black hairs flared from his nostrils. "So how do you explain those sister accounts that brokers use on the floor of the Stock Exchange? Hah! They got enough sisters down there to fill a dozen nunneries! Sisters, my bare ass! Dummy trading accounts! So another guy, a salesman maybe for a brokerage house, he takes a finder's fee and says nothing to the house. You know what he got, one fellow I know? A hunnert and fifty grand, that's what." Spiegelman snarled. "So maybe you can't use that kinda money, you're so almighty proud or somethin'. I'll tell you what you are." He leaned back. "You're a *schlub.*"

Israel Padawer longed to reach across the table and smash that face with his fist. Anybody else, he was thinking in torment, anybody else but Saul Spiegelman would talk to him this way and he would hit the man, the Lord be his witness! But this man with the red eyes and the skin of a potato had him dead to rights; he could read Izzy as well as Izzy's own father read the scholarly books in Hebrew. Yes, he admitted to himself, that is why I am sitting here now in this chair instead of smashing him in the face. The world did not fool Saul Spiegelman. He saw what he wanted and he reached out for it. Israel Padawer saw it and he had no guts.

"Here," said Spiegelman, his voice suddenly gentle, and pushed the plate of crackers toward Izzy. "The cheese is Brie, the best Brie you can get . . . and it's free."

"Th-thank you," Izzy said. He stood up with an effort. "Could you excuse me one minute? I'll be right back."

"The men's room," announced Spiegelman, pointing over his shoulder with a spoon that was balancing a wedge of Brie, "it's the first door on your left. But if you want real fun, I'd take the second door."

Izzy left the bar still smarting under Spiegelman's assessment of him. The man was right, of course. Despite his vulgarity, despite his Jewishness. You had to cut a corner or two. Or else you never really made it big on the Street. Isn't that what he had done by getting his cousin to smuggle out the lists of UJA contributors? Yes, but that was years ago. Now he could not afford to take such a chance. He had too much at stake. He had grown used to playing it safe; why, that was the essence of his investment approach. And now with the partnership . . . one wrong step and it would be finished for him. He might even have to leave Kimbridge & Co. The thought made him feel cold and he hurried into the men's room.

When he was ready to wash his hands, he stepped up to the mirror. The attendant was a little Italian who reminded him of the shoeshine man at Kimbridge & Co. He felt vaguely cheated; the attendant should have been a more imposing person in a restaurant such as this. Yes, in a special men's room uniform. Izzy stopped in astonishment. The attendant had filled a bowl for him with hot, steaming water and then turned away to busy himself at another bowl. He was slowly twirling a tin can, stripped of its label, in hot water. When Izzy was ready to dry his hands, the attendant stopped long enough to hand him a towel. Izzy, who considered it ridiculous for one grown man to help another grown man wash his hands, stood staring at the can.

"My supper," the attendant said, shifting his own eyes to the can. He took back the towel from Izzy and used it to wipe the basin. "Spaghetti and meat-balls. Heat it up like you see and eat right here." He twirled the shiny can.

Izzy was so touched—his own ego seemed somehow to be restored by this encounter—that he took a dollar bill from his wallet. "Keep the change," he said, trying to appear nonchalant. The attendant looked as if he might suddenly cry into the crumpled towel in his hand.

Izzy lingered a moment before passing through the alcove; for the first time he examined the bar closely. The dozen or so tables were all filled now and the room was pulsing with a quiet merriment. It was like walking suddenly into a fairyland world where there were no cares or competition or problems about money. Everyone seemed to be having such a splen-did time. The fabric on the walls was a rich purple velvet. The velvet fabric and the cigarette smoke and the intimate clink of glasses—all these things touched him and, yes, excited him. He heard a woman's voice ask, "Do you mind if I call Igor Igor?" It was the per-fect thing to say in this room somehow. He wished suddenly that his cousin Alec could see him. He nod-ded gravely to the Cossack officer and the man snapped his heels and said, "How are you this eve-ning, sir?"

Squaring his shoulders, Izzy strolled toward the table where Spiegelman sat waiting.

As he approached, he noticed that the party at the adjoining table were in evening clothes. He supposed these people would be going into the restaurant afterward for dinner. One of the women in the party caught his eye. She had reddish hair that was coiled atop her head and her skin seemed as white and soft as the Brie. She was so lovely that Izzy felt his pulse skip a beat, then another beat. Then Spiegelman said, "Where ya been? Washing your car? C'mon, I'm three ahead of ya in the drink department." He was busy on another King Alphonse and a new white mustache line.

Without hesitation Izzy picked up his glass and drank the Scotch. Miraculously, he felt no pain in his stomach—only a warm sense of well-being. It was truly amazing. He, Israel Padawer, began to enjoy a glowing kinship with the soft lights and the sound of laughter and the richly dressed people in this room. And no one appeared to mind that he was here.

Spiegelman was a smart salesman; he knew when not to push too hard. He extracted a wooden match from the box bearing the crest of the restaurant and patiently began to dig wax out of his ears. Izzy noticed for the first time that his ears were enormous and had black angry hairs matching the hairs in his nostrils.

"Why not somebody else?" Izzy asked. "Why not some . . . some Indian who belongs to the Society of Security Analysts?" He had a feeling that if he accepted Spiegelman's offer now he would be invited inside for dinner.

"Hah!" snorted the other man. "The Guild for the Jewish Blind. There everybody is cribbing from his neighbor. I know that place. You go there at lunch and first thing you know somebody's eaten your salad, they're so used to cribbing. No, thanks!"

Spiegelman began to talk about his advisory services. "First thing I got for myself was a cable address. For class, you know. Hell, I was in business four years before I received a cable. I didn't even know what it was at first. But now"—he replaced the match carefully in the box—"I'm big enough to have my own auditor. Even my own foundation. Mostly I give grants to prospective clients—*big* prospects with maybe fifty mailings—and to my friends who got their own foundations. That way everybody wins . . ."

The man was utterly repulsive, yet he conveyed a life force that Izzy found himself envying. There was no doubt about the fact that Spiegelman knew how to make money, a lot of money. And there was no doubt that he, Israel Padawer, could use more money. Newyorkitis.

". . . sweetest profit curve you ever saw in a business," Spiegelman was saying. "After you hit the break-even point you bring practically everything down to net. Except you got to allow for paper and postage. And the stepladder payments. But everybody wins, including me."

Izzy could imagine this grotesque man describing his business prowess to anybody who would listen. His wife, the members of his pinochle club, his rabbi even.

So Izzy listened and sipped his Scotch. But he grew increasingly conscious of something else. The woman at the next table, the redhead. She was sitting with her back against the black cushion and the effect, her red hair and white skin and the black cushion, was hypnotic. He listened to Spiegelman's rasping voice and, from the corner of his eye, he could watch the woman. . . .

Israel Padawer had never permitted himself to lust completely after a *shiksa*. He had developed a certain technique. He would glance quickly at some woman who met his fancy, extract some choice part of her anatomy and then, in his mind's eye, he would turn this around and around as a jeweler might feast upon some rare stone. He could, even at this moment, conjure up fragments of beautiful women he had glimpsed in recent months, all of them *shiksas*. The soft crook of an elbow on Nassau Street. The waxy nostrils of a bank teller. A slender throat swaying in the subway car. The tenderly bulging thigh of a girl in Riverdale carrying a bag of groceries. This past summer, as soon as short skirts became the style, he had concentrated for a period on the backs of women's knees. The knee itself was all knobs and ugliness. Ah, he thought, but the back of the knee where the creases formed in the shape of a beckoning H, sending his dreams upward along the swelling, soft promises of the thigh . . . there was, of course, another advantage. He could examine the back of a woman's knee on the street without attracting her attention.

Suddenly he thought of his wife and how, after the birth of Abraham, the varicose veins had surfaced in her legs, never to disappear. They clung to Sarah's legs like fat purple worms. Some months after they were married he had gathered up the courage to ask his wife to shave the coarse black hairs that covered the front of her thighs. She neglected to carry out his wishes and Izzy never mentioned the matter again. But there were times now when he saw a beautiful woman that he would suddenly hate her. He wanted to destroy her simply for being beautiful.

There was a movement at the next table. Izzy nodded to Spiegelman to show that he was listening attentively.

Izzy shifted in his chair and then, quite casually, his glance fell upon the woman's knees. Her legs were crossed. Izzy followed the white, tantalizing flesh down to a black pump. He stared at the clefts between the toes, where they disappeared into the shoe. He had never seen anything quite so lovely. Those clefts, he thought, I will carry the image of them for years. . . .

"Lookahere!" cried Spiegelman and he reached down into a brief case at his side. Spiegelman was waving two sheets of paper in the air and talking excitedly as he leaned toward Izzy. His breath was like sour milk. "You just got to give John Q. Public what he wants," said Spiegelman. "This one is the latest issue of my *Ivy League Trader*. Take a look at it."

Izzy picked up the sheet and read the heading: "Seven Stocks to Double by Christmas."

"Now this one," declared Spiegelman and placed the other paper on the table. "*The SS Theorist*," he added proudly.

The blocks letters glared out at Izzy: "IS THIS THE END OF THE GREATEST BULL MARKET OF ALL TIME?"

"I don't understand," said Izzy, shaking his head. "Are you bearish or bullish about the stock market?"

"I'm both! I give the public what it wants. That's the ticket!"

Izzy was appalled. Why, the man himself knew nothing about the stock market! His judgment was no better than that of Izzy's father.

Something dropped to the carpet. It was the black pump. Now the woman's foot was swaying, ever so gently, and Izzy thought he would go mad with desire.

Then Izzy felt the pain. He had been a fool to

340

drink the Scotch without Pepto Bismol! But that would have made Spiegelman laugh at him. The Scotch was turning to cut glass in his stomach—

"Whatsamatter?" growled Spiegelman. "You gonna be sick? In a swell place like this?" He seemed incredulous.

The room began to turn before Izzy's eyes. He imagined the woman's foot sticking in the platter of Brie cheese . . . and now Spiegelman was licking the woman's foot.

He fought down the nausea and, half dead with pain, pushed his chair away from the table.

"Where ya going?" demanded Spiegelman. His red eyes were hot with anger. "We got a deal or no?" he shouted at Izzy.

Izzy swallowed and there was a terrible taste in his throat. Of course not, he thought wildly, he could never agree to Spiegelman's offer.

Saul Spiegelman's thick, ugly mouth came forward, a still point of focus in the spinning room. *Schlub.* His mouth formed the word noiselessly. Like some terrible curse. But then Spiegelman spoke. "One stock just," he said.

Izzy struggled to his feet. He was amazed at the man's tenacity. Spiegelman was a specialist at extracting the last ounce of flesh. "Sears!" croaked Izzy. "Sears, Roebuck! Take it for free! But leave me out! Sears, Roebuck . . ."

26

"But, Noel! They *need* the exercise. All day long they sit in front of those switchboards—"

"Turrets," he corrected.

"—turrets, then. And they stare at those little blinking lights. Why, on a busy day your over-the-counter traders don't even go out for lunch!"

"So what?" said Noel. "Kimbridge & Co. has a hot lunch sent in on a tray. And what's more, the firm pays for it."

He watched Deirdre uneasily. She would never cease to confound him, not if he knew her for a thousand years.

The movie line in which they were standing moved slowly toward the ticket window. Noel flipped his cigarette into the street, a brief red arc in the night.

This silly business about the over-the-counter traders, he was thinking. The traders had one special talent: the ability to communicate with their counterparts at the other brokerage firms. Half of them were

Italian and they all managed to look as if they'd just crawled out of a cement mixer. Traders—baloney! The only thing they had to do was to keep lying to each other—"I'll open up to ya, Joey boy, we're interested in picking up a thousand shares that stock," which could mean five hundred or two thousand shares, depending on the trader—in a consistent pattern so that nobody would get crossed up. And what was Deirdre now proposing to do? Ask her father to sponsor a group membership for the Kimbridge & Co. traders at some downtown health club so they might exercise after the market closed. God!

"Noel. Don't scowl so. You'll scare the little children."

"They ought to be home in bed anyway," he said. "Okay. Have it your own way. Who knows? Those traders, they might all turn into weight lifters for the next Olympics."

Deirdre touched his coat lightly. "I'm going to speak to Father about it," she said.

Yes, he thought wonderingly, she has a strange quality—a childlike desperation concerning Kimbridge & Co. It was as though the firm itself were a living thing to Deirdre. He could understand this attitude in her father, but somehow it became far more immediate and touching in her.

Perhaps his own father had felt the same way toward Bigelow, Quigg. But a fat lot of good it had done him! Well, the score was going to be evened up. Noel Bigelow was going to take over the helm at Kimbridge & Co. one fine day. And Deirdre—she was going to be his first mate. Correction. His *second* mate.

"That's better, Noel. When you smile, your horns disappear."

He took out his wallet and extracted a crisp ten-dollar bill. The wallet, made of baby alligator skin and tipped with gold at the corners, was the most expensive one he could find at Mark Cross. It was a present to himself, bestowed on the day his divorce became final. "Two, please," he said to the woman at the ticket window.

His courtship was running smoothly although it progressed on Deirdre's terms. They had been to four movies in the past two weeks. "You've no idea how I missed American movies in Paris," she had told him on Monday. "A good slam-bang Western with John Wayne and what happens? They've dubbed it so he's talking in French. *John Wayne*, by glory! Once they got so careless with the dubbing that his horse was talking in French."

But to Noel's intense disgust, he was also becoming an authority on the Gallic character of Joan of Arc. Whenever he lured Deirdre out for supper she insisted on carrying part of her main course back to the cat in a paper bag. He knew, too, that the cat derived great pleasure from watching Deirdre bathe and on hot afternoons Joan of Arc chose to nap on the cool porcelain of the tub. That god-damned cat! There were times when he would imagine her pressing against his leg in the board room. . . .

But Saturday now drew closer. The day promised something special: Deirdre had swept the decks clean of other commitments and the two of them were driving out to the country.

In the car she sat close to him, their thighs touching briefly around the curves, and once she leaned her head against his shoulder. The car radio was playing an old Glenn Miller tune and Noel could feel Deirdre's head nodding in time to the beat. They stopped for a traffic light in a small Connecticut town.

"Alive," she whispered, so softly that he might not have heard her if the car had been in motion. He turned in the seat and when he saw the look in her eyes he bent his head. Her lips, full and moist, met his with a passion he had not experienced in Deirdre. He felt the muscles tighten in her neck when he touched her. He knew that he would remember this kiss as long as he lived. A horn began to sound impatiently and, returning his hands to the wheel, Noel nosed the car through the crowd of noontime shoppers.

Deirdre had been waiting for him on the sidewalk in front of her apartment when he drove up that morning. She was wearing a raccoon coat that was much too long for her and he wondered when he saw it if the coat once belonged to her brother. But he said nothing; he was learning how to handle her at last.

An hour later they were driving through back country roads. It was a superb October day and the maple trees, blazing red and gold, were at the height of their beauty. The woods were ablaze, too, with the rich yellow of birch leaves, and they would see an occasional poplar tree, squirrel gray alongside one half of the trunk and black on the other side where the autumn rain had run down. There was the smell of burning leaves in the air in the small towns and once when the car slowed down its wheels rustled against the fallen leaves.

"Hungry?" Noel said at last.

She nodded her head obediently. And then she curled up against his shoulder and went to sleep until he found the old coaching inn he wanted.

On the veranda a sign said: "The Bear's Paw." They went inside, past the gift shop, and the inn seemed to retreat into time by two centuries. Large black pots hung on iron hooks in front of the brick fireplace; the beamed ceiling was scarcely eight feet high and the heart pine flooring, mellowed to the shade of a lion's mane, was set with wooden pegs. It was a place he had thought she would appreciate.

"Why, Noel!" she exclaimed. "It's perfectly wonderful!" She clapped her hands together in a spontaneous movement that quickened his pulse.

"Yes," he said. "We're in luck today. Here, let me take your coat."

She was wearing a dress designed in the style of the twenties, a flapper dress with a low waist and a short skirt with tassels. The dress was blue, it had no sleeves, and on Deirdre Kimbridge it looked magnificent.

They ate black bean soup, piping hot, followed by lobster salad stuffed in long rolls, and they drank beer in pewter mugs, beer with a glorious head of creamy foam. The dessert was deep-dish apple pie; their conversation was ambling, relaxed, and cheerful, the kind of conversation that should come with solid food in the country on a bright autumn day.

After lunch they browsed through the collection of old penny banks in the inn and, in the gift shop, Noel bought a small painted china bed for Deirdre. "George Washington was here," read the legend across the headboard, "but he wasn't asleep."

Noel was feeling so good that he summoned up an indulgent smile when Deirdre cried: "Oops! I forgot about Joan of Arc!" She raced back to the kitchen and had the waitress wrap up some lobster salad in wax paper. She placed it inside her purse.

They spent the remainder of the afternoon meandering through back country roads. Deirdre busied herself with remodeling old farmhouses as they drove slowly past.

The car neared a sagging gray house with twin chimneys on either end. "Oh, Noel," she cried delightedly, "can't you just visualize it if the front porch were sheared away? And that horrid gable—it's *perfectly* useless!"

"We unload the gable," declared Noel, responding to her mood. "We sell it to the highest bidder."

"And the roof line," said Deirdre, staring at the house. "You need to cut back the roof line, oh, just about four feet, and change the position of that center window . . ." She twisted in the car seat, furiously renovating the forlorn house in her mind, and watched until it disappeared through the rear window. "Brown, don't you think?" she said, settling herself again beside him. "Brown paint. But with character."

"Brown paint it is," he said. "With bright yellow trim. Boat painter Noel Bigelow at your service, ma'am."

"Oh, yes," she cried, "yellow trim!"

It was dusk when they returned to Manhattan. The lights of the city, bedecked for the revels of a Saturday night, winked expectantly as they crossed the Triborough Bridge. Deirdre had unbuttoned the raccoon coat and she kept one hand resting lightly on his knee during the return trip.

He found a parking place half a block from her apartment. Deirdre said suddenly, "Avis wrote me a letter. Noel, I think she's still in love with you." She took her hand from his knee. "How do you feel about her?"

"Divorced, I feel very divorced about her." He snapped off the ignition. "Now let's forget about Avis, shall we?"

"All right, Noel. I just wanted to make sure, that's all. Avis is a very good friend."

They went upstairs and Deirdre unlocked the door. She never bothered to double lock the door and she refused to follow Noel's advice and install a stronger lock. When he mentioned this to her, she had replied lightly, "Why, in Paris I didn't even *have* a lock."

"Murr-rr-roah." Joan of Arc leaped into Deirdre's arms when the door swung open.

"You poor dear one," she crooned. "I'll fix your supper in a jiffy." She stroked the cat and then, putting her gently on the floor, she tossed her coat on a chair. "Noel," she called over her shoulder, "be a dear and fix the drinks for us."

He took the bottles out of an antique sewing cabinet that Deirdre had bought to use as a bar. He poured gin and a splash of vermouth into a silver shaker and waited for her to come out of the kitchen. On reconsidering, he added some more gin to the shaker. His mind was already drunk with the promise he had perceived in Deirdre. . . .

She cupped the ice cubes in her hands. Noel dropped the cubes—"Fire one," he said. "Fire two"—into the shaker.

They clinked glasses. The martini tasted perfect, Noel thought with satisfaction.

"What would you like?" she said, watching him.

"You mean right now?"

"Oh, no, I mean some *thing*, silly. You have an eyelash on your cheek." Deirdre came close to him and carefully took the eyelash between her fingertips. "Now blow it," she commanded, "and make a wish."

He did as he was told. She was sipping her drink, a half smile around her lips, and waiting for him to say something. "Well?"

Noel frowned. "All right," he said finally. "I've got it. At least, if it has to be a thing. Expense is no object?" She shook her head.

He set down the martini glass and ran his hand slowly over the top of a teakwood table. "A boat," he said. "I'd like a custom-made job, a boat nobody else in the world owns. An eighty-foot yawl with a teak deck and a real galley and a shower." He paused. "The trim all stainless steel. A boat that could sleep eight or nine people in comfort. This boat would draw, oh, maybe nine feet over all. But it would be a shoal draft job so I could navigate in shallow water. Say, in Chesapeake Bay. And ground tackle—I'd want the finest ground tackle money could buy." He could see the boat in his mind's eye as he described it to her. With Deirdre at his side, the boat seemed suddenly possible.

"Well," she said, "you certainly know what you want."

He drained his glass. He picked up the shaker and said to her, "Better drink up. You're falling behind in this race."

She moved restlessly about the room. She sat down suddenly and looked up at him. "Do you think Father is getting old?" she said.

"I don't know," he said evasively. "I was talking with him yesterday and he seemed to be right on top of things."

"What were you talking about?" She had detected the edge in his voice.

"An idea of mine. A friend of my father's here in town asked me to handle his brokerage business. It's a Swiss bank account. But no trick at all on our part. This man has made his own arrangements with the bank in Switzerland. We'd simply receive a letter from the bank authorizing us to accept orders from a client with a numbered account. Then this man would telephone his orders. No written communications. All the confirmations and statements, even the dividends, go directly to the Swiss bank from Kimbridge & Co. What happens between the bank and its client is their concern."

"And Father turned it down?"

"Yes. A big account like that and he turned it down!"

Deirdre nodded slowly.

"I have the strangest idea sometimes," she said. "I wonder about going into Kimbridge & Co. myself." Her eyes were bright and serious. "Oh, I know it isn't a popular thing for a woman to work as a partner on Wall Street but"—she played with a tassel on her dress—"sometimes I feel tempted to try it, all the same. Just for my father's sake."

Noel became alarmed. It would be just like her, he thought. There was the sudden realization, too, that Deirdre might just be able to pull it off. She actually might succeed in running the firm after her father and the other partners passed out of the picture. . . . Noel lighted a cigarette, took one puff, and snubbed it out.

"Oh, Noel, don't glower so. Why, my father would probably have a fit if he knew I ever entertained such a thought. Noel, come over here and sit down."

He knelt beside her on the floor. He could smell her rich apple scent, warm and intimate. He noticed that Deirdre had removed her stockings.

"Murr-rr-rroah!"

The god-damned cat! Supper was over and Joan of Arc was rubbing against Deirdre's other leg. Noel fought back the desire to sneeze.

"Oh, you jealous cat," said Deirdre, laughing.

"How good is Joan of Arc at obeying orders?" asked Noel. He moved a tassel experimentally across Deirdre's bare knee.

"Well, of course, she's Gallic. So you can never

tell." Deirdre clapped her hands and the cat's ears flicked forward. The huge emerald eye stared at each of them in turn. "The kitchen," Deirdre commanded. "No, Noel. Don't point. That's not fair. Joan of Arc. Listen to me now. The *kitchen*."

To Noel's amazement the cat glided softly across the carpet and disappeared through the door to the kitchen.

What the hell, Noel thought, and keeping his eyes on the door he slid his hand under Deirdre's dress. He felt the goose pimples forming as he gently caressed her thighs. She did not move. He bent forward and now he could smell the fabric of the dress mingled with the scent of apples.

"Give me three minutes," she said, very quietly.

She ran from the room and Noel sat riveted to the floor.

After all this time, all the time and the agony and the scheming, "something chemical" had happened between them. He picked a cat hair absently from the carpet and saw that his hand was shaking.

"Ed-*die!* Eddie, wait for me-e-e!" Through the open window he heard a girl calling on the sidewalk below. The night sounds of the city, the sounds of love and promise and far away the faint wail of an ambulance siren, these sounds sent the blood pounding through his temple.

And then he heard Deirdre's voice. "Noel? *Hurry*."

He scrambled to his feet.

"Hurry, Noel." He stopped at the bedroom door, hesitating for an instant. "I have a short fuse, my darling," she said.

The room was dark and the shades had been pulled down. Then his eyes began to adjust to the darkness.

Deirdre was lying in bed under a sheet. From the way her head was turned he knew that she was

351

watching him. She raised her knees and he heard the crisp whistling of the sheet.

He flung off his clothes and groped for a chair. He could hear Deirdre moving in the bed to make room for him and then she laughed.

"Why, silly," she said, "you've still got your socks on." She reached out and touched him. "No," she said urgently. "Don't bother." And then, "*Silly.*"

He found it almost impossible to breathe and he sat upright in the bed for a few moments. She was kissing his ribs, one by one.

Then he touched her bare shoulder, purposely delaying the exploration of his hands. He became ecstatic; her flesh was indescribably lovely, like fire and ice mingling together.

He began to talk then, not knowing what he was saying. But the warmth of her body, yielding now to his touch along her heavy breasts and the smooth, hot sweep of her inner thighs, so delighted Noel that he felt an inexplicable desire to express himself. He was like a sinner in a confession box.

He kept babbling, and then she reached up and pulled his head down to her lips. She kissed him and he stopped talking.

"Hurry. Oh, my goodness, *hurry!*" she cried.

That single word so stripped Deirdre of her defenses! A tiny stream of saliva dribbled from the corner of her mouth and now he was kissing it dry with his lips. He felt her fingers lacing across his back and his own hands were moving quickly, expertly. He felt himself stiffening.

There was a dampness now between his fingers and with the dampness a new smell. One palm lightly traced the warm hollow of her buttocks and it was as if his hand had caught on fire. She shifted position slightly and the pressure of her breasts was amazingly heavy against his body.

He tried to kick the sheet free. He heard it rip. "Don't mind, don't mind!" she cried breathlessly, but something made him turn his head. And then he froze.

There on the wall beside the door, crouching against the old dressing mirror that he knew once belonged to Deirdre's grandfather, he saw the black outline. It was Joan of Arc peering at their reflection in the glass.

"Hur-*ry!* Oh my God, oh my God!"

But he was powerless to act. As he froze above Deirdre he watched the cat slowly turn her head. And then there was that huge emerald eye, sparkling and gleaming in the darkness like the distillation of all evil. The cat flicked out her tongue; the eye remained steadily upon the two figures in the bed.

Noel's blood began to chill. Suddenly the emerald was gone!

Joan of Arc had leaped onto the bed. The cat landed on Noel's ankles and he could feel Deirdre turning below him in stunned surprise.

Noel felt the claws tearing at his lower legs. He swung at the cat clumsily and then he screamed, "Get it off, get that god-damned thing away from me!"

Deirdre did not move. The cat scratched Noel's thigh and then, "Mrrr-mrr-mrr," the cat slid under his legs and stretched out beside Deirdre.

The golden time was over for Noel Bigelow.

He watched in disbelief as Deirdre climbed slowly from the bed. She was standing on the other side of the bed, cradling the cat between her breasts and stroking her slowly.

He saw her head move, and he knew once again

that she was looking at him. But he could not see her eyes.

"I think you'd better go." That was all she said.

He turned toward the door and bumped his knee against a candle-stand. It toppled to the floor. Then he wheeled around and started toward Deirdre.

"Murr-rr-roahh." Calm and peaceful.

That cat's purring decided him. She could go to hell, he told himself savagely, and take the damned cat with her. Noel swept up his clothes with one hand and stalked from the bedroom.

In the living room he thrust himself into his shirt and pants in a blind fury. He jammed his stockinged feet into his shoes. A trickle of blood ran down the side of one shoe.

He was holding the suit jacket under one arm when he slammed the door to the apartment as hard as he could. He heard the vestibule door open downstairs and a woman's voice saying, "Harry, we forgot to get cottage cheese at the deli. Harry, now you know I told you cottage cheese."

Noel struggled into his jacket. He could hear the couple climbing the stairs. He stood panting in the hallway. On the floor below there was the sound of a lock turning and the couple went inside.

When Noel Bigelow reached the street, it was bitterly cold.

27

Word had gotten around the home office of Kimbridge & Co.

Poke Jeffers had topped every other salesman in production for the past two months and now in early November with the stock market turning suddenly weak he kept widening his lead. In a race with no starter's gun and no chalk lanes on the track he was running like a man possessed. He was applying his kick down the home stretch and he seemed to gain momentum with each passing day.

In a world where rumor wedded fancy every few seconds, where production was king, the word was out. In the back office, in Purchases & Sales, in the Margin Department and in the typing pool, in the Wire & Order Department, the word was: watch Poke Jeffers. In the computer room the odds had shifted in his favor. After all, wasn't Thatcher Kimbridge himself stopping by for a chat every few days?

"Ho!" cried out Poke at his desk. A dozen feet away

a tape watcher ducked his head instinctively. Again, "Ho!" Poke had known a hurdler who yelled just before each hurdle; the teammate was convinced this gave him an extra lift. The tape watcher flashed a dark look and Poke smiled benignly. An ecstasy of power, the feeling that he had become as strong and tireless as the stock tape, was flowing through him.

"What have you got, for Christ's sake?" demanded Noel Bigelow irritably. "Your own private Ouija board? Merriam finally gave me a stock after I kept badgering Research for some merchandise. And what happens? The stock moves beautifully. Only it keeps going down and I'm long the stock with a dozen customers. Merriam called his contact yesterday and guess what? A big holder has been dumping his stock on the open market. The damned fool! He doesn't have enough sense to do a secondary offering. All that money and no brains!"

For several days Noel had been so morose that he did not even bait Izzy Padawer. He appeared somehow to have lost his zest.

Eat my cinders, Poke thought to himself, and aloud he said, "Tough luck, fella." He turned his back to Noel and dialed a number. "Hi there, Mr. Grosvenor," he said easily. "Well, I've got a stock for you that should do every bit as well as Emerson Coal. This company's in the baby-food business and it plans to bring out a new line for old people. Actually, it's the same product mix but with different labels. The announcement won't be made until next week. Right, right. The company is aiming at customers at both ends of the age scale. Stock is selling at thirty-nine this morning. Good. Three hundred shares. Three hundred at the market. What's that, Mr. Grosvenor? Sure, I'll be glad to talk with your sister. You just send her in to see me, or I can call her. Whichever is more convenient. Many thanks."

As he wrote out the order, Poke found it hard to believe that he once had doubted Carol's ability as an analyst. She was providing him with one or two ideas every week now. "A spy has no character," she had said to him laughingly. "He merely assumes one. That's the way I am when I research a situation that might show promise."

She uncovered one oil refiner with the earmarks of a takeover candidate and, sure enough, Wall Street was buzzing with these rumors after Poke had taken a position for his customers. Carol found another company with a tax-loss carry forward and a tantalizing balance sheet; the cash on hand was equivalent to the market price of the common stock. She pointed out another company one week before its directors voted to pay off dividend arrearages. "I did somebody there a favor once," she explained to Poke, "and now turnabout is fair play." One situation she discovered was a Detroit manufacturer of heavy equipment that had just completed a five-year program of building new plant facilities. "This fiscal year the depreciation alone will be enough to cover capital outlays and that means the company can bring a lot more money down to the bottom line," Carol said. "The order backlog is up 40 per cent over a year ago. That stock looks ripe for a move." Another stock was an over-the-counter company that received a feasibility contract from the government for missile work. The market in the stock was thin but Poke managed to buy 3,000 shares for his customers without moving up the price; then within two weeks the stock rose nine points, aided in part by the secrecy surrounding the government contract. One of the customers Poke put into this stock was Mrs. Witherspoon. She agreed to sell a small number of IBM shares after Poke confided to her, "I understand the man in charge of this new program is a Christian Scientist. But, of course, it's all very hush-hush." Percy Scovill's mutual fund began to funnel an increasing amount of its commission business through Kimbridge & Co.

Carol was giving Poke something more than a list of select investment opportunities—namely, the confidence that these stocks could perform strongly in an erratic market. And Poke, a salesman now armed with the necessary ammunition, succeeded in conveying this confidence to his customers. He kept holding his breath; surely Carol's string of successes could not last. One night he asked her how much money she made at Hillyer & Hunt and he was shocked when she told him the amount. It amounted to a mere fraction of his own income.

"Do you know why you're such a good salesman?" she asked.

"Sure," he said. "Because of Carol Tracey."

She shook her head. "No," she said. "It's because you know the needs of the people you deal with."

But the most miraculous thing of all was that Poke found himself forgetting about the Monster more and more. Even the stump did not pain him so often. He was running hard on Carol Tracey's legs.

He picked up the telephone.

"Hi, there," a voice said. It was Carol; she was even beginning to talk like him.

"You're supposed to be in Los Angeles," he said.

"I *am* in Los Angeles, darling. I just wanted to hear your voice before I left the hotel, that's all. I spent yesterday going through a micro-circuit plant. You know what I saw?"

"Lots of micro-circuits."

"That's just it, Poke. I *didn't*. I kept looking at the

production line and all I could see was your face in front of me. Oh, my darling . . . I miss you so.".

"When does your plane get in?"

"Tomorrow night. Seven-fifteen. Flight four-oh-two."

"I'll meet you at the airport."

"Oh, darling!"

"I miss you, too."

"I feel like flying home this minute. Oh, Poke?"

"Yes?"

"There's something I ran across out here that looks very interesting. The company has only a million two of common outstanding and a debt of forty-seven million. That's tremendous leverage. This is the way I see it . . ."

On Wall Street the tempo of the market suddenly was quickening. Volume began to rise on the Stock Exchange and in a single week during November the Dow-Jones industrial average plunged 23 points. A combination of falling prices and rising volume, the technicians intoned, was a bad sign. At last the market was no longer "making a line." But the implications appeared forbidding. Two nationally prominent advisory services warned subscribers of an impending bear market in stocks. Another well-known analyst shifted his position from "long-term bullish" to "intermediate-term neutral." Market letters were sprinkled with phrases of caution: "Upgrade your portfolios . . . conserve some cash . . . watch truck production—often a better advance indicator of the business outlook than auto output. . . ." *Time* magazine's cover depicted a bear and a bull bedecked in ticker tape and glaring at each other across a plank laid over a narrow gorge. The buildings of Wall Street were etched into the sides of the abyss and the

359

streamer on the cover said: "Which one wins this time?"

Ursula Leone gave birth to twins and a girl in the Proxy Department won the date pool. A customer of Kimbridge & Co., a Navy captain with an account in Richmond, informed the firm he had devised a faultless technique for charting stocks of consumer industries. Another customer in St. Louis watched seven stock certificates float out of the glove compartment of his car at the height of a flash flood. In Providence a client received the monthly statement of another customer by error and, being a somewhat nervous person, he regarded this as an omen and proceeded to sell every stock in his account. Priscilla Hooker began collecting dinosaur tracks; she had geologists all over the world sawing up rocks for exorbitant fees and shipping them to her for placement in the front lawn of the new estate. And Fred Lincoln broke an expensive golf club over his knee when on a par-3 hole he watched his ball sail unerringly for 185 yards and then stop one inch short of the cup.

Inside 50 Wall life went its varied ways. A bomb threat was received by telephone at the travel agency; the entire floor was vacated but no bomb was found by the police. The following week an elevator stalled in a blind hatch and one woman on the way to her dentist proceeded to faint in a standing position between two company executives. A messenger for one of the brokerage firm tenants was robbed in the corridor of $400,000 in negotiable securities; he received nine proposals of marriage by letter.

The excitement and urgency of a moving market affected the other producers in the board room like an epidemic. One customers' man drummed up business by estimating cash flow on stocks—invariably a more optimistic figure than current earnings. Another salesman decided that he wasted valuable time in dialing. He proceeded to dismantle his telephone and, with the aid of a soldering iron and a kit of tools, succeeded in speeding up his dialing technique.

The salesman who commuted to 50 Wall daily from his home in Philadelphia made an extraordinary discovery: he happened to notice that a morning fog on the Jersey meadows coincided to an uncanny degree with days when the stock market managed to climb. For one happy month he predicated his business on this basis and then, quite unaccountably, a solid week of foggy mornings proved his undoing.

Another customers' man took to polishing his shoes endlessly in his cubicle. One afternoon he bent over and found he could not tie his shoelaces. Mental fatigue—that was the diagnosis of the firm's Medical Department on the twenty-eighth floor. There ensued an active scramble for his accounts by producers in the adjoining cubicles. His client list included an eminently successful madam with an establishment on Central Park South. Eighty-five per cent of her portfolio, which ran high into six figures, was kept always in oil and electric utility stocks.

In the Charlotte office a salesman was found to have diverted customer funds to his own account. Thatcher Kimbridge permitted the salesman to turn in a formal resignation after making full restitution to the client. In St. Louis another man was fired, following testimony by a handwriting expert, for having taken the qualification test for a friend who had joined another brokerage house.

But for Noel Bigelow there existed finally a different sense of excitement. He was no student of the Bible but the phrase, "an eye for an eye," had taken on new meaning for him. On the afternoon when he left the board room early—on the pretext of visiting a client—he felt a delightful shiver of anticipation dance along his spine.

After riding the subway to Grand Central, he made a purchase at a delicatessen and then went across Vanderbilt Avenue to the Biltmore Hotel. He took the elevator to a floor where he knew there was a free lavatory; he was carrying his brief case and a paper bag. Inside one of the booths he spent five minutes. He washed his hands carefully and when he walked out of the lavatory he was carrying only the brief case. His next subway ride took him to within two blocks of the building where Deirdre lived. He glanced about casually as he approached the vestibule. He gave the appearance of a businessman returning home from the office.

Extracting a credit card made of celluloid from his pocket, Noel worked it expertly against the snap latch of the vestibule door. His practice on the door to his own apartment rewarded the effort quickly; there was a clicking sound. He turned the knob and stepped inside. The hallway was deserted. It smelled faintly of Brussels sprouts.

He walked swiftly up to the third floor and stopped in front of Deirdre's apartment. Once again he slid celluloid between the door and the frame, breathing a prayer of gratitude for Deirdre's nonchalance over locks.

Noel had placed a clean white handkerchief over the doorknob. His palms were covered with perspiration. "Goddamit," he muttered under his breath, and then the latch snapped open. A moment later he was standing inside the living room.

He reviewed his strategy. He knew that Deirdre should be at the shelter for nearly another hour. Noel had timed everything very carefully. But suppose she came back to the apartment early? After all, you could count on Deirdre to do the unexpected.

The living room was empty. He set down the brief case and made a quick inspection of the other rooms. He frowned. Where the hell was Joan of Arc? The only sound in the apartment was the faucet dripping in the bathroom sink. This was Deirdre's solution for providing fresh water for her cat. Under the sink was an old roasting pan filled with cat litter. Noel looked again around the living room. He began to curse silently and his armpits were wet with perspiration. Joan of Arc was nowhere to be found.

Then he glimpsed a movement above his head. Noel looked up and there was the cat, crouching on the figurehead above the door. The emerald eye was fixed upon him; the gray tail was twitching slowly.

"Hello, Joan of Arc," Noel said amiably. "You'll never guess what I have for you."

The tail grew still. But the cat did not move from her perch.

Noel laughed and clapped his hands. A blur of gray fur pounced to the floor. Joan of Arc began to rub against his trouser leg and he could hear her deep throat rattle.

Noel snapped open the brief case. First, he removed the fresh copy of *Paris Match* and spread it out on the carpet. Then he took the bologna sandwich and pulled it gently apart. He was careful not to cut his hands on the particles of glass he had kneaded into the bologna.

"Merr-rr-owr!" With a final caress against Noel's leg, the cat lifted her tail and walked daintily toward the food.

Through the window he could see the roof of the apartment building across the street. Shirts and towels were hanging stiffly on a clothesline. The black curved pipes of air vents, protruding above the roof line, seemed to lean forward like curious pallbearers.

He looked down at the cat. Joan of Arc was attacking the bologna sandwich with swift, neat gulps.

Noel wiped his hands with Kleenex tissues which he tossed into the open brief case. He could hear the chewing sounds distinctly. Above the cat's head he saw the bold type of an advertisement. *L'aspirine qui se prend—*

He walked to the bedroom door while waiting for it to happen. He glanced toward Deirdre's bed and then he heard the new sound. Like the crying of a baby, he thought. And then the cat began to thrash about. Noel retraced his steps and stared down in fascination. Joan of Arc's claws ripped into the paper; the cat was thrashing more violently now but the crying sound had stopped.

Finally the body lay still. The paper was smeared with saliva and the stain of bologna. Noel leaned forward hesitantly and as he did so the emerald eye flicked open to stare up at him. There was no pain or anger in the eye. The cat seemed to be trying to smile at him.

He heard a final deep rattle inside the cat and he knew then that the end had come. The eye was still open but the stare had turned to glass.

Carefully, he lifted the cat from the tattered paper and deposited it on the carpet. The soft gray body hung limply in his hands. Moving more hurriedly now, he crumpled up the magazine and placed it inside the brief case which he snapped shut.

He stood erect, not wanting to look again at Joan of Arc, and the sound of dripping water from the bathroom seemed to swell in his ears. Suddenly he sneezed.

Noel glanced at his watch. He had entered the vestibule eleven minutes ago.

He gave a final look around the apartment to make sure everything was in order. There were cat hairs on his trousers; he would brush those off later. A last look at Joan of Arc. He saw the blood on the long white whiskers and he shivered.

He let himself out of the apartment. The hallway was empty, thank God. A minute later, on the street, he was swinging his brief case. The sidewalk sparkled with tiny crystals of quartz. An immense sense of victory flooded over Noel Bigelow and he began to hum a tune from an old Triangle Club show.

28

". . . . no trouble at all, Mr. Goodman. I will tell the Cashier's Department to set up your wife's account for the automatic payout of dividends." Izzy Padawer scribbled a note on a yellow pad. "Already I am reminding myself," he said.

"You know how they are, these women," a guttural voice came over the telephone. "A wonderful firm like Kimbridge & Co. and my wife has to be suspicious. She tells me, 'So why should I wait until the end of the month to get my dividends?' So it's a big deal. Now she gets the dividends maybe a week earlier. You would think she is balancing the budget in Washington, my wife."

"Yes, Mr. Goodman." Izzy paused expectantly. "Anything else I can do for you?"

"Dayton Laboratories. Know anything about it?"

"A pharmaceutical company. A quiet, steady stock. Hasn't done a thing in the market, not for the past year."

"Huh. Maybe you should watch it now. Tell me. How're they making that stock on the floor?"

"Right with you, Mr. Goodman." Izzy pressed the "hold" button and picked up another telephone. He listened to the automatic quotation service, nodding his head. Then he was back on the line to Mr. Goodman. "Twenty-five bid, a quarter offered. Last sale 25. Volume only four hundred shares so far today."

"Okay. Buy me in the margin account for Goodman Brothers three hundred shares at the market. Call me right back."

Izzy put through the order. Five minutes later he was talking to his customer again. "You just bought three hundred shares at 25¼," he said.

"Buy for me four hundred more. Same account. I'm waiting for your call."

Then, "Mr. Goodman? You got two hundred shares at a quarter, the other two hundred at three-eighths."

"Okay. You should watch that stock. What time is it?"

Izzy squinted at the wall clock in the board room. "Five minutes past two," he said.

"Huh. If my information is correct"—the guttural voice had become more casual—"that stock you should see at 27, maybe 28. Before three o'clock. You call me then and we take a look. Okay?"

"Yes, Mr. Goodman."

At precisely three o'clock Izzy was back on the line. "Mr. Goodman? You've done it again. Three hundred shares just crossed at 27¾."

"Huh. How're they making the stock now?"

Then, "It's 27⅞ bid, 28¼ offered."

"Sell three hundred. Call me. I want out before the bell."

Ten minutes later Mr. Goodman had sold his entire 700 shares at an average price of 28. He had made a profit of approximately $1,400, after commissions, in little more than one hour.

At his desk, Izzy was shaking his head in wonderment. The Robin Hood Group had done it again. That was his private name for the clique of wealthy Jewish businessmen who seemed to work magic in the market. They picked a stock, these people, just before it was set to move. Not only that. They were able with amazing consistency to predict the price at which the stock would sell at a certain time of the day. Now *that* defied every law in the market. Izzy kept shaking his head. Sometimes these people stayed with a stock for several months; sometimes they were out the same day, as Mr. Goodman had just done. How, how? Mr. Goodman was Izzy's only customer in the Robin Hood Group. The others were spread across the country in cities such as Chicago, Miami, Atlanta, Los Angeles, Dallas, and Las Vegas, cities where rich Jews talked in country clubs and in card games and in cabanas. They talked to company officials who were friends or relatives and they talked to each other. Their money—the rich, informed Jewish money—moved with a force that seemed irresistible; it caught up the centuries of barter, usury, and cunning, then rolled on like the ocean. Izzy called them the Robin Hood Group because the name sounded so Anglo-Saxon. But there was one difference: these men kept what they made in the stock market.

He was proud of their uncanny market ability. Yet he also feared these people. Were they rigging the market? Impossible. Was some terrible scandal about to unfold and involve these men? Of course not. Then how did they do it? He shook his head. Mr. Goodman's family concern manufactured rubber bath mats —and here he was suddenly an expert in pharmaceuticals.

Whenever Izzy saw in the newspaper that a man with a Jewish name had been arrested for robbing a bank or had gotten involved in some divorce scandal, he felt shame for his entire race. There were other times when Jews made him proud; when they received an honorary degree from Harvard or won the Nobel Prize or were appointed to some high position in Washington. For the Robin Hood Group his reaction was one of awe blended with wild suspicions. But such a customer! The commissions he made from Mr. Goodman!

That evening, as he was walking toward the subway station, Izzy saw a man who reminded him of somebody. A customer? No. Then who? The man had a head just like Saul Spiegelman. Izzy made a face. Such a terrible man, Saul Spiegelman. And yet, he thought longingly, the money he might have made by climbing the stepladder of Saul Spiegelman. Yes, it was a Jacob's ladder, anchored on Wall Street and reaching up to heaven.

It was his custom to wait in the board room until six o'clock so that he would avoid the subway crush. The germs you could pick up just from breathing! Izzy heard the grumble of thunder and felt the charged weight of the atmosphere. Through the grating in the sidewalk came the answering rumble of a subway train. Under the darkened sky the sidewalk gray melted into the gritty gray of the buildings. It was Friday evening and the people scurried past Izzy Padawer. The weather had turned unaccountably warm—it was an Indian-summer day.

Izzy sighed wearily. He had sent his family off to the Catskills for a holiday and now the thought of returning to an empty house seemed depressing. Should he stop off in Times Square and eat a grilled-cheese sandwich? Grilled cheese was safe to order any place;

369

he could measure his life by an endless procession of grilled-cheese sandwiches.

He pondered this as he trudged down the stairs and was swallowed up by the subway entrance. He passed the newsstands and resolutely kept his eyes from caressing the magazine covers on the special rack. There they waited, he knew, an arm's reach from *The Commercial & Financial Chronicle* and *Forbes* and *The Northern Miner*. Cover photographs of fetching nude models. Models who were bending forward or kneeling or looking sideways, always smiling softly, always with rounded breasts so tantalizing, breasts that seemed about to fall right out of the magazines. . . .

At first Sarah had protested that he should not stay alone. But Izzy had insisted. "I must work," he told his wife. "There are many reports to read. So go and enjoy."

The bulging brief bag—an old-fashioned upright type rather than the attaché case carried by Noel Bigelow—now was proof of his determination. In his other hand he carried a Sears, Roebuck catalog. He meant to examine it in hopes that the act, like reading the Torah, might somehow bolster his faith. This week Sears, Roebuck stock had dropped 8½ points and no less than a dozen customers had called to pass along the news that the stock was weak. Where did they think he was—in some Foreign Legion fort? Izzy sank down on a bench and waited for his train. An old man was sitting on the same bench. Izzy told himself he must remember to buy a new *tallis*, a prayer shawl, for his father.

"So go and enjoy." The family had left that afternoon for the most expensive Jewish resort hotel Izzy could find. "Inspect, inspect," he had told his father. "If you like this hotel, next April for Passover I will send you there again. Everything is kosher, the manager guaranteed it." Secretly, Izzy wondered how the splash parties and the new sauna baths advertised by the hotel could be kosher. He shrugged. Perhaps it was part of the American Plan. "An opera star from the Metropolitan, he comes to the hotel to conduct the *seder*," Izzy had told his father. The old man nodded and said, "For the Passover I am thinking I should invite Levon Stepanian. The music he would love." So off his family went to enjoy.

A train clattered into the station and Izzy struggled to his feet, clasping his brief bag and the heavy catalog. By the time he boarded the train all the seats were taken. He braced his feet and leaned against one of the upright poles. Directly in front of him a filthy-looking woman was sitting with her knees wide apart. Izzy closed his eyes in disgust and listened to the wheezing sigh of the fan.

He almost fell asleep on his feet—the train jolted to a stop at 14th Street. The doors clicked open, then closed, and the train started again.

"Pardon me," a voice said. It was a woman who apparently had just boarded the train. Izzy leaned clumsily forward, arching his back so that the woman had room to grasp the pole. Once he felt her knuckle graze his spine and he arched until he thought his back would break. So much room in the car, he thought, so why does she have to stand right behind me? The knuckle grazed his spine again and, in desperation, he shifted position, standing completely away from the pole. When the train screeched around a curve he stole a look at the woman. She had long, auburn-colored hair and a line of freckles—a necklace almost—just below her throat. Her looked away but irresistibly his eyes drifted back to the woman. She wore an open-neck peasant blouse and her shoulders were round and white as cream. Israel Padawer sighed. He did not dare to look at her face. She might be ugly and somehow he did not think he could stand that. He thought automatically of Sarah and her gaunt bosom. The Sears, Roebuck catalogue was so heavy that he felt his arm muscles fluttering.

The chin, Izzy argued with himself, the chin only. With the air of a man surveying a subway car for the first time, he gazed about him and ended with a brief glance at the woman's chin. Ach, such a chin! Cool and white like a lily it was.

A few minutes later, just as the train was pulling into Times Square, something very strange happened. The subway cars jolted together and Izzy thought, there is a madman at the controls. The woman twisted with the impact and fell heavily against Izzy. Her head brushed his shoulder.

"Oh," she exclaimed. "Oh, I'm so *sorry!* Look—I've gotten lipstick on your coat!"

Izzy peered down in confusion. It was true. A bright streak of red had appeared just over his heart.

"All right, all right," he stammered. "Pay it no attention—"

"But it's *not* all right! You poor man—look what I've done to you!"

She bent forward to examine the damage. Izzy felt the auburn hair graze the side of his chin. He flushed and wondered if he were going to faint.

"I know!" the woman said triumphantly. "I can fix that in a jiffy!"

The subway doors were open. Before Izzy realized what was happening, the woman had pulled him out of the car. His hands were weighted so that it was impossible for him to struggle. They were standing on the platform at Times Square.

"What—what are you doing, what?" stuttered Izzy.

He felt utterly confused. A film of steam crept up his eyeglasses. He was aware that the filthy-looking woman on the train was staring at them accusingly. Then the train was gone—the woman with the auburn hair was dabbing with her handkerchief at the lipstick stain.

"It's getting worse!" she cried. "I don't live far from here. I'll get it off for you. You've got to take a stain like that out right away!"

There was something in her voice, a warm urgency, that puzzled him. He looked into her face for the first time. There were freckles also on her wide cheekbones. She had large hazel eyes and a nose that was like finely molded wax. There was a softness to her face—a white softness, Izzy found the phrase forming in his mind—and of course the chin, so white and cool. Despite the whiteness of her skin, there was a sort of tropical beauty about the woman.

Israel Padawer proceeded to drop the Sears, Roebuck catalog which landed with a sharp cracking sound. He jumped forward.

The lovely hazel eyes were regarding him with amusement. She touched his arm and said softly, "Your book."

He did not trust himself to speak. Besides, what to say? He felt as if he were on another planet. He bent over to retrieve the catalog and in his confusion he bumped his head against her thigh. It was an exquisite sensation, like pressing against warm silk. When he straightened up he actually could feel a hammering in his ears.

She took the brief bag from his other hand. "Come on," she commanded, "we're wasting time." He followed her in a daze across the platform and up the stairs. She was a large woman, several inches taller than himself, and he stared at the dress gliding above her smooth bare legs.

They passed a hot-dog stand and for a dozen paces the rancid smell seemed to envelop the passage. Then suddenly they were on 42nd Street and it was starting to rain. Huge drops splashed around them, darkening the sidewalk.

"Come on, come on!" the woman called. "We'll get soaked!"

Izzy ran to catch up with her. They passed under the winking bright lights of the movie marquees and in this unreal setting his mind finally began to function again. Who was she? What did she want with him? There was a mutter of thunder. Was she leading him to some place where her partner was waiting? Where they would beat him up and rob him? He had heard such stories. In sudden fear, he clutched his wallet with his free hand.

"Wait!" he shouted. But she paid no attention to him. He watched his bag swinging through the crowd. She was a half-dozen steps ahead of him. They began to cross Eighth Avenue and a taxi splashed water on Izzy's trousers.

And then they were walking along a quiet street where the rain beat against the canopies of small French restaurants. She veered suddenly under the stoop of a building and took a key from her pocket.

Run! his instincts commanded him. Run, Israel, for your life—

But instead he followed her meekly inside the building and then she unlocked a second door and Izzy stood there quite ridiculously, waiting for the club to descend upon his head from behind.

"Well," she said, setting his bag on the floor, "I never thought we'd make it. Just listen to that rain." Gusts rattled the apartment windows, as if in affirmation, and then the rain began to sweep along the street in solid gray sheets.

The woman shook loose her hair. It was somehow an intensely feminine motion. She turned on a lamp and Izzy felt a curious longing to touch the damp dark strands.

"Give me your coat," she said. "I'll fix that lipstick stain with spot remover."

Still dazed by what was happening, he placed the catalog on the floor. It fell open to a page filled with corset displays and he hastily closed the catalog. He began to struggle out of his coat.

Now was the time, he thought desperately, for her confederate to come out of hiding and pin back his arms in the coat. . . .

But there was nothing—only the woman with her hand outstretched and those glorious hazel eyes and the rain beating against the windows. And then she had disappeared into another room with his coat, calling back to him, "Make yourself comfortable. There's sherry in the armoire. Help yourself."

Left alone, Izzy could only think, she is a *shiksa*, such a lovely *shiksa*. He looked about him as if plotting an escape route.

It was the strangest living room he had ever seen. The room had parquet floors and a high ceiling but it was almost barren of furniture. There was a table and several straight chairs at the far end of the room and, near the windows, two grand pianos. The pianos faced each other so that their curved shapes fitted together. Like lovers in an embrace, Izzy thought to himself. Behind the pianos was a row of shelves filled with phonograph records. Then he noticed the loudspeakers of a stereo system placed in opposite corners under the high ceiling. The ceiling itself, he saw now, was decorated with terra-cotta scrolls and floral patterns. The room was clean and dusted and he noticed that the floor seemed freshly waxed.

Izzy walked over to the nearest piano, taking care not to slip on the smooth floor, and stood looking down at it. He pressed a key and started back as a deep, rich note suddenly filled the room.

"Do you play?"

He turned around. The woman was watching him curiously. He had not heard her enter the room. No wonder! She was dressed in a bathrobe and her feet were bare!

She came toward him and he could sense her smooth white feet caressing the floor. Izzy stepped back and promptly sat down on the piano seat.

"No, no," he said quickly. "I'm not musical."

She threw back her head and laughed. Her laugh had a rich, warm ring. She came up to him and his eyes were fixed upon the belt of her robe. It was knotted like some huge exotic flower.

"You still have your things on," she said softly. "Don't you find me at all attractive?"

Izzy's hands gripped the edge of the piano seat. He swallowed and nodded dumbly, continuing to stare at the belt. It was green and made of velvet, the same material as the robe. He could see the swelling of her stomach and her thighs. He forced his head away and inspected the webbing on a loudspeaker in the far corner.

"Don't worry," she said. "I'm not going to attack you."

Then she gave a soft laugh and moved toward the window. He followed her now with his eyes, devouring her body at this safe distance. There was not a sound in the room except the rain beating against the glass. She stood looking out at the rain.

"I have to go," he said, finally finding his voice. "My coat—please, my coat."

"It's in the bedroom," she said. She seemed to have forgotten he was there. "Help yourself." She sat down at the other piano—the one facing into the room—and began to play. It was a melancholy tune and she seemed to grow sad as she played. She was no longer looking at him.

Izzy went into the bedroom. His jacket—perfectly clean now—was spread out neatly on the bed. A *round* bed! There was a round blue blanket on the bed and it appeared newly made up. The faint odor of cleaning fluid lingered in the bedroom like stale perfume.

He picked up the jacket—and then he understood. There was no trap, no sinister confederate. She liked him, she actually *liked* him. But why? It was crazy, all so crazy. The old fear welled within Israel Padawer and he hated himself for it. He began to curse himself in Yiddish. He should die, he was such a coward. He stood beside the bed holding the jacket and he could hear the piano. What was she playing? He wished suddenly that he knew something about music; he longed to be able to sing beside her as she played.

He draped the jacket over his arm and walked back into the living room.

The woman kept playing. Her auburn hair was dry now and a lock had fallen across her forehead. "You can't go out yet," she said matter-of-factly, her words falling in time with the sad piano notes. "Wait until the rain stops. You'll get drenched if you go outside now." She nodded toward his bag on the floor near the catalog. "Go ahead," she said. "Do your homework. I won't eat you alive."

"I—I don't want to do my homework," he said.

377

She looked up. "What do you want to do?" she asked, still playing.

He shrugged helplessly. The old fear fought with something else inside him. "I don't know," he said.

"Well," she replied, "if you don't know, then I certainly can't help you."

He stumbled over to the armoire and opened the door. There was a sherry decanter and some glasses on one shelf. Without understanding why, he seized a glass and placed it carefully on the parquet floor. Then he smashed the glass to bits under his shoe.

"Stop that!" she shouted.

"No," he said stubbornly and reached for another glass.

She stood up and hurried toward him. Her legs scissored free of the green robe. Her legs were long and white and full—they seemed possessed of some electric quality.

"Wait!" he cried out. "Stop there! You'll cut your feet!" Izzy moved away from the armoire. He dropped the glass in his hand and it fell with a musical tinkle. The woman started toward him again and now she stopped, so close he could hear her breathing. He raised his arms as if to defend himself from her blows. "*Who are you?*" he cried out in anguish.

She smiled and shook her head ever so slowly. "Does it matter?" she asked. She was watching him closely; the irises of her eyes were flecked with black. "Only one thing really matters . . ." She drew nearer. "Isn't that true?" Then she said, "You can tell genuine crystal by touching it."

Izzy uttered a moan. He reached out like a drowning man grasping for a raft. He pulled the belt and her robe fell free. She stood naked before him.

He caught his breath. He had never dreamed a woman's body could be so idyllically formed . . . no longer could he restrain himself. Her eyes, half closed now into the shape of almonds, kept watching him, daring him. The long, curved lashes, dark as the iris flecks, quickened his desire. "I want you," he said with a desperate groan. "I may be damned for it, *but I want you—*"

He touched one thigh tentatively as if to convince himself she was real. And then the pressure of his hand traced a faint rosy course, up along her hips and the swell of her stomach, up to the rich white curve of her breasts.

"My, my," she murmured, taking off his glasses and holding them in one hand. With the other hand she tugged sharply at the tight curls behind his ear. She pressed against him and he closed his eyes.

He smelled the richness and warmth of her body, a *shiksa* body, and he thought: I am like a snake shedding its old skin.

And then in the round bed. The bed became an island they filled with their love-making.

But with this woman it was all so different, marveled Izzy. She was tender and passionate by turns and there was such a supreme sense of joy on her part that the last vestige of remorse fell away from Izzy. He had dared, he told himself. He had finally committed a genuine act of daring and in his daring he achieved heaven.

In the great round bed she stroked his body and kissed the glossy hairs upon his back. She even kissed him *there*—such kisses—and the ecstasy was almost more than Izzy could endure.

But the greatest surprise of all was his ability to make love under her patient and tender tutelage.

"No-o-o. Not yet, not yet," she whispered and bit the lobe of his ear playfully. "Ah-h-h, that's my sweet one. My sweet, sweet metronome." She took his lower lip between her teeth. "Stay in me, stay quietly. You'll be amazed how long you can stay. Just concentrate, concentrate quietly." She laughed then, a low and tropical laugh, and the sensation for Izzy, feeling his power respond and grow with this woman, was indescribably wonderful.

She had a tiny red vein alongside one nostril and somehow this hint of ugliness served to heighten her sensuous effect upon him. He touched the vein with his nose. There was a sweet, wonderful smell to her body. Myrrh, he thought, myrrh and frankincense. For the first time words he had heard all his life became reality.

"Thy lips are like a thread of scarlet," he whispered, "and thy speech is comely." He kissed her forehead. "Thy temples are like a piece of pomegranate within thy locks."

"What's that?" she said. "I like it."

"The Song of Solomon. It's from the Bible."

"Oh."

"Thy two breasts are like two young roes that are twins"—he touched her breasts with his lips—"which feed among the lilies."

"You are my Solomon?" she asked.

"Yes. I am your Solomon." He sighed. "Yes, *yes!*"

Later—it was early Saturday morning and the rain had stopped—she told him about herself. It is the *Shabbat*, Izzy thought for a fleeting moment, and then touched her hair where it thinned slightly above the temple. Her hair is like softly spun bronze, he thought.

Her name was Gwen Overland and she gave piano lessons at home during the week. Her husband worked as a saxophone player on a cruise ship that would return in thirty-three days from the Mediterranean. When she mentioned her husband Izzy felt neither remorse nor jealousy. She gave herself to him so completely that somehow they seemed to be the only two people alive in the world.

"I always go down to the pier when Ralph sails," she said. "He comes out on the deck and plays a final serenade for me. There's such a sad tone to a tenor sax without any accompaniment. Did you know that?" Izzy shook his head. "Well, it's true," she said. She turned her head to the wall and he watched the jugular vein swell in her neck.

"What is it?" he murmured. "You seem so troubled all of a sudden . . ."

"Troubled, yes," she said finally, turning back to stare at him. "That's as good a word as any." She wet a finger and touched it to a curl on his neck. "The truth is," she said slowly, "that for the past month Ralph has been a perfect failure in bed. Nothing happened for him, absolutely nothing. It's driven me crazy." Her voice reminded Izzy of the mournful tune she had played on the piano. "Then when I saw you on the subway . . . well, I'd been thinking, 'maybe it's me, maybe it's me.' I saw you then and I wanted you more than you can know. And I wanted to find out about myself. Well . . . I found out." She reached out for him. "Kiss me, darling—oh, my darling one."

They remained inside the apartment for the entire weekend. They ate yogurt and fresh fruit on the bedside table and they made love. She taught him how to eat ripe mangoes, scooping the pulp out from between the skin and the long, flat seed. He had never eaten a mango before and the fruit reminded him of the texture of her breasts. To Izzy's surprise he found that food stimulated his sexual appetite. His pulse had dropped to a slow, even beat and there was no skipping whatsoever, not even after making love.

"You," she said on Sunday morning, biting into a peach. "Your job?"

"I work in Wall Street. I sell securities."

"I own ten shares of American Telephone. An aunt left them to me. I keep the stock certificate out in the living room. In the jacket of a Vivaldi record." She touched a napkin to her mouth to catch the juice. Her movements delighted him; every gesture was so utterly feminine and filled with grace. Even when she would raise her elbows preparatory to blowing her nose, it sent a shiver of delight through him.

"That's very dangerous," he said with mock solemnity. "Your stock certificate you should keep in a safety-deposit box."

"I know. But I love chamber music. So, if anything, it's a tribute to American Telephone." She put down the peach and stretched luxuriously. Her breasts lifted above the top of the sheet. "Who needs stocks anyway?" she said. "There's too much wonderful music to buy."

Early Sunday afternoon the rain began again. They made love while Vivaldi's music strummed lustily in the stereo set. "This is called 'The Seasons,'" she said, rocking her head on the pillow in time to the rhythm. He listened to the muted strings and felt a sudden longing to become a violinist. She gripped his arm. "Listen," she said. The tempo was speeding up. "This is the pastoral dance for shepherds and their nymphs," she said, and then, "Ah-h-h, my sweet one . . . slowly, slowly, slowly."

She had closed her eyes and, still embracing her tightly, he kissed her eyelids.

Later she put on a bathing suit. It was a black bathing suit with scallops in the side that heightened the electric quality of her skin. "I'm an indoor bather," she said and laughed. "I *hate* the sun. It wrinkles my elbows."

"I want to put on a bathing suit myself," he demanded.

She found a pair of trunks that belonged to her husband, shockingly bright trunks with madras patches. The other man had drifted from reality; Izzy felt only compassion for him, as for an old friend who had drowned at sea.

They joked about all the annual reports and papers in the brief bag that Izzy had not opened. He began to nuzzle her bathing suit. "Stop it!" she cried with pleasure. "You're tickling!"

There was a brass button on the front of her suit connecting the top and bottom. He worked at the button with his teeth, keeping his hands planted on the bed sheet. Finally the button gave way and he pulled the suit free with his teeth. . . .

When he prepared to leave the apartment early Monday morning, there was something of the poignancy of a soldier's farewell as he regarded her.

"I will call," he said. And then, "You."

"Yes." She patted the coat where the lipstick smear had been.

"I must see you—oh, how I hate to leave now," he said. Izzy shook his head. "But I must have time to think. Plans I must make for us. You understand?"

"I understand." She was adjusting his tie. "There is one thing," she said slowly, her lashes lowered.

"What is it? Anything. Anything you ask."

"The Sears, Roebuck catalog. Can I keep it?"

He nodded and suddenly tears filled his eyes. The time clock in his mind had started to turn relentlessly. He knew that he must go to the house in Riverdale and perform certain chores—perhaps even manufacture excuses for the weekend—before his family returned at noon from the Catskills. "Yes, yes," he cried. "Keep it, keep it."

He touched her once more, quite tenderly, on the temple. It was as if he meant to bless her. Then he stooped quickly and picked up his brief bag. He did not trust himself to speak again.

Outside, the sun was shining and the street was filled with little pools of still water. For some reason, he looked down at his tie. She had tied it so that the initials CM were showing. Israel Padawer, squaring his shoulders, let the tie flutter gently in front of his belt buckle. It is our flag, he thought, our flag of love.

29

The moment Poke stepped inside the board room he sensed something was wrong. He thought suddenly about Korea again; he saw bodies frozen into grotesque shapes and he could smell the stench and the disinfectant.

"It's Voorhees, Seth Voorhees!" Izzy was yelling at him.

Izzy ran out of his cubicle and gripped Poke by the arm. Izzy's face was white as chalk.

"What happened?" said Poke.

"Heart attack! Voorhees just had a heart attack. On the floor, on the floor! They just picked him up in an ambulance." Izzy took off his glasses and waved them in the air.

Poke gave a low whistle.

"Mouth to mouth," Izzy said wildly, "they gave him mouth to mouth right there on the floor."

"Is he dead?" asked Poke.

"No, at least not yet." Izzy followed Poke into his

cubicle and sat down forlornly beside the desk. "I haven't heard anything more," Izzy added. He put on his glasses but his face was still the color of chalk. "The other partners, they're all in Mr. Kimbridge's office right now."

Noel Bigelow swung around in his chair. "This does it for me," he announced to Poke. "I'm giving up cigarettes—for good this time. Christ, I heard last week that some partner dropped dead in the back office. But his firm kept that part out of the papers."

"What do we do?" pleaded Izzy.

"Do?" replied Poke. "What can we do? We go right on with our jobs, that's all. You'll hear something soon enough." He clapped Izzy on the shoulder. "So take it easy. Okay?"

Izzy nodded uncertainly.

There was the crackle of cellophane. Poke saw Noel crush a pack of cigarettes in his hand and, with a ceremonial air, deposit the mass in the wastebasket. "Two points, Princeton," sang out Noel.

"Nice shot," said Poke dryly.

An hour later the partners were filing quietly out of the office of Thatcher Kimbridge.

"Howard," the managing partner said, "I'd like a word with you."

Howard Merriam retraced his steps. "At least," said Thatcher, his hand resting on the telephone, "what the doctor just said is encouraging. It's a stroke. The doctors have agreed on that. Seth has a good chance of pulling out."

"Sure he'll pull out. Don't you worry about Seth. He's too mean to die yet."

"Meanwhile," said Thatcher, "life goes on—"

"This does it, you realize," said Merriam. "This ends the opposition to your incorporation plan."

386

"Yes," said Thatcher slowly. "Yes, I guess it does at that." He rubbed the side of his nose wearily. "But I would have ended it one way or another. Seth simply took the wrong stand. That's all there is to it."

Merriam looked at the other man for a few moments. "You're right," he said finally. He ran a finger along the glass top of the desk. "I think Seth realized it, too," he said. "He knew he was wrong. But he just had to keep fighting." He scowled at the stock tape spilling into the basket.

Thatcher took a deep breath. "Howard, I'm going down on the floor."

"You're *what?*"

"I'm going to take Seth's place on the floor. I think we need our own man down there to run things. We owe that much to our customers."

"But I thought we just worked that out! I thought we agreed to let Tatum, Rollinson handle our floor business. Why, they're the top firm of two-dollar brokers. They can take care of things for us just fine!"

"Can they?" said Thatcher. "They've got their hands full already. Sure, they'd be tickled pink to take us on. But would we get the best executions? I don't think so. I think Tatum, Rollinson will take care of their present clients first—and Kimbridge & Co. next." He held up his hand. "Oh, sure, I know we agreed on it. And for a few days, anyway, it won't make too much difference. But that's what I wanted to talk to you about. What do you think of my going down as the floor partner for Kimbridge & Co.?"

"I'll tell you! I think you're crazy. Good Lord, Thatch! Get that old dream out of your head. What the hell are you trying to prove? That you're just as good on the floor as Seth? Or your father? Don't you realize what's happening in this business? The floorman isn't what he used to be—why, Thatch, in a few

387

years they're going to be handling the floor transactions out of computer consoles! Even now it's a routine down there. The floor is just a place for the highest-paid messenger boys in the world to strut their stuff!"

"No, Howard, I don't agree with you. At any rate, I've made up my mind."

"And who's going to run things up here? Tell me that. This is where you're really needed. Hell's bells, Thatch! Who do you think built up this firm to what it is today? No, now don't interrupt me. It wasn't Jared and it certainly isn't Seth. It's you, Thatch. You! Can't you get that through your stubborn head? You've got the talents of a true administrator. So you can't trade stocks, so who the hell cares! I can go out and hire you a dozen crack traders before nightfall. One just as good as the other." Merriam paused, the concern for his partner showing plainly on his face. "Do you realize what Jared's concept of cost control was? Telling the last man who leaves each office to turn off the lights, that's what."

Thatcher Kimbridge sat listening. "I'll tell you what, Howard," he said at last. "I won't do anything about it for a few days. But I'm going down on the floor and take a look around. Let's leave it at that right now, shall we?"

The telephone rang.

"Yes?" Thatcher Kimbridge said. "What is it?"

"I have Mr. Lincoln on the line in Palm Springs," Miss Donahue said. "No, I didn't tell him a thing. He told me, though, that November is the best month for a vacation. He shot a hole in one this morning."

The managing partner nodded impatiently. "Put him on, if you please. Fred? Bad news—"

"Thatch? Darling, where are you?"

388

"Here, Edith. In the library."

Thatcher got up from the armchair to kiss his wife. "Well," he said, "how is he?"

"Well, he asked his wife today for the latest quote on their apartment in River House."

"That means he's feeling better."

"Yes, I think so."

"Seth called up the office this morning," said Thatcher. "He wanted some order pads sent up. That's another good sign. He's making quite a recovery."

Edith rearranged the roses in a vase absently and then she said, "I know. When I saw him he was practicing on them. He put the pads under the blanket just as I came into the room. But I saw him writing—with his left hand." She looked at her husband. "What have you been doing?" she asked. "You don't usually sit in the library before dinner unless you want to think."

He smiled fondly at her. "That's just what I've been doing," he said. "Thinking. I've been thinking how odd it is about life that nobody ever rings a bell when a crisis suddenly comes up." He shrugged. "And there's no bell when a crisis is over. It's almost as if some things never really happened. A week ago I was all set to tangle with Seth and now it's all over, finished. But then there's something else, too . . ."

"What?"

"The feeling I still have," said Thatcher slowly. "The feeling that I've been cheated somehow by the stroke Seth had. Do you know something? I *wanted* to fight him. I really wanted to fight him."

Edith was silent. Then she picked up a rose petal from the table and said, "The doctors allow Seth only one visitor at a time. When I got there all four of his wives were standing outside in the corridor. His second wife had flown in from New Orleans. How odd it was! There they were all in a row and they looked exactly like sisters! Except that there must be about ten years between each one of them. And then . . . Seth wanted to see me last of all. Wasn't that strange? His wife came out of the room and told me what he had said about River House and then I went inside. In sort of the place of honor."

"What did he say to you?"

"Oh, he thanked me for the presents. He thought it was remarkable that I remembered his liking plum jam. He even unscrewed the top and tasted the jam while I was there." She reached out and took Thatcher's hand. "But it's what he *didn't* say, what I could see in his eyes. I think he wanted to ask me something but was too proud to do it. I think he wanted you to keep the floor partnership open for him."

"But it will be six months, six months at least, before he can come back to work. Maybe longer."

She nodded. "I think he realizes that—and all the other obstacles." She drew back her hand. "Just as I was about to leave, he reached under his pillow. The way a little boy hides something precious. He said to give you this."

Edith Kimbridge opened her purse and took out a worn bronze coin. It was Jared Kimbridge's tossing coin.

30

Thatcher entered the Stock Exchange building and found his excitement quickening at the prospect of what lay ahead. He passed through the corridor flanked by elevator doors—the same corridor where Seth Voorhees had been rolled out on a stretcher—and stopped at the entrance to the trading floor.

This is where it all is, he thought, this *is* Wall Street for men like his father and Seth. The floor. Nothing else mattered. Even Thatcher, as an office broker, an "upstairs" broker, may as well have worked in Mozambique as far as a true floorman was concerned. When Thatcher was elected a governor of the Stock Exchange—an "upstairs" governor—his father had scoffed: "It takes the board of governors ten years to make a decision. Three different committees take turns looking at something. Their terms run three years apiece. Then it takes them another year to vote." How wrong his father had been. Jared Kimbridge's will had stipulated that the Kimbridge & Co.

membership remain in his name as long as the firm itself existed—quite contrary to the rules of the Stock Exchange. But Thatcher had pushed a special dispensation through the board after his father's death. He fought, wheedled, and pleaded with his fellow governors. The opposition was formidable. But he won out. It had taken two months, not ten years.

A husky guard gave Thatcher an incurious glance at the entrance. The guard was dressed in a tan shirt, olive-drab trousers, and a matching cap. He carried a pistol in a brown holster and he was standing on a small mat.

Thatcher wrote out his name on a form and handed it to the guard who stepped, almost reluctantly, from his mat to summon Rex Banta from the floor. From beyond the swinging glass doors, the view blocked completely by a wide bulletin board, came a strange, relentless sound.

He had telephoned Rex Banta to arrange for this visit. It was as though he were seeking some answer from the floor itself. . . .

Rex was an old friend, a member of the same Skull and Bones delegation at college. In his younger days Thatcher had been a welcome visitor to the Banta mansion in Tuxedo Park and had dated Banta's favorite sister before he met Edith. One dawn he and the sister had stolen out to the pool for a swim; they debated endlessly on the best procedure for trapping a bat and smuggling it inside the bedroom where Rex lay asleep. It seemed a glorious adventure, and for a few moments Thatcher remembered how they crept hand in hand through the stable with its cool, intimate smells, and how the scattered straw delicately spiked his bare feet. My Lord, he wondered, attempting now to match the impassive expression on the face of the guard, did that ever really happen?

"Thatch! You rascal, you! Where the *hell* have you been hiding?"

Rex Banta, grayer and thinner than Thatcher wanted to see, suddenly was pounding his back, shaking his hand, pinning a Visitor badge on his coat, and drawing him through the door, all in a single swirling motion. The sound of the trading floor—like pounding surf—filled Thatcher's ears.

"Hello, Rex. It's good to see you."

Banta paused beside the bulletin board. "Tell me. How is Seth? Will he make it—or is that just window dressing from the medics?" There was a frown on Banta's lined gray face. "My God, Thatch. I was standing no more than six feet from him, I was trying to unload a thousand Kennecott, I saw the whole thing happen. Seth had flipped his coin to see whether he or Paul Gentry was going to get a block they hit the bid on. Seth bent over to pick up the coin and—well—he just kept going until he smacked the floor. A Merrill Lynch man stretched him out and loosened his tie. Christ, those fellows are all *over* the lot these days. By the way," he said as an afterthought, "Seth won the toss. But then I suppose you know that. Now tell me. How is he?"

"He's going to pull through, the doctors say."

"Thank God for that."

"He needs a lot of rest. That's the order right now, plenty of rest."

"The good men are popping off like flies this year. Maybe it's this damn market that does it to them. I don't know. And who takes their place?" Banta snorted. "Ninety-day wonders, that's who. First thing they want to do is fill out an application for the luncheon club. You'd think they've been starving since puberty." He stopped to glare at a notice on the bulletin board proposing a new member. "Now tell

393

me. What do you want to see? Anything in particular? Been a fairly routine morning so far. I like the feel of Avon Products. It's yeasty."

"Oh, nothing special. It's just that I haven't been down here for years and thought it was time I took a look around. Can we just walk around a bit? And before I leave I'd like to stop in at the Kimbridge & Co. booth. Just to see how things are going. How do you stand on time?"

"Like Rudy Vallee. My time is yours. That's the advantage of having three other partners on the floor."

They walked out into the main trading room.

The room was cavernous, like an immense armory. Thatcher's gaze, pulled upward as if by some powerful magnet, was drawn to the ceiling. The coffered ceiling shone resplendently in its solid gold leaf. It gave a celestial elegance to the huge room.

His eyes dropped finally to the floor. It was littered with scraps of paper, pink and yellow and white and blue, shredded order slips, quotation blanks, a corner of some market letter, bits of newspaper, and—incongruously—an empty wrapper of Juicy Fruit chewing gum. He moved his shoe and a pink slip of paper caught his eye: "Please Quote." The loose piles of litter gave the room a careless, unkempt appearance, not unlike debris deposited by hordes of picnickers.

"Squad!" At Thatcher's elbow a broker was bellowing, a slip waving in his uplifted hand. "*Squad!*" A page in a tan jacket hurried past and expertly extracted the slip.

Scattered about the floor were some two thousand men, brokers, pages, specialists, traders, supervisors, telephone clerks. They moved in a sort of swaying football scrimmage bound by a universal rule of the game: a fine of up to fifty dollars for running.

Thatcher found an empty patch on the floor. In

front of him was a neatly dressed man wearing a Tattersall vest. The man sat on the collapsible seat of a trading post. Apparently he was a broker with nothing to do at the moment. He sat nonchalantly with his legs crossed, leafing through a newspaper with the undisturbed air of a bench sitter in Central Park.

The *sound* of the room, that was the most eerie part of it to Thatch. A throbbing sea of sound that rushed continually through the vast marble-halled space, a muscled amorphous sound that seemed to rise right out of the hardwood flooring. A steady sea noise distilled from hundreds of outcries, from questions that invariably started "How is—?" or "What're you making—?" or simply the name of a stock blurted out and answered in curt, noncommittal tones by the specialist; a sound compounded of shouted bids and offers, the slow, deliberate tearing of an order blank by a disgusted trader, the urgent whisper of leather along unpolished tongue-and-groove maple. And above it all the imperious clacking of the annunciator boards, hanging huge and gray on opposite walls, going *slap! slap! slap!* as numbers flipped into view, a kind of sea monster summons that sent brokers who made $90,000 a year scurrying to their telephone booths like carhops at a drive-in restaurant. Hurry, hurry, hurry, the twin boards slapped in a raucous beat, grab your orders and get them filled.

The old-timers on the floor liked to say that once you got used to the sound you never even heard it. But Thatcher did not believe that. He remembered that his father could step onto this floor and, without looking at the tape or going into a crowd, tell what the market was doing just by the sound. When the market turned strong, a certain expectant note overlay the rolling ocean roar; when stock prices were headed down on heavy volume, another sound took its place, a deep sighing sound that at times achieved the pitch of some monstrous inhuman wail.

Behind him Thatcher heard a broker say: "I get so cold—if I like a stock I want to see it open down." Another voice said: "How was it at the opening?" The first broker said: "Up. The damn stock was up." The second broker: "You still like it?" The reply came: "No, I decided then I don't like it."

Thatcher felt a tug at his elbow. "Want you to meet one of my partners," Rex Banta said.

With a start of surprise, Thatcher realized how few of the men in this room he actually knew. There was something about the floor that drew together its inhabitants in a clannish, almost primitive, sense. Some critics called this place "a club," but that did not bore into the truth of the matter. No, it was something that reached far deeper, a sense almost of a band of men who relished standing together against the rest of the world. This suspicion of all other persons emanated from the specialists and the traders; it caught up the two-dollar brokers and it even fanned out among the commission brokers whose prime allegiance was to their member firms. Thatcher often had sensed this divided loyalty in his father and in Seth. And he felt it, as real as the sea noise throbbing about him, in Rex Banta whom he had known since college.

Thinking again now about his father, Thatcher watched the tall man with the hawk eyes who was approaching. Banta's partner, wearing the white plastic badge of a Stock Exchange member on his lapel, peered sharply at Thatcher as the introductions were made. The man seemed to relax slightly when he heard the Kimbridge name. Thatcher had the sensation of having passed some guarded initial test but it was only the tiniest of advances.

"Volume's picking up," the partner said crisply to Banta.

Banta nodded in assent. "Motors up a quarter," he verified.

The partner started to pull Banta away for a moment, then evidently decided his message was permissible for Thatcher to hear. "I just spoke to the specialist," the partner said, "to tell him our buyer is no longer interested in picking up that forty thousand shares. My guess is that he did it off the board. Now that I've alerted the specialist, he knows we're pulling back. If some other buyer comes in, he won't be afraid to—"

Thatcher Kimbridge, impelled by a sense of propriety, walked a few paces away until he was out of earshot. He glanced around for the broker in the Tattersall vest but the man had disappeared.

At the next post a specialist was flipping the pages in his book. Some of the specialists, Thatcher knew, simply traded numbers. They did not care a hoot for the company, for its new products, its employees, its capital spending plans, the study on decentralizing management controls. It was all there in the numbers, these specialists said, everything about the company was reduced to the arithmetic on the tape. That's all you had to trade, the numbers.

The timbre of the floor's sea sound—Thatcher wondered, had it changed in his new position? He cocked an ear but he could detect no difference in the pounding roar. Men hurried past him and he felt oddly out of place, as if he had stumbled by mistake into a sacrosanct temple of some mysterious cult. He rubbed the side of his nose furiously and looked up at the huge tape cutting high above one corner of the floor. He picked out Telephone, Motors, Steel, IBM, the handful of stocks that men on the floor watched warily as a gauge of the general market. The clock suspended near the balcony blinked and its orange bulbs said eleven-thirty-one.

Thatcher imagined himself at the Kimbridge & Co. booth thirty minutes before the market opened. At that hour the floor would be hushed, tense, expectant, stirring with its own restless electricity. First, he would straighten out any DK's left over from the previous day's trades. The DK's—Don't Knows—that failed to identify the brokerage firm on the other side of the trade. Then he would parcel out the limit orders and the open orders to the two-dollar brokers. The main market orders, the important ones where executions were so vital because the clients were professionals who would be watching the tape, he would handle himself. By this time he would have checked with the specialists to determine whether they had light books or heavy books in the stocks for which he held large orders. He must remember to call the office as soon as possible after the opening to keep the clients informed of his progress. Once the market orders were filled, he might get some client to come down an eighth or maybe a quarter so that he could get rid of an entire block at what he considered to be a good price. He would have to learn, he told himself, the specialists he could trust, the ones he could open up to and not be afraid of being massacred. He knew that Seth Voorhees could stand in a crowd and tell the difference between some broker's buy order covering a short and another broker's buy order to establish a long position. That type of delicate judgment took time to develop and some men on the floor never really got the hang of it in a lifetime. But he would! He vowed to limit himself to twenty-minute lunches his first weeks on the floor, no lunch at all if necessary—

"WAIT TILL THE SUN SHINES, NELLIE . . ."

The words, springing up unaccountably at some post, boomed across the floor, suddenly drowning out the throbbing ocean sound. Thatcher looked around the room. On every side of him the men appeared to drop whatever they were doing to join in the chorus. "—AND THE CLOUDS GO DRIFTING BY."

A reedy voice sounded strangely familiar. Banta! He hadn't heard Rex Banta sing since the Thursday-night meetings at Bones, and here again was that unforgettable nasal intonation. Everybody in sight was singing. Banta's partner, bawling lustily, was swinging his pencil as though it were a baton.

"YOU AND I—I—I . . ."

Another chorus began, and the singing swelled. The entire floor had been transformed into an impromptu glee club. The singing tugged at Thatcher. He opened his mouth to join in—and then suddenly decided against it.

That was a strange thing about the floor, he mused, standing quite still among the singing throng and trying not to appear foolish. The floor had that inexplicable quality that kept it forever darting between stuffy conservatism and the level of prep-school pranks. "WE'LL BE SO HAPPY, NELLIE . . ."

When a person watched this performance, Thatcher was thinking, he could believe the old stories about the horseplay. Pinning a paper cup on the tail of a member's coat and filling it with water. Hazing a new broker by sending him into a crowd with orders to buy a fictitious stock. Attaching a donkey tail to a coat and trailing the victim around the floor with shouts of "Hee-haw! Hee-haw!" In the old days, when trading got dull, some brokers would practice drop-kicking a football into the Visitors' Gallery. Or they would set fire to a pile of papers on the floor and then step aside, cheering as the fire brigade of pages rushed into action. Why, not too many years ago average trading volume had dropped below one million shares a day. Good Lord! Suppose that happened again! Every man in the room would be out of business. In more recent years a new prank had made its appearance—the Countdown. "Ten . . . nine . . . eight . . ." the voices would boom. "Three . . . two . . . one . . . ZERO!" And colored balloons filled with helium would go sailing up from a dozen trading posts, bobbing at last against the majestic gold ceiling that was five stories high.

"BY-Y-Y . . . AND . . . BY-Y-Y-Y."

The singing stopped instantly, the figures on the floor began moving again, the shouts began to rise and die, the ocean roll of sound flowed back onto its wooden shores.

Rex Banta stood beside Thatcher, red-faced and grinning.

"Well," said Thatcher, "what the hell caused *that?*"

"Du Pont," panted Banta. "A twenty-thousand-share block. On an uptick."

"Oh," said Thatcher. "I honestly didn't notice it on the tape." Du Pont, he admonished himself, he must remember to keep watching it, too.

"Want to visit your booth?"

"Yes, let's do that," replied Thatcher. "I'd like to see how things are going—if there are any problems. We've got Tatum, Rollinson handling our trades now that Seth is out of action."

"Good outfit," said Banta, nodding his approval. "One of their best floormen—he started out here as a page but he had that Irish push that you can't miss— used to stutter years ago. Scared out of his wits that he'd stutter when he got into a crowd with a big order to fill. But the first day cured him. Never stuttered since." They were dodging their way across the floor. "That's the way it goes," said Banta. "You either make it or you don't. It's just like taking your solo flight."

Banta had been in the Air Force during World War II, having twisted the proper arms all the way up to the top. Thatcher went to Banta's send-off party at the Brook Club. He had wanted desperately to join up, but his father had persuaded him that running the home office of Kimbridge & Co. was a more important duty.

They approached the booth of Kimbridge & Co.— marked by a small sign beside the battery of wall telephones. Above the telephones was a row of metal spikes that speared the orders for that morning. The booth also contained an opened bag of potato chips resting on a ledge, several newspapers, and a crudely-painted slogan on a box top for shoes that read: IF YOU CAN KEEP YOUR HEAD IN THE MIDST OF ALL THIS CONFUSION . . . YOU DON'T UNDERSTAND THE SITUATION. These telephones, connected to the firm's order desk at 50 Wall, linked the booth to the outside world. An order clerk in a linen jacket was standing with his back to the floor, a telephone cradled on his shoulder as he made notes on a pad. The clerk was nodding his head automatically.

Thatcher stood to one side, waiting for the young man to finish. He recalled the time he had telephoned his father at this same booth. The news tickers had just flashed word that the Japanese had occupied the Philippines. "Buy the Philippine sugars!" his father had shouted in response. "The Philippine sugar stocks trading on the West Coast exchanges! Buy all you can get for the house account—across the board. Let's see a second." He could visualize his father inspecting the vest-pocket notebook where he kept a record of all trades for the account of Kimbridge & Co. "Your buying limit is three hundred and twenty thousand dollars. You got that? Those sugars must be dropping like blazes right this second. But they'll come back someday. And come back big! Thatcher, you call the Coast yourself." Thatcher had started to object. His feeling was that if the stocks seemed such a good speculation the Research Department should fire off a bulletin for the firm's aggressive trading accounts. But his father would not listen; he could not stomach the prospect of competing with his own customers and thereby probably paying higher prices for the stocks he wanted. So Thatcher had called the Coast. As his father had anticipated, the Philippine sugar stocks were being dumped on the market in wild activity. Checking by telephone for the lowest offers he could obtain, Thatcher found a strange exultation creeping over him. He spent the afternoon buying stocks three thousand miles away, virtually catching the securities in bushel baskets, and by five-thirty he had reached the limit; Kimbridge & Co. had invested nearly one-third of a million dollars of its own capital in less than four hours. The following day Thatcher refrained from sending out a research bulletin because the firm had already established a position in the sugar stocks. That was a fine point of morality over which Jared Kimbridge normally would have scoffed; but his father had been too jubilant to care. And, of course, time eventually proved out the wisdom of his father's spot decision; Kimbridge & Co. cashed in its position with tremendous profits.

The clerk had completed the call. Thatcher Kimbridge stepped up to the booth and asked politely, "Things running smoothly? No problems?"

The clerk looked at him blankly. "Sure," he said finally. "We always got problems." His eyes flicked over the Visitor badge. "But what the hell is it to you, mister?"

Thatcher's face reddened. Suddenly he understood. *The youth did not recognize him!* Thatcher turned away to hide his embarrassment. Rex Banta started to say something angrily to the clerk but Thatcher silenced him with an upraised hand. "God damn . . ." sputtered Banta.

The chief order clerk hurried up to the booth. "Why, Mr. Kimbridge," he said in surprise. "Why, good morning, sir."

The young clerk, having realized his mistake, dropped a handful of orders on the floor. With an agonized face, he tried to mumble an apology to the managing partner.

"That's all right, son," Thatcher said. "You go right on with your job." He stooped over. "Here," he said, "I'll help you pick these things up. We can't keep our customers waiting, can we?"

A few moments later Thatcher Kimbridge turned away from the booth. His eyes had a strained look; he did not seem to notice the figures scurrying around him in their ghostlike scrimmage. Finally he let out a long breath. So—at last—the floor had given him its answer. It was like getting the word from the Delphic oracle. Yes, he thought, Howard was right. He had no business down here. His place was in the office. That's what he was—no more and no less—an upstairs broker.

He gave a tight smile to Banta. "I'm all through, Rex," he said. "Thanks for the tour."

The two men walked quickly across the floor. Thatcher glanced up at the tape but the prices did not register in his brain. At the entrance he surrendered his badge to the guard.

"Look," said Banta, still sharing Thatcher's embarrassment, "give me ten minutes. Then we'll pop upstairs for lunch. Even buy you a drink, old-timer. How's that?"

Thatcher shook his head. "I've got a pile of desk work to tackle back at the office. My regards to the family."

"Okay," said Banta, eyeing him carefully. "But remember—it's an open offer. You just hit it whenever you're ready."

"Yes," replied Thatcher, "I'll keep it in mind."

He turned away from Banta. Yes, he was thinking now, the trading floor held a quality he had never realized before. That smell, it was almost exactly like the dank coolness of a stable.

31

After leaving the apartment with Joan of Arc huddled on the floor, Noel had walked for half a block and then climbed inside a cab as a precaution against being seen on the street by Deirdre. The prospect of going back to his own apartment somehow did not appeal to him; he was still too keyed up. Without quite knowing why, he gave the cabdriver the address of the saloon on Third Avenue.

The place was much the same as on the night they first met. The long, decklike reach of the bar, the smell of beer and old wood, the same travel posters of Ireland, if anything a bit more grimy now. But the bartender was new: a thin man with long black sideburns who twitched his mouth experimentally each time he served a drink. Noel consumed a number of martinis, still fifty cents apiece, and did not complain about the quantity of vermouth which seemed to have increased somewhat.

He drank steadily, trying to erase the memory of

both Deirdre and the cat from his mind. He stared stupidly at the paper daffodils and he cursed his ill fortune. Everything had been going so beautifully for him until that god-damned cat jumped into the bed! By his sixth martini he was gloating in the recollection of blood on the whiskers of Joan of Arc.

The following morning his mind had cleared considerably. There was still a chance with Deirdre, he told himself. However, he must plot his moves with the greatest of care. It would be very ticklish sailing.

He must call her soon, otherwise it might appear suspicious. He waited another day, and that evening in his apartment, fortified by a small pitcher of his own martinis, Noel picked up the telephone. The proper approach, he rehearsed his strategy once again, was to depend upon the Big Lie.

"Yes?" Deirdre's voice was muffled, as though she were talking with a handkerchief at her nose.

"Greetings! This is the old sailor. Home from the sea. Speaking of which, when can I see you?"

"Oh, Noel, the most terrible thing has happened."

"Deirdre! What's the matter? What's happened?"

There was a sob and then she said, "It's Joan of Arc. She's *dead!* Oh, Noel, I came home and there she was. Just lying on the floor."

"How did it happen?" Careful, he told himself, careful.

"I don't know-w-w. She seemed perfectly all right when I left in the morning. The vet wanted to perform an autopsy. But I couldn't stand the thought of that. He thinks it might have been poisoning. But how? How? And then last night I thought I heard her. Rustling around in her litter pan. I jumped out of bed and ran to the bathroom—"

"Oh, darling, that's terrible. I know how you must

feel. Can I come over? I could shoot over there right now!"

"No, no. You're sweet, Noel. But, well, I just don't feel like seeing anyone."

"Tomorrow night then?"

"No, please. Maybe later. Maybe next week. But just now . . ."

Jesus, he thought, she's retreated into mourning. Deirdre Kimbridge was the all-time world champion for mourning. This time she was setting up a litter pan for a gravestone. Damn her, anyway!

Then he pictured her sitting beside the telephone, and he knew how badly he wanted her. That lovely body . . . and no one around to console her. He felt a desperate urge to keep talking; that was one way of reaching out to her. So he changed the subject. He told Deirdre something he had been careful never to mention. Maybe it would cheer her up.

"You remember that night I met you in the bar?" he said.

"Yes," she replied with a sniffle.

"Well, I was getting pretty fed up with things at the bank, let me tell you. That same day I did something to get even. I walked out of the bank during my lunch hour and put through an anonymous phone call to the manager of the safe-deposit vault. I told him I was a very disgruntled customer and there was something he should know about. I told him I had put a fish in my deposit box, a dead fish. I told him that in another couple days his whole vault would be smelling of old fish! Isn't that just great!"

"Did you really do it?"

"Of course not. It was just a hoax. But can't you just see him downstairs in that precious vault with its thick gold carpet! They must have run around like madmen, wondering if they dared to open up every one of the boxes and find the fish. And, of course, they couldn't do *that*. What a stink *that* would make. Isn't it great?"

"Yes," she said slowly, "it is kind of amusing."

At least, he thought, she's quit crying.

"I'll call you soon, darling," he said. "And that's terrible, terrible about Joan of Arc. There's nothing I can do?"

"No," she said in a dull tone, "there's nothing you can do." A pause. "But thank you, Noel. You are sweet to care."

He heard a sigh, and he thought exultantly, there's still a chance for ole skipper Bigelow to pull it off! He'd have Deirdre Kimbridge yet—and the partnership, too.

And then Deirdre said, "I talked to Father about the over-the-counter traders. He's going to arrange for a health club membership. At least that's something, isn't it, Noel?"

There it was again! Deirdre's motherly attitude toward Kimbridge & Co. She would blow up the Stock Exchange—on Sunday, of course, so that no one would be injured—if it would benefit Kimbridge & Co.

"Yes," he said thickly, "that's something." He decided to mix another pitcher of martinis when he hung up.

Poke executed an imitation soft-shoe dance after he let himself into the apartment in Brooklyn Heights. He had his own key now.

"Sweetheart?" Carol called out from the bedroom.

"Front and center!" he yelled back. "Got a present for you. I tell you a grown giraffe is very hard to find in this town. Very hard to find."

She hurried into the living room, blotting her lipstick.

"For me? Oh, Poke, you shouldn't!" She tore the wrapping from the small box he handed to her. "Dearest!" she cried. "Oh, it's lovely!" She held out the gold case and fingered the sapphire clasp.

"Go ahead," he said. "Open it. Eighteen small men come marching out. They're a little bowlegged."

"Why, it opens right into a clock—a travel clock!" She threw her arms around him. "Ummh," she said, "you taste good." Then, "How did you know I've always wanted a clock like this?"

"Well, when you were out in California it struck me suddenly that you might need a clock. So you'd remember to come home. You like it?"

"I *love* it." She placed the clock on the carpenter's bench and pulled the alarm plunger. "It even *sounds* beautiful," she said. "Just for that you get eighteen kisses."

Some moments later he pulled himself free and said laughingly, "I'm just in a buying mood, that's all. I've been selling so much stock lately I thought it only fair to buy something myself. I'm even thinking of getting wheels again. Any special kind of car—it has to be a foreign make, you understand—that you prefer?"

"No, dearest. Anything you like is fine with me." She regarded him fondly. "My," she said, "you are in a jubilant mood. I wonder if you know how much you've changed lately."

"Knock on wood," he said and rapped the Monster.

"Well I've never seen you do *that* before. Oh, Poke, I almost forgot. We ought to keep our eye on the weather in California this winter. A cold snap would be very bullish for the canning companies. Those processors out West have been loaded down with crop surpluses for three years in a row. But a freeze now would start coining money for them. Give them the makings of a real turnaround situation."

"Consider it done," he said. He filled his cheeks and blew the wrapping paper off the carpenter's bench. "How's that for a wintry blast? I just leveled fifty thousand acres of tomatoes." He grinned at her. "What's new in your shop?"

"Today was a wonderful day. Mr. Hillyer got thrown out of a bookstore on Fulton Street. He kept badgering people in the store to buy his book on church bonds and the proprietor tossed him right out on his ear. Anyway," she said happily, "I think it's a lot more fun to work for Kimbridge & Co. That's what I'm doing incognito, isn't it?"

"Sure it is. You said once you feel just like a spy when you research stocks. By the way, I've got a complaint for you. A customer called up today and said one of the stocks I recommended last week hasn't gone up. In fact, the stock is down a point and a half from where he bought it."

"Which stock?"

"Gerald Home Equipment."

"Tell your customer to be a little patient. That stock has all the right ingredients. Small capitalization, a rising backlog, the best management in its industry, a good depreciation picture—and the company's board has approved a plan to buy up to fifty thousand shares in the open market. For acquisition purposes. Once the company starts to dicker with another corporation, that will become an added kicker. And besides—two pension funds started to nibble at it this week. So all your customer has to do is wait."

He nodded. "Don't get me wrong," he said. "I'm not complaining. And guess what customers' man got an offer today from a big wire house?"

410

"You did? Oh, dearest, that's wonderful! Tell me about it."

He looked around the room. "No hidden microphones around here? Okay, I'll tell you what happened. This man called up, the vice president in charge of personnel. He said he had heard about my work and would I possibly be interested in joining another organization."

"But that's raiding! I thought it wasn't done on Wall Street."

"He explained that, too. Very neatly. He said that if I saw my way clear to join his organization, they would run an ad in the newspapers after we reached an understanding. You know the sort of thing. 'Liberal commissions and excellent fringe benefits, chance to grow with forward-looking firm, weekly telephone hookups with Research Department to bolster your production.' The gimmick is that if I went over they would place the ad and make it appear as though I had answered it. Good guys, huh?"

"What did you say?"

"I told the man—and I was very polite about it—that I happened to be happy right where I was."

"You didn't tell him he was talking to the next partner of Kimbridge & Co.?"

"No, ma'am. I figured that was none of his business."

"Oh, Poke, you have so much confidence." She traced a finger along the line of his chin. "I think that's wonderful, to have so much confidence."

"I have you. That's what I have."

"Oh, my dearest . . . if you only knew how frightened I get sometimes. How afraid that some situation we talk about will go wrong." She shivered. "I grow cold all over when I think about that. It's like getting stage fright on opening night. Only I feel that way with every single stock."

He watched her carefully but said nothing. She had become so possessive that it frightened him at times. He knew that when she prepared some new dish for dinner now that she would try the recipe in advance and then throw out the food; she tried to protect even his enjoyment of meals in the apartment. And she savored the tiny details of his personal habits. One morning she had watched him with fascination in the bathroom. "You wash your face with one hand," she said. "You have such strong hands." And when he met her at the airport after her return from Los Angeles, she had sobbed with relief all the way to Brooklyn Heights in the taxi. She could become quite stubborn also. Once, after he had criticized a dress she was wearing, she refused to speak to him until they went to bed—and then she insisted on unbuckling the Monster from his stump. He did not know whether that was her way of hurting him for what he had said or whether she was asking his forgiveness for her behavior.

She appeared to be tired tonight. There were dark areas under her eyes and when the light fell on her face at a certain angle it made her look like an old woman. She was letting her hair grow longer so that it had lost the helmet shape he first remembered; he had said once, quite casually, that he did not think short hair made girls look particularly feminine.

"Come on," he said suddenly. "I'll take you out to dinner. We'll celebrate."

"What are we celebrating?"

"Well—we'll celebrate my not leaving Kimbridge & Co. How's that for an excuse?"

She shook her head, smiling at him a little sadly. "You're sweet," she said softly and pulled back a lock of hair that had fallen over her forehead. "If you don't mind . . . let's stay in tonight."

"Okay. Then I'll cook. What's the matter? You didn't like the last supper I prepared for us? Why, that was a Jeffers special. You can't get it at the finest restaurant in New York City."

"No wonder. Cold tuna, mayonnaise, raisins, cocktail sauce, chopped olives . . . let's see. And lemon juice."

"The pecans," he said. "You forgot the papershell pecans. That's part of my specialty. I remove the pecans from the shells first."

She was smiling at him, appearing happier now, the hair swinging gently across one cheek. Then she doubled over with pain. "Oh, Jesus," she moaned. "Oh, Jesus, Jesus . . ." Her hands were locked over her stomach.

"Carol! What's the matter? Honey, tell me what's wrong!"

She rocked slowly back and forth. Her eyes were squeezed shut and her face was twisting. Finally, with a gasp, she opened her eyes and straightened up. She blinked back the tears. "I'm afraid it's an old, old problem for us girls," she said. "Don't look so fierce, dearest. It will go away. Just like clockwork when the time comes." She reached out her hand and when he kissed the palm she closed her eyes again. "Oh-h-h . . .J e*sus!*"

"Pills," he said urgently. "Don't they have pills for this sort of thing?"

She turned her head away from him for a few moments. "Oh, yes," she said finally, "they have pills, all right. The only trouble is that I've never found any pills that help me." She gestured helplessly. "Usually the cramps aren't this bad," she said.

"Is there anything I can do? Do you want me to leave?"

"No, no." She reached out to grip his hand. "Stay with me—please!" Her lips were gray around the edges of the lipstick.

"All right. Whatever you want. But there must be something I can do. I can't just stand here and watch you suffer."

"The heating pad," she gasped and bent forward again. "That seems to help a little."

"I'll get it. Just tell me where."

A little while later she was lying on the bed. The heating pad, a rather frayed pad the color of mustard, was draped across her stomach. Poke sat on the edge of the bed watching her closely.

"You're feeling a little better?"

"Yes. I think the worst is over now." She started to smile but it was a wan effort.

Bending forward gently, he kissed her cheek. He could feel the heat from the pad pressing against his thigh.

"When I was a little girl I thought that's where babies came from," she said in a low voice. "From being kissed." She closed her eyes. The eyelids were dark gray and puckered with fine wrinkles. Then, without opening her eyes, she said, "Something happened to me today, too. Nothing like your job offer but it was strange."

"Yes?"

"I was walking past Trinity Church and just then the big doors opened up. A noontime service was ending. But the oddest thing happened at that very instant. I heard the organ strike a chord and I could see the altar way inside the church." Her eyes fluttered open and fixed upon his face. "It was exactly as if"—her voice dropped very low—"I were walking down the aisle of the church . . ."

He stared across the room at the mahogany dresser with the huge curved legs; he had never liked that dresser because it was so ungainly. She began to kiss his hand and he knew that she was crying now because his fingers were wet.

"Oh, my dearest," she said, "don't you know what I'm doing? I'm proposing to you."

He stared at the dull sheen of the mahogany and he thought: it's so close, it's so close. The tape stretched white across the finish line; he was out ahead and his kick was going perfectly. Oh, God, he prayed, give me just a little more time. It's so close . . .

Poke turned his head so that it was lost in shadow when he finally looked down at her. "Remember that first night?" he whispered gently. "About us being adults and—well—living a little? Isn't that what you said?"

A little cry escaped her lips, and he could feel her body stiffen under the heating pad. "You make it sound like a pact with the devil," she said slowly. "Oh, my dearest, am I that bad for you?" Then her voice grew stronger. "Yes, I remember. But it didn't turn out to be that simple. If you knew, if you only knew how I crave to be with you . . . but I guess I have my answer now, don't I?" Her eyes looked past him toward the ceiling. "It doesn't require a whole lot of analysis," she said. Her face seemed to have aged twenty years.

The room grew silent. He heard the faint, familiar buzz from the electric clock on the dresser. His lips were moving silently. Just a little more time. It was so close, so close now. He could almost feel the tape snapping against his chest. . . .

32

On the following Monday the Dow-Jones industrial average rose 14 points while volume increased by 2,000,000 shares. This broke a solid row of "Blue Mondays" that had seen the market decline all during autumn on the first day of the week. The action brought some cheer to Wall Street, but one eminent broker, a man who wrote his market letters every Monday afternoon simply to set himself apart from the traditional Friday composers, warned his readership: "One swallow does not make a summer."

On Tuesday turnover on the Stock Exchange climbed by another 2,000,000 shares. The industrial average spurted ahead 16½ points. After the close of trading a large wire house dispatched this bulletin to its offices around the country: "The remarkable performance of the stock market cannot be attributed to any new development on the economic or political scene. The DJI is now within striking distance of the 'line' it had formed throughout this spring and summer. However, we would caution clients against chasing stocks at this particular time. The technical pattern suggests that a consolidation phase is now in order. It would, in fact, not be too surprising to see the market retrace two-thirds of its recent gain before a further advance gets under way. We call attention to our Recommended Lists of stocks for Growth, Income, and Safety of Principal."

On Wednesday the tape ran late from the opening bell. The average was up 9 points in the first hour; volume rose sharply above Tuesday's pace. In the second hour the market continued to advance on a broad front. At noon radio stations in New York inserted special broadcasts on the stock market into their program schedules. A woman's club at Rye, coming into the city to attend the matinee of a Broadway musical, voted to spend the afternoon instead in the Kimbridge & Co. board room on Park Avenue. At 50 Wall something even more remarkable occurred: a tape watcher stood up, walked around to the cubicle of Noel Bigelow, opened an account, and purchased 500 shares of U. S. Steel—at the market.

By one o'clock on Wednesday the "line" had been penetrated decisively on the upside. The word spread like wildfire. The board rooms of Wall Street milled with people who were shouting, pushing, and exchanging stock-market strategy. Two dentists in 50 Wall canceled all appointments for the rest of the afternoon and came downstairs to stand in their white coats along the aisle of the Kimbridge & Co. board room.

The switchboard was flooded with incoming calls. The voices of customers clamoring, pleading, testing, demanding to know their buying power.

"You double up on your winners and cut your losses. That's the way to make money in the market.

This electronics stock, what do you think of it right here?"

"The volume yesterday equaled the volume for all of last week. I like that in a stock. Buy me three hundred shares."

"I hear another outfit is going to make a tender offer for this company. You hear anything? Way I figure it, the stock's good for ten points at least. Who knows? Maybe twenty points."

"On Tuesday I was thinking I'd wait until the market flops back. The time to buy stocks is when nobody else wants 'em. But there might not be a second chance the speed this market's moving at. I'm going into the glamour stocks. Now here's what I want you to buy for me—"

"So I told my wife only last week we ought to buy some more stocks and she says, 'No, Henry, we have to set aside money for Maxine's college.' You know what? She just got hold of me at the plant—Christ, I was in the john—and she yells, 'Henry! The market! Shoot the works!' I yell back, 'Maxine's freshman year?' 'No, no!' she yells. 'All four years! Invest the money for all four years. She'll probably get married anyway her last year in high school, Maxine. She'll get married and go away and forget all about her poor parents. So we should starve for her sake? An ungrateful daughter like that? Buy stocks, Henry, buy stocks!' Okay, so what do you like? You're my broker."

And the brokers responded, their voices cajoling, soothing, analyzing, commiserating, advising. The voices of service responding to the call.

The board room quivered, a room in rapture over the market. "Kodak's on the move! . . . Seven-eighths for Burroughs! . . . The pressure's off that stock! You know why? That big block lifted the supply over-hanging the market, that's why!"

The message wire of Kimbridge & Co. picked up the chant. "BUYERS IN XEROX ON FLR. NO IN-DICATION YET OF OPENING PRICE."

With the rapture there came moments of confusion. Two tape watchers engaged in a brief, but remark-ably fierce, fist fight over a choice seat under the mag-nified tape. Memphis queried the home office: "CAN U SUGGEST INVESTMENT STRATEGY FOR BANK TRUST ACCT?" The teletype operator, an employee with only a week's experience on the firing line, picked up a message intended for the bulletin board on the twenty-ninth floor. The reply clacked back urgently to Memphis: "PLS INSERT YOUR PAPER NAPKIN INSIDE COFFEE CONTAINER TO ABSORB COFFEE RESIDUE BEFORE DIS-CARDING CONTAINER."

The clock on the tower of Trinity Church stopped for the first time in twenty-two years and, for some unknown reason, an order for 100,000 shares of Amer-ican Telephone reached the Stock Exchange floor at the same moment. On Wednesday trading boomed in American Telephone; the stock was the most active issue of the day as it gained 3 points.

Atop 50 Wall scrambled the toy figures of work-men, partially obscured by delicate floating clouds. For the first time in its history the building was being steam blasted. In the Margin Department of Kim-bridge & Co. there sprang up an office pool on when the next building on Wall Street would begin its cleaning.

But for Israel Padawer Wednesday was simply an-other day of anguish. He watched the quotations board ripple with new prices and what he saw was

Gwen Overland's body turning gently to him, the round white thighs and the full delight of her breasts. Beneath her armpits lay the dark auburn tips of shaven hairs; kissing these hairs was like sucking bone marrow. He smelled the cigarette smoke and the relighted cigar stubs in the board room and his nostrils quivered to the scent of myrrh and frankincense.

The first day he had not called her because of the remorse that suddenly filled him, a remorse tinged with the lingering wonder of that glorious time. They had made an island with their love and yet when he had stepped away he seemed once more to slip into the old skin of Israel Padawer the coward. He! A man who turned sideways when he replaced dead light bulbs so they would not explode in his face. He was going to make plans! What plans? He was going to climb up on a white horse and ride up to the West Side and sweep her into his arms? He, Israel Padawer, who once in Central Park fell off a horse on the merry-go-round while his son Abraham, galloping like Roy Rogers, had doubled over with laughter. Laughter, yes, and was there shame also for his father?

The next day had passed, then another. Izzy did not even eat during those first days of anguish; he kept himself alive with the memory of that exalted time. And then another fear possessed him, the fear that he might forget even the smallest detail. Once, just before the market closing, the telephone had rung and when he picked it up there was no voice on the line. He knew somehow that it was she and she was waiting for him; he felt his flesh quiver and he longed to shout her name, to shout her name and leap out from his cubicle! But he had done nothing. He had repeated, "Padawer, Padawer here," and then he heard the click. It was as if all the joy in his life had pulsed to an end.

In his anguish he did a strange thing. At night, in the cold bed at Riverdale, he turned to his wife with a lust she had never known in him. And Sarah, with her shrunken breasts and her bony thighs matted with black hair, had responded with an eagerness that was so pathetic he thought he would weep.

And then Seth Voorhees had suffered his stroke— "the heart," Izzy's father had said, "the rich man's sickness"—and Izzy was swept by a new fear. Suppose he should dare, yes, suppose this instant he should go to Gwen—and suppose he had a stroke in that glorious round bed. Such things happened, oh, yes. Once it had happened to a customer of his, with a lingerie model in a Times Square hotel, *The Daily News* had told all about it. And Izzy remembered the shame he had felt, a shame for his entire race. "If she calls me again," he made a pledge to himself, "I will go to her. The risk I will take." He pictured her giving a piano lesson to some child with bored eyes and he wondered, "Does she step on the pedals with her bare feet?" Her toes were so white and perfectly formed. And then—suppose he had this stroke at the height of their love-making? He saw the headlines: WALL STREET BROKER STRICKEN IN LOVE NEST. Oh, yes, such reading, such shame and such reading. And he, Israel Padawer, who was going to become the next partner of Kimbridge & Co.

Each day he marked a Y on his desk calendar, a Y for You. Ah, there was still time . . . he could see the jugular tensing in her neck and he bent to kiss the vein.

His hand reached out for the phone. The rimless glasses began to fog with anticipation. He touched the cold plastic and it was like dead flesh.

The phone rang and his voice answered in a scream: *"Padawer!"*

"So the bull is back, the bull market. You shout so loud maybe I can save money. Maybe I don't have to use the telephone."

"Hello. Hello, Mr. Goodman."

"So hello. Pioneer Chemicals. What do you know?"

Izzy scowled. He tried to concentrate but his mind was a blank. Feverishly he thumbed through the Standard & Poor's stock guide. He rattled off the price range for the year and the company's financial position. "Current assets to current liabilities look good," he said lamely. "Three to one, that's a good ratio."

Mr. Goodman gave a short laugh that held no humor. "A good ratio, that's what you're telling me? Well, maybe I should tell *you* a little something. Rust spray . . . Yes, that's right. Rust spray. Pioneer Chemicals has developed a new rust spray that's guaranteed to hold for ten years, at least that's what its lab technicians claim. Spray it on anything. Pfft! Iron fences, tin roofs, barbed wire, tax collector's teeth. Ten years it lasts, this spray. You spray it on old rust and even the old rust looks like silver, it's that good. Current assets to current liabilities—hah!"

"Yes, Mr. Goodman."

"So check the market on Pioneer Chemicals. Outside I have three people waiting. They want to buy maybe a boatload of bath mats. So-o-o, I will accommodate."

"Mr. Goodman? That stock's 44¼ bid, a half offered. Last sale at the offered price. Volume is—"

"The volume forget. Today I am in a hurry. It is my pinochle day. Buy for Goodman Brothers, the margin account, five hundred shares. Then wait ten minutes and buy another five hundred. Call me soon as you clean it up."

"Yes, Mr. Goodman." Izzy wrote out the order. He saw Gwen's teeth—so white and even, they were—smiling up at him from the order pad. In his anguish he blurted out: "Mr. Goodman? Do you see that stock for a one- or two-day play? Or longer maybe?"

There was a sudden silence, and he could almost hear Mr. Goodman's mind at work. A gamble like this, Izzy thought desperately, what was he doing? Why, Mr. Goodman might close out his account! But then he heard a low chuckle. "So maybe you're interested? So all right. It is good we should stick together." A pause. "That stock is good for seventy. But three, four months maybe. Next month the announcement comes from Chicago. Then the fireworks start. I gotta go. Call me."

So they were off and riding again, thought Izzy, the Robin Hood Group was on the move. This time Pioneer Chemicals. How unlike some of his other customers these people were! So many people climbed aboard a stock just as the ride was about to end. They threw away good stocks like banana peels, just to pay for their ride. And when it was all over, so many of them blamed the broker.

Izzy Padawer delivered a silent lecture on the techniques of investing. Patience. One word only. The hardest rule to follow in the market. Job, he thought, such an investor he would make! Now there was a man who understood patience. Yes, Job should come to Kimbridge & Co. They would talk of patience, he and Job—and they would make money in the market.

In the Research Department Thatcher Kimbridge looked thoughtfully out across the board room. From this vantage point he felt somewhat like the captain of a ship standing on the bridge.

Waiting for Howard Merriam to finish talking with

one of the analysts, Thatcher glanced down at the Dow-Jones ticker. The ticker was chirping merrily, as if in tune to its message of optimism. Thatcher ran the white paper through his hands. Then he pulled the sheet free of its glass cover and read:

N Y—DJ—AT TWO FIFTY THE MARKET IS STILL STRONG AND ACTIVE. ADVANCES OUTNUMBER DECLINES BY THREE TO ONE. THE RAILS CONTINUE TO HOLD THEIR GAINS. THE TAPE IS RUNNING WITH DIGITS DELETED. GENERAL MOTORS IS UP $2\frac{1}{2}$, US GYPSUM UP 3, WOOLWORTH UP $1\frac{1}{8}$, AMERICAN TELEPHONE UP 1, US STEEL UP $1\frac{3}{4}$, WALL STREET BROKERS ATTRIBUTE THE S

T
R
E
N
G
T
H—

"Just a second, I'll see," he heard Merriam say. He glanced up. The analyst had returned to his desk and Merriam was cupping the telephone with a palm and calling out to him. "Thatch! It's CBS. They're planning to do an inside study of a brokerage firm in this bull market. They want to shoot tomorrow morning for this news report and they want to know if we're interested in cooperating. Are we interested?"

The managing partner shook his head. Merriam spoke into the phone: "No, I'm very sorry. It's just a matter of firm policy. But thanks for thinking of us."

Merriam walked over to the glass partition and stood beside Thatcher. "You know what you sounded like?" Thatcher said. "As though you were turning down a syndicate participation."

"I know some brokers," said Merriam mildly, "who'd have given both their thumbs for a chance like that. Television exposure would mean tremendous publicity for the firm."

"That's quite true," Thatcher agreed. "But we're going to get along without it."

The two men watched the figures moving in the board room.

"Well," said Thatcher finally, "what do you think of this market? If you tell me you're not flabbergasted, I'll never believe another word you say."

"Oh, I'm flabbergasted, all right." Merriam shook his head but there was a smile playing about his lips. "We're all like blackbirds sitting on a telephone wire. One flies off and all the others follow. I've learned one thing after all these years. It's very simple, Thatch. The market creates its own atmosphere. Up, down, or sideways. You and I—and all the others— we're just plain old blackbirds."

"I won't disagree. But what are you telling our customers? Not, I hope, that we're all blackbirds in this thing together?"

"I sent this out on the teletype twenty minutes ago," said Merriam, handing him a slip of paper. "It's an occasion," added Merriam. "Our first buy bulletin since last February."

Thatcher read the bulletin:

ALL OFFICES
RE MARKET
   PRESSURE STILL UP AND TAPE ACTION LOOKS GOOD.
WOULD USE DIPS TO BUY FOR TRADERS.

He handed the paper to the research partner and said, "So it's all systems go?"

"Yes," repeated Merriam softly, "all systems go—

and I hope to goodness we're right." The two men watched the board room in silence and then Merriam said, "Somewhere out there is a future partner of Kimbridge & Co. You've been giving that a lot of thought, I suppose."

"Yes," said Thatcher, "yes, I have. Another few weeks and I'll have made my decision."

"Whoever it is, he can't bring much money into the firm."

"Oh, he'll bring in a little," said Thatcher. "A hundred thousand, perhaps two hundred thousand. But, of course, we'll have to arrange a bank loan for him. And we'll see that he gets the prime rate."

"He'll bring one thing that money can't buy. He'll bring youth. And youth," said Merriam, carefully creasing the message and placing it in his pocket, "is cheap at any price."

"Amen," breathed Thatcher Kimbridge.

"Yes, Rabbi," intoned Israel Padawer. Rabbi Stern was calling for the second time that day.

"Such a *bar mitzvah* it will be," said Rabbi Stern. "And send me the menu if you have it finished. I have a friend in the printing business. He can fix it up for you at a nice price. A coat of arms even."

"The menu I will send, Rabbi."

"The market looks good, don't you think? Buy for me a hundred shares, Israel. Any stock you pick. I trust you. And—ah—the payment. We can handle that in the usual way?"

"Yes, Rabbi. The usual way."

Izzy wrote out an order slip for Sears, Roebuck and in his misery he thought: you are so brave you think of capturing a woman who is paradise to you. And what do you do? You lie down so a rabbi can milk you, that is what.

But what to do? He could not bring disgrace upon the head of his own son. No, that was unthinkable. He must stand fast against temptation for the sake of his Abraham. His own happiness did not matter. The young must live.

Abraham be damned! The whole world be damned! Heaven waited at his fingertips and he, Israel Padawer, was a coward.

He took out a card and his fingers were trembling as he dialed the number.

"Hello?" he said. "Mr. Spiegelman, please. Tell him Mr. Padawer is calling. He will know." During the brief pause he fought to keep from hanging up. "Mr. Spiegelman? Yes, yes. Thank you. About that stepladder we were talking about? Yes, I have a name for it. Pioneer Chemicals . . . Let's see, it's now 45½ on the tape . . . Thank *you*, Mr. Spiegelman . . . Yes, yes, I'll think about some other names."

33

On Thursday the market opened strong for the fourth consecutive day. It was front-page news in *Variety*. The market absorbed some profit taking by traders in the second hour, then forged ahead with renewed strength. Even the utility stocks were posting gains of better than a point. The message wires sang with inquiries. The word was fanning out from Wall Street to the entire nation. Almost everyone was ready to believe it: another bull market suddenly had gotten under way.

An exchange of words took place on Thursday morning that was of interest primarily to one corner of the board room of Kimbridge & Co. Noel Bigelow, pausing for breath shortly after eleven o'clock, called out over his shoulder: "Hey, Max! Have you heard the one about—" He was cut off by a snarl from Israel Padawer: "Go to hell, damn you! Cut out the crap or stand up and fight." Bigelow, stunned as much by this response as by the emergence of the bull market, snapped his head around to stare at Padawer. Then Bigelow shrugged and said: "Sorry, but I'm too busy filling orders to bother with you." Israel Padawer had tasted his first blood.

Poke Jeffers spun about in his chair and moved his hands in a silent burst of applause, then spun back to his desk. He moved with blinding speed this morning; his hands formed a blur across the order pad and his voice was taut and swift on the telephone. Taking his calls, he would stare up at the tape and repeat soundlessly to himself: Easy, easy, easy. Run, baby, run. He felt a singular thrill. At last he had caught up with the moving tape; he was part of it; his own muscles were crammed now with the fierce pulsating power of the tape. He felt the old lost joy—that he was strong enough to run forever. And there was an added kicker, something hypnotic and strange. The sensation that his entire life had been leading up to this race he was now running. "Easy, baby, easy. Easy does it." He began talking to himself softly between the phone calls.

The steady, rhythmic thump of the stock ticker—the pulsing beat of the market—swept across the board room. The tape was sprinting. It caught up customers and customers' men alike in its spell. Thump, thump, thump, went the tape, its downbeat steady and irresistible.

A customer with an unlisted telephone number called Poke to buy 1,400 shares of over-the-counter stocks. A woman on Park Avenue telephoned him to announce that her pet parakeet had picked up a new refrain: "Stocks have stopped to fluctuate! Grab your socks—the market's going up!" A geologist who had missed out on the last mining boom in Canada put in an order for three sulphur stocks. An Army intelligence officer stopped by at noon to check the account of one of Poke's customers who was being screened for an important position in the Pentagon; the officer tarried long enough to open an account for himself and to buy 200 shares of an aircraft stock. "You have time for lunch?" asked the officer. "Sorry," replied Poke, "but not today."

The officer tossed a salute and walked smartly out of the board room. There had been times, Poke reflected, watching the officer disappear through the door, when he felt a burning resentment against his customers. They made money by not moving a muscle, by not losing a drop of sweat—the market did their work. He felt scorn for his customers at these times because they were no better than armchair athletes. But lately even this feeling had evaporated in him. "Easy, easy, easy," he said softly as the phone rang.

"—and for those canning companies," Poke said easily, the telephone a willing muscle atop his shoulder, "a cold snap ought to be pretty bullish."

"I agree, I agree," said Mr. Watkins, the senior vice president of a bank. Mr. Watkins proceeded to conjure up the coldest California winter of the century in his mind. "I'd like to buy six hundred shares," said Mr. Watkins, naming a stock.

"Now?" said Poke. "Maybe we ought to keep an eye on the weather for a while."

"Now," repeated Mr. Watkins firmly. "I want to get in there ahead of the crowd."

Yes, it was true, thought Poke as he swiftly wrote out the order, customers were coming out of the woodwork. People reacted to the tempo of the market. When the market was sleepy, they were content to let their investments drift. But when the market boiled, they wanted one thing: action. Okay. So you couldn't afford to be stubborn at the wrong time as a customers' man; you had to know when to give the customer his head.

But you had to be careful of some people. The sharpies had smelled the action, too. They were the trickiest of all to handle. Yesterday at two-thirty he had received a call from a man he did not know.

"I'm in the building," the man said. "I want to stop up after the close today and open an account. But first I want you to do a piece of business for me. Buy five hundred shares," and he named a fast-moving stock that had gone up 11 points since Monday. The man's voice was assured; he sounded far more prosperous than Mr. Watkins, the banker.

Poke thought quickly. He had two choices. He could accept the order and run the risk that the man would fail to show up—a disavowal for which Kimbridge & Co. would be responsible. Or he might refuse the order and thereby lose a potential client. He weighed the alternatives; the man's voice sounded sincere, that was one indication. There was something else: it was very hard for a salesman to turn down an order served on a platter.

"I'd like very much to accommodate you, sir," Poke said. "But this procedure is a little unusual. We have our new clients fill out a form. Now if you could just give me a little information about yourself. In fact, it would be a good idea for you to drop by here—as long as you're in the building—before we put through the trade. It's a mere formality, you understand."

"Listen to me," the man said, "and don't hand me that drivel." His voice had turned decidedly nasty. "I know how you brokers work. You want my business or not? Now put that order through!"

Poke held his temper. "We can buy that stock for

you tomorrow morning," he said soothingly, "in case we don't get an execution before the close today."

"You're not going to take my order this minute? You want me to report you to the managing partner for insolence?"

"I'm afraid I cannot accept your order," said Poke in an even voice.

There was a ripe curse, then the sound of a receiver being slammed down hard.

A sharpie, thought Poke, one of the floating population. Now he could guess the man's technique: place an order through Kimbridge & Co. to buy 500 shares and place another order as quickly as possible through another brokerage firm to sell short 500 shares of the same stock. If the stock went up in the final hour of trading, the man would honor the trade made for him by Kimbridge & Co. while standing away from the other transaction. "The customers' man misunderstood my instructions," he would say, or something like that. On the other hand, if the stock moved down, the man would scuttle his order with Kimbridge & Co. and cover the short sale. There were enough brokers in the business, Poke reflected, green guys or scared guys, to make this man's method pay off surprisingly well.

But now, at one-thirty on Thursday, he was not thinking about the sharpie. He was concentrating on a new idea to boost his production. Starting Monday morning he would send out letters—over his personal signature—to suggest year-end tax switches. A lot of people would be willing to accept losses now on certain stocks and switch into securities that appeared likely to perform profitably for them in the months ahead. Yes, he thought, a market like this is made to order for tax selling. As a broker he would receive commissions both ways—through the sale and then through the buy order utilizing the proceeds from the sale. He would talk to Carol about it over the weekend; she could help him to draw up a list of suggested stocks.

He had eaten lunch at his desk; he sent out for a milkshake and a package of raisins. When he finished lunch, he flipped rapidly through his order tickets. He grinned. The biggest single production day of his career was shaping up.

Shortly before two o'clock his phone rang.

"Poke Jef-*fers!*"

"Mr. Jeffers, this is Miss Donahue. Mr. Kimbridge would like to see you in his office. Right away."

"Can he hold off, Miss Donahue? I'm really swamped out here. Can't he wait until after the close?"

"I'm sorry, Mr. Jeffers. He said, 'Right away.' Those were his exact words."

"I'll be there in three minutes flat. Just have to call the floor. I've got a block that needs special handling."

"Very well, Mr. Jeffers. I will tell him. Three minutes—flat."

Thatcher Kimbridge snapped into the telephone, "No calls, please, Miss Donahue." Then, impatiently, "No, no. It will have to wait until later."

The office was bathed in sunlight with a peculiar density; it was as if light rays were playing upon particles of moisture in the air. Now, suddenly, the light darkened, as it does when the sun passes behind a cloud, and artificial light from the ceiling molded Thatcher's face in sharp relief. There was something about the resolute thrust of the head that puzzled Poke as he stood before the desk.

"You sent for me, sir?"

The managing partner took a deep breath. "Yes," he said. "Yes, I sent for you."

He picked up a sheet of paper, regarded it for a few moments with a look of intense distaste, then thrust the sheet toward Poke. It was a typewritten letter. "This just arrived," Thatcher said. "Go ahead," he commanded. "Read it."

Poke glanced automatically at the signature and his mouth went dry. The letter was signed "(Miss) Carol Tracey." Poke looked up. Thatcher walked across the room and now he stood near the window, his arms folded, watching Poke carefully.

Easy, boy, Poke told himself, she's applying for a job at Kimbridge & Co. But what a fool thing to do without telling him!

And then he began to read the letter.

"Dear Mr. Kimbridge," the letter began. "It is my understanding that Mr. Poke Jeffers, a registered representative in your main office, is under consideration for a general partnership at Kimbridge & Co.—"

My God! What was she doing?

Poke forced himself to continue reading. A chill came over his body.

"There is something I should like to call to your attention. I am an institutional research analyst for the firm of Hillyer & Hunt and during the past three months I have been assisting Mr. Jeffers—unknown to any other parties—in selecting certain stocks for recommendations to the clients of Kimbridge & Co. A list of these stocks follows."

There were thirteen in all, from Emerson Coal to Gerald Home Equipment, with the original dates given for each recommendation.

"Inasmuch as Mr. Jeffers, who had led me to believe that we were to become engaged, has chosen to break off our relationship, I no longer feel bound to keep this matter a secret. It is not my intention to mention this matter to any party other than yourself, but if Mr. Jeffers does, in fact, become the next partner of Kimbridge & Co., I shall inform the proper authorities of his activities concerning the source of his stock-market information as enumerated above."

The letter ended, "Cordially yours, (Miss) Carol Tracey."

Poke lowered the letter. So this is the way the race ends, he thought. He felt numb.

Slowly he placed the letter on the desk and then stepped back.

From a great distance came the voice of Thatcher Kimbridge. "Is it true?"

He looked at the man beside the window and he realized the pain that Thatcher Kimbridge was experiencing.

"Yes, sir," he replied. A leaden weight was dragging his stump down. "It's true. Except for the part about our being engaged. She—well—she sort of oversold herself on that point. But the business about the stocks, that's all true."

The older man gave a quick nod. "Yes," he said. "I was looking over your production record on the computer printouts just before you came in."

"She has a very good memory," Poke said. "Usually she doesn't even take notes during interviews." Then he added, as if this explained some mystery, "She's not a very good speller."

"I see." Thatcher Kimbridge walked slowly back to his desk. He rapped his knuckles against the glass. "Damn it all!" he exploded. "Why did she have to do this!" He glared down at the letter and then placed it inside a drawer. "Let me ask you something," he said to Poke. "Did you ever split any commissions with her?"

435

"No, sir. There was never anything like that. She gave me the stocks she liked and the story behind them. I passed the information along to my customers . . ." His voice trailed off. His mind seemed to be locked on some distant thought.

The sun had come out again and the shadow of a pigeon suddenly was flung magnified against the opposite building.

Poke became conscious, at last, that Thatcher Kimbridge was staring at him. No, not exactly at him but as if someone else were standing in his shoes. Why the hell should he be so bugged? Poke thought, with anger stirring now inside him. After all, the reputation of Kimbridge & Co. was going to remain unscarred.

When the managing partner spoke again, his voice seemed almost gentle. "You are the man I would have picked," he said quietly. He cleared his throat. "Yes," he added, "without any question. And now—you're out of the running."

Poke shifted his feet. The stump was beginning to throb.

"Mr. Kimbridge—" The whole world could go whistle, he was thinking as the rage grew and spread through his body.

"Yes?"

"I want to resign. Call in your secretary. I'll dictate a letter of resignation. Effective immediately." His voice was rising now with the rage spitting inside his stump. "I've even got my replacement. A customer called up this morning—an engineer with a good job —and he wanted to know how he can go to work here as a salesman."

"Dammit, Poke! Shut up! No, I won't call in my secretary. And I'm not going to let you resign. Who the hell said anything about resigning? You're too im-

436

petuous. You're just as impetuous as my son was. He hitchhiked to Greenwich one night in the snow when I wouldn't let him have the car. He was only fifteen then. Already proud as a peacock."

"But I want—"

The managing partner held up a hand. "Now you simmer down." He began to play absently with the drawer latch. "After all," he said after a pause, "I'm involved in this matter, too. You seem to forget that I purchased some Emerson Coal for my own account. Yes, and three of the other stocks you suggested. Good Lord, boy! You think we both ought to resign from the firm?"

"No, sir. I never said that."

"Well, take some advice from an old man and stop thinking so much." He shook his head and a weary chuckle issued from his throat. "Hillyer & Hunt," he said musingly. "Of all the firms on the Street. You can't appreciate how ironic that makes it. A small, small world."

"I ought to be getting back," Poke said brusquely. "I've got to check on a block I was working on."

Thatcher Kimbridge did not appear to hear him. "You were in Korea?" he asked.

Poke gave a puzzled nod.

"Combat?"

"Yes—combat." What the hell was the man getting at?

"Yes," repeated Thatcher Kimbridge absently. "I thought so." Then he shook his head. "Let me tell you a funny story," he said. "I don't want you to think you're the first broker in history to obtain market advice in—well—an unusual way. What would you say if I told you that I once hired a stargazer?"

"A stargazer? Why?" He's old, Poke thought, he's old and tired and now he's trying to humor me.

"To pick stocks, that's why. It was 1930 and, believe me, the world was falling about our heads. It was Doomsday. I persuaded my father to take on this man who published a horoscope. On retainer—as an adviser to Kimbridge & Co. My father was convinced I had gone crazy."

"What happened?"

"What happened was that this stargazer picked seven winners in a row. Right out of the hat. Or right out of the sky, if you prefer. Then on his eighth try he picked a lemon. Oh, what a lemon! You know what we did?"

"No, sir."

"We fired him, that's what." Then he added softly, "But for a while there we had a real sweet deal going for us. Until we ran into the lemon, my father was beginning to think that there was hope for me in this business, after all."

There was a silence in the room. The stock ticker had been turned off. Thatcher Kimbridge appeared lost in memories. Then he nodded toward a snapshot under the glass top of the desk. "That's my son," he said with an effort. "He was in Korea, too."

"Yes, sir. I know."

For a moment the two men stared down at the husky figure in the swimming trunks. "I've been thinking," Thatcher said finally, "about getting an assistant. An assistant to the managing partner." He waved a hand around the room. "There's so much to be done around here that a man needs an assistant, a good one. Would you be interested? I can assure you there will be no reduction in your income."

"No, sir," Poke said stubbornly. "I wouldn't be interested. Maybe I'll go out West and—well—raise cattle or something. I like to be out-of-doors."

"I understand, I understand. Look. There's no hurry

438

about deciding anything. People always keep rushing into things. When the market goes up, they buy stocks as if money were going out of style. Just think it over, that's all I ask." He gave a short laugh. "First I tell you not to think and now I'm telling you to think. Sounds as though I'm hedging my bets, doesn't it?" He snapped his fingers. "I have an idea. Are you free for supper Sunday night?"

"I don't think so."

"Sure you are. Dammit, that's an order!"

Why the hell should this mean so much to the man? Poke wondered. He shrugged. "All right."

"Fine! Once a month my family gets together for supper. It's a sort of tradition with us. But nothing fancy. Just my wife and I—and my daughter. You've never met Deirdre?"

Poke shook his head.

"Well," said Thatcher Kimbridge, "I wish I could say you have a treat in store. But with Deirdre it's very difficult to predict things. Except that she does condescend to come around once a month to see her parents. Good! Then it's settled. I'll send a note around to you with the time and place."

Poke turned without saying good-by. When he reached the door he was drenched with sweat and he knew he was limping badly.

Poke dialed the number as soon as he returned to his desk. The stock tape floated before his eyes—a taunting, formless mass of fat tissue—and the board room sounds were reduced to a distant sighing.

"Yes?"

"You told me once you wanted to go on the Staten Island ferry," he said evenly. "I'll take you tomorrow. Tomorrow at noon."

"Oh, Poke!" A pause. *You know about the letter*. I can tell by your voice."

"Yes, I know about the letter."

"Poke, dearest, let me explain! I didn't know what I was doing when I wrote it. I was going out of my mind with the thought of losing you. I kept thinking about what you said that night. Why, as soon as I mailed the letter I wanted to climb right inside the mailbox and tear it up. Oh, my darling! I've been going crazy all morning. I spent an hour interviewing a company treasurer and I can't remember one thing he said. Forgive me, Poke. I just . . ." Her voice choked.

"Noon tomorrow," he said. "The Staten Island ferry."

"All right," she replied dully. "I'll be there."

34

Poke leaned over the railing and the stiff breeze parted his hair into haphazard furrows. He heard the clanging of a bell buoy and smelled the salt air. When the wind shifted there was the oddly enticing odor of soup and sweet rolls from the small galley beyond the sliding doors of the ferry.

Off to the right the Statue of Liberty drew nearer, growing grayer against the blue sky. The harbor was alive with boats. Empty tankers rode high on their rusting hulls and tugs puffed importantly and a string of railroad freight cars rode silently past on a barge. The deck shuddered gently with the steady rumble of engines and he could feel the throbbing pass up through the Monster and into the stump of his left leg. He raised the heel of his shoe but the throbbing would not be stilled.

Carol was watching him. She wore a wool coat and her hands were jammed deep into the pockets. The wind played with her hair; occasionally she would take a hand from her coat and pull back the wayward strands.

"Are you cold?" he said.

"No, I'm all right. I like it out here."

He stared at a gull wheeling away from the ferry. With a shrill cry the gull spun down into the foaming wake and then curved away out of sight.

"Yes," he said slowly. "You want anything to eat?"

She shook her head. She glanced toward a young couple sitting on a wooden bench halfway down the deck. Red life jackets on the roof formed a canopy over their heads. The boy was kissing the girl and her feet lifted from the deck. Carol forced her eyes away. She said, "You hate me, don't you?"

"Hate you?" He turned to look at her. "No, I don't hate you. I only hate myself. That's all. I've hated myself ever since—well, it's been awhile."

He stared out again at the Statue of Liberty. Finally he said, "In sports—if you cheat—you are dead. It's an unwritten rule and somehow there's no way of getting around it. Yesterday afternoon, when I was in Mr. Kimbridge's office, that's what I kept thinking to myself. If you cheat, you are dead."

"Oh, Poke, you mustn't torture yourself like this! Why, when I was in high school there was a man who lost one arm in a plane crash. He turned out to be one of the best golfers in Columbus. And then he went on to become a big success in business. Just look what he did!"

Poke smiled thinly. "I'm sorry," he said, "but I don't play golf."

Neither of them spoke for a few minutes.

A strange quiet had settled over him, a calmness he could not explain. He wanted to tell Carol about it— perhaps it would be a debt payment of sorts—but he was unable to find the right words. No, he did not

442

hate her. His feeling toward her was—well—like a vacuum now. And with this feeling of emptiness had come a realization: the pretense finally was ended. He had run the race and he had lost. But with his losing he seemed to sense some newly won freedom. At last he was on his own again.

Then Carol said, trying to keep her voice light, "I bought two hundred shares of a stock this morning. For my own account."

"Oh? I thought you didn't play the market because it might bring you bad luck."

"Yes-s-s." She blinked her eyes. "Well, I suddenly had the urge to *do* something. So I bought a stock."

"Welcome to the club."

"Maybe that's what's wrong with the market today," she said. "The Dow industrials were down eight points when I left the office. Mr. Hillyer asked me if I thought the bull market was over. The four-day bull market."

"What did you tell him?"

"I—I said I didn't know. Those are the three hardest words in the English language for an analyst to say. 'I don't know.'"

"Well, you gave him a very honest answer."

"Yes. But he seemed quite disappointed when I said it. Oh, Poke"—tension tightened in her voice—"what will you do now?"

"I'm not sure—and that's a very honest answer."

"Suppose I went to see Mr. Kimbridge," she said hurriedly. "Suppose I told him to forget the whole thing, my letter and what I wrote. Wouldn't that help? He'd be willing to do that, wouldn't he? And then maybe you could still become a partner. Someday, anyway. I could tell Mr. Kimbridge you have a wonderful way with people."

"You're not going to see him. I won't let you." He

443

ran a hand over the railing. "Something will work out," he said. "I've just got to sort things out, that's all."

The ferry bumped into its slip at Staten Island. They joined the crowd sweeping toward the exit and immediately boarded another boat bound for the return trip to Manhattan.

Once a black-winged gull swept close to the railing and Carol said, "We have a neighbor at home who scares away the pigeons by beating on a dishpan. She comes out on the front lawn and beats on a dishpan with a wooden spoon." She spoke again in a few moments. "I never thought I'd miss anything about Columbus," she said, "but last night I kept remembering how my mother irons the ribbons after every Christmas and puts them away for another year. She irons the wrapping ribbons. That's an odd thing for me to remember, isn't it? Poke?"

"Ummh?"

"You know what I found myself doing this morning? Right on the street?"

"No, what?"

"Oh, Poke, I was talking to myself! Remember what I told you about coming to New York and noticing all those people talking to themselves? And now I'm doing it!"

He nodded silently. Manhattan was drawing nearer. The buildings of the financial district, at first an indistinct mass, had separated now into their individual shapes. He could see the top of 50 Wall. The white building gleamed like a beacon among its grime-encrusted neighbors.

The pain in his stump had become sharper with the relentless throbbing of the engines.

"The market is like you and me," Carol was saying

444

softly. "It lives continually in hope or dread." But he made no reply.

They could see the slip now dead ahead. They could see the workmen waiting on the dock and the automobiles that would ride on the ferry to Staten Island. The scene was very clear; it was like a glossy photograph with every detail sharply imprisoned.

"Carol?" It was the first time he had used her name.

"Yes? Oh, yes, my darling?" She turned quickly from the railing and took a tentative step toward him. "Yes, Poke?"

He reached out and she raised her arms. His hand brushed against the shoulder of her coat and—very gently—touched the lobe of her left ear. "Your earring is missing again," he said.

"Oh, *Poke*—" And then she turned away, bending her head so that he would not see the tears.

"Yes, yes, Alec. That is good to know. That lime green is the big color for next spring. Yes, green like money."

"*Thy lips are like a thread of scarlet,*" he whispered to himself.

"Alec, please. I'm busy. There is no time to hear about the corset buyer and the Supreme Court justice. No, Alec, not even if he owns stocks—"

"*Thy temples are like a piece of pomegranate within thy locks.*" Izzy moved his lips silently.

Finally, his cousin was off the line and Israel Padawer sat huddled in his cubicle wondering if he possessed the courage . . .

He telephoned his home to say that an unexpected business trip would take him out of town for the weekend. "It's for a finder's fee if the deal works out," he told Sarah. "The money we can use, the way bills build a pile. No, no. Clothes I'll manage. So I buy a new Arrow shirt. There is not time to pack a bag." His wife was solicitous; she did not protest. "Monday morning probably I'll return," he said. "I'll call you from the office when I get back. So kiss Abraham for me."

Late that afternoon he would stop by Tiffany's. He knew exactly what he was going to ask for: a pin or a charm shaped like a book. A thousand dollars it could cost, he did not care. Their Sears, Roebuck book.

He blinked his eyes; he thought he saw scarlet lips appear on the front glass of his cubicle. "Let me be damned for this, oh, Lord," he kept repeating under his breath, "let me be damned."

He was not really conscious of having made a decision. All he realized was that if he did not see Gwen Overland again he would turn to dust.

So finally he had come to this. Did disaster wait for him? He did not know. What of the partnership in Kimbridge & Co.? Partnership, smartnership. He rocked back and forth in his chair with the pain.

He watched Poke Jeffers entering the board room. It was nearly two o'clock.

That Jeffers! The commissions he was piling up! For a moment envy flared within Israel Padawer and then he forgot again about Kimbridge & Co.

Long enough he had delayed making the telephone call. Suppose she was not at home—or maybe she would refuse to see him. That would be a sign. Yes, that was it. His final escape route.

He picked up the telephone and regarded the instrument with fascination, as though he were seeing it for the first time.

Her husband would not return for awhile—he had counted the exact number of days—so suppose she had gone off to visit a friend. Omaha, suppose.

Izzy stared at the receiver and was tempted suddenly to tear out the wires. Tabloid headlines, hard and black, swirled momentarily before him. Then a mist covered his eyeglasses.

He knew only one thing: that he would lay down his life for another golden time with her.

The number was ringing.

Then, "Hello?"

"*You*," Izzy said hoarsely.

"Yes-s-s?"

"*You*," he said again, more slowly. "I—I am coming this evening. It is all right?" He waited for what seemed an eternity.

"It is all right," she repeated softly. That was all she said. Like a prayer almost. He could see the smile playing about her face now and he reached out to caress the cool white chin. . . .

35

The four of them were standing in the library. The introductions had been made and now Thatcher Kimbridge was rubbing his hands expectantly and saying, "Well, let's call this meeting to order. Poke, what would you like to drink?"

"Bourbon would be fine, sir. Bourbon and a little water. But no ice, please. I want to try a change of pace."

Thatcher nodded. "I'll join you," he said. He seemed in a jovial mood, as if the cares of Kimbridge & Co. had been lifted from his shoulders. "Deirdre and her mother are confirmed martini drinkers," he added.

"It's the color of gin, dear," said Edith Kimbridge sweetly. "We like the color of gin."

The maid who had been hovering at the door disappeared. Poke looked about him.

The library was a neat, snug room. It was lined with leather-bound editions and in one corner stood an antique sewing table on a carved pedestal. The room reminded Poke somehow of the two elder Kimbridges; warm and courtly, it carried its riches without ostentation. He glanced again at the sewing table. On the table was a faded photograph in a polished silver frame. It showed a little girl on a blanket laughing, with her face turned up to a tow-headed youngster who was apparently her brother. The girl in the photograph had a pony tail.

Poke was conscious of Deirdre Kimbridge, standing beside her mother and watching him quietly. She had not said a word other than a polite "How do you do?" when he entered the house. Her dark hair was braided and it hung in a short pony tail behind one ear. He realized then how short the three Kimbridges were; he seemed to tower above the family group.

"Mrs. Kimbridge," he said, "your daughter has something to look forward to." There was a faint drawl to his voice.

"Yes?" said Edith Kimbridge.

"If she's lucky—if she's very lucky—she's going to look like you someday."

"Why, Poke! Aren't you sweet." A touch of color rose in her pale face. "My, my," she said, cocking her head to one side, "and I thought gallantry was dead on Wall Street."

"Ah," said Thatcher, rubbing his hands again. "Now we can attend to the first order of business. I should warn you, dear," he said to his wife, "that Poke comes from the South. A Georgia gentleman."

The maid served the drinks and left the room.

"Well," said Thatcher, raising his glass, "what shall we drink to?"

Deirdre spoke up suddenly. "The future," she said. "Let's all drink to the future."

"To the future," they chorused softly.

Poke let the Bourbon seep deliciously into his throat. How odd, he was thinking. He had been in the house for only ten minutes and yet he felt the most unusual sensation—there seemed to be on the part of all three Kimbridges a heightened awareness of something that puzzled him. It was as though the three of them were peering at a drama that he could not see clearly. Especially Deirdre. She kept looking at him with such fixed concentration that he kept his eyes consciously averted from her. Strange. He shook his head and smiled at Edith Kimbridge who had plucked the olive from her glass and stood chewing it approvingly.

There was a second round of drinks and then they went into the dining room.

Deirdre was seated opposite Poke at the table. A break-front cabinet framed her head and the grained mahogany inlays between the glass rose up behind her like miniature Gothic arches.

"What do you do, Deirdre?" Poke asked.

"Oh," she said, "Deirdre sounds so formal. Call me Deedee. Would you mind that?"

"Not at all," Poke said.

Thatcher Kimbridge, helping himself to a slice of roast beef, dropped the serving fork. The fork clattered on the silver tray and he muttered, "Sorry," to the maid. Thatcher glanced quickly at his daughter and then busied himself again with the roast beef.

"I really don't do much of anything," said Deirdre. "I work at a shelter. A place for unwed mothers," she added, and Poke nodded understandingly. "At least it's a useful sort of thing to do with one's time," she went on. "But I'm not—well—productive in any sense."

"You do keep trying, dear," said Edith Kimbridge with a laugh. She turned to Poke. "Before you arrived

450

this evening, my daughter was trying to convince us that we should will this house as a shelter."

"Yes, she's pretty hard to deter once she gets an idea into her head," observed Thatcher Kimbridge. "Of course, I think she takes after her mother in that respect. Only last week"—amusement contested with affection in his face as he looked at his daughter—"she wanted to go downtown and talk with my lawyers. She was all set to place a bid on an old city firehouse. She wanted to buy it and convert it into a shelter—"

"Oh, Father, that's not fair! That firehouse would have been perfect. I went down and took the measurements. The firemen were very nice about it."

"Remember what I told you, Poke?" said Thatcher, chuckling. "I told you that Deirdre is difficult to predict."

"That's a woman's privilege, dear," said Edith. "The next thing you'll tell Poke is that we women are as difficult to fathom as the stock market."

"The market isn't hard to handle, Mrs. Kimbridge," said Poke. "You just give the market its head, that's all. And you remember not to be surprised by anything—anything at all—that happens."

"Well put, well put." Thatcher nodded.

Poke had the feeling that he was coming out of anesthesia. He felt a sensation of freedom, of forgetting slowly some ancient pain. Part of it, oddly enough, came from the realization that he no longer was racing for the partnership at Kimbridge & Co. He had been scratched, disqualified. At first this knowledge left him numb; it was as if his entire body had no more feeling in it than the Monster. But after leaving Carol at the ferry—they had walked away, as though by prearrangement, in opposite directions—he began to experience a strange feeling of weightlessness.

451

And then, a little while ago in the library, there had been something else. Looking at the rows of books he had been reminded suddenly of the yellowed law-books in his father's office. How he had loved that old office! He could smell the slightly honeyed odor of pipe tobacco and he heard the steady tapping of the bowl into the artillery shell casing that had served his father as an ash tray. A forgotten scene from child-hood awakened in his memory.

His father, wearing the frayed seersucker jacket with a torn pocket, was defending a Negro on trial for first-degree murder. There were round worn spots on the wall behind the jury box; the spots, almost the size of cannon balls, had been rubbed on the wall by the heads of countless jurors. He remembered his father asking a witness if he knew Walker Allen, and the witness had replied: "Why, I know him better'n his own folks. I've gone fishin' with him." Years later Poke understood what the man had meant.

A chocolate éclair was placed in front of him. The rich yellow custard oozed from a pore. He was con-scious of the laughter rippling around the table. It was a family group, he thought, and somehow he seemed to slip quite naturally into it. Or was he fool-ing himself? Was the real reaction to his defeat yet to make itself felt?

"Remember the time," Thatcher Kimbridge was saying, "when Deirdre wanted to set up a foundation for dining cars?" His glance invited Poke into the dis-cussion. "A special grant that would encourage strangers on diners to speak to each other?" He was laughing now, and a speck of chocolate moved mer-rily up and down on his lower lip.

"Oh, Father," broke in Deirdre, "that's enough about me! Tell Poke about the broker in Boston. You know—the sure thing?" She was peeling an apple on

452

her plate expertly with a knife and fork. She looked up at Poke and said, "My one accomplishment from years in Paris."

"Yes, yes," said Thatcher. "Boston . . . you might be amused, Poke. A man my father knew up there was the biggest bull you ever saw in traction stocks. This was back in the early nineteen hundreds. He had his accounts loaded up with traction companies. The way he figured it was this: if business remained good, people would ride the street railways to work and if hard times came they would continue to ride into town to look for jobs. Well, what happened to the traction stocks a few years later would have turned your hair white."

Deirdre had dispensed with the apple. "Poke, do you play bridge?" she asked.

"Afraid not," he said. "The only card game I know is poker. And it's hunting-camp poker at that."

"Well, Deirdre was practically a riverboat gambler at college from what I heard," said Edith Kimbridge. "Only she played bridge. She'd play bridge between breakfast and her first class." Edith Kimbridge rose from the table. "I think we'll take coffee in the library," she said to the maid.

As the two men went into the front hall, Deirdre followed her mother back to the kitchen. The maid was in the dining room, clearing the table. "I'll fix the coffee, Mildred," Edith called to the maid. "You know how particular Mr. Kimbridge is about his coffee on Sunday night."

The kitchen door swung closed and Deirdre leaned back against it. "Mother," she said, "I can't believe it's happening. It's just as though—" Her voice faltered.

"Can't believe what, dear?" asked Edith Kimbridge, measuring out the coffee for the percolator.

"Oh, Mother, you must feel it—you must! He has—I

453

don't know—a *pull* to him. I know Father feels it."
Deirdre moved slowly toward the counter. "From the
way he was talking at the table. And laughing. Why,
I haven't seen Father laugh like that in years. Oh,
Mother," she pleaded, "he's come back to us! *Don't
you see?*"

Deirdre's body began to move convulsively. She
threw herself into her mother's arms, causing loose
coffee to scatter over the floor. "Mo*ther!*" she said bro-
kenly and then she began to sob.

"There, there, dear," said Edith Kimbridge softly.
She held her daughter tightly and after a few moments she began patting her on the back. "Those
tears have been a long time coming," she said. "That's
when I always used to worry about you as a child.
When something bad happened and you didn't cry,
that's when I would worry."

Deirdre pulled herself free. She was gulping for
breath now and she groped for a handkerchief.

"Mother? Do you believe in love at first sight? At
being swept right off your feet! No, Mother, I've
never been so serious in my entire life. Do you?"

"Dear, I didn't say you weren't serious." Edith Kimbridge had reached for a broom. She began to sweep
up the coffee grounds. Then she stopped, and there
was the grating sound of coffee against her shoe. "Yes,
dear," she said tenderly, "I'm a prime example when
it comes to love at first sight. I don't suppose you
know this, but I was practically engaged to Seth
Voorhees at one time."

"What happened?" asked Deirdre, dabbing at her
eyes.

"What happened was that I met your father. It was
love at first sight—simply that."

"Oh, Mother, what shall I do? I don't even know if

454

he *likes* me. He seems so, well, stern in a way. Mother?"

"There's only one bit of advice I can give you. Don't lose him. Don't rush things, dear . . . but don't lose him now."

"Oh, Mother! Can I read your love letters?"

Edith Kimbridge placed the broom carefully in its closet. She turned around to regard her daughter with faint amusement. "No, you may not," she said. "But if you find any letters in my things after I die, you have my permission to read them once—before you burn them."

She crossed the kitchen and put a hand lightly on Deirdre's shoulder. "Oh, my darling," she said, "remember the last time you were here? You wanted to adopt a Negro baby."

"I'm sure of myself," Deirdre replied quietly. "About Poke. Just as sure as I'm alive. And now," she said with a mock curtsy, "shall we join our gentlemen?"

An hour and a half later Poke was standing outside the front door. He had thanked the Kimbridges for their hospitality and now he stood alone with Deirdre.

"Good night," she said, touching a place on his coat where the button was missing.

"Good night," he said. "Good night, Deedee."

She raised up on her toes suddenly and kissed him. Then, without a word, she stepped back into the house and closed the door softly.

This scene was witnessed by one other person who sat motionless in a parked car half a block away.

Noel had taken his station shortly after Poke entered the Kimbridge house. In the intervening hours, as he sat torturing himself with visions of what might

455

be going on inside the house, he had broken his pledge not to smoke by consuming an entire pack of cigarettes. The trees, outlined against a street light, laced their spidery leaf patterns upon the hood of the car while he sat huddled against the cold. The car was blue with smoke; he lowered the window a bit. He felt completely foolish—like a private eye in one of those impossible movies—and Noel Bigelow was not a man who liked to regard himself as ridiculous.

But he had been consumed by curiosity ever since Thursday afternoon when Miss Donahue emerged from the bull pen to place a manila envelope on Poke's desk. A tremor had passed through Noel in the adjoining cubicle. Was that envelope the tip-off? Had Jeffers been selected as the next partner? Somehow it seemed plausible. For the past hour or so Jeffers had been acting rather strangely; he seemed, well, he seemed no longer to be driven by demons. He just sat at the desk, very quietly, and stared at the magnified tape. The kike, well, that was something else. Max had turned into a crazy man on the telephone in the final hour of trading on Friday.

Noel's chance had come late Thursday afternoon.

Shortly before four o'clock Jeffers had gone out to the men's room. The envelope lay beside the telephone on Poke's desk. Noel got up and sauntered over to the drinking fountain. On the way back to his own desk he had stepped inside Poke's cubicle, ostensibly answering the telephone. He glanced about. Nobody in the board room was paying any attention to him. As for Max, he appeared completely exhausted; he was resting face down on the desk, the eyeglasses pushed up onto his forehead. Holding the dead receiver to his ear, Noel moved his lips in pantomime. His hand brushed the manila envelope to the floor and he stooped over to retrieve it. Then, hidden from

456

view, he swiftly opened the envelope with his free hand and extracted the paper.

"Memo from Thatcher Kimbridge," ran the printed heading and there it was! The time and the address. Noel easily read between the lines. An invitation for Poke to appear for Sunday-night supper with the Kimbridges. The holy gathering of the clan—the invitation for which Noel had thirsted so long. But of course! That was just the way Thatcher Kimbridge would choose to reveal Poke's selection as the new partner—in the privacy of his immediate family. The employees of Kimbridge & Co. had come to realize some time ago that the next partner would represent the personal selection of Thatcher Kimbridge. So Poke Jeffers was going to be the man. . . .

And now he had Deirdre kissing him, too! No wonder she had refused to see Noel despite his repeated calls. Their chemistry had turned somehow into oil and water. Noel was not superstitious but he was almost ready to believe that the evil eye of Joan of Arc had managed to put a hex upon their courtship. Deirdre was tossing him over for the winner—for Poke Jeffers. How long had something been going on between these two? He gripped the wheel of the car as tree shadows danced gently upon the hood.

Watch it! Jeffers was coming down the sidewalk toward the car. Noel ducked swiftly below the dashboard. He held his breath, feeling the cold plastic of the wheel on the back of his neck. Good! Jeffers had not spotted him.

Noel listened to the light, measured tread moving past him, only a few feet away. It was amazing the way Jeffers walked; you'd never know he had a peg leg. Noel was cursing silently. Jeffers would pay, oh, yes, how he would pay. Noel Bigelow was not about to lose the partnership *and* his girl to the same man and let him get away with it.

The footsteps died away. The light above the entrance to the Kimbridge town house was dark now. Noel sat up, rubbing his cold hands together. He switched on the ignition and already his mind was beginning to turn.

36

On the following Saturday the lounge of the New York Yacht Club, dimly lit and gloomily luxurious, was as quiet as the hold of a deserted ship. You could almost hear the creaking of timbers, Noel Bigelow was thinking.

Sailing peacefully along the high walls were the small smooth wooden hulls of prize boats. Noel peered at the model above his head. *Sweet Gambol I.* What had become, he wondered, of his father's schooner? Suddenly he was glad he did not know. This tiny red hull represented defeat.

He had chartered out *Sweet Gambol II* after the divorce and right at this moment his boat was lazing somewhere in the Caribbean. He stood for a little while lost in thoughts, utterly at ease in this huge dark lounge with its ornate gargoyled mantel. The mantel was ghostly gray, like the belly of a fish.

His mind strayed back to his college days and he thought now, with a smile beginning to play on his lips, about the incident during freshman year. Several of his friends had contributed a pot of $100. The agreement was for Noel to go to New York one Saturday night and get laid by a dance-hall hostess. In return for their donations the other freshmen were to be treated later to every detail of the incident. They received their money's worth; Noel had obliged with a glittering account. What they did not know was that Noel had pocketed their money after meeting a girl from Sarah Lawrence at the Biltmore. Her attentions had been offered free of charge; she even paid for the hotel room.

Yes, he reflected, that was one of the extra dividends of being a sailor. You could make plans. The thought pleased him. You set your plans just as carefully as if preparing for a cruise; you checked the gear and supplies and, always, the sails. And you had to be willing to adapt, to change course.

Breaking Jeffers' good leg—now there was a plan that brought him greater anticipation than any cruise! It was such a *right* move. Had he not been somewhat afraid of the man's physical strength, he would have liked to attend to it personally. But that was out of the question. He must preserve his anonymity.

He was humming now as his eyes caressed the smooth lines of *Sweet Gambol I*. Yes, once Jeffers became no better than a cripple he would see how the wind blew with Deirdre. Noel always appreciated a plan with leverage.

Leverage. His thoughts flicked briefly to the stock market. It had turned soft again this week for no apparent reason. "How's the market?" his customers kept asking him. "Down and dirty," became his standard reply. The Dow Theorists on Wall Street who kept looking for bullish indicators were becoming frantic. But then that was the trouble with these market technicians: they merely reacted to outside events without taking any direct action. No, they did not know how to plan properly.

Noel Bigelow touched the bell. He would toast his new plan. An attendant materialized out of the gloom, hurrying forward like a competent steward on shipboard.

"The Special Dividend," repeated Henry Eustis with a hearty chuckle. "That's very good—just the name for a drink. Sort of fits the financial district, you might say." He beamed at Noel Bigelow and surveyed the glazed catacomb interior approvingly. "Lucky you made this for Wednesday, uh, Noel. I'm on duty in the vault this afternoon. Not up on the main floor. Otherwise, all I'd be drinking now is water."

"Yes," said Noel softly, "I thought of that." He took care not to flinch when the man addressed him by his first name. This was a level of camaraderie reached after three "SDs" apiece at Alberto's.

Henry Eustis was a guard at the bank where Noel had worked. A barrel-chested man with the drooping jowls of a bloodhound and—as became apparent when he reached for the martini carafe—dirt crescents under his fingernails.

"Another one?" asked Noel. "Before we order?"

"No, no." The crescents deployed upon the table-cloth regretfully. "I'm already feeling these."

For Noel the martinis had brought a heightening sense of anticipation. In a few moments he would spring the question.

Henry Eustis was an obliging talker in such congenial surroundings. He had provided Noel with the latest gossip at the bank. A clerk in the Bond Department had been dismissed for refusing to trim back his long sideburns. One of the vice presidents in Customers' Service was busy arranging a wedding for a Texas banker who was coming into New York to claim, with proper discretion, his fifth bride. An officer in Personal Trust had created a mild revolution by requesting for his new office a stone sundial instead of one of the Remington paintings favored by the board chairman.

Noel glanced appraisingly at his luncheon companion. He had in the past arranged a small number of favors for Henry Eustis. He had shown Henry how to save $700 in interest payments on his house mortgage. Every Christmas there arrived at the bank for Henry two bottles of domestic brandy with the compliments of Noel; the brandy was a present to Noel from one of his customers at Kimbridge & Co. He happened to detest domestic liqueurs. Yes, thought Noel, weighing the accounts in his mind, Henry Eustis remained clearly in his debt. But he must be very careful in broaching the subject.

Henry Eustis was a man destined to rise no higher than a bank guard. He was an ex-Marine and this was sufficient to assure him of his present station. But he also once served as a New York City patrolman. There had been a scandal about some assault-and-battery case—Noel never knew all the details—and Henry was discharged from the police force. This was the clue that Noel was depending on; Henry should have access to the kind of information he was seeking. If he would only talk—

"Say, Henry, I was wondering . . ."

"What about, Noel, ole Noel? Say-y-y. Just look at the knockers on that babe over there. They're practically falling into her soup. Sure would like to get her down in the vault this afternoon. I'd sure clip *her* coupons."

"I was wondering if you could help me on something." Noel hunched forward. "Could you give me the name of someone you know who could provide me with—well—some muscle?"

"Muscle?" The man's bantering tone grew suddenly suspicious. His hands formed into huge ham fists on the tablecloth. "What exactly"—he was talking very slowly—"do you mean—muscle?"

"Oh, it's just a gag," said Noel quickly. "Don't worry. A friend of mine, he's getting married. You know, like the banker from Texas. Well, there's a bachelor party I'm getting up and I want to do something a little different. A chorus girl popping up out of a cake isn't very imaginative any more. I want to hire some people—some genuine tough types—to rough him up a bit. Not really hurt him, just throw a scare in him. Just for laughs." He paused. "By the way, I've got some Scotch, a case of Scotch someone sent to me. You drink Scotch?"

"Drink Scotch?" Henry Eustis was offended. "Hell, I drink *anything*. When I was a kid I started out with antiseptic. Now you take two aspirins and shake them up in a bottle of antiseptic. Whew! What a kick! And at discount rates." There was a silence as Henry Eustis regarded Noel. Finally he said, "What if I do happen to know a certain citizen . . . You don't mind a jig?"

"A jig?"

"A nigger. This one's got green eyes. But don't let that throw you. I knew him when I was on the force and we've sort of kept in touch. Yes, he's muscle, if you want to call it that. The best. Only he's not cheap. Not even for a bachelor party. I don't think you could say he offers discount rates. A bachelor party," Henry Eustis repeated. "That's a bit out of his usual line."

463

Noel tried to control his excitement. The hook had been taken!

The two men talked quietly for several minutes and then Henry Eustis wrote out something on a bank-deposit slip. He handed it to Noel.

As he pocketed the slip, Noel picked up the large glazed menu. He shook it, and there was a cracking sound like a rifle shot. "What about ordering some lunch?" he said with a wide smile.

"Yeah, okay. You go ahead, Noel, ole Noel. You order for us both. You know what's good here. And there's nothin' too good for us. Right, Noel, ole Noel?"

"That's right, Henry."

"Say, you got out of the bank in the nick of time. Know what they're doin' this week in Credit Audit?"

"No, what?"

"The vice presidents are taking turns. They're monitoring the phone calls. All the way up to assistant vice president. How's that for the limit?"

Deirdre turned her head sleepily. "Ummh," she murmured, "what time is it?"

"Thursday. It's still Thursday night, Deedee."

"Ummh, you're a calendar watcher. Is that what they taught you to do down in Georgia? To watch calendars?"

"No, not all the time. Sometimes we just watch girls who ought to get up and eat. Do you realize we haven't had any supper?" He looked at his watch. "And it's nearly midnight?"

"Ummh . . ." She reached out for him.

Poke rolled over on the bed. "Oh, no, you don't," he said, and then he stood up on one leg.

He hopped over to the dresser. Then he sat down quickly on a chair. Slipping on a pair of white shorts, he thought about the past few hours. It was uncanny.

464

With this girl he felt no self-consciousness about the stump. Everything they did seemed smooth and natural. He shook his head. Easy, easy, easy, he cautioned himself. He ought to be gun-shy as hell. He knew that, and yet with this girl—

"How are you on sardines?" he said. "I'm off to the kitchen to reconnoiter."

She opened one eye. "Come over here," she said, "and I'll tell you a little secret."

"No, ma'am."

"You're a coward."

"That's right."

"And I love you."

"Deedee," he said patiently, "how are you on sardines?"

She closed the eye again. "Wonderful," she whispered. "We'll have a midnight snack. Sardines for two. It just might start a trend."

A few minutes later he heard her calling from the bedroom. "Can I put on a pair of your pajamas?"

"Help yourself!" he called back. "Bottom drawer of the dresser! But they'll be a little long for you!"

He took inventory of the two plates he had prepared: sardines, tomato slices, lettuce, mayonnaise, bread, chocolate pudding, lemon cookies. A feast. He remembered the small bottle of white wine in the refrigerator and he opened this, too, and found two wineglasses.

"Poke?" The voice, less sleepy now, seemed to come from the living room.

"Yep?"

"Come out here."

"You ready to eat?"

"Not just yet. Come out here—*please*."

"Okay." He poured the wine and set the bottle down on the counter.

465

"Well?" she said.

She was standing in the middle of the living room. She was wearing only the top to a pair of red-striped pajamas that fell almost to her knees.

"Great!" he said. "It does things for you it never did for me. Anyone ever tell you that you have beautiful knees?" It was amazing, he thought, everything about this girl.

She watched him closely. "I *know* you," she said in a low voice.

"Your father been talking about me?"

"Oh, goodness, no! But I *know* you. I just do."

"Well, let's just take it a bit easy, Deedee."

"Yes," she said. "We won't rush things. We have a long, long time." She seemed to be smiling to herself. She twirled about suddenly and the pajama top flared up around her rich full buttocks. "What a lovely room!" she exclaimed. "What a lovely room for me to redecorate!"

"Hey!"

"Oh, you can't help yourself now," she said. "When the women in my family get an idea into their head nothing can stop them. You should see Mother. She carries scissors in her purse—just to trim plants when she visits places. I think she's barred perpetually from the Bronx Botanical Garden. All the guards there carry her photograph."

"Are you ready to eat?"

"Yes," she said and sat down on a chair, primly smoothing out the pajama top over her thighs.

"The sardines," he observed a bit later, "are delicious—if I say so myself."

"Mmmh," she murmured, chewing. She swallowed and took a sip of wine. "Poke, let's take the day off and we'll—"

"Now what would your father say if I didn't show up at the office?"

"Oh, I don't think he'd mind really. You could catch—let's see—a virus. A twenty-four-hour virus. How's that?"

"No, Deedee. You just said yourself we have a long, long time. Tomorrow I report for work as usual. Not that I'll be in condition to do much for Kimbridge & Co." He picked up a sardine with his fingers. "In Korea," he said, "there were gangs of civilians who tunneled into the Army warehouses. You know what they were after? Tuna. Those South Koreans just loved canned tuna."

She crossed her legs and leaned toward him. "Tell me about Korea," she said softly.

On the sidewalk below Noel Bigelow stopped pacing the instant the light went on in the living room. All evening long he had been in agony. He could picture what must be going on inside.

Now he walked up to the stoop of the building across the street and tried to peer beyond the curtains. God, it was cold! But he saw nobody—not Deirdre or that bastard Jeffers.

He retraced his steps and kicked savagely at a newspaper lying on the curb. The paper was opened to the financial section and the headline said: MARKET STILL MOVING IN SAWTOOTH PATTERN. He kicked at the paper again and cursed. He would get the peg leg! Tomorrow he had an appointment. An appointment with the Duke.

That was the only name Henry Eustis had used— the Duke. And at lunch Noel had gotten certain dis-

tinct impressions. One was that Eustis himself har-
bored a deep fear of this man, the jig as he had called
him, and another was that the name kept changing,
from something else to the Duke now and then from
the Duke to some unknown name in the future.

Noel was wondering about this as the taxi turned
into 125th Street.

"Buddy," the driver said, "you know what you're
doin' up here?"

"Just find the address," Noel said.

"Okay, buddy. It's your funeral. But I'll tell you one
thing. My 'Off Duty' sign is already on. And if it don't
make you no difference, you can pay me right now
what's on the meter and add your tip to it. When I
stop, you get out fast, buddy." The driver kept shaking his head.

The address was a small shop with a sign—HOSIERY
—painted across the window. The shop was in the
middle of a block of tenements with cocoa brick
walls; fire escapes spilled down the front of the buildings like the straggly hair of old women. It was already dark and Harlem had begun to stir expectantly
with the sudden mysteries of a Friday evening. A
trash can had been overturned near the curb where
Noel got out of the taxi. He stepped gingerly onto the
sidewalk. Near the shop door was an armchair,
plainly abandoned, and its seat had exploded into
dirty cotton padding. Noel caught a glimpse of a
black tail scuttling inside the chair—was it a rat?

On the sidewalk nearby was a Negro with glistening
kinky hair; he was swaying like a drunk and then he
touched the elbow of a girl passing by. He said something to her and she shook her head quickly. The man
snapped his fingers. "Shoot," he said thickly, "I can be
twice any other man!"

The girl was thin and high hipped; she wore black

cluster earrings and dark glasses. Noel could sense her eyes fastening upon him as the girl came forward. He felt sudden hot panic. What a fool he was! He started back toward the curb but his taxi had disappeared. Wheeling about, he half ran to the shop, hearing the tinkle of a bell and the high, giggling laughter of the girl announce his entrance.

Inside, the dim lights shone upon truncated manikins with figures like polished eggplant. Noel stopped in front of an armless manikin adorned with a filmy red brassière. There was a sharp, familiar smell in the shop.

The only person there was a teenage boy wearing a leather jacket. Apparently he was the clerk.

"I want to see the Duke," said Noel nervously. When the boy did not move, he added, "I have an appointment with him here."

The boy bestowed a quick, hard stare upon him. Then, quite deliberately, he turned his back to Noel and tenderly lifted a stack of pink panties onto the top of the glass counter. "Rear door," the boy said with an almost imperceptible nod.

Noel hurried to the back of the shop. He opened the door and the smell was stronger now. Suddenly he remembered: pop skull. He had not smelled popskull whisky since that dedication of a chemical plant in Kentucky years ago.

The back room was small and it had no windows. The only furniture consisted of two wooden chairs and a small wooden table which at the moment was being treated to the sawing motion of a murderously long switch-blade knife.

"Sit down, Mr. White," said the man with the knife.

"My name is—"

"No names in this room, Mr. White. You understand?"

Noel nodded slowly. The pop-skull smell had begun to work into his head but there was no bottle in sight. Maybe there is a whisky still right under this floor, he thought. He sat down and looked across the scarred table at the Duke.

He was a big man wearing a woolen turtleneck sweater and the skin stretched tight across his bald head like a dark blue drum. He had huge calloused ears and a long, triangular jaw. The Duke did not look at Noel for several minutes. He kept notching the edge of the table with his knife, grunting now and then with satisfaction as he twisted the blade. Wood shavings littered the floor and the Duke occasionally would brush one shoe across the shavings. This scraping sound also appeared to give him satisfaction because he would grin savagely down at the table, revealing a row of top teeth capped with gold.

"About our arrangement," the Duke said finally and then he stopped. His voice seemed to float about the room. It was a faintly cultured voice, like that of a bell captain in a resort hotel, and he pronounced his a's with the broad, gentle inflection of a Jamaican.

Noel realized this was his cue. "Well," he began, "it's really for a bachelor party, a joke we're playing on this friend of mine who—"

"Mr. White, I got no time to fool with you." The eyes flashed up from the table. The eyes were green, a lustrous green, and they were glinting now at Noel. Strange how the eyes reminded him of Joan of Arc. Noel felt the man's hatred for him tighten within those eyes. "Why?" The word came out with the sharpness of a knife blade.

"It's a joke—"

"Why?" The Duke ran a finger meditatively under the row of gold-capped teeth. "Folks don't pay me for jokes. Nothing is *that* funny."

Noel decided upon another tack. "By the way, what do you charge for this—arrangement?"

"Three thousand dollars."

"Three *thous—*"

"You want to leave, Mr. White? I think maybe you better leave. You probably got other things to do."

"No, no." Noel swallowed with an effort. "It's just that—well, isn't three thousand dollars a lot of money?"

"For a joke, sure. For an arrangement, no. Remember. You don't take any risks. You just pay up." The knife carved out a huge notch. "For you, Mr. White, the ante has just gone up. You came here in a cab. Well, my meter's still ticking. Four thousand. Now you want to talk or get out?"

"I'll talk," said Noel quickly. He felt the hatred of this man for himself—and for all white men. The sensation was far more real than the sharp whisky smell. "What do you want to know?"

"*Why?*"

"Why am I doing this?" Noel's voice turned suddenly hard. "All right, I'll tell you. I want to get even with a guy. I want him roughed up—but good. I want the job done by professionals. I want his leg broken. His right leg broken below the knee." He wet his lips. "There," he said, "that's what I want."

"So that's what you're ordering," the Duke murmured. "My, my, that *is* an arrangement."

"Can you deliver?" Noel's fingers gripped the edge of the table. Was the Duke going to back out?

"Mr. White, *I* don't deliver personally. But I can arrange it, yes." There was a low rumble in his throat—the sound of animal amusement. "Maybe you should know, Mr. White, how I arrange an order of this kind. I use only Mr. Whites for the job. *Your own kind, Mr. White,*" the Duke said, and the hatred in

471

his voice seemed to fill the room. "Subcontracting, you might call it."

"Do—do you mind not using that knife? While we're talking? It—well, it makes me nervous."

"Yes, Mr. White, I *do* mind." A neat wedge, the suddenly exposed wood white as flesh, fell to the floor. "It helps me think, Mr. White."

Noel could feel the sweat standing on his forehead. His instincts were to bolt from this ugly room with its stench of pop skull. But he had gone too far to turn back now. The green eyes seemed to track the thoughts inside his head. "About the payment," Noel blurted. "Will new bills be all right?"

"New bills?" The eyes shone with surprise. "You mean fresh lettuce? No, Mr. White"—the huge bald head shook slowly in chastisement—"that would never do. Old bills. Nigger bills, if you please. In fives and tens, Mr. White."

"All right." God, thought Noel, old bills. Somehow that was the worst part of it, old bills. "Suppose I pay you half before the, uh, arrangement takes place? The other half after it's done."

"What's the matter, Mr. White? My word not good enough for you?" The calloused ears appeared to twitch slightly. "You won't take my word?"

"Sorry, I'm sorry," said Noel, pressing back against his chair. "All right. You tell me how you want it handled. I'll pay any way you want. But remember what I ordered. The right leg—broken below the knee."

Noel did not see the movement. But suddenly the switch-blade knife was quivering on the table top. It had bitten half an inch into the wood. He watched the quivering knife in fascination. Very slowly the knife grew still and then the Duke said, "That's the way I seal my arrangements. Now if you have some

472

ideas about your order, I'm listening to you." His tone had turned brisk, the voice of a businessman.

"Yes," said Noel. "I've been giving this a whole lot of thought. I can get the man in position for you. Just leave that to me. Another thing—it's got to happen in Wall Street." He leaned forward, pressing his elbows against the table, and said, "The way I see it . . ."

37

At twilight, on this Sunday in December, Noel Bigelow lighted a cigarette. The moment finally had arrived for him to launch his plan. The scheming, the watching, the last wheedling phone calls to Deirdre when his voice almost choked with jealousy—all these faded from his mind. Now his single regret was that the $4,000 would not be tax deductible.

Seated beside the telephone in his apartment, he exhaled a thick gray ring of smoke and then stuck his finger through it. "Poke," he said and smiled with an immense satisfaction.

At first the Duke had been dubious; he had wanted to work out the arrangement his own way. But Noel kept insisting and, on his second visit to the back room on 125th Street, his plan had prevailed. Even the Duke ultimately seemed to appreciate its finer points.

For a moment the green eyes of the Duke emerged into focus—the green eyes and that long, devilish knife. Noel shivered. He could hear the knife blade biting into the table. "Mr. White," the Duke had said, "we won't be seeing each other—*ever*. I always move on to a new location after completing an arrangement. Don't try"—the voice turned into cold steel—"to get in touch with me. You understand what I'm telling you, Mr. White?" Noel had nodded and his eyes dropped to the worn bills on the table between them.

Noel snubbed out his cigarette. What was it Tim McVay had once called him—the best mimic ever to take the stage for a Triangle Club show?

His throat muscles went into a brief, silent rehearsal as he thought again about Deirdre. She had told him when he had insisted on seeing her again that she planned to attend a wedding in Brooklyn this evening. One of the girls Deirdre had befriended at the shelter was getting married. Deirdre had sounded so excited. Yes, she was going alone to the wedding. No, she could not see him later . . . she had a date.

He picked up the phone and dialed Poke's number.

"Hello?"

"Poke? Oh, darling, I've got to see you—right away."

"Deedee, what's the matter? I thought you said you'd be tied up until after eight o'clock."

"Something's happened. I can't explain it now. But I want you to meet me. Can you come right away?"

"Sure. But where? What's all the trouble? Are you all right, Deedee?"

"Yes, yes. I'm fine." There was a brief pause. "Meet me at seven o'clock. I'll come over to Wall Street. Meet me right at the entrance to 50 Wall—"

"Fifty Wall? Why there?"

"Oh, darling, I can't explain it all now." The voice turned frantic. "Seven o'clock?"

"All right. See you then. Take care of yourself, Deedee. You need money or anything?"

"No, darling, all I need is you. I've got to go now. Please be on time." The line went dead. Perfect! exulted Noel.

He quickly dialed another number. When the voice answered, he said, "It's all set. Where we planned it. Seven o'clock." There was no response—but that, too, was part of the arrangement.

Noel set back in the chair and closed his eyes. Everything was shipshape, he thought with satisfaction.

He began to picture Poke Jeffers walking along Wall Street. The peg leg was about to get what was coming to him. In a little while now, in less than an hour.

And best of all, thought Noel, nobody could trace anything to him. Jeffers would end up with his good leg busted. And then maybe Deirdre would see the light. . . .

Yes, yes. He fumbled for another cigarette. Nobody knew for sure what lay beyond tonight. But Noel had the sensation that he would be back in the running for Deirdre. After all, he was her kind of guy. The god-damned peg leg—he was nothing but a passing fancy.

Poke raced up the subway steps two at a time and hurried out on to Broadway. He heard the chimes of Trinity Church high above him and then the loud, solemn bonging of the bell. His brain automatically ticked off the count—seven o'clock. The church formed a large dark eminence off to his left. There was not another person visible on Broadway; the avenue was still and cold, its lampposts like frozen sentinels with helmets of light. On Sunday night even the automobiles had forsaken Lower Manhattan. When the church bell stopped ringing, the silence hung like a shroud. The stillness of the churchyard seemed to have spread over the entire area.

He turned right into Wall Street. It, too, was completely deserted. The stone buildings stood huddled in the cold. The chill began to tickle his stump and he lengthened his stride. He felt a sudden breeze on his face, cold and slightly damp from the river.

What was wrong with Deedee? he wondered again. There had been something odd about her voice when she called—his customers' man ear, with an awareness for nuances, had detected that—but he could not puzzle it out. He had quelled the doubt itching his mind and simply reacted to her summons. What could have happened? And why did they have to meet here of all places?

He hurried past the dark gray masses of stone. Polished steel doors were drawn tight across the bank entrances and the street lights glinted gray and ghostlike upon the doors. From above there drifted the clucking and cooing of invisible pigeons.

He smiled then as he began to wonder again about Deedee. What a girl—she came at you like a tornado. Only she enveloped you with her warmth and love instead of any destructive force. And yet there was a certain hesitancy about her, almost a kind of shyness as if she could not quite believe what was happening between them. That hesitancy was in a way her saving grace. He knew that because he recognized the same feeling in himself.

Now he was only half a block from 50 Wall. He began to wonder about the car parked in front of the darkened building. His steps echoed in the gray cold stillness but suddenly his pace changed. A door of the car swung open and a man emerged from the driver's side.

Poke narrowed his eyes. What was a car doing here at this hour? And where was Deedee? Was she in the car?

The man was waiting on the sidewalk. He was about Poke's height and he was wearing a sheepskin jacket cut just above the knees.

"Mr. Jeffers?" the man asked. "Mr. Poke Jeffers?" There was a cold, metallic formality in the voice.

"Yes," Poke replied. "What do you want?" He stopped in front of the man.

"We have a message for you, Mr. Jeffers," the man said. On the other side of the car another man got out. He walked around the car, passed behind Poke, and then stood with his arms folded, leaning casually against the recessed entrance to 50 Wall.

The two men appeared oddly like twins. They were about the same height and they both wore sheepskin coats with the collars turned up. From their catlike movements they also conveyed the impression of supple strength.

"Yes?" Poke said impatiently. "What's the message?" He was starting to worry about Deedee. Was she in some kind of trouble?

"Oh, there's no real rush now, Mr. Jeffers," the first man said with elaborate politeness.

Poke tried to make out the man's features in the half darkness. He had a pale, blunt face.

The man reached inside his coat and, with the precision of a vaudeville act, his partner followed suit. They each extracted a small slender piece of metal. Slowly each man pulled out his metal piece and then collapsed it. An automobile aerial. The second man was circling back around him now and Poke turned slightly to keep both men in his view. Neither of the

478

two men spoke; each one simply kept working the tube of metal.

"That's a nice tie you've got there, Mr. Jeffers," the first man said, moving closer as though it were impolite to address a stranger from a distance. And then the aerial darted through the air and neatly flicked the tie free of Poke's coat.

Poke ignored his tie which now stirred ridiculously in the breeze. "What the hell have you done with Miss Kim—"

The second man hit him from the side. It was a solid blow, laid below the hips like a body block, and Poke went crashing against the building. The stone scraped the back of one hand and he did not have to look to know that the hand was bleeding. He crouched against the wall like a dazed prize fighter kneeling on the canvas.

He shook his head as the two men, their aerials bending and sighing like foils, advanced upon him. He looked quickly into their faces but their features were as impassive as stone.

Well, well, well, Poke thought. A couple of hoods. Whatever they were up to didn't seem to concern Deedee at all. He glanced sideways along the street; nothing else stirred.

Th aerials began to play within a few inches of his face. He could hear the metal rods singing and then he felt a sharp, stinging sensation along one cheek.

"*Behind you!*" Poke yelled at the top of his voice.

The bluff gave him the split second he needed. Both men turned instinctively.

Poke had set himself. He sprang up and hammered the side of his right hand, a chop blow that did not travel more than eight inches, into the neck of the second man. The man fell grunting to the pavement and his aerial went skidding into the street.

479

Poke hopped over the prostrate body and turned toward the first man who was coming at him fast.

And then a strange thing occurred. Poke realized that if he chose to run at this moment he could shake himself free of these men. It was like barreling through an opening between two runners and forcing yourself out in front. His mind worked it out with lightning speed: he could sidestep the first man and then hightail it toward a side street and then the tunnel near the entrance to the barbershop. He knew that he could lose them there in the maze of darkness.

But he was feeling the fine film of sweat coming over his body and with it a sense of exultation. He was in full command of his muscles. *He did not want to run.* "Hey, hey," he said softly and beckoned with his hands for the first man to advance.

The man stopped in his tracks. His aerial flicked out again and this time Poke caught it and pulled the man toward him. "Hey, hey," he said again, and the man was mouthing obscenities. The man began to tug at the aerial and Poke suddenly let go. The man fell backward, losing his balance, and Poke slid forward.

His body was like a splendid single nerve. The perspiration of his body became a lubricant and he felt that long-forgotten thrill, the free-running thrill, surging through him—

There was a tug at his right foot and Poke realized, a fraction of a second too late, what was happening. The man on the sidewalk had grabbed his foot. Poke twisted suddenly to break the hold, his mind and body moving in unison, and then there was this snapping sound . . . he actually *felt* the pain as though it were a bone breaking in his body. The nerve ends in his stump cried out. The anchor bolt of the Monster, the bolt governing the movement in his left pumpkin foot, had broken. He pitched forward.

Something hit him brutally on the right leg, below the knee; that feeling, too, registered in his mind as he was falling. And then he saw something streaking before his eyes as plain as daylight, a scene etched from his childhood. The highway that ran through the middle of his home town. The broad band of asphalt ran past the houses and the city hall and the post office and the courthouse and then the Episcopal church and its clipped lawn where on Sunday mornings the choir youngsters hung outside until the last possible moment, looking like black-and-white butterflies in their fluttering robes. The highway ran past the filling stations and the stores plastered with tin signs exhorting the populace to drink Coca-Cola and finally past the sign, standing alone in grandeur, that said simply: "Come Again. People Here Are Folks." That highway held an indisputable life force the way it came hurtling out of the red hills that were like huge Christmas hams and charged through town and then lit out again, always changing and yet never changing, a hard asphalt ribbon that seemed to bind the whole world together.

And then the hard, cold darkness folded him in its arms and he lay quite still.

Poke did not see the first man, panting and wiping the sweat with a sleeve of his sheepskin coat, as he bent over him. In two minutes, working with savage precision, the man had finished with his right leg while his partner retrieved the aerials. He telescoped the rods neatly and placed them inside his coat.

"There, that takes care of the leg," the first man said, grunting from his effort. "As ordered. Broke as nice as you please."

Nor did Poke see the second man approaching now. "His neck," the second man said, the voice suddenly quickening, "it looks sort of funny." The second man bent over and felt his pulse. Then he touched Poke's eyelid. "Marty," the second man said, "it's a bigger order than you think. His neck is broke. He's dead, Marty."

38

The good die young . . . the good die young . . . the
good die young . . .

For the thousandth time this phrase tormented
Thatcher Kimbridge. Now he sat alone in the library,
tapping his palm on a chair arm in time to the hammering litany. He had turned out the lamps and occasionally the passing headlights would flicker eerily
upon the frosted windows. It was eleven o'clock on
Sunday night and the snow had been falling steadily
since noon.

With a rush of helpless anger he struck his fist
upon the chair. Why did Poke have to die? He
cocked his head as if waiting for an answer in the
dark, silent room. Outside the falling snow lulled the
street and softened the harsh city edges. Manhattan
seemed a remote Alpine village. But there was no
answer to Thatcher's question, only the insistent tapping of snow against the windowpanes.

He scowled furiously. What did he know for certain? He knew that the bourbon highballs at the Union League Club were weaker than the ones served at his downtown club. But after that? Thatcher Kimbridge began to run out of certainties.

So much had happened so swiftly. The old need time to adjust, he thought. Philosophy was poppycock —and the good die young. Exactly one week ago at this hour he was standing in the city morgue, where he had gone to identify the body. The police had been surprisingly gentle; they sent a squad car around to fetch him and later, when he left the morgue, the questions were put quickly and neatly. The detective was an alert, well-dressed man and as Thatcher sat talking with him he thought how much like a security analyst the detective seemed. Did Mr. Kimbridge know what the victim was doing on Wall Street at that hour? No. Possibly he might have been driven there? Possibly. The police had checked; the victim did not presently own a car. The detective began thinking out loud. Apparently it was a mugging, but there was very little to go on. The victim's wallet had been rifled and—this was the single strange element—his right leg had been forcibly broken below the knee. A break like that could not have come from the fall that apparently killed him. But what did it mean? The detective shook his head in perplexity and Thatcher Kimbridge simply sat in the straight-backed wooden chair feeling the shock roll over him.

Thatcher had broken the news to Deirdre and—he shook his head now—he would not think of that, no.

The following day Deirdre had taken over the final arrangements. She had moved as though in a trance but she insisted on attending to every detail. She had ridden in the baggage car beside the casket all the way to Poke's home in Georgia and she had remained there for one day with his aunt after the funeral.

When she flew back to New York on Friday, she had called her parents. She did not want to see them, not just yet. . . .

Thatcher rose wearily and walked through the silent house. He paused near the kitchen and looked outside. The garden lay clumped with snow; ordinarily he would be thinking now about setting up a spruce in the garden so that Pinckney could hang the Christmas lights. He decided this year there would be no tree.

He heard a soft step behind him and he turned.

Edith was standing there in her robe. Neither of them spoke for a few moments; they simply looked at each other. And then she touched him on the arm and said, "I'm going up to bed, dear. You're sure you are all right?"

"Yes, I'm all right."

"You don't think we should telephone Deirdre?"

"No. She'll come around to us. But I think it's important to let her choose the time."

"All right, dear. Whatever you say."

She kissed him, and her fingers suddenly tightened on his arm.

"I'll be up in a little while, Edith. Good night."

"Good night, my dearest."

He stood there for perhaps another ten minutes, staring out at the snow-white garden but not really seeing anything. How peculiar it was, he thought, that Poke's death should in some strange way ease the burden of grief he carried for his own son. He shook his head; nothing in life made sense, nothing at all. He felt like an aged officer whose finest young soldiers had died in battle.

In time he, too, would pass on, and then what would remain? After he and all his partners had gone? Kimbridge & Co., Inc. The new name seemed to form in coals upon the snow for his inspection. He repeated the name and it came awkwardly to his tongue.

Kimbridge & Co., Inc. Yes, thanks to the legal wonders of incorporation, his money could remain in the firm after he died. There would be no danger of dislodging the keystone in the firm's capital structure. Even the Estate of Jared Kimbridge shortly would feed its funds into Kimbridge & Co., Inc. What his father would have hated and fought against—Thatcher could imagine his father mouthing the word "incorporation" in disdain—would in the long run become a blessing. The secret lay partly in a new item in the profit-and-loss statement: earned surplus. How strange it all was! How simple and yet so strange.

The incorporation would take effect with the new year. Already the machinery had been set in motion. On Friday he had seen a proof of the new letterhead. Three little letters—"Inc."—seemed so innocent in print. The name change meant a bonanza to the printers. Every paper form used by the firm was to be changed. In a gesture that would seem extravagant to the outsider, Thatcher intended to have every sheet of paper in the home office bearing the name Kimbridge & Co. destroyed in the shredding machine. He could save several thousand dollars simply by stamping "Inc." at the end of the name, but no. There was something especially fitting in the destruction process. Yes, he reflected grimly, it was like burying household treasures with the Pharaoh.

Through slips of paper we achieve life everlasting in the twentieth century, Thatcher Kimbridge kept thinking. He shook his head in disbelief.

Thatcher Kimbridge walked stiffly back into the library. He sat down and rubbed a finger furiously against the side of his nose. The time had come; he had to decide upon the next partner of Kimbridge & Co.

He swore under his breath. If only he could shut out the memory of Poke as easily as the sight of his sheet-covered body gliding back into the refrigerated wall of the morgue. One of the casters in the long steel drawer had cried out, almost like a human voice expressing pain, as the body disappeared with the slow-motion pull of a sailor slipping into the ocean.

Finally, in the darkness of the library, Thatcher succeeded in tearing his mind away. He did it with the help of his mistress—the stock market. The market had turned strong again from the opening bell last Monday. There had been no special news out of Washington over the weekend; the foreign situation had not changed; prospects for business remained the same. But once again the market had turned suddenly, heeding its mysterious inner voice, and after it began to move everyone seemed to throw caution to the winds. Even some institutional clients of Kimbridge & Co. forsook their pattern of buying stocks on a scaledown and began to put in orders for large blocks at the market. The year-end rally was in full cry. It resembled, thought Thatcher, some maddened outing of the Maryland Hunt Club. Buy, buy, buy. Now, now, now. Even Howard Merriam had returned to his beloved charts like some penitent monk going back into his cloisters after an excursion into the outside world. Howard's market letter last week had recommended no less than a dozen stocks for immediate purchase—and he had the charts to back his wisdom.

The headlights of a passing automobile flickered against the windows and Thatcher thought about the customers' men of Kimbridge & Co. Miraculously, they had become the keepers of the kingdom. Selling stocks on Wall Street was fashionable—what younger people spoke of now as the "in thing"—once again. How strange it all was! The words of a friend, a partner in another brokerage house, sprang into his mind. They had eaten lunch recently and the friend, not normally a reflective man, had said suddenly: "I was thinking this morning as I looked at the volume figures about those three awful years starting with the '37 break. For our firm those years were worse even than the Crash. God, we had"—the voice shook with incredulity—"*no business*. Why, there were days when I remember one of my partners—we all had our desks in one big room then—making airplanes out of P & S sheets and sailing them out of the window. He won a quarter from one of the clerks in the cage by betting he could get the most distance with a paper airplane. My partner practiced for a solid week before he made that bet! And I remember reading the want ads one morning. You know what, Thatch?" The man's fingers twisted the crisp linen tablecloth. "I suddenly discovered I wasn't worth ten dollars a week to anybody. It was a horrible feeling. *There was nothing I could do to earn a decent living.* So I stayed on the Street and kept borrowing money from my father-in-law to keep my family alive. My God—I didn't even pull out of debt until 1950!"

Yes, thought Thatcher, the good die young. But on Wall Street a chosen few from the ranks would walk on to glory. In time the young, too, would grow old; the market had its own way of aging a man.

Which man? The question that had tantalized his mind for so long was insisting for an answer.

Israel Padawer? Or Noel Bigelow? The choice for the partnership logically narrowed down to these two men. He said their names aloud, one at a time, and they echoed strangely in the still house.

Why not pick some other man? Why not throw a

surprise into the entire organization? His mind ticked off the best office managers. The man in Boston showed great promise as an administrator. The manager of the Park Avenue office would make a good partner for any firm; he was young and bright and aggressive. And there were a half-dozen fine producers in offices outside of 50 Wall.

Padawer was still the largest producer in the firm. For the past few weeks, in fact, his production had soared. Padawer should get the nod; it ought to be that simple. But it wasn't. The world did not turn on such clear logic. The fact remained—and Thatcher felt a positive disgust for himself as he grappled with the dilemma—that Israel Padawer was a Jew. Thatcher tried to tell himself that it made no difference, that the man he selected as the next partner of the firm could be a Jew or a Bolivian or an Eskimo. The most important consideration was the man's own merit. But a Jew . . . Kimbridge & Co. picks its first partner in nearly twenty years and the man turns out to be a Jew. It was the sort of thing that the Street would notice immediately. The other firms would begin to wonder. "What on earth is happening over at Kimbridge & Co.?" people would say, and then they would shake their heads. Dammit, he didn't care! He detested prejudice of this sort.

What would a man like Rex Banta say? An incident from his college days floated into his mind. It was spring and Bones was drawing up its list for Tap Day with a self-conscious gravity that indicated the fate of mankind hung in the balance. Thatcher's choice was a Jewish boy he had gotten to know in the Shakespeare seminar, a brilliant, intense fellow with octagonal-framed glasses and skin almost as dark as rubbed walnut. "Sure, he's different, that's just my point!" Thatcher had argued one Thursday night with the other members of his delegation. "I say, it's about time we broke away from the mold! Let's be venturesome. Let's pick someone who doesn't own a dinner jacket but who might someday become a justice of the Supreme Court—even if he is a Jew!" But he might as well have been debating with the wind. Rex Banta did not want a Jew and Rex, as the last man to be tapped in their delegation, knew the weight of his own opinion. He caressed a football between his palms, nodding slowly while Thatcher spoke. "Yes, yes," Rex had said finally, "you have a point, Thatch. But think of this—what would the Old Guard say?" The other seniors in the room gravely nodded their agreement. Everyone was staring now at the football, perched dramatically upon the knee of Rex Banta. Yes, yes, the silent voices agreed, such a choice was unthinkable. The man to the right of Thatcher then dug an elbow into his ribs—just to show him that the others respected his rights as an individual. After all, wasn't that the essential idea behind Bones—to improve the individual member through team effort? Years later, when Thatcher had gone down to Washington to find a new manager for the Kimbridge & Co. office there, he ran into his Jewish acquaintance on Pennsylvania Avenue. Thatcher had lost touch with the man; he knew vaguely that the man was some minor attorney submerged in the Department of Commerce. Thatcher moved forward quickly, his hand outstretched, and called out the man's name. And then Thatcher stopped in his tracks. The man looked right through him and kept on walking.

Dammit, he didn't care what Rex Banta thought or even what his partners might say! Selecting a new partner was his private decision. A gust of wind flung snow fiercely against the windows. For a moment the sound resembled the staccato beat of a stock ticker. It was the same sound his father used to make when he cleared his throat. Jared—what would his father say? He wrestled now with the ultimate ghost of his mind. In the darkness he could visualize his father's face peering at him, the bright hawk eyes waiting expectantly for him to commit some grave mistake. A humorless smile fluttered across Thatcher's mouth. Yes, yes, he knew quite well what his father would say at a moment like this. His father would never forgive him for permitting a Jew to become a partner of Kimbridge & Co. His father would rather see the firm go bankrupt! He sat resignedly in the chair. Then he raised his hand in a signal of defeat and he said, half aloud, "All right, all right." So Israel Padawer was out. He tried not to think what the partnership would have meant to Padawer, not merely the money but the exhilaration and confidence that would flow through the man. "All right, all right," he said again, and this time there was a cruel Jewish inflection to the words. Thatcher Kimbridge permitted the self-hatred to seal inside him. So his father finally had prevailed again. And Seth, he had probably saved Seth from a second heart attack.

The choice would be Noel Bigelow. There was a helpless rattle in Thatcher's throat—dammit, dammit, dammit. What was there about young Bigelow that he did not quite approve of? Something . . . a feeling he had about the man that lifted the hairs along the back of his neck. Nonsense! You're getting old and feeble, Thatcher told himself angrily. Bigelow would be a good choice; he would *belong*. He thought then about Noel's father, whom he had known slightly, and how the two of them so many years ago had been filled with hope and the relentless drive that were deemed to be so important to success on the Street.

Yes, the world downtown once had been their oyster, too—but for Noel's father it all had ended so swiftly. Life had a way of playing such tricks.

Thatcher rose from the chair and walked slowly into the hallway. As he turned out the hall light, his mind was planning the pattern of the next morning. First, he would inform his partners of the decision and later, a decent interval before the market opened, he would ask young Bigelow to step into his office.

His mind toyed with the wording of the advertisement that would appear in a few days in the financial pages. "We are pleased to announce that Noel Bigelow has been admitted as a general partner." That was all the advertisement would say, except for the standard acknowledgment at the bottom, "Kimbridge & Co., Members New York Stock Exchange, Other Principal Security and Commodity Exchanges."

Yes, Noel Bigelow's name would appear duly in the space that once had been intended for Brittin Kimbridge. Thatcher began to climb the carpeted stairs. How Wall Street treasured its sacred rites, he was thinking as his hand gripped the banister. The stark tombstone advertisements heralded the new partners and when they died there would appear the final pronouncement, "With deep sorrow we announce the death of our Friend and Partner . . ."

The phone began to ring. Who would be calling at this hour, at midnight? wondered Thatcher. He moved quickly to the extension at the head of the stairs so that the sound would not awaken Edith.

"Hello?" he said.

39

Noel crushed out the cigarette and almost immediately he broke open another pack. Crumpling the cellophane in his fingers, he thought desperately: This is my third pack today. I've *got* to get hold of myself!

He rose from the armchair and went over to the window. The snow was still falling late Sunday afternoon. It had covered the parked automobiles along Ninth Street hours ago and now they resembled huge white sleeping beetles. The falling flakes twirled frenziedly against the street lights and then twisted away.

He went back to the armchair and as he sat down the insistent terror curled up with him again.

On Monday he had gone to the office half an hour early, already reveling in what he knew he would hear that morning. The excitement had built up within him to such a degree that he could not bear even to read the papers. He sat in his cubicle, building the scene in his mind with all the craft of a stage manager.

493

And then he let the dialogue filter through. At first it would come in bits and fragments like a stock-market rumor. Poke Jeffers had been hurt—did you hear the news?—a mugging, they're not sure—imagine! right in front of 50 Wall—his right leg broken—isn't it *terrible?*—such a handsome man, too—the doctors say he will be out for months—

His telephone rang. It was Marion Parker. The Happy Hippo—that was Noel's private name for the chief operator.

But on Monday morning Marion Parker had been anything but happy.

"You're the first one in," she said.

"Yes," replied Noel. "I have a feeling the market's going up today and I want to be ready for it."

"You—you haven't heard?" She had begun to cry.

"Heard? Heard what?"

"About Poke."

"No-o-o. What about Poke?" In the empty board room Noel's heart began to sing.

"He's dead."

She was joking . . . she *must* be joking.

Noel was silent for a few moments. He fought to control his voice and then he said, "What do you mean? What are you talking about?"

"You haven't seen the papers?"

"No, not yet." A cold knife blade of terror began to press against his spine. *Had something gone wrong?* Impossible. The Duke was a professional.

"Well, take a look."

The quotations board began to tilt in front of Noel's eyes. The board was pitching like the bow of a ship caught in a sudden squall.

"What—what do I do about his calls this morning? You want to take his calls?"

"No, no!" stammered Noel. "No," he repeated and

his voice became calmer. "Give his calls to Max. I mean, Izzy Padawer."

"All right," said Marion Parker in a whisper. "But I don't think I could bear to walk inside the board room."

That had been the beginning of it. Later, as the other customers' men reached their desks, a blanket of grief seemed to settle upon the room. Instead of the clamoring urgency that normally accompanied the opening of the market, there was a strange, deathly kind of silence. Izzy Padawer had sat perfectly motionless, staring straight ahead at the empty cubicle in front of him.

One of Noel's clients sent a stock power in the morning mail. In his confusion he tore up the sheet of paper. By eleven o'clock he had garbled three orders and some clerk in the back office was on the phone complaining nastily. Noel lost his temper and then, for the first time in his life, he became nauseated. Seated in the board room of Kimbridge & Co., the master sailor began to vomit into his wastebasket.

He had gone home at noon, feigning an attack of flu, and remained in his apartment for two days. Then on Wednesday afternoon, unable to bear the suspense any longer, he returned to the office. The orders flooded in—everybody was buying stock. His cousin's pension fund purchased a large block but Noel felt absolutely numb as he wrote out the order. Just before the market closed, Izzy Padawer told him that Thatcher Kimbridge personally had attended to cleaning out Poke's desk.

Since Wednesday evening he had remained in his apartment.

He kept waiting . . . and nothing happened.

The Duke did not telephone. The police did not arrive on his doorstep. Nothing.

He slept fitfully. One night he had a nightmare about the stock market—every issue was dropping because some arch criminal had sold short and then tampered with all the Stock Exchange tickers—and he imagined several times that he heard the voice of Poke Jeffers calling out to him. "Hey, lad, how's it going?" Jeffers had a way of alternating between a Southern drawl and clipped accents. A good customers' man always matched the voice of his customer.

Noel began to hate the apartment that had become his prison. And to think he had once been so proud of this place. "Fix it up like the lounge of an ocean liner," he had instructed the decorator. "The most luxurious liner afloat." The decorator, who also happened to be a customer of Noel's, had performed magnificently. Later he had slept once, briefly and without passion, with the decorator's assistant who attended to the details. The assistant had looked just like the room—fashionable and expensive.

Why didn't someone come?

He had begun to fashion an alibi in these last few days and at times he would find himself mumbling bits of it aloud. The Big Lie, that's all he had to remember, the Big Lie. He was innocent, completely innocent. Who would suspect anything? Deirdre? Of course not. How could she?

Suppose the plan had worked out just right—then might she not have suspected something? She would have talked to Poke, of course. Ah-ha-ha. He began to chuckle mirthlessly. That, too, was part of his plan. The two of them would have been mystified. And finally they would quarrel; they would break up; Poke would be a cripple, a helpless cripple. And Deirdre would belong once again to him. Yes, Noel had the whole thing worked out ever so carefully.

If only he could talk to someone!

But no, no. That would be a mistake. If he were careful, time would begin to work in his favor. Why, even now there were moments when he felt his old confidence returning. He stared craftily about the room. Admit it—he believed in traveling only one way. First Class.

He went into the bathroom and peered at the mirror. A hermit, he thought, you look just like an old hermit. He ran his hand across the light stubble of beard. Yes, if he shaved he might feel better. He ran hot water into the bowl and began to lather his face. The accumulation of several days' beard came off neatly. He began to hum, and then he nicked himself with the razor. Goddamit! For a few seconds he watched the blood drop swell from the tiny cut with fascination. Then he applied a styptic pencil and felt the quick hair's edge of pain.

He wandered back into the living room. Perhaps tonight he would not need a sleeping pill. He had begun taking the pills from a bottle Avis had left behind long ago. He used to laugh at her about these pills but later, when he found the bottle, he could not bring himself to throw it away. After all, that bottle had cost four dollars.

For a brief interval, like a child teasing the cover from a bakeshop surprise, he let his mind dwell upon the hope that had begun to stir anew: the death of Poke Jeffers meant that someone else would become the next partner of Kimbridge & Co. Yet just now things were a bit too tricky to explore that possibility—

The buzzer sounded, and Noel whirled about.

Who could that be? The police? Had they discovered something—some clue? Had the Duke come to blackmail him?

Perhaps the best thing was not to answer. Then

497

whoever it was might go away. But no! The lights in his apartment—they were visible from the street.

The buzzer sounded again. He stood by the window and looked down, half expecting to see a squad car with the red light spinning on its roof. But he saw only the huge white beetles parked along the curb.

His heart was pounding as he went slowly to the door and pressed the button. He listened, and shortly there was the sound of the elevator mechanism. He heard the elevator door opening and then footsteps.

"Noel?" a voice asked tentatively. "May I come in?"

It was Deirdre!

"Just—just a minute," Noel called. He looked quickly around the room. He straightened some chairs and emptied the ash trays. He carried a pile of newspapers out to the kitchen. Then he went back to the door. For just a second he hesitated.

He turned the dual cylinder lock and next the spring lock just above the doorknob. He opened the door and saw Deirdre standing alone. "My," she said, looking at him with a forlorn smile, "you certainly have a lot of locks. But I suppose you can't be too careful around New York these days."

"Hello, Deirdre," he said.

What did she mean by that remark? Why was she here?

He stepped back and she walked unsteadily into the room. She was wearing an orange wool cap and a heavy plaid coat with a scarf thrown around the neck in the manner of an Oxford undergraduate.

A snowflake was clinging to her cap. Noel watched the snowflake melt, turning suddenly dark like a drying drop of blood.

"My feet," she said almost inaudibly. "I'm afraid my feet are wet." She had on a pair of low leather boots.

His first thought was that she had been drinking.

This was a ruse to get her inside the apartment. But no—he saw now that she was shivering. She clasped her arms tightly in front of her in a gesture that reminded him of Avis. Her gloveless hands were blue with cold and even the pocketbook over her arm was shaking.

"Come on," he said gruffly. "Let's get you out of these things." She let him take the coat and scarf—they were soaking wet—and she then looked about uncertainly. "Take your boots off," he commanded, and she obeyed meekly. She was wearing thick woolen socks but no shoes. "The socks, too," he said. "I'll hang these things for you in the bathroom."

"I'm sorry to barge in on you like this," she said, lifting her shoulders helplessly. "But I was wandering down Fifth Avenue in the snow—and I thought you might not mind."

"Don't be silly. Why should I mind?"

"Well . . . it's been a long time."

She had on a red woolen sports shirt that was much too large for her. The cuffs of the shirt had been folded back but the sleeves were still too long for her arms. The shirt was tucked in bulges into her black skirt.

He took the wet clothes into the bathroom and when he returned she was standing in front of the etching of yachtsman's knots. "That," she said, pointing, "is a buntline hitch."

"Yes," he said. "I had to fight hard to put that print there. I had some—well—some help in fixing up this place. The decorator was all for a picture of a balloon ascension."

"Well," she said, "I'm glad you won." She looked about the room. "It's really very nice, Noel."

"Here," he said and tossed her a towel. "Sit down and dry your feet. Can I get you a drink?"

499

"No, no, thanks. You're sure I'm not intruding?" She sat down on the rug and began rubbing her feet with the towel. "You're really very sweet to take me in like this," she said. "I've been walking around in the snow all day. When I saw the snow starting to fall, well, I thought I ought to go out and walk around in it, that's all."

Her smooth brown feet were glowing from the fierce massage. Noel longed suddenly to touch Deirdre's feet. The phrase ran through his mind: as warm as cinnamon toast. He felt his caution ebbing. The old feeling—the absolute shock thrill of even being in the same room with her—had begun to take hold of him.

She looked up suddenly. "Noel?"

"Yes?"

"Can I have some soup, please? Some tomato soup if there's some around? I just remembered . . . I haven't eaten anything all day but one hot dog."

"A hot dog—where?"

"Central Park. I walked around in the snow for a long time and then I went to Central Park to visit the animals. That's where I ate the hot dog—"

"You've been out in that"—he lifted a hand to indicate the snow—"all day?"

She nodded. "Oh, I did go to a movie for a little while."

"An Errol Flynn movie?"

"Yes." Then she frowned. "But it was the one picture of his that I don't like. It has a very sad ending."

"Make yourself at home," he said, moving his head nervously, "while I fix you some soup."

"Can we have a fire? Oh, Noel, you use *The Wall Street Journal* under the kindling! I'll light it. You go ahead."

The oak logs were sawed in quarters, their open
500

sides splintery to the touch. From the kitchen he could hear the first tentative pops.

When he came back into the living room Deirdre was gazing into the fire, her eyes almost closed. There was something about the stretch of her body—a kind of suspended vitality—that reminded him oddly of Joan of Arc. That damn cat! he thought, and almost spilled the soup.

"Noel? You look so serious all of a sudden."

"Don't mind me. I was voted the Class Gloom at Princeton. You want to eat this at the table?"

"No. Right here, thank you." She patted the rug and he set the tray down. "Rug-side service," she murmured. She spread cheese on the crackers and, biting into a cracker, she said: "I've been renovating your fireplace. I've decided on Dutch tiles. Windmills and cottages and flowers. Dutch flowers, I guess." She paused a moment and chewed in concentration. "Blue tulips. Mother would approve of that. And right up there in the center a tile showing the figure of Christ." She began to eat the soup. "You're not hungry?" she asked.

"Unh-uh. I fixed myself a roast-beef sandwich a little while ago." He watched her as she sat with her legs crossed. Her skirt was pulled up over one knee; the dark line between her thigh and calf curved into the shape of a question mark. The blue light from the snow outside filtered into the room. Noel felt a tiny vessel begin to pound in his forehead. He must get hold of himself! Deirdre wasn't going to make a fool of him again.

"There was a soup stock that I pushed last year," he said gruffly. "I heard the president of the company ate soup for breakfast. I never knew if it was true or not, but it was enough to convince some of my customers they ought to be in the stock."

"I've just been down South," she said slowly. "Down around Atlanta. Some of the people drink Coca-Cola for breakfast."

She was staring wide-eyed into the fireplace. Her eyes were dark and shining and he knew that she must be thinking about Poke. In a minute or so she picked up the spoon and began to eat again.

She was, he reflected, like food herself, a child's image of some glorious dessert. Pistachio and vanilla and strawberry ice cream, pressed together and topped with a twisting cap of whipped cream, served up with spicecake. He forced his eyes away from her and scowled furiously at the blond furniture.

"Noel," she said softly.

He was standing in the middle of the room and he turned quickly.

"What a wonderful name for this season of the year —Noel. It's funny, though"—she shivered—"I don't feel like Christmas at all."

She was looking into the fire as she spoke. He stood quite still and watched the flames begin licking up along the sides of the logs. The splinters burst into long, burning brands, flaring briefly like lighted matches. The flames crept blue and yellow across the thick bark at the top; they slowly encircled the logs like the arms of a lover. There were the hiss of escaping sap and the snapping of the burning logs.

He looked at Deirdre now. She seemed utterly defenseless. Her mouth was open and the flames shone against a tiny film of saliva upon her lower lip. She raised a hand to brush away a loose strand of hair and for an instant the signet ring on her little finger gleamed golden against the flames. Suddenly Noel found it difficult to breathe; it was as though the fire were sucking the oxygen from his lungs.

A knot exploded in the fireplace, and Noel gave a

start. Deirdre did not move; the fire seemed to hypnotize her.

Noel picked up the tray and carried it into the kitchen. When he came back he said, "I'm going to fix myself a martini. Would you like a drink?"

She turned then, slowly, catlike, and nodded. "Straight gin, please. That's what I drank the first time we met." There was a different look in her eyes now—or was his imagination playing tricks?

A few minutes later he handed her the gin in an old-fashioned glass. She touched his fingers when she took the glass. "Please sit by me, Noel." She ran her hand through the long amber and black hairs of the rug. "It's a lovely rug," she said absently.

"It's jackal," he said. "From Greece. The skins are sewn together and backed with leather. This decorator," he added, grateful for the chance to talk about some neutral subject, "told me animal skins are the latest things in rugs. I had to fight off bearskins for this one."

Deirdre nodded her head. She did not appear to be listening.

He sank to his knees and the pounding in his forehead intensified. Her bare knee was only a few inches away.

Was she merely toying with him? No, no, no, the hammering in his forehead answered. It was something else. Deirdre was slowly leaving her grief and venturing back into the world of reality, like a butterfly emerging from its cocoon. He felt this conviction with a positive physical force. But some instinct made him hold back.

For a long time they watched the fire without speaking. Ash began to form along the tops of the logs almost like snow. The flames crackled and molten drops fell into the glowing coals heaped between the andirons.

He turned finally, stretching his body. His hands and face were quite warm but his spine had become chilled. His palm brushed against the hairs of the jackal rug.

He touched Deirdre's cheek ever so gently. She did not move. He began to run his hand slowly along her face and throat. She turned finally, looking straight at him. Her eyes were like oil slicks. He smelled the cidery warmth of her and his fingers touched her lips. She kissed the tips of his fingers. "Noel," she whispered, "you've been so understanding . . . about everything. You do forgive me?"

"Yes, yes." Forgive her? What an idiotic question! His body began to ache with desire.

She looked into the fire again. "The Kimbridges are an old whaling family," she said, speaking as though to the flames. "Did you know that?"

"No, Deirdre."

"Well, it's true. They used to name their whaling ships after the women in the family."

"Like the Moran tugs."

She smiled faintly, and the fire glowed against her throat. "I suppose so," she said.

Whaling. Why was she talking about whaling at a time like this?

"Noel?"

"Yes?"

"My great-great-grandfather made his bride take an oath on their wedding night that she would never marry again if he were lost at sea. The oath was inscribed inside her wedding band." Deirdre's voice was almost inaudible. "He was a sea captain and he left her a widow at twenty-one. She waited four years —and then she married again. She broke the oath."

Deirdre was leaning with her weight on one arm. She twisted toward him fiercely. "Oh, Noel!" she cried. "Hold me! *Hold me tight!*"

His arms closed about her, and he felt the moans under his palms. Very slowly his hands began to stroke her back. His hands moved across the woolen shirt, and in this moment of triumph he realized suddenly that the shirt had belonged to Poke. And now Deirdre was his, Deirdre was his. . . .

He kept stroking her back, and she grew heavy in his arms. He unhooked the snap of her brassière through the shirt and moving now with frantic haste he pulled the brassière free. A button popped against the andirons, a tiny pinging sound, and spun into the coals. Deirdre's superb breasts, richly tanned and insolent, swung free, and he lowered his head to kiss the goosefleshing nipples. The hammering had moved to the base of his skull and Noel Bigelow was transported with a joy he dared not question. Her body became the fire.

Finally, gasping for breath, he managed to say, "I think—well, we would be more comfortable in the bedroom."

She did not resist. He took her hand and led the way. Then he said, "I'll be out in a minute," and he disappeared into the bathroom. He brushed his teeth and undressed.

He was wearing only a dressing gown—it seemed fitting somehow, as though this were the first night of their honeymoon—when he came back to the bedroom.

Deirdre was sitting naked on the edge of the bed. Her back was toward him and she was combing her hair. The room was gray bright from the snow shining through the window.

"Leave it loose," he said. "I like it that way."

She obeyed quietly, putting her comb in the purse on the bedside table. She darted quickly beneath the blanket and pulled it up to her neck. When Noel approached, she raised the blanket like the opening to a tent filled with some wondrous mystery. The dressing gown fell to his feet and he kicked it away.

He felt the coolness of the sheet settling upon his back. And beside him Deirdre's body was like fire. She did not say, "Hurry, hurry!" this time. He felt her waiting for him, and he delighted now in his mastery. She ran a hand along his hips and there was the tiny shock of the ring—Brittin Kimbridge's ring—against his flesh.

Deirdre did not utter a sound. She stared at him with wide and unblinking eyes as he slowly shifted position. Her hair lay across her forehead in tangles and he kissed it away. He could sense her growing desire. She bit his cheek suddenly and began to murmur his name, over and over again.

He raised his body above her and she said excitedly, "Noel, oh, Noel! You'll be my bridge?"

"Yes, oh, Deirdre! Yes, yes!"

His hand went down expertly and now he could smell a moist new odor mingled with the warm scent of apples.

Noel was in such utter ecstasy that he began to babble. The words fell from his lips like a penitent before the altar. She had asked his forgiveness and yet it was she who must forgive him. It became terribly important that she understand how it happened, that he had not intended for Poke to die. Noel was obsessed with the idea as the pounding in his brain cried out: Tell her! Tell her this instant! Yes, yes. His happiness with Deirdre, their life together in the years to come, depended upon her understanding this very clearly.

His bed became a confessional for Noel Bigelow. He pulled the sheet aside so that he could feast upon her body as he explained it all. Poised above her, stretching out his arms, he felt his leg muscles quivering as the words tumbled forth. He told her about the Duke . . . about his plan . . . about how Poke's good leg was to be broken—that was all . . . about the agony he had experienced for the past week . . . something had just gone wrong . . . God knows what . . .

She shook her head dumbly. She did not seem to understand what he was saying.

"I did it!" he cried out. "I planned it!"

But she did not believe him. "No, no," she said as in a trance. "It's not true. You couldn't do a thing like that, Noel! You couldn't!"

She had to understand it all exactly.

His muscles were shaking now and he lowered one knee to the bed to sustain himself. His hand kept stroking her, and the moist perfume of her body became almost overpowering.

Her voice, he thought in sudden desperation. He began to mimic her voice; he repeated the entire conversation with Poke last Sunday evening.

And then she began to comprehend. He had the sensation that her eyes actually made a clicking sound. Yes, the conversation, that was the missing link. Thank God, now she believed him.

She understood! An electric thrill passed through Noel. Deirdre's body seemed to swim below him. He felt like a bull, yes, that was it exactly—

"Noel?"

It held a new edge, this voice, but Noel Bigelow in his ecstasy did not perceive it.

"Yes?" he said hoarsely. His forehead was slick with sweat.

"You'll be my bridge, Noel?"

"Yes, yes."

"All right, my darling," she said. "But I want us to be exactly right. Just a moment, Noel, while I slip off this ring. I won't be needing it."

The ring! Yes, now he was about to become Brittin and he would be Poke, too. Her entire life!

She turned swiftly on her side. The sweat dripped into his eyes, blinding him.

He heard the clasp opening on the purse. "Hurry, Deirdre!" he cried out. "Dammit, I can't see!"

"Just close your eyes, my darling. Yes, that's right. Oh, Noel, I'll make it so good for you. You've never dreamed how it can be."

In his confessional, one hand clutching the pillow, Noel Bigelow shuddered with joy. He did not see Deirdre's fingers steal inside the purse.

The ring dropped gently, almost reverently, and there was the rustle of satin. When her hand emerged from the purse it gripped another object. Her fingers moved deftly and the reflected light of the snow outside shone against the opened razor of Jared Kimbridge.

Noel fought desperately to keep his eyes shut. At last, at last. The hammering at the base of his skull was so powerful that it seemed about to touch off an explosion inside him. He felt Deirdre turning again under him and the excitement of her flesh was almost more than he could bear.

"All right, Noel. You can look now."

His eyelids flew open as he let out a sigh of rapture. And then—

"What are— My God, Deirdre! *That razor!* Have you gone crazy? No, no! *Keep that thing away from me!*"

"Get up, Noel. We're going into the living room.

Slowly, very slowly." She flicked the razor at him and he shrank back. "That's a good boy, Noel." He retreated across the sheet and almost fell off the bed. His bare feet found the floor.

Deirdre came creeping across the bed like a hunter stalking the kill. Her voluptuous body had become obscene to behold.

The two figures, naked, twisting in the half shadows, moved in their slow, tortuous dance. They were framed in the doorway.

And then she said, "My, my. What a chance to use this trusty heirloom. You could imitate eunuchs over the telephone. How would that be, Noel?" She threw back her head and laughed.

He backed into the living room as he thought in terror: My God, she's just crazy enough to do it!

He did not trust himself to run. Deirdre was a jungle cat. "What—what do you want?" he cried at last, almost gagging. For a terrible instant he imagined this tickle of pain and then the sucking sound of his own blood.

Across the room the coals were tinkling delicately, the sound an ornament-laden Christmas tree makes when its branches are rustled.

Deirdre did not speak. She kept stalking him, a slow step at a time, waving the razor ever so slowly. He stared at the blade and heard the faint, merry tinkle of the coals.

Suddenly she kneeled swiftly and then stood up, backing away a step. She had propped the razor, blade up, against an ash tray taken from a table.

As if in a dream, he remembered the razor in his father's stiffened fingers. His father was floating on his back in the tub; his own father had become a proud shattered ship. . . .

Grab the razor! his brain shrieked in torture. *Go ahead! You're stronger than she is!*

But his legs—they had turned to stone battered by a pile driver. His legs had become the broken limbs of Poke Jeffers.

"Deirdre, Deirdre . . ." Noel babbled in penitence. Painfully, he sank to his knees. The whole thing was so monstrous—to come so close to winning Deirdre forever and then to lose her. "Deirdre, please, please. *I beg you—*"

"You might throw yourself on it, Noel," she said encouragingly. "Soldiers do that. They fall on hand grenades to save their comrades. Sometimes they even get the Medal of Honor, Noel. Please," she crooned, "won't you do it for me?"

He shuddered. In the light her body had become an avenging angel in bronze. He tried to speak but his tongue was numb with fear.

Then, with a nimble movement, Deirdre swooped down and snatched the razor.

"Sit down, Noel. The chair by your desk. That's right. That's a good boy." Her voice was like the razor —gray and cold and utterly without emotion.

A zombie, he thought wildly, she's become a zombie. Her eyes were huge in their sockets.

He was groveling now before her. "Du-Du-Ddd—" He could not speak. The prayers clogged his throat.

"Now pick up the phone, Noel. You're going to call my father. You're going to tell him exactly what you told me. About Poke. How it all happened. All right, Noel?" The razor weaved in tantalizing arcs.

He longed to shout, to do something, to flee from this room, and to lose Deirdre forever.

She came a step closer.

"Now here is the number . . ." She whacked her thigh with the flat of the razor.

510

It was a dream, a wild dream, a nightmare from which he would awaken in full command of his senses. Yes, that was it, a nightmare. Once again Deirdre would be his. *Oh, God!*

Noel Bigelow began to dial. Somehow he could imagine the telephone ringing now in the quiet town house. Yes, yes, at this very moment Thatcher Kimbridge would be walking toward the telephone. . . .

The final stroke of midnight dripped majestically from Trinity's tower. The falling snow seemed to muffle its sound and then silence—a white, intense silence —settled upon Wall Street.

The snow softened the Gothic edges of Trinity and curled upon the bare branches in the churchyard. It fell softly upon the ancient flaking tombstones and scooped tiny hollows beneath the hedges. The snow settled its crown upon the head of Christ and heaped along the outstretched arms. The statue on the cross appeared to hover above the churchyard.

There was not a sound; the dead spoke to the dead. Already the snow was gathering a faint crust of soot. In one corner the unread sign proclaimed: PLEASE DO NOT FEED PIGEONS ANYWHERE IN CHURCHYARD. In the early morning hours the pigeons would come to joust with stiff-legged sparrows but now not a living thing was to be seen.

In front of Trinity a single glass eye snapped red.

Wall Street itself became an extension of the churchyard under the mantle of snow. The red eye stared down the Street, and in the tomb of silence the cold buildings stood like grave markers under the falling snow.

ELIA KAZAN
the arrange-ment

— is about Eddie Anderson, a tough-minded, dynamic ad executive and a brilliant writer, married to Florence and obsessed by the much younger Gwen...

— is the devastating story of Eddie crashing out of his arrangement.

"It is a great book. When you touch it you touch a man."   Henry Miller

IT HAS ALREADY STUNNED NEARLY THREE MILLION READERS. IT JUST MIGHT JOLT YOU OUT OF YOUR ARRANGEMENT!